Une discipline sans douleur

Dire non sans marchandage,
sans cris et sans fessée

De la même auteure

Rêves & Créativité
Comment atteindre ses objectifs par les rêves
Préface de Roger St-Hilaire
Éditions Le Dauphin blanc - 2003

Recueil de postulats
500 demandes pour induire des rêves-réponses
et trouver des solutions tout en dormant
Éditions L'ABC des Rêves et du Sommeil - 2005

S.O.S. cauchemars
Techniques pour s'en libérer
Préface de France Castel
Flammarion Québec - 2005

Mon premier journal de rêves
Outil simple et original pour vous aider
à vous souvenir de vos rêves
et à les comprendre
Éditions L'ABC des Rêves et du Sommeil - 2007

Le rêve et ses bénéfices
Découvrez-les à travers des témoignages
Préface de Nicole Gratton
Éditions L'ABC des Rêves et du Sommeil - 2007

Mieux dormir... j'en rêve !
Stratégies pour bien dormir
adaptées à la femme et à l'homme modernes
Préface du Dr Jean Drouin
Les Éditions de Mortagne - 2009

Comment aider mon enfant à mieux dormir
De la naissance à l'adolescence
Préface : Germain Duclos
Les Éditions de Mortagne - 2009

Brigitte Langevin

Une discipline sans douleur

Dire non sans marchandage, sans cris et sans fessée

ÉDITIONS DE Mortagne

Catalogage avant publication de Bibliothèque et Archives nationales du Québec et Bibliothèque et Archives Canada

Langevin, Brigitte, 1964-

Une discipline sans douleur : dire non sans marchandage, sans cris et sans fessée
Nouv. éd.

ISBN 978-2-89074-927-6

1. Enfants - Discipline. 2. Éducation des enfants. 3. Enfants - Modification du comportement. I. Titre.

HQ770.4.L36 2010   649'.64   C2009-942314-6

Édition
Les Éditions de Mortagne
Case postale 116
Boucherville (Québec)
J4B 5E6

Distribution
Tél. : 450 641-2387
Téléc. : 450 655-6092
Courriel : info@editionsdemortagne.com

Tous droits réservés
Les Éditions de Mortagne
© Ottawa 2010

Dépôt légal
Bibliothèque et Archives Canada
Bibliothèque et Archives nationales du Québec
Bibliothèque Nationale de France
1er trimestre 2010

ISBN 978-2-89074-926-9

1 2 3 4 5 – 10 – 14 13 12 11 10

Imprimé au Canada

Nous reconnaissons l'aide financière du gouvernement du Canada par l'entremise du Programme d'aide au développement de l'industrie de l'édition (PADIÉ) et celle du gouvernement du Québec par l'entremise de la Société de développement des entreprises culturelles (SODEC) pour nos activités d'édition. Gouvernement du Québec – Programme de crédit d'impôt pour l'édition de livres – Gestion SODEC.

Membre de l'Association nationale des éditeurs de livres (ANEL)

*À ma fille Karelle,
pour son amour inconditionnel
qui m'incite chaque jour à devenir
une mère toujours meilleure.*

REMERCIEMENTS

Ma reconnaissance va tout d'abord à tous ces parents qui, le réclamant avec tant d'insistance, m'ont motivée à mettre au monde ce bébé littéraire.

Un merci particulier à mon père et à ma mère, qui ont appris le métier de parent « sur le tas » et qui m'ont donné tout ce qu'ils pouvaient.

Un merci rempli de reconnaissance à toutes ces personnes qui ont croisé mon chemin et m'ont soutenue dans mon rôle de parent, et ce, sans jugement, malgré les maladresses, les bévues et les faux pas que j'ai commis dans les premières années de vie de ma fille.

Un merci rempli de gratitude à mon coach professionnel, Chantal Beaulieu Lynch, pour son soutien et ses encouragements à me dépasser continuellement autant dans l'écriture de ce livre que dans la vie en général.

Un merci du fond du cœur à Carole Fortin pour son inestimable travail de correction et à Claire Lesage pour son œil de lynx, qui a repéré les moindres coquilles lors de la relecture finale du manuscrit.

De doux mercis à mon amoureux Éric. Sans sa générosité et son dévouement aux tâches familiales, il m'aurait été difficile de mener à terme ce projet.

Un merci tout spécial à l'équipe des Éditions de Mortagne qui a fait évoluer ce livre vers sa forme actuelle ! Il est devenu un bijou à lire... et à relire !

Enfin, un merci vibrant d'amour à ma fille Karelle. Sans sa présence dans ma vie, je n'aurais pu écrire ce livre.

TABLE DES MATIÈRES

Introduction 15

Chapitre 1 : Témoignage personnel 19

Chapitre 2 : Le rôle de parent 23
- Un dur métier 23
- Être parent 25
- Besoins et désirs 28

Chapitre 3 : La discipline qui fait mal 33
- La fessée 34
- La gifle est partie 36
- Rouge de colère 38
- Le marchandage 41
- L'ingérence de nos propres parents 47
- Les abus verbaux 49

Chapitre 4 : Éduquer sans douleur 59
- Poser fermement des limites 59
- Commander sans en culpabiliser 62
- Accepter d'être détesté 66
- Accepter de frustrer 68
- Laisser pleurer 73
- Résister à l'envie de céder 76
- Exprimer sa colère 78
- Le laisser s'exprimer 81
- Écouter et nommer 84
- Encourager et complimenter 86
- Dire je t'aime 90
- Persévérer avec les ados 91

Chapitre 5 : Stratégies d'intervention 99
- Conséquence naturelle 102
- Conséquence logique 103

- Renforcement positif 105
- Adapter le milieu 107
- Le hors-jeu 108
- 1... 2... 3 ! 110
- La diversion 112
- L'exemple 113

Chapitre 6 : Pour l'avenir de nos enfants 117
- Éviter le chemin de la délinquance 117
- Avoir ou ne pas avoir d'enfant 119
- Savoir qu'il n'est jamais trop tard 122
- Ressources en cas de crise 123

Conclusion 129

Annexe : Aide-mémoire 131
Bibliographie 135
À propos de l'auteure 137

*En tout enfant,
il y a une personne unique
et merveilleuse qui n'attend qu'un adulte
ayant foi en lui et le traitant comme un être digne
pour apprendre à bien se comporter
et à s'épanouir au contact des autres.
En tout parent,
il y a une personne
qui aspire profondément
à donner le meilleur de soi-même
et à être un modèle de réalisation pour son enfant.*

Brigitte Racine
La discipline un jeu d'enfant

INTRODUCTION

Ce charmant bébé que nous tenons dans nos bras est tout l'amour de notre vie. Nous lui donnons de l'affection et répondons à ses besoins et à ses moindres désirs. Il est si petit et il a tant besoin de nous, ses parents ! Et puis, les jours passent et cette relation parent-enfant tant idéalisée tourne trop souvent au cauchemar. Les parents se rendent alors compte que leurs attentes ne correspondent pas à la réalité.

Plusieurs parents m'ont fait part qu'avant la naissance de leur premier enfant, ils s'imaginaient à table avec leurs enfants, mangeant presque silencieusement, échangeant calmement tout en s'amusant ! Au lieu de cela, ils se voient obligés de lancer des ordres : « Assieds-toi comme il faut... Ferme ta bouche en mangeant... Arrête de faire du bruit avec tes ustensiles... » Ils avaient bien remarqué, chez les enfants des autres, des crises, des désaccords et des comportements désagréables, mais ils se berçaient de la douce illusion qu'ils échapperaient à cela avec les leurs et que, pour les calmer, ils éviteraient de recourir aux cris, aux menaces et aux fessées. Ils sont donc grandement déçus des agissements de leur bébé et de leurs propres réactions. Par ailleurs, à voir le comportement calme et respectueux de certains enfants, ils s'imaginent que les autres parents réussissent tellement mieux qu'eux.

Une discipline sans douleur

Tout d'abord, précisons un point important : un parent parfait, cela n'existe pas. Cependant, je crois au plus profond de moi qu'il est possible de devenir un excellent parent. Le mot *perfection* est écrasant parce qu'il ne laisse aucune place à l'erreur. Viser l'excellence, c'est se donner le droit à l'erreur, tout en se responsabilisant et en faisant tout en son pouvoir pour développer ses habiletés parentales, en matière de discipline ou d'éducation. C'est d'ailleurs ce qui est mis en lumière dans le témoignage personnel que je livre au premier chapitre.

Malheureusement, « faire » un enfant ne nous donne pas automatiquement la sagesse et l'efficacité nécessaires à l'art d'être parent. Lorsque les parents ont de « bons » enfants, ils se sentent compétents ; mais lorsque ceux-ci résistent à leur autorité, ils se remettent en question et doutent alors de leur compétence. Le chapitre 2 aborde le rôle crucial et exigeant des parents et la nécessité de bien différencier les « besoins » et les « désirs » des enfants.

Lorsque les enfants défient leur autorité et transgressent les limites mises en place, tout parent risque de réagir plus fortement qu'il n'est souhaitable de le faire en matière d'éducation, à un moment ou à un autre. Les menaces, les cris, les abus verbaux, les accès de colère, etc., peuvent nous échapper. Le chapitre 3 décrit ces attitudes, ces paroles et ces gestes qui sont loin de reposer sur l'amour et la compassion et qu'il faut éviter. La fessée et le marchandage figurent aussi au banc des accusés, afin de susciter une réflexion quant à leur utilisation.

Rassurez-vous ! Une éducation sans douleur est possible, encore faut-il savoir comment s'y prendre. Le chapitre 4 en détaille les principes essentiels. Le gros bon sens y est à l'honneur. Peut-être même vous reconnaîtrez-vous et cela vous confirmera-t-il votre façon d'être et de réagir.

INTRODUCTION

Afin de vous soutenir dans votre démarche, le chapitre 5 offre quant à lui un éventail de stratégies efficaces tant avec les jeunes que les moins jeunes.

Que vous soyez parents depuis peu, depuis déjà quelques années ou en voie de l'être, ce livre s'adresse à vous, de même qu'à tout adulte qui se sent concerné par les progrès en éducation.

Si votre motivation à devenir parent, ou à avoir un autre enfant, se fonde sur le plaisir de tenir un bébé dans vos bras, sur l'espoir de sauver votre relation de couple ou sur celui de vous sentir moins seul, le chapitre 6 vous mènera droit à une réflexion percutante sur l'immense responsabilité qui incombe à chaque parent et éducateur envers les enfants. Des ressources précieuses en cas de crise sont aussi indiquées.

On croit trop souvent que l'éducation des enfants est complexe. D'ailleurs, la majorité des livres traitant du sujet le laisse croire par le nombre faramineux de pages qu'ils comptent. En écrivant ce livre, je l'ai voulu pratique et concis pour que le parent trouve rapidement des réponses à ses questions. D'ailleurs, vous trouverez une série d'énoncés servant d'aide-mémoire en annexe. Affichez-les à la vue sur le réfrigérateur. Tout comme l'enfant, l'adulte a aussi besoin de rappels !

Enfin, ce livre, comme tous ceux qui traitent d'éducation, ne peut être qu'un ouvrage général par rapport à VOTRE enfant. Un parent connaît son enfant mieux que personne, c'est pourquoi, si vous lisez certains passages qui vont à l'encontre de vos sentiments de mère et de père, oubliez ce que dit le livre et suivez votre instinct. Certains parents ont parfois surmonté une étape difficile dans l'éducation de leurs enfants en agissant envers et contre tous et les résultats ont été hors du commun. Ils méritent l'admiration de tous !

Puisse la lecture de ce livre faire la différence au sein de votre famille, dans vos relations et dans votre vie.

Note : Quand j'écris « l'enfant » ou « le bébé », j'évoque le garçon aussi bien que la fille. Quand j'écris « le parent », je m'adresse à la mère autant qu'au père. Même si les deux parents diffèrent en matière d'autorité, il me semble évident que cette réflexion les concerne au même titre.

Chapitre 1

TÉMOIGNAGE PERSONNEL

Je suis l'aînée d'une famille de trois enfants. Ma sœur est de onze mois ma cadette et le benjamin est arrivé huit ans après ma naissance. Dans ma famille, pour éduquer, il était normal de frapper ses enfants.

La coutume voulait que ce soit le père qui, en rentrant du travail, frappe les enfants, après que la mère eut révélé les « fautes atroces » commises par eux durant la journée. Pendant le repas du soir, haussant fortement le ton, mon père résumait les actions méritant une correction et, après avoir baissé nos pantalons, il nous administrait à tour de rôle une fessée.

De temps à autre, il arrivait aussi que ma mère y mette du sien durant la journée. Son rôle se limitait cependant à nous pincer, à nous taper avec la tapette à mouches ou à nous punir en nous agenouillant dans un coin. Non seulement, je ne me sentais alors pas aimée, mais cette façon de nous discipliner me laissait croire que mon père était méchant et sans cœur. Par ailleurs, en tant que petite fille, je ne voulais pas du tout jouer le rôle de mère un jour dans ma vie, puisqu'il ne semblait guère plus reluisant que celui de père.

Une discipline sans douleur

Déjà, très jeune, vers l'âge de quatre ou cinq ans, je comprenais que ces méthodes d'éducation étaient injustes et surtout humiliantes. Étant donné que j'avais très peur de mes parents, il m'était impossible de leur exprimer ce que je ressentais et encore moins d'en parler à qui que ce soit d'autre. Tout au long de mon enfance, j'ai accepté la fessée et les punitions sans jamais rouspéter, mais je pleurais en silence.

Lorsque j'ai commencé l'école, je ne comprenais pas pourquoi les autres enfants étaient si effrontés. Comment osaient-ils remettre en cause les directives d'un adulte ou pire encore, lui désobéir ? Ne craignaient-ils pas la fessée ? Par ailleurs, je voyais des parents si affectueux avec leurs enfants que j'aurais aimé être la leur ! J'en venais à croire que j'avais été adoptée !

Avec le temps, j'ai dû me rendre à l'évidence : j'étais vraiment leur fille. Ma ressemblance physique avec l'un de mes parents me le rappelait quotidiennement. Je me suis donc fait la promesse de ne jamais agir de la sorte si je devenais mère un jour.

Les années ont passé, je suis devenue fonctionnaire au sein d'une municipalité, j'ai rencontré un homme, je me suis mariée et, cinq ans plus tard, je suis devenue enceinte. J'avais alors vingt-cinq ans.

En comprenant que j'allais devenir maman, la détresse s'est emparée de moi. Je me suis mise à bégayer et j'ai perdu confiance en mes capacités. Accomplir des tâches simples devenait un défi de plus en plus lourd à surmonter. Les seuls moments jouissifs de ma grossesse ont été ceux où j'ai su que j'étais enceinte, où je l'ai annoncé à tous et où j'ai accouché, c'est-à-dire lorsque j'ai constaté qu'un être si petit et si parfait avait pu se créer à l'intérieur de moi et en sortir sain et sauf.

Ainsi, neuf mois plus tard, j'étais devenue une maman. Incapable de faire face à cette réalité, je me suis inscrite à des cours au cégep pour fuir mon rôle et, surtout, pour sortir de la maison. Pourtant, ma fille n'avait alors qu'un mois et j'étais en congé de maternité. Mes parents la gardaient le jour et son père ou moi allions la chercher le soir venu. À l'âge des premiers mots, elle nous appelait papa, son père et moi ; pour elle, il n'y avait pas de maman dans sa famille.

Vous devinez sans doute la suite : je me suis mise à l'éduquer comme je l'avais été. Fessée, pincettes, bras tordus, punitions à genoux dans un coin ont ainsi fait partie du quotidien de ma fille jusqu'au jour où, agacée par l'affront qu'elle venait de me faire en me répliquant, je l'ai frappée en plein visage. Elle avait alors un peu plus de quatre ans. Ce geste inacceptable a été l'un des déclencheurs qui m'ont poussée à consulter une psychologue. Fort heureusement, il me restait encore une parcelle de conscience et, sans aucun doute, beaucoup d'amour pour mon enfant.

Six mois plus tard, je prenais une ferme résolution : plus jamais de violence dans ma vie ni dans celle de ma famille. Je me suis alors séparée, non pas parce que le père de ma fille était menaçant, mais plutôt parce que je l'avais épousé pour la mauvaise raison, c'est-à-dire pour quitter la tyrannie de mon milieu familial. Rejeter la violence demandait aussi de me choisir. J'ai aussi impliqué ma fille dans ce cheminement en l'informant que dorénavant je m'interdisais de la frapper, de la punir et même de crier contre elle. Elle m'a alors regardée du haut de ses cinq ans, les mains sur ses hanches et m'a dit : « Mais qu'est-ce que tu vas faire ? » Elle avait déjà compris, à son âge, que mes stratégies éducatives n'avaient d'autre but que de démontrer mon pouvoir afin de reprendre la maîtrise d'une situation. J'étais renversée ! Je lui ai alors expliqué que si elle avait un comportement répréhensible, il y aurait des conséquences pour elle, mais des conséquences en lien direct avec son manquement. Elle m'a fait un signe affirmatif de la tête : elle avait saisi. Il me restait maintenant à mettre ma résolution en pratique.

Au moment où j'écris ces lignes, ma fille a près de dix-sept ans. Je suis encore émue en pensant à ses premières années de vie. Désormais, une certitude s'est ancrée dans ma tête et dans mon cœur : tout ne se joue pas avant l'âge de cinq ans, il est toujours possible de se rattraper. Si je n'avais pas travaillé avec acharnement à modifier mon attitude, mon comportement et ma façon de penser, il est fort probable que ma fille, qui a une forte personnalité, serait aujourd'hui une délinquante ayant décroché, sans doute aux prises avec une dépendance quelconque (drogue, alcool ou sexe).

Ce travail, très exigeant dans les premiers temps (ne nous le cachons pas !), m'a demandé une énorme dose de courage, de patience et de tolérance. Cependant, l'amour que me porte ma fille m'a donné, jour après jour, la force de persévérer. La récompense est grandiose car, chaque fois que je l'entends m'appeler *Maman*, je suis alors envahie d'un sentiment de fierté et de réussite. Je suis finalement devenue cette maman, cette mère que chaque enfant aspire à avoir. Je vous souhaite de vivre ce profond bonheur !

Maintenant, tournez cette page et voyez comment vous pouvez vous aussi passer à l'action.

Chapitre 2

LE RÔLE DE PARENT

Un enfant qui vient au monde, c'est un univers de sourires, de gestes tendres et, surtout, une vie qui prend sa place dans le cercle familial. Un enfant qui vient au monde, c'est une invitation à donner le meilleur de soi. Très tôt, toutefois, il est nécessaire de faire preuve de discernement afin de répondre adéquatement à ses besoins, mais pas nécessairement à tous ses désirs.

UN DUR MÉTIER

Notre société offre peu d'occasions d'apprendre le métier de parent. On n'introduit pas tout à coup une hygiéniste dentaire dans un cabinet de dentiste sans lui avoir appris le maniement des outils buccaux, en lui disant simplement : « Vous êtes hygiéniste, allez-y ! » Pourtant, lorsqu'un couple devient parents, c'est comme si la société lui disait de but en blanc : « Vous êtes parents, nous ne vous avons pas appris grand-chose de ce métier, mais allez-y, faites de votre mieux ! »

Dans tous les domaines d'activité, les gens travaillent en moyenne huit heures par jour. Ils ont, chaque jour et chaque fin de semaine, des heures régulières de loisirs. Ils

Une discipline sans douleur

prennent chaque année des vacances. Pas nous, les parents ! Il n'y a pas de travail plus ingrat dans notre société que d'être ce parent travaillant vingt-quatre heures sur vingt-quatre, sept jours par semaine. La venue du premier enfant, et plus encore celle du second, est un tremblement de terre pour le couple qui doit continuer son chemin en terrain inconnu. Les grasses matinées, la tranquillité en sirotant son café, les moments de tendresse au coin du feu, les longs repas au resto cèdent la place à la course folle des préparatifs du matin, à la planification et à la préparation des repas, aux devoirs, aux discussions interminables avec les enfants pour obtenir leur collaboration aux tâches, à la répétition des consignes afin de garder l'harmonie et le respect au sein de la famille, etc.

Au premier abord, même si les propos précédents semblent décourageants, leur but est de faire prendre conscience des exigences du rôle de parent. De fait, en posant des limites, l'adulte joue son rôle ; en protestant, l'enfant joue le sien. Ne soyez donc pas surpris d'avoir parfois envie de tout laisser en plan et de partir. Vous êtes tout à fait normal !

Certains passages de ce livre vous feront dire : « J'aurais souhaité lire ce livre il y a quelques années. Je comprends maintenant toutes les sottises que j'ai commises. J'ai fait telle ou telle chose, maintenant je vois que cela n'était pas la meilleure chose à faire. » De grâce, ne demeurez pas dans la culpabilité. Aucun parent qui fait de son mieux ne mérite d'être blâmé (que ce soit moi, vous, les miens ou les vôtres !). Nous essayons tous d'éduquer nos enfants de notre mieux. Si l'on considère que la plupart d'entre nous ont peu ou pas de connaissance du métier, nous faisons sans doute un travail tout à fait convenable dans l'ensemble ! Aussi, j'espère que vous serez indulgent envers vous-même à propos des erreurs que vous pensez avoir commises. Et surtout, décrochez de cette phrase souvent entendue au cours des vingt dernières années : « Tout se joue avant six ans. » Beaucoup de choses se jouent avant six ans, mais certainement pas tout. Il est possible de rectifier bien des choses. Cependant, il faut savoir que, plus un parent attend avant de changer ses méthodes éducatives, plus la résistance de son enfant sera grande. Commencer à discipliner son enfant à l'adolescence est un défi frôlant la folie !

ÊTRE PARENT

Être parent, c'est être responsable d'un autre que soi, d'un être en processus d'apprentissage et en quête d'autonomie. Que représente cette grande responsabilité ? En voici les cinq grandes lignes :

1- Être parent, c'est d'abord éduquer, enseigner les bonnes manières selon les usages et les traditions de la société, mais aussi répondre aux besoins des enfants. Les besoins primaires sont :

   a) d'ordre physique, qu'il s'agisse de la faim, de la soif ou du sommeil ;

   b) d'ordre relationnel, impliquant les diverses interactions entre l'enfant et son entourage ;

   c) d'ordre sécuritaire, en particulier sur le plan émotionnel. L'enfant a besoin de stabilité pour construire sa personnalité harmonieusement. La discipline comble ce besoin en lui fournissant un cadre de référence sur lequel il peut s'appuyer, afin de savoir comment il doit agir.

2- Être parent, c'est trouver le juste milieu entre autoritarisme et laisser-aller. Il n'y a pas si longtemps, plus les parents étaient autoritaires et avaient du pouvoir sur leur progéniture, plus ils étaient jugés compétents. Et puis, il y a eu un revirement. De nos jours, la tendance sociale est de laisser les enfants faire tout ce qui leur plaît, en plus de répondre à leurs moindres désirs, de crainte que leur estime de soi en souffre. Le résultat en est lamentable. Nous avons ainsi créé la génération des enfants-rois, ces bambins qui mènent leurs parents par le bout du nez. Et voici qu'une nouvelle génération d'enfants vient d'apparaître, celle des enfants explosifs, qui n'hésitent pas à frapper leurs parents ou leurs professeurs pour avoir gain de cause.

Afin de vous situer, voici quelques-unes des attitudes du parent qui intervient trop, de celui qui n'intervient pas du tout et de celui qui se situe au juste milieu.

Trop intervenir	Non-intervention	Juste milieu
Imposer ses règles et son raisonnement.	N'imposer aucune limite ou restriction.	Mettre en place des limites en fonction de l'âge de l'enfant et les faire respecter.
Être centré davantage sur les punitions.	S'attendre à ce que l'enfant se responsabilise tout seul.	Comprendre la cause du comportement de l'enfant et agir en conséquence.
Ne rien laisser passer et désirer contrôler tous les comportements.	Désirer que l'amour prime sur toute contrainte.	Être souple dans ses décisions et dans sa façon de les appliquer.
Être intolérant et très exigeant.	Demander la permission de l'enfant.	Être sûr de ses exigences.

Trop intervenir	Non-intervention	Juste milieu
Aller jusqu'à frapper ou humilier publiquement l'enfant.	Être contre toute autorité.	Trouver une conséquence qui incite l'enfant à apprendre afin de ne pas reproduire le comportement indésirable.
Fonctionner selon ses humeurs.	Acheter la paix.	L'aider à agir seul.
Juger, dévaloriser, dénigrer.	Trop valoriser l'enfant.	Applaudir aux réussites de l'enfant.
Vivre les relations en fonction d'une lutte de pouvoir.	Rechercher une relation « ami-ami » avec l'enfant.	Faire la distinction entre ses besoins, ceux de son couple et ceux de ses enfants.
Critiquer les autres adultes y compris l'autre parent.	Défaire l'intervention de l'autre parent.	Être cohérent avec l'autre parent et faire équipe.

3- Être parent, c'est couvrir son enfant d'amour sans le laisser nous envahir pour autant. Consacrer à son enfant des moments privilégiés constitue un puissant moyen de lui manifester notre amour. Lui consacrer tout son temps ? Non ! Un enfant doit développer un minimum d'autonomie. Selon son âge, il devrait pouvoir faire certaines choses ou s'occuper de lui-même pour un certain nombre de minutes. Par exemple : un nourrisson* peut patienter quelques minutes dans son lit lorsqu'il pleure la nuit ; un bébé peut jouer quelques minutes sans que son parent soit nécessairement près de lui ; un enfant peut patienter avant un repas sans

---

* Bébé de moins de douze mois.

qu'inévitablement on le « branche » devant la télé ; un adolescent peut prendre l'autobus pour rendre visite à ses copains, etc.

4- Être parent, c'est servir de guide à son enfant, lui proposer des solutions, être ouvert à la communication, être capable de l'écouter tout comme de s'affirmer, lui proposer des activités agréables, lui démontrer sa confiance, le recevoir, lui apprendre, partager avec lui, évoluer à ses côtés, l'aimer, en être aimé...

5- Être parent, c'est rendre son enfant autonome. S'il est une responsabilité importante qui nous incombe, c'est bien celle-là. Les enfants constituent notre trésor collectif, les adultes de demain. Ils gouverneront notre monde dans l'avenir. Si nous voulons qu'ils soient des citoyens consciencieux, qu'ils transforment pour le mieux la société, c'est notre devoir de leur donner le meilleur de nous-mêmes et de les responsabiliser.

Afin d'accomplir notre rôle au meilleur de nos connaissances, il convient de faire la distinction entre les besoins et les désirs de nos enfants.

BESOINS ET DÉSIRS

Quand les parents confondent besoins et désirs chez un enfant, voici les conséquences qui les attendent : ils transforment les enfants en consommateurs et ils entretiennent l'illusion qu'il faut combler tous leurs désirs pour avoir leur amour. Il en est souvent ainsi parce que les parents cherchent à se déculpabiliser de ne pas leur donner suffisamment d'attention, et ce, en répondant à toutes leurs demandes ! La discipline se vit alors très mal de part et d'autre.

Ces dernières décennies, un certain courant de pensée laissait croire aux parents qu'ils risquaient de traumatiser l'enfant ou de nuire à son développement s'ils ne répondaient pas à toutes ses attentes, qu'il s'agisse de besoins ou de désirs. Ce qui est inexact. Apprendre à distinguer besoins et désirs devrait faire partie des apprentissages parentaux. Voyons de quoi il s'agit.

Le propre d'un besoin est de nécessiter une réponse, plus ou moins différée, qui comblera l'attente, apaisera la tension ou la souffrance du manque. Les besoins de l'enfant se doivent donc d'être satisfaits le plus tôt possible, sinon cela pourrait nuire à son développement. Lorsque les parents satisfont les besoins physiques et affectifs de l'enfant, ce dernier a le sentiment d'être important. Ainsi, l'estime de soi se bâtit chez l'enfant lorsque nous répondons à ses besoins.

L'enfant a besoin de limites sécurisantes qui lui indiquent où s'arrêter, comme le font les arrêts aux coins des rues. L'absence de sécurité nuit à son développement. En plus d'avoir besoin de se sentir en sécurité, un enfant a besoin de se sentir aimé, capable, compétent et libre de faire certains choix. Il a aussi besoin d'éprouver du plaisir en compagnie de ceux qui prennent soin de lui.

Le propre d'un désir, c'est qu'il demande à être entendu, reconnu ou valorisé, ce qui ne veut pas dire satisfait. Gardons présent à l'esprit que certains enfants sont très habiles pour présenter leurs désirs... comme des besoins. Le rôle du parent est de les entendre et de les reconnaître, sans les satisfaire tous.

Par exemple, manger est un besoin ; manger des frites, un désir. Dormir est un besoin ; se coucher avec son parent, un désir. S'exciter, pour un enfant, est un besoin ; passer trois heures au parc, un désir.

Aussi est-il souhaitable de rappeler que les parents sont là pour :

- répondre aux besoins matériels et relationnels des enfants, au moins jusqu'à un certain âge ;

- favoriser l'acquisition d'une autonomie suffisante, afin que les enfants puissent à leur tour, tôt ou tard, répondre à leurs propres besoins ;

- entendre les désirs des enfants et, éventuellement, les aider à en réaliser quelques-uns, quand ceux-ci sont recevables ou conciliables avec la réalité.

Désirs des enfants	Réalité
Les enfants veulent s'amuser, tout le temps si possible, même en mangeant ou en marchant.	Il y a un temps pour jouer et des moments plus sérieux pour ramasser ses jouets, faire son lit, ses leçons ou encore sa lessive.
Les enfants veulent regarder la télévision du matin au soir.	Une limite est établie en fonction de l'âge de l'enfant (1 heure de télévision par année : 6 ans = 6 heures de télé par semaine ; 10 ans = 10 heures ; etc.)
Les enfants veulent beaucoup de choses et les veulent tout de suite.	Il faut attendre la fin du repas pour le cornet de crème glacée. Il faut attendre son anniversaire pour un jouet spécial. Il faut apprendre à économiser pour acheter un jeu électronique ou un vêtement griffé.
Les enfants veulent leurs parents pour eux tout le temps.	Les parents organisent des activités pour les enfants, et aussi pour leur couple !

Que l'enfant exprime de nombreux désirs est un signe de bonne santé et de vitalité. Le rôle des parents est de lui apprendre que tout désir a un prix et que d'y accéder demande des efforts. Il faut juste se rappeler qu'un enfant dont les désirs sont pris en considération sans être pour autant satisfaits à tout coup vit une frustration. Toutefois, cette frustration est formatrice et lui permet de se projeter dans l'avenir. Par ailleurs, il apprend ainsi la réalité de la vie. Certains de ses désirs seront donc satisfaits, d'autres non. Quelques-uns le seront rapidement (un nouveau jeu pour sa fête qui approche), d'autres le seront plus tard (un cadeau dispendieux pour Noël) et certains, peut-être jamais (demander une petite sœur ou un petit frère). Lorsque ses désirs sont entendus et reconnus, l'enfant se sent important, compris et aimé. Ce sentiment a beaucoup plus de prix à ses yeux que les jouets achetés pour éviter une crise ou pour maintenir la paix. Se sentir important, compris et aimé est un besoin.

Lorsque la relation parent-enfant s'envenime, on ne sait plus où donner de la tête et perdre la maîtrise arrive très vite et trop souvent. La fessée, les cris, les injures et le marchandage (je te donne ceci, si tu fais cela) sont-ils des solutions ?

Chapitre 3

LA DISCIPLINE QUI FAIT MAL

Bien des parents semblent croire que des remontrances hystériques inciteront les enfants à bien se conduire. Nous avons tous eu le « plaisir » de voir des parents exploser devant leurs enfants. Tout d'abord, leur visage s'empourpre et leurs veines se gonflent. Ensuite, ils perdent toute maîtrise d'eux-mêmes et tiennent des propos qui dépassent leur pensée. Ce comportement ne changera malheureusement pas l'enfant qui a un comportement répréhensible. Peut-être même aura-t-il apprécié votre spectacle ou aura-t-il remporté un pari avec son petit frère sur le nombre de veines qui allaient saillir de votre visage. Votre accès de colère peut même lui faire très plaisir et témoigner de son influence en tant que personne. En fait, peut-être vous a-t-il aiguillonné simplement pour obtenir la réaction que vous croyez qu'il craint.

Je me souviens d'un matin où j'étais pressée et pendant lequel ma fille, qui avait trois ans à l'époque, a renversé son verre de lait. J'ai crié si fort qu'on aurait pu croire que la maison venait de prendre feu. Un enfant ne devrait pas voir ses parents sortir de ses gonds si cela peut être évité. Le risque est alors de prononcer des paroles blessantes qui pourraient rester à jamais gravées dans sa mémoire ou, pire encore, de le frapper malgré vous. Bien sûr, nous sommes humains et ne sommes pas toujours bien disposés, mais un adulte qui perd la maîtrise de sa colère peut causer une souffrance affective et physique à un jeune.

Voyons de plus près les manifestations d'une discipline qui fait mal.

LA FESSÉE

La fessée blesse et humilie l'enfant. Elle sert à défouler l'adulte, à évacuer son irritation, à réaffirmer le pouvoir qu'il a perdu et à mettre fin au comportement de l'enfant. En fait, elle est toujours un aveu de faiblesse, un comportement par lequel un adulte révèle que ses autres recours ont échoué et qu'il se sent pris au dépourvu. Par ailleurs, la fessée ne s'en prend pas au comportement ou à l'acte répréhensible, elle s'en prend à la personne : c'est là tout le problème.

Les mains des parents sont faites pour tenir l'enfant lors de ses premiers pas, pour l'inciter à découvrir les merveilles de la vie, pour le soigner et pour le caresser. Bref, pour exprimer tout leur amour. Les mains des parents ne sont pas faites pour lui infliger de la douleur.

Interdire tout châtiment corporel à l'égard des enfants est, selon moi, une mesure préventive afin d'éviter le risque d'escalade, qui peut survenir même chez les parents les moins violents. Imaginons qu'un parent, sous le coup de la colère, gifle son enfant. Il est fort probable que ce dernier réagisse. Face à une protestation de l'enfant, la colère du parent pourrait augmenter d'un cran et il risquerait alors de frapper plus fort, peut-être à la tête, voire de le projeter contre un mur. La gifle du début, qui pouvait paraître anodine, aboutit ainsi à une agression brutale et dangereuse pour l'enfant. Il est d'ailleurs prouvé que les formes mineures de punitions corporelles augmentent les risques de dérapage vers des formes plus violentes et abusives.

Même les nourrissons encourent la violence de leurs parents. Entendre pleurer son bébé est une épreuve très pénible pour les nerfs. En effet, les cris d'un bébé peuvent atteindre 85 décibels, soit l'équivalent d'une rue très animée ou du rugissement d'un lion. C'est également éprouvant psychologiquement, car le père et la mère ont alors l'impression d'être de mauvais parents, impuissants à soulager leur bébé.

Lorsque vous sentez la moutarde vous monter au nez, voici cinq moyens de ne pas craquer :

– Passez le relais, surtout si vous êtes à bout de nerfs. Confiez votre bébé à quelqu'un de confiance (compagnon, copine, grand-mère). Essayez de penser à autre chose et de vous détendre avant de retourner le chercher.

– Allez prendre l'air. Si personne ne peut prendre le relais, installez l'enfant dans son landau, sa poussette, son kangourou et promenez-vous tous les deux pendant au moins une demi-heure. À l'extérieur, les cris de votre bébé perdront de leur intensité.

– Ne culpabilisez pas en imaginant que vous n'êtes pas un bon parent. Sachez qu'un bébé qui pleure beaucoup n'a pas pour autant une mère ou un père moins bien qu'un autre.

– Gardez une attitude positive et accordez-vous le droit d'être fatigué et énervé.

– Si vous sentez la colère monter en vous (mâchoires serrées, points dans le dos, etc.), prévenez-la. Avant de perdre la maîtrise, respirez profondément et déposez votre bébé en lieu sûr. Sortez de la pièce et téléphonez à une personne fiable qui saura vous écouter. Il est préférable de laisser votre enfant seul quelques instants, plutôt que de le secouer et de le regretter ensuite... toute la vie.

LA GIFLE EST PARTIE

« Le plus aimant et le plus bienveillant des parents peut à l'occasion s'énerver et commettre des erreurs. Il faut alors reconnaître la faute et non la justifier en prétendant qu'il s'agit d'une méthode éducative efficace. En disant à l'enfant que nous nous sommes trompés en manifestant notre colère par des coups ou des claques, nous lui démontrons que même un adulte peut avoir tort, mais surtout que l'usage de la force pour exprimer la colère ou pour obtenir gain de cause est inacceptable[*]. »

« Il ne s'agit pas toutefois de taire notre déception, notre mécontentement ou notre colère. L'enfant se rend bien compte que l'adulte est en colère. Il sait très bien décoder le ton de sa voix, son attitude corporelle. Chez le tout-petit, ce double message peut être interprété de telle sorte qu'il apprend que la colère est répréhensible, qu'il doit la réprimer puisque même l'adulte n'ose la dire. Il est essentiel que l'enfant sache ce que l'on pense de sa conduite[**]. »

---

[*] BOURCIER, Sylvie et Germain DUCLOS. « La fessée au banc des accusés », *Magazine Enfants Québec*, novembre 2004.
[**] *Id.*

La gifle est partie : on se sent vraiment moche ! Que faire ? Faut-il lui demander pardon ? Il ne s'agit pas tant de « demander pardon » mais plutôt de s'interroger : que s'est-il passé ? Par quoi s'est-on laissé emporter ? Quand on a trouvé la réponse ou des éléments de réponse, on peut en parler à l'enfant, non pour lui demander pardon, mais pour lui dire que, même si ce n'est pas une méthode d'éducation que l'on approuve, on a été amené à gifler « parce que... ».

Personnellement, lorsque j'ai giflé ma fille, je me suis interrogée sur ce qui était venu me chercher. C'était tout simple, injustifié mais tout simple. Je lui avais demandé de s'habiller en vue de rendre visite à sa Mamie (ma mère). Nous y allions régulièrement les fins de semaine, deux à trois fois par mois. Cette journée-là, elle n'était pas très chaude à l'idée d'y aller, elle préférait demeurer à la maison et s'amuser avec ses jouets. Elle s'est alors tout simplement mise à rechigner puis, finalement, à crier tout en refusant d'obtempérer. Étant moi-même exaspérée de consacrer régulièrement une journée de ma fin de semaine à visiter ma mère, ma colère a fait un bond. Je me suis élancée et je l'ai frappée en plein visage. Comment, à quatre ans et demi, osait-elle m'exprimer son désir et me dire non, alors que je n'y arrivais même pas avec ma propre mère ? Quelle bévue !

Les parents irrités par des obligations devenues insupportables perdent plus facilement la maîtrise d'eux-mêmes. Et les enfants le ressentant, ils expriment par des pleurs, de la résistance ou des crises ce qui ne va pas chez le parent ou l'adulte qui prend soin d'eux. Soyons conscients de nos limites, de nos besoins et de nos propres désirs, afin d'éviter de faire des gestes répréhensibles ou de dire des paroles très regrettables.

Parfois, il arrive que l'enfant lui-même s'emporte car la violence n'est pas le propre de l'adulte. En effet, les actes ou les paroles de certains enfants peuvent aussi être d'une grande violence. Il faut les aider à en prendre conscience en leur disant, par exemple : « Tu supporterais, toi, quand tu demandes quelque chose de normal, qu'on te dise "non", qu'on te dise des bêtises ? Nous, tes parents, nous ne le supportons pas non plus... »

ROUGE DE COLÈRE

Vous êtes sur le point de voir rouge ? Voici des stratégies* pour garder votre sang-froid :

- Exprimez clairement votre désaccord en épargnant l'amour-propre de l'enfant. Même si sa conduite vous déplaît, il doit pouvoir sentir que jamais son comportement ne diminuera l'amour que vous lui portez. Les mots blessants frappent eux aussi et tuent peu à peu sa confiance en lui et la confiance que lui inspire votre relation. Par exemple, de telles affirmations sont aussi préjudiciables qu'une fessée : « Tu n'es plus ma fille... Tu es méchant... Tu me tombes sur les nerfs, va-t'en... »

- Agissez, réagissez avant d'atteindre le point de non-retour où la fessée devient inévitable. N'attendez pas d'être à bout avant d'exprimer votre désapprobation.

- Extériorisez votre colère. Par exemple, vous pouvez vous isoler quelques instants dans la salle de bains et porter une serviette à votre visage pour crier cette colère, ladite serviette assourdissant le son de votre voix afin d'éviter d'inquiéter quiconque pourrait

---

* Inspirées du livre *Responsabiliser son enfant*, de Germain Duclos et Martin Duclos, aux Éditions du CHU Sainte-Justine.

entendre. Si vous le pouvez, prenez la voiture, roulez lentement et criez tout votre saoul, les fenêtres fermées, en frappant le volant s'il le faut. Une autre technique consiste à vous isoler dans votre chambre et à vous coucher, à plat ventre, le visage enfoncé dans un oreiller. Faites votre crise, criez, frappez des bras et des pieds : c'est tellement libérateur ! Cependant, si ces gestes ne font qu'attiser votre colère, employez d'autres stratégies.

— Prenez une douche légèrement chaude et réduisez progressivement la température de l'eau jusqu'à un niveau confortable.

— Retirez-vous quelques minutes dans une autre pièce. Fermez les yeux. Inspirez lentement et profondément. Expirez par la bouche. Faites une courte pause (les poumons à vide) avant la prochaine inspiration. Laissez votre souffle s'apaiser. Si possible, ouvrez grand la fenêtre pour aérer la pièce et buvez un grand verre d'eau fraîche. Cette courte pause vous permettra de réfléchir.

— Prenez vous-même du recul au lieu d'envoyer votre enfant dans sa chambre pour un moment de réflexion. Il ne saurait réfléchir dans un tel état d'agitation. Si vous choisissez plutôt de le mettre à l'écart pour qu'il se calme, par exemple dans une autre pièce ou sur une chaise, soyez toutefois conscient que l'utilisation systématique du retrait ne lui apprendra pas à mieux exprimer ce qu'il ressent. Il est donc important de faire un bref retour après la tempête afin de le rassurer sur le lien d'amour qui vous unit. Ce retour permettra une réconciliation et deviendra constructif dans la mesure où vous lui apprendrez comment il aurait pu agir ou s'exprimer au lieu de faire une bêtise ou une crise.

– Communiquez avec l'éducatrice ou l'enseignante de votre enfant. Le partage d'expériences et d'observations vous permettra de mieux cerner les besoins de ce dernier et ainsi de déterminer les moyens d'y répondre. Des stratégies éducatives cohérentes à la maison et dans le milieu scolaire favorisent un changement de comportement chez l'enfant.

– Donnez-vous des temps de répit. Le stress relié à une vie trépidante exacerbe l'impatience. L'exercice, le plein air, la lecture, l'écoute de musique, un long bain chaud ou un bon café en agréable compagnie vous permettront de reprendre contact avec la femme ou l'homme qui existe toujours derrière le parent. Par ailleurs, il est indispensable pour la santé du couple de séparer vie conjugale et vie familiale. Par exemple, passez « en amoureux », sans les enfants, une soirée par semaine, un week-end par trimestre, une semaine par an. Les enfants vont protester : ils sont couramment jaloux des liens qui unissent leurs parents. Mais ils en seront profondément rassurés. Rien n'est plus sécurisant pour un enfant que de sentir que ses parents s'aiment et forment un couple solide. Pour les plus jeunes, cela éloigne la crainte d'une séparation, pour les ados, cela leur permet de gagner en autonomie. Pour tous, cette image d'un couple unit servira de référence plus tard.

– Travaillez en équipe avec votre partenaire de vie à la maison ou avec une collègue au travail (éducatrice, conseillère pédagogique ou autre personne dont le mandat est de prendre soin des enfants). Convenez d'un code pour indiquer à l'autre qu'il est temps qu'il (elle) prenne la relève ou que vous avez tout simplement besoin d'aide. L'enfant constatera que vous partagez les mêmes valeurs. Fixez les mêmes limites et la ronde épuisante des négociations avec l'un et avec l'autre diminuera grandement.

— Demandez de l'aide si votre enfant vous fait sortir de vos gonds régulièrement. Si vous envisagez de recourir à la fessée ou si vous développez une aversion pour votre enfant (un sentiment humain mais non éducatif !), n'attendez pas que la situation dégénère. Allez chercher de l'aide ! C'est ce qui m'a le plus aidée, car j'ai eu l'occasion d'échanger avec un professionnel sur les méthodes éducatives susceptibles d'aider mon enfant, et ce, sans être jugée.

LE MARCHANDAGE

« Si tu ranges ta chambre, tu auras un cadeau... Si tu ramasses tes jouets, nous irons nous amuser dans les aires de jeu au restaurant... Si tu t'habilles, tu auras droit à un bonbon... Si tu ne lances pas ta nourriture, tu... » La tentation d'employer ces petites phrases existe. Il s'agit ni plus ni moins de marchandage. Ce procédé ne marche qu'un temps. Il conduit à une escalade de menaces qui se termine trop souvent par une guerre de tranchées qui épuisera nerveusement les parents. Non seulement le marchandage ne donne pas de repères à un enfant, mais il lui retire ceux qu'il peut avoir. Par exemple, lui promettre une gâterie (chocolat, cornet, friandise, etc.) s'il ramasse ses jouets exerce une pression sur lui, alors que cette tâche pourrait constituer un moment de bonheur partagé entre ses parents et lui. De plus,

Une discipline sans douleur

il doit comprendre que les exigences de ses parents ne sont pas des fantaisies. Ils lui demandent ce que tout parent demande à ses enfants, c'est-à-dire des choses qui sont des conditions *sine qua non* pour que la vie en famille soit possible et agréable pour tous. Voici quelques situations où le marchandage devient tentant et des stratégies d'intervention pour l'éviter.

Situations	Stratégies d'intervention
Sortir du bain.	Utilisez l'humour au lieu de marchander. Entrez dans la salle de bains, regardez votre enfant avec stupéfaction et dites : « Non, je rêve, ce n'est pas mon enfant qui est dans le bain ! Ce n'est pas possible puisque je lui ai demandé trois fois de sortir. Mon enfant est très obéissant, donc ce n'est pas lui ! Il est forcément dans sa chambre en train de mettre son pyjama. Donc, celui-ci n'est qu'une illusion, je vais vider l'eau du bain et il va disparaître avec... » Et vous retirez le bouchon du bain. Vous verrez votre enfant rire et filer dans sa chambre mettre son pyjama.
Se brosser les dents.	Encouragez-le ! Par exemple, dites-lui ceci : « Qu'est-ce que je suis content que tu te brosses les dents ! Tu as de belles dents bien blanches, je suis fière de toi ! » Ou encore, dites-lui : « J'étais chez une connaissance hier soir, elle a dû ordonner trois fois à son enfant d'aller se brosser les dents. Cela m'a fait plaisir de penser que toi, tu le fais chaque soir sans que j'aie besoin de répéter. »
S'habiller le matin.	Préparer les vêtements la veille. Au moment de s'habiller, utilisez une minuterie (celle de la cuisinière par exemple) et faites un pari. « Je te parie que tu n'es pas capable de t'habiller avant que la minuterie sonne : je la règle sur 10 minutes. »

Situations	Stratégies d'intervention
Ranger les jouets.	Faites-en un jeu ! Par exemple, les enfants font les wagons (ils se placent l'un derrière l'autre en se tenant par la taille) et vous faites la locomotive. Vous passez ensuite tout près des jouets afin que les enfants puissent les ramasser, puis vous vous dirigez vers le coffre à jouet où chacun y met la marchandise trouvée !

Par ailleurs, en respectant des règles de vie, on ne fait que remplir son devoir d'être humain vivant avec les autres. Pourquoi doit-on s'habiller ? Parce que dans notre société, cela fonctionne ainsi ! Pourquoi ne doit-on pas lancer de nourriture ? Parce qu'elle est d'une importance vitale, elle n'est pas un jouet. Pourquoi doit-on ranger ses affaires ? Parce que si chacun laisse tout traîner dans la maison, la vie y deviendra rapidement intenable. Celui qui ramasse ses affaires n'a donc pas à être gratifié d'une récompense pour cela. Que recevez-vous, vous les parents, pour avoir préparé les repas, fait le lavage ou tondu la pelouse ?

De plus, pratiquer le marchandage revient à mettre l'enfant en position de toute-puissance. Puisqu'on quémande son accord et qu'on est prêt à le monnayer, il devient le maître du jeu. Ce n'est pas son rôle et c'est destructeur pour lui. En effet, chaque fois que vous lui promettez un cadeau, des friandises ou de l'argent afin qu'il exécute une tâche ménagère ou autre, vous engendrez une dépendance psychologique : l'enfant associant effort et récompense. Il doit comprendre qu'on participe aux tâches ménagères non pas pour gagner quoi que ce soit, mais parce que, dans une maison commune, chacun a des droits et des devoirs. Il doit découvrir qu'un bon comportement renferme ses propres récompenses.

Une discipline sans douleur

Cette problématique survient aussi lorsque l'entourage (grands-parents, tantes, oncles, amis de la famille, etc.) pratique le marchandage, parfois de façon subtile, auprès de vos enfants. Dans ce cas-ci, bien que vous soyez sensibles aux conséquences négatives de ce procédé, votre famille immédiate ou vos amis ne le sont pas du tout ! Comment intervenir pour faire valoir vos valeurs et vos convictions sans blesser les mamies, papis, beaux-frères, belles-sœurs, parrains, marraines, amis, etc. ? Vous vous doutez sans doute qu'il s'agit d'un défi de taille.

Voici quelques situations et des stratégies pour intervenir :

Situations	Stratégies d'intervention
Vous êtes chez une amie avec votre poupon de 6 mois. Il vient de manger, sa couche est propre et il est l'heure de la sieste. Dans une pièce sombre, vous le déposez dans son parc, afin de reproduire ses conditions habituelles d'endormissement. Il pleurniche un peu selon son habitude, mais vous savez qu'il s'endormira rapidement. Votre copine intervient sur un ton culpabilisant en vous disant qu'il a peut-être encore faim ou qu'il vient probablement de souiller sa couche.	Dites-lui qu'elle n'a pas à s'inquiéter, que le comportement de votre bébé est normal et que vous comprenez que cela lui déchire le cœur d'entendre votre bébé pleurer. Tentez de lui changer les idées en abordant un sujet qui la passionne. Évitez surtout de vous sentir coupable. Vous connaissez votre bébé et vous êtes la meilleure maman pour lui.
Vous êtes en visite chez votre mère. Il est bientôt l'heure de souper et elle offre un biscuit à votre fils de 3 ans qui pleure, alors que vous venez de lui dire non à deux reprises en lui expliquant que le repas sera servi dans quelques minutes.	Penchez-vous et regardez votre enfant droit dans les yeux (en prenant soin d'éviter qu'il voit sa mamie qui pourrait avoir un regard réprobateur à votre endroit) et dites-lui : « Je sais que tu as faim et mamie l'a compris aussi. » Ensuite, faites diversion en lui offrant

Situations	Stratégies d'intervention
	papier et crayons pour lui permettre de patienter. Vous pourriez aussi demander à votre mère de lui offrir un morceau de carotte ou de céleri en attendant le repas. Ne faites pas allusion au biscuit et ne blâmez pas votre mère du regard. Prenez soin de remettre le biscuit dans le sac et rangez-le.
Lors d'une rencontre familiale à votre domicile, votre enfant arrive en pleurant, car le chiot d'un proche vient de gruger son jouet, récemment acheté au magasin à 1 $. Le proche en cause, qui ne supporte pas d'entendre un enfant pleurer, lui dit alors : « Arrête de pleurer, je vais t'en acheter un autre. »	Regardez votre enfant en lui parlant et dites-lui que vous comprenez sa peine et qu'il a le droit de l'exprimer en pleurant. Faites-lui comprendre que le chiot est un bébé chien et que, comme tous les bébés, il porte tout à sa bouche. Faites le tour de la pièce avec votre enfant afin de ranger les autres jouets pour ne pas qu'ils subissent le même sort. Vous pourriez aussi, votre enfant et vous, remettre le chien à son propriétaire pour qu'il le surveille. Quant au jouet, s'il se répare, vous pourriez l'en aviser et, s'il est complètement détruit, attendez que votre enfant soit prêt à s'en débarrasser avant de le jeter, à moins qu'il ne soit devenu dangereux.
Votre fils de 10 ans, en visite chez parrain et marraine pour le week-end, arrive avec ses plus beaux habits pour leur faire plaisir. Juste avant votre départ, l'un deux lui dit que s'il reste bien propre dans ses beaux habits, ils iront prendre le dessert chez un marchand de glaces votre départ après le repas du soir. Votre fils vous lance un	Prenez votre fils par la main, faites-lui un clin d'œil et expliquez à parrain et marraine combien votre fils adore leur faire plaisir en portant de beaux habits et en même temps combien il apprécie venir les voir pour l'occasion qu'il a d'aller jouer au parc aussi longtemps, car marraine peut le surveiller de son balcon. Ensuite offrez

Une discipline sans douleur

Situations	Stratégies d'intervention
regard désespéré, car il adore jouer dans les aires de jeu au parc situé juste derrière la maison.	une solution de rechange : par exemple, il pourrait se changer avant d'aller au parc et garder ses vêtements propres pour le repas du soir et pour la visite chez le marchand de glaces.

Évidemment, les situations ne sont jamais les mêmes d'une visite à l'autre, mais il importe de respecter les mêmes principes de bases. Que votre enfant soit en visite ou que quelqu'un soit en visite chez lui, vous devez conserver la même attitude à son égard. Toutefois, il peut être agréable de permettre de petits changements dans ses habitudes de vie.

Certains comportements, tels que des crises de rage, ne sauraient être tolérés nulle part. Cependant, certaines choses peuvent être modifiées sans que cela ne cause de problème, comme la façon de préparer un plat ou d'établir une routine durant la journée. Ces nouvelles habitudes de vie seront l'occasion pour lui de découvrir de nouvelles façons de faire. Il est même possible d'envisager des exceptions : par exemple, chez les grands-parents, mamie pourrait lui lire une histoire avant la sieste de l'après-midi, même si, chez lui, cette activité n'est réservée qu'au soir. Cela lui procurera beaucoup de plaisir.

À l'inverse, il s'apercevra qu'il y a ailleurs des limites qui ne s'appliquent pas chez lui : par exemple, dans la maison de parrain et marraine, tout le monde enlève ses chaussures en entrant et il est interdit de sauter sur les lits. L'enfant apprend alors que chaque maison a ses règles. Inutile de recourir au marchandage : après l'âge de trois ans, l'enfant est tout à fait capable de saisir la différence entre ce qui est accepté à la maison et ce qui ne l'est pas ailleurs.

Enfin, il arrive parfois que les parents doivent s'opposer à la famille ou aux amis. Si vous ne parvenez pas à reprendre la situation en mains, car la parenté ou l'environnement (amis, voisins, collègues de travail) ridiculisent vos valeurs et vos convictions, il faut parfois en arriver à espacer les visites ou à être moins disponible pour les recevoir. Éduquer ses enfants, c'est parfois faire des choix difficiles.

L'INGÉRENCE DE NOS PROPRES PARENTS

Tous les parents ont en commun le besoin primordial d'être rassurés quant à leurs compétences parentales. « Suis-je une bonne mère, un bon père ? Est-ce que j'adopte la bonne attitude ? » Avec tous ces questionnements, il est normal de se tourner vers ses propres parents. Cependant, certains grands-parents, en voulant bien faire, en arrivent à juger et à critiquer au lieu de prêter une oreille bienveillante, ce qui peut être mille fois plus utile que des tonnes de conseils. Malheureusement, les parents se trouvent trop souvent aux prises avec des grands-parents qui s'ingèrent dans les habitudes de vie ou dans l'éducation de leurs propres enfants. Cette ingérence peut même semer la discorde au sein du couple et de la nouvelle famille. Parfois, les parents ne développent pas leur confiance en eux et s'en remettent trop aux nouvelles stratégies qu'on leur conseille au lieu d'agir en fonction de leurs valeurs et de leurs convictions. Les enfants finissent inévitablement par en souffrir. L'ingérence peut prendre différentes formes[*].

---

[*] Tiré du livre *Grands-parents aujourd'hui, plaisirs et pièges*, de Francine Ferland, aux Éditions du CHU Sainte-Justine.

1. Il peut s'agir de commentaires insidieux, pleins de sous-entendus.

    - Il est pâle et ne dort pas assez, non ? (Sous-entendu : il a l'air malade, vous n'en prenez pas bien soin.)
    - Je lui ai fait une purée de légumes et il a tout mangé en un rien de temps. (Sous-entendu : moi je sais le nourrir adéquatement.)
    - Tu veux lui faire percer les oreilles ? Tu l'envoies déjà à la garderie ? (Sous-entendu : vous ne prenez pas les meilleures décisions pour l'enfant.)

2. Elle peut se manifester par des propos plus directs.

    - Tu prends le bébé dans tes bras dès qu'il se met à pleurer, tu vas le gâter !
    - Il n'est pas encore propre à seize mois ? Toi, à quatorze mois, je t'avais déjà entraîné à la propreté.
    - Il choisit lui-même ses vêtements ? Il va finir par penser qu'il est le roi de la famille et il va vous mener par le bout du nez.

3. Elle peut se manifester par des initiatives déplacées prises sans consulter les parents.

    - Je lui ai acheté une nouvelle sorte de couches : elles semblent plus confortables que celles que tu utilises.
    - Je lui acheté un petit téléviseur pour qu'il puisse écouter ses émissions dans sa chambre ; il aimera ça, j'en suis sûre.
    - J'ai pensé que la compagnie d'un petit animal serait bénéfique pour lui, alors j'ai décidé de lui offrir ce chiot. (Pourtant, avoir un animal domestique représente une décision importante qui revient à la famille.)

Vos parents se justifient en disant qu'ils veulent vous éviter toute erreur ou toute difficulté, mais ils vous empêchent ainsi de trouver votre propre façon de faire et vos points de référence. Si vous vous sentez jugés et critiqués, faites-leur part de ce que vous vivez, dites-leur que vous serez plus enclins à discuter avec eux de vos inquiétudes si vous bénéficiez d'une oreille attentive. Par ailleurs, invitez-les à souligner vos compétences parentales lorsque vous en doutez vous-mêmes, cela vous aidera à prendre confiance en vous et surtout à transmettre ce sentiment à votre bébé.

Enfin, vous pouvez aussi leur dire que lorsque vous sollicitez leur aide pour garder votre enfant, il serait sage de faire les choses comme vous le désirez. S'en soucier constitue une manifestation de respect et une reconnaissance de votre rôle de parent.

LES ABUS VERBAUX

Si les coups et les châtiments corporels peuvent être aisément qualifiés de sévices, les abus verbaux sont plus subtils et sont considérés comme moins dommageables. Et pourtant, les paroles peuvent causer des blessures morales tout aussi profondes et dévastatrices. Une langue acérée peut faire autant de mal que des coups ! Des attaques verbales répétées coupent la communication entre un jeune et son parent, détruisent les liens affectifs, suscitent du ressentiment, de la colère et de l'hostilité. Elles sont dévalorisantes pour l'enfant. La crainte de les subir engendre le mensonge pour y échapper. Elles amènent l'enfant à se croire mauvais, stupide et inutile. Le sentiment de rejet et la faible estime de soi qui en découle risquent de perdurer et d'affecter toute sa personnalité. Les abus verbaux à bannir sont :

1. **Les menaces**

Les menaces, même lorsqu'elles ne sont que des paroles en l'air, détruisent le sentiment de sécurité de l'enfant. Il faut comprendre qu'un enfant fait entièrement confiance à son parent. Il accepte toutes ses déclarations comme des faits. Certains propos frisent la cruauté : « Je vais te donner si tu es tannant... Si tu touches encore ton pénis, je le coupe... Je vais te coller les fesses sur la chaise si tu ne cesses pas de bouger durant le repas... Arrête ça ou bien je te descends de la voiture et je continue sans toi... » De telles intimidations, loin de calmer un enfant, ont pour effet de le rendre plus anxieux, et par conséquent, plus agité. On n'éduque pas un enfant en le menaçant ou en lui faisant peur.

2. **Les humiliations et les moqueries**

Pénible et dégradante, l'humiliation donne lieu à un refoulement et apprend la dissimulation à un enfant. La personne qui utilise ce moyen cherche à rabaisser l'autre, à l'écraser. Les sarcasmes, les railleries et la dérision sont tout aussi néfastes. Ces agressions sapent l'estime de soi d'un enfant et ne lui enseignent pas une conduite adéquate. L'humiliation et la moquerie s'expriment à la maison de mille et une manières, toutes aussi blessantes les unes que les autres. Vos enfants se dénigrent entre eux ? Édictez une nouvelle règle. Dites-leur : « La prochaine fois que quelqu'un dira une phrase blessante, il devra s'excuser et dire que c'était de lui dont il parlait ! » Généralement, ce genre de propos cesse en moins d'un mois si vous faites respecter la règle. Assurez-vous cependant de donner l'exemple !

3. **La culpabilisation**

La culpabilisation, quant à elle, jette le blâme sur un enfant : « Tu fais de le peine à maman ... Tu vas me faire mourir... C'est à cause de toi si je suis malade... Tu devrais avoir honte ! » L'enfant modifiera parfois son comportement de crainte de ne plus être aimé, ce qui laissera malheureusement croire que cette stratégie est valable. En réalité, cette forme subtile de dévalorisation nuit à l'estime de soi d'un enfant et mine ses relations avec les adultes.

4. Les critiques

Une critique devrait faire ressortir les qualités d'une personne ou d'une chose (un livre par exemple), mais le plus souvent, elle souligne ses défauts. Un parent qui exige la perfection et qui critique sans cesse les efforts de son enfant aura tôt fait de le décourager et de l'énerver. Une abondance de commentaires négatifs, comme ceux qui suivent, amèneront un enfant à douter profondément de lui : « Arrête de froncer les sourcils comme ca... Tu es encore en retard... Si tu regardais ce que tu fais... Tu as vu comment tu as laissé ta serviette ? » Une autre manière de critiquer consiste à être sans cesse sur le dos de son enfant. Par exemple, le fait de reprendre constamment le langage de l'enfant, de souligner ses erreurs de syntaxe ou de désapprouver sa lenteur à exprimer sa pensée finit par produire un effet contraire à celui recherché. Cela ne l'aide absolument pas à s'améliorer, bien au contraire. Assurez-vous, par un examen médical, que votre enfant a une bonne audition. Parlez-lui lentement, avec des mots simples puis écoutez-le sans l'interrompre. Ne l'accablez pas pour qu'il parle plus vite, qu'il parle davantage ou qu'il développe un vocabulaire plus étoffé.

5. Les conversations inopportunes

Voici un exemple de ce que j'entends par conversations inopportunes. Imaginons que vous êtes réunis autour d'une table avec des amis ou des membres de la famille tandis que les jeunes enfants âgés de deux à cinq ans, qui ont déjà mangé, s'amusent dans la pièce voisine. Une discussion sur l'un des enfants débute. Par exemple, un convive vous fait part de son inquiétude quant au développement de votre enfant, car il ne trouve pas ses aptitudes langagières assez développées pour son âge. Étant inquiète vous aussi, vous participez activement à cette conversation. Croyez-vous que les bambins dans l'autre pièce n'entendent pas ce que vous dites d'eux ? Ils entendent certainement !

Trop souvent, les adultes tiennent des conversations entre eux sans se soucier de la présence des enfants. Voici une anecdote qui le démontre. Je me souviens d'avoir discuté avec ma sœur des problèmes de santé (sans conséquences) de notre mère, tandis que nos filles de trois et quatre ans jouaient ensemble. Au bout de quelques minutes, ma fille est apparue dans l'embrasure de la porte et m'a demandé les larmes aux yeux : « Est-ce que mamie va mourir ? » Il m'a fallu plusieurs jours pour la rassurer. Si elle n'avait pas fait irruption dans notre conversation, je n'aurais jamais su qu'elle entendait. Lorsque plus tard, j'ai divorcé de son père, nous avons été prudents dans nos échanges (parfois très orageux) afin de s'assurer qu'elle n'en soit nullement témoin. Les mots d'adultes blessent, inquiètent, dévalorisent et perturbent les enfants. Sachez qu'ils entendent et comprennent tout, même s'ils ne sont pas dans la même pièce que vous. Soyez vigilants !

Enfin, avant de clore ce chapitre, il me semble opportun de faire la distinction entre des paroles menaçantes, du marchandage, une punition ou une conséquence. Lorsque je donne des conférences aux parents, il arrive souvent que ces mots sèment la confusion. Même si les punitions et les conséquences font l'objet d'un autre chapitre, voici un tableau démontrant la différence entre chacun de ces termes à partir d'un même exemple et selon différents groupes d'âges.

ENFANT DE 2 ANS

Paroles d'un parent	Catégorie	Objectif
Si tu es gentille chez tante Annie, je te donnerai un biscuit.	Marchandage	Le parent tente de charmer son enfant pour se faire écouter.
Si tu es tannante chez tante Annie, je ne t'y amènerai plus jamais.	Menace	Le parent tente de faire peur à son enfant pour se faire écouter.
Si tu es tannante chez tante Annie, je t'enlèverai ta suce pour dormir.	Punition	Le parent tente de priver son enfant d'un plaisir pour se faire écouter.
Chez tante Annie, tu peux jouer dans le salon et la cuisine, mais pas dans les chambres, sinon, je devrai te garder tout près de moi.	Conséquence	Le parent tente de responsabiliser son enfant pour se faire écouter. Le fait d'expliquer le comportement attendu peut l'aider.

ENFANT DE 4 ANS

Paroles d'un parent	Catégorie	Objectif
Si tu ramasses tes jouets, nous irons au parc.	Marchandage	Le parent tente de charmer son enfant pour se faire écouter.
Si tu ne ramasses pas tes jouets, je vais les jeter.	Menace	Le parent tente de faire peur à son enfant pour se faire écouter.
Si tu ne ramasses pas tes jouets, tu ne pourras pas écouter la télévision ce soir.	Punition	Le parent tente de priver son enfant d'un plaisir pour se faire écouter.
Je règle la minuterie et si tes jouets ne sont pas tous ramassés d'ici 5 minutes, demain, tu ne pourras en sortir qu'un seul à la fois et tu devras le ranger avant d'en sortir un autre.	Conséquence	Le parent tente de responsabiliser son enfant pour se faire écouter. Le fait de lui donner un repère temporel peut l'aider.

ENFANT DE 8 ANS

Paroles d'un parent	Catégorie	Objectif
Si tu vas au lit dans 15 minutes, je te ferai ton petit déjeuner favori demain matin.	Marchandage	Le parent tente de charmer son enfant pour se faire écouter.
Si tu n'es pas au lit dans 15 minutes, je me débarrasse de ta console de jeu.	Menace	Le parent tente de faire peur à son enfant pour se faire écouter.
Si tu n'es pas au lit dans 15 minutes, il ne sera plus question d'aller jouer chez ton ami samedi matin.	Punition	Le parent tente de priver son enfant d'un plaisir pour se faire écouter.
Si tu n'es pas au lit dans 15 minutes, il sera trop tard pour te lire les 3 histoires que tu as demandées.	Conséquence	Le parent tente de responsabiliser son enfant pour se faire écouter. Lui rappeler la raison de la consigne peut l'aider.

ADOLESCENT DE 14 ANS

Paroles d'un parent	Catégorie	Objectif
Si je cesse de recevoir des plaintes de tes professeurs parce que tes devoirs ne sont pas faits, je t'achèterai une bicyclette neuve.	Marchandage	Le parent tente de charmer son enfant pour se faire écouter.
Si je reçois une autre plainte de tes professeurs parce que tes devoirs ne sont pas faits, je te mets à la porte.	Menace	Le parent tente de faire peur à son enfant pour se faire écouter.
Si je reçois une autre plainte de tes professeurs parce que tes devoirs ne sont pas faits, je te prive de tes jeux électroniques pour un mois.	Punition	Le parent tente de priver son enfant d'un plaisir pour se faire écouter.
Si je reçois une autre plainte de tes professeurs parce que tes devoirs ne sont pas faits, c'est signe que tes amis prennent le pas sur tes études et que je devrai réduire tes permissions de sortie.	Conséquence	Le parent tente de responsabiliser son enfant pour se faire écouter. Lui montrer ce qu'il croit être la source du problème peut amener une discussion afin de bien saisir l'enjeu.

Depuis plusieurs années, je me suis engagée personnellement à rayer la discipline qui fait mal (physique, verbale et affective) de ma vie et de celle de ma fille, de même que de celle de tous les enfants. Dans ce but, j'offre des formations aux parents et éducateurs afin de leur fournir les outils nécessaires pour une éducation incitative. Je crois qu'il est de notre devoir à tous de mettre tout en œuvre pour éviter que les adultes heurtent les enfants (en coups et en mots), par respect pour leur dignité. Je vous invite donc à tourner la page pour découvrir comment on peut faire de la discipline... sans douleur !

Chapitre 4

ÉDUQUER SANS DOULEUR

Quand les adultes ont peur de causer des frustrations à leurs enfants et ne savent quand poser des limites ou des interdits, alors le prix à payer se révèle très élevé. Ces enfants sont souvent comblés sur le plan des désirs, mais incroyablement frustrés dans leurs besoins relationnels, auront un seuil de tolérance très bas à la frustration. Par conséquent, une réalité décevante ou limitative déclenchera chez eux une agressivité incontrôlable. Beaucoup d'enfants insupportables sont en réalité en manque de limites. En apparence, ils s'opposent à ces limites, mais comme ils en ont besoin, ils les recherchent et, la plupart du temps, ils le font en multipliant les méfaits.

POSER FERMEMENT DES LIMITES

Au temps des grandes familles où frères et sœurs se retrouvaient nombreux sous un même toit, pour ne pas dire dans la même chambre, les relations familiales étaient différentes. Les parents ne pouvaient guère accorder beaucoup d'attention à chaque enfant. Ils donnaient ce qu'ils pouvaient et la marmaille s'en contentait, quitte à se le partager ou à se le disputer, selon les mœurs de la maison.

Une discipline sans douleur

De nos jours, les familles sont moins nombreuses et un enfant reçoit beaucoup d'attention. Il vit dans un petit royaume. Il découvre rapidement qu'à la maison, ses parents lui sont entièrement dévoués. Il voit qu'on lui accorde beaucoup d'importance. Haut comme trois pommes, il le comprend déjà. De plus, lorsque les deux parents travaillent à l'extérieur, il est fréquent qu'ils cherchent à compenser leur absence en acquiesçant à toutes ses demandes. Ils auraient l'impression d'être de mauvais parents s'ils n'écoutaient pas ses diverses requêtes. D'autres, sans même avoir besoin d'être absents, ont une propension à répondre aux moindres désirs de leurs enfants. Dans ces conditions, il n'est pas rare de voir les parents se sentir dépassés, impuissants et démunis devant le comportement de leur enfant, comme s'ils étaient les victimes de leur progéniture.

Lorsque j'explique à ces adultes qu'ils auraient intérêt à être plus fermes avec leur enfant ou avec celui qu'ils ont à charge, ils me répondent trop souvent : « Il est trop petit pour me comprendre. » Ou bien : « C'est trop difficile de dire non, il va se mettre à pleurer. » Ou encore : « J'ai peur de lui parler sur un ton dur. »

Combien d'enfants – et j'entends aussi par là des bébés de trois mois ou plus – font des crises dans leur bassinette à l'heure du coucher et se mettent pourtant à sourire et même à rire dès que leur parent entre dans leur chambre ?

Si ces enfants sont capables de tels comportements à un jeune âge, ils sont tout autant en mesure de comprendre rapidement ce que leurs parents attendent d'eux. Ils peuvent répondre aux exigences parentales. Et si personne n'intervient de façon plus soutenue et concrète dès maintenant, ils risquent de devenir, pour reprendre l'expression populaire, des « petits monstres ». Parlez-en avec d'autres parents !

Vous verrez combien les enfants sont brillants et astucieux quand il s'agit d'attirer l'attention et de combler leur désir d'exclusivité.

Tous les professionnels de la petite enfance admettent l'importance de fixer des limites pour le bon développement de l'enfant. Au risque de vous décourager, poser des limites à ses enfants tout en restant d'un calme olympien est un idéal difficilement atteignable. Si tant de parents en viennent aux cris, aux menaces, à la fessée ou au marchandage, ce n'est pas le fruit du hasard, mais bien des réactions de défense de leur part. Ceux-ci se heurtent à la résistance (normale) de leurs enfants et ils se sentent parfaitement impuissants à y faire face. Bien souvent, ils finissent même par douter de la légitimité de leurs attentes.

Tous les parents se sentent mal à l'aise dans pareille situation. Et tous les parents se sentent coupables. D'autant plus coupables qu'ils sont persuadés – comme je l'ai été d'ailleurs – que les autres parents se débrouillent mieux qu'eux. Ce n'est pas vrai ! Fixer des limites à ses enfants n'est simple pour aucun parent. Ce n'est pas magique : c'est un travail continuel, à toute heure du jour.

Certaines écoles de pensée nouveau genre ou certains intervenants (souvent sans enfant !) laissent croire aux parents qu'il existe une seule et bonne « recette » qui réglera miraculeusement tout. Cette promesse illusoire ne fait que renforcer la croyance en un idéal qu'il faudrait atteindre à tout prix. Face à cet idéal inaccessible, les parents se sentent encore plus misérables et démunis. Il est exact de dire que tous les enfants sont différents, mais ils ont heureusement des traits psychologiques communs qui peuvent servir de base à une réflexion sur la manière de les éduquer. Ensuite, c'est la connaissance fine de chacun qui permet aux parents de s'adapter à leurs enfants en tenant compte de leur propre personnalité. Bien souvent, les difficultés éducatives que rencontrent les parents n'ont rien d'inévitable, mais viennent de ce qu'on pourrait appeler un malentendu dû à une méconnaissance de l'enfant. Les parents ignorent trop souvent comment fonctionne leur enfant. Savoir ce qui le touche, ce qui le met en colère, est indispensable pour bien le comprendre, surtout à un âge où il ne s'explique pas !

COMMANDER SANS EN CULPABILISER

Poser des limites implique inévitablement de commander. Les enfants ne l'apprécient guère et la majorité semble ne pas entendre les directives énoncées. Si vous devez répéter cinq, six ou sept fois à votre enfant d'aller se coucher, vous êtes dépourvus de toute autorité, vous n'êtes qu'un perroquet.

D'ailleurs, certains enfants vont même jusqu'à demander : « Pourquoi c'est toi qui décides ? » Il est important de leur rappeler que les parents commandent parce qu'ils ont plus de vécu et ont appris à connaître les règles. Le fait de se coucher n'est pas une fantaisie, c'est une règle d'hygiène de vie essentielle. Tout comme interdire à un enfant de boire du vin à cinq ans.

L'adulte qui exerce son autorité signale à l'enfant de demeurer à sa place. Il lui démontre que ce sont les adultes qui ont la responsabilité d'enseigner et d'appliquer les règles. Toutefois, ça ne veut surtout pas dire que les adultes ont tous les droits. Il importe de tenir compte de la parole de l'enfant, mais dans de nombreuses situations, les adultes doivent décider. Le parent favorise ainsi le lien affectif avec l'enfant, le soutient dans ses expériences et ses découvertes, et respecte ses perceptions (par exemple, si l'enfant déclare ne plus avoir faim, il ne l'oblige pas à terminer son assiette). Il fait preuve de sensibilité à l'égard de l'enfant.

Par ailleurs, un enfant que ses parents laissent « commander » a tendance à angoisser et c'est normal. Comment pourrait-il se sentir protégé par des parents incapables de l'envoyer se coucher ? Beaucoup d'enfants qui ont peur la nuit cessent d'avoir peur quand on leur dit que les voleurs ont peur des papas et des mamans. Encore faut-il que les parents soient crédibles et, pour l'être, ils doivent exercer une autorité sur l'enfant.

Cependant, le parent ne doit pas imposer « sa » loi. Tout enfant, par exemple, doit manger des légumes. Mais, s'il y a à table des carottes et du brocoli, il doit avoir le droit de choisir. On n'a pas à lui imposer les épinards sous prétexte que l'on est friand de ce légume. On peut ainsi tenir compte des principes d'une saine alimentation et également de ses goûts personnels. En fait, pour savoir si l'on est ou non dans l'arbitraire, il faut se demander : est-ce que j'exige de lui ce que tous les parents (ou une majorité d'entre eux) demandent ?

Une autre façon de vérifier si vous n'êtes pas en train d'imposer à votre enfant des règles purement subjectives et fantaisistes consiste à vous poser deux simples questions :

1. Est-ce dangereux physiquement pour lui ou d'autres, est-ce nuisible pour l'environnement, les meubles, etc., si je n'interviens pas ? En d'autres termes, va-t-il blesser quelqu'un d'autre, se blesser lui-même ou risque-t-il de briser quelque chose ?

Une discipline sans douleur

2. Si je n'interviens pas, cela aura-t-il un impact dans sa vie plus tard (dans dix ou vingt ans) ?

Si vous répondez « non » aux deux questions, vous devriez tolérer son comportement. Par contre, si vous répondez « oui » à l'une ou l'autre des questions, vous devez intervenir chaque fois que votre enfant répète ce comportement.

Par exemple, un garçon de trois ans bouscule sa sœur ou ses parents parce qu'il est contrarié. Ses parents ne tolèrent pas son comportement et le mettent en retrait. Ils se demandent alors s'ils agissent correctement. Est-ce dangereux ? Non, puisqu'il ne leur fait pas mal. (S'il avait quinze ans, la réponse serait toutefois différente.) S'ils n'interviennent pas maintenant, cela aura-t-il un impact sur sa vie, ne serait-ce que dans dix ou vingt ans ? Oui, car ils ne lui auront pas appris le respect des autres. Ils doivent donc intervenir chaque fois que leur fils reproduit ce comportement, afin qu'il comprenne qu'il est inacceptable. Ils devraient aider leur garçon à mettre des mots sur ses frustrations en lui disant, par exemple : « Dis-moi que tu n'es pas content de quitter la garderie, mais ne me frappe pas ! »

Un autre exemple : une fillette de cinq ans aime choisir ses vêtements. Plus ils sont colorés, plus elle est fière de les porter. Un matin, elle veut partir pour la garderie avec des bas de couleurs différentes. Sa mère ne veut pas la laisser partir mal affublée. Frustrée, sa fille se met en colère. Sa mère l'envoie alors réfléchir dans sa chambre. Elle et son conjoint se questionnent alors sur la conduite à adopter. Est-ce dangereux ? Non. Cela aura-t-il un impact dans sa vie, dans dix ou vingt ans ? Non. Ses parents devraient donc la laisser faire et tolérer son caprice. De plus, en évitant d'intervenir à tout propos, ils auront plus d'impact lorsqu'ils le feront.

Pourquoi est-ce si difficile, pour des parents, de laisser leurs enfants aller à la garderie ou à l'école habillés de façon extravagante ? Parce qu'ils craignent la désapprobation de l'éducatrice, du professeur ou des autres adultes. Toutefois, lorsqu'ils choisissent de donner plus d'importance à l'avis des autres qu'aux goûts de leur fille, celle-ci a le sentiment que son opinion a peu de valeur. Un petit truc, chers parents, pour vous aider : mettez sur ses vêtements un autocollant sur lequel vous aurez inscrit : « J'ai choisi mes vêtements moi-même ce matin ! »

Évidemment, il en serait autrement si la fillette avait douze ans et voulait porter, pour aller à l'école, un chandail décolleté ou laissant le ventre à découvert. Serait-ce dangereux s'ils la laissaient faire ? Non. Cela pourrait-il avoir un impact plus tard (dans dix ou vingt ans) ? Oui, parce qu'ils ne lui auront pas enseigné que chaque situation ou contexte comporte certaines règles vestimentaires. Ils devraient donc intervenir.

Personnellement, lorsque ma fille est entrée à l'école secondaire, j'ai édicté une règle vestimentaire précise : interdiction de voir la naissance de ses seins ou le haut de ses fesses. En ce qui concerne les *strings*, ces sous-vêtements constitués de ficelles dont l'une passe entre les fesses, je n'y voyais aucun problème en autant qu'ils n'étaient pas visibles.

Malgré cette règle, ma fille avait tout de même le sentiment de gérer ses choix vestimentaires. Elle s'y est donc très bien conformée. Cependant, un jour, une de ses amies est venue à la maison. C'était en janvier et elle gardait son manteau même à l'intérieur. J'ai alors demandé discrètement à ma fille ce qui se passait : faisait-il trop froid dans la maison ? Elle me répondit : « C'est mieux qu'elle garde son manteau ! » Vous devinez sûrement que la jeune fille portait des vêtements qui ne correspondaient pas à la règle de la maison !

Les parents posent des interdits et énoncent des règles qui facilitent la vie de tous en société. En exerçant leur autorité sans culpabilité et dans le respect de l'enfant, ils le rassurent et lui rappellent sa place.

ACCEPTER D'ÊTRE DÉTESTÉ[*]

Et si, à force de trop aimer les enfants, on les préparait mal à la vie adulte ? Et si c'était normal, pour un adulte, de se faire détester par eux ? Il ne s'agit pas de moins les aimer, mais de supporter qu'eux puissent ne pas vous aimer et, parfois même, vous détester.

Il est évident que l'enfant réagira négativement aux interdits et aux privations. Ce serait trop beau s'il vous répondait : « Tu as raison de m'empêcher de voir ce film, je me range à tes arguments. Merci de prendre si bien soin de moi... » Non seulement, il insistera pour vous faire changer d'avis, mais il argumentera, protestera, piquera une colère ou fera la tête, selon son âge et son caractère. Le conflit est parfois inévitable. Cela ne signifie ni qu'il est véritablement malheureux ni qu'il ne vous aime plus. Rappelez-vous : vous êtes l'adulte, donc vous donnez les consignes ; il est l'enfant, donc il proteste. Chacun joue son rôle. Vouloir que votre enfant aime la discipline et les limites que vous lui imposez est utopique et vous compliquera sérieusement la tâche.

---

[*] Tiré du livre *Grands-parents aujourd'hui, plaisirs et pièges*, de Francine Ferland, aux Éditions du CHU Sainte-Justine.

L'amour idéalisé que certains adultes portent aux enfants peut devenir nocif. Ce sentiment tend à occuper toute la place dans leur relation avec le petit, au détriment d'autres éléments essentiels comme l'autorité et la transmission des valeurs. D'ailleurs, selon un sondage effectué pour *L'Express* (une revue d'actualité en ligne), à la question « Qu'attendent les parents de leurs enfants ? », 32% des participants ont répondu : « Qu'ils les aiment » !

L'amour est un sentiment beaucoup plus complexe qu'on veut bien le croire. Les gens qu'on aime le plus sont aussi ceux à qui on en veut ou ceux contre qui on se met en colère. C'est « l'ambivalence des sentiments ». Les enfants expriment très facilement cet état : quand nous leur interdisons une chose, ils répliquent par un « Je te déteste ! » puis, une heure plus tard, ils nous soufflent un « Je t'aime ». Croire que les enfants ne nous aimeront plus jamais est bien sûr un leurre !

De nos jours, les adultes craignent qu'un enfant se croit mal aimé s'ils se montrent autoritaires avec lui et, surtout, ils s'imaginent qu'il les aimera moins. Bien sûr, un enfant qui se fait gronder n'ira pas en remercier son parent. Il le fera peut-être dans dix ans mais, sur le coup, il réagira en tapant du pied, en faisant la tête, en pleurant... Or, comme nous souhaitons trop souvent une reconnaissance immédiate, nous faisons de la démagogie parentale permanente en favorisant les sentiments au détriment de l'autorité.

En fait, nous, les parents, devons donc arrêter de nous mettre à la place de l'enfant. Plus question d'empathie déplacée : nous n'avons pas le même âge que lui ! Si nous nous mettons toujours à sa place, nous ne pourrons pas maintenir longtemps une interdiction. Nous devons donc rester à notre place d'adulte, qui est aussi faite de contraintes. En fait, c'est comme si nous voulions éviter à l'enfant les choses auxquelles nous avons nous-mêmes du mal à nous résigner. Être sévère n'est plus à la mode, c'est vrai. D'ailleurs, sévère rime souvent avec réactionnaire. Aussi, pour être dispensés d'agir avec autorité, les adultes aimeraient que les enfants acceptent les règles et les appliquent d'eux-mêmes.

Par ailleurs, c'est une situation que l'on retrouve souvent à l'heure du dodo. Les parents souhaiteraient tellement que leur bambin aille au lit sans discuter, négocier, argumenter ou pleurer. Avouons-le, très peu d'enfants acceptent au premier abord d'aller dormir sans tenter d'en retarder le moment. Un parent qui ne met pas en place les limites indispensables se verra vite confronté à un défi de taille à l'heure du dodo. Afin d'éviter d'agir avec autorité, certains parents vont jusqu'à demander à l'éducatrice en garderie de supprimer la sieste de leur enfant. Ainsi, trop épuisé à l'heure du coucher, l'enfant ne trouve même plus la force de protester...

ACCEPTER DE FRUSTRER

Plusieurs parents croient qu'une attitude permissive leur vaudra d'être aimé de leur enfant. Qu'ils se détrompent ! Il est évidemment beaucoup plus agréable de dire « oui » à son enfant et de voir la joie briller dans ses yeux. Cependant, les parents qui pensent que les enfants sont naturellement bons et qu'ils deviendront sans effort des citoyens responsables et des humains altruistes et raisonnables se trompent. Ils devront, un jour ou l'autre, leur fixer des limites et accepter de les frustrer. S'ils ne le font pas, la société s'en chargera !

Deux motifs peuvent expliquer les difficultés de certains parents à dire « non » à leurs chers enfants et leur propension à être trop permissifs avec eux.

- La première est un manque de connaissances en matière d'éducation. En effet, bien des parents ignorent les pièges d'une telle éducation. Encore aujourd'hui, ils ignorent les conséquences négatives qui en découleront tôt ou tard.

- La seconde raison expliquant la difficulté des parents à s'opposer à leurs enfants se cache dans les profondeurs de leur âme : il s'agit du désir impérieux d'être aimé de leur enfant.

Pourtant, répondre à tous les désirs d'un enfant ou omettre de les réfréner lorsque c'est justifié, mènent rarement à cet amour, et ce, même si nous croyons justement être permissifs par amour. Nous n'avons qu'à observer l'attitude des enfants pour nous en convaincre. Très jeunes, ils manifestent différents comportements spontanés mais pas toujours souhaitables : jalousie, manque de respect, égoïsme, indifférence, violence, manipulation, agressivité et colère. De fait, ces manifestations ne font pas toujours la joie des parents. Notre rôle consiste à tempérer ces conduites. Trop de permissivité avec nos enfants encourage indirectement ces comportements qui sont loin d'être des manifestations d'amour. Savoir leur dire non, au bon moment et de la bonne manière, est certainement un meilleur gage d'amour.

Les enfants élevés de manière trop permissive développent les problèmes suivants :

– Une faible connaissance des valeurs.

– Une moindre appréciation de ce que nous faisons pour eux.

– Un manque de respect.

- Une tendance à être davantage manipulateur.

- Une propension à être plus capricieux.

- Une inclination pour la violence, verbale ou physique, lorsque leurs désirs ne sont pas satisfaits.

- Un penchant plus prononcé à l'égoïsme et à l'indifférence.

- Une plus grande désobéissance et indiscipline.

- Une tendance à recourir aux menaces pour obtenir ce qu'ils veulent.

Certains parents croient qu'un enfant n'est heureux que sans limites et que toute limite est nécessairement répressive. Ce n'est pas vrai. Cependant, certaines limites le sont en effet : celles qui n'ont aucun sens et que l'adulte met pour son plaisir ou pour affirmer son pouvoir.

Il y a aussi des limites indispensables : celles qui permettent à l'enfant d'avancer. Ainsi, un enfant ne peut pas téter toute sa vie. Ces limites-là n'empêchent pas son bonheur. Au contraire, elles le favorisent. Elles lui déplaisent néanmoins et il leur résiste (du moins, tant qu'il n'a pas compris leur nécessité), mais elles sont garantes tant de son bonheur que de son plaisir. Par exemple, si l'on veut apprendre le piano, il faut s'astreindre à faire des gammes. Si on ne les fait pas, on n'y arrivera jamais et on ne découvrira jamais le plaisir de jouer de la musique.

Certains parents considèrent que les interdits briment l'enfant dans sa personnalité et sa créativité. Une maman me racontait que, lorsque son enfant lançait sa cuillère par terre, elle la ramassait sans rien dire, car un enfant connaît tellement d'interdits qu'elle ne voulait pas lui en ajouter un.

En fait, il y a un âge où ce peut être normal et constructif pour un bébé de jeter les objets par terre pour que sa mère les ramasse. Ce jeu permet aussi à la mère de communiquer avec son enfant et de nommer les objets qu'elle lui rend. Mais plus tard, cela peut devenir une façon pour l'enfant de faire de sa mère son « esclave », de se persuader qu'il a tout pouvoir sur elle. La mère doit alors lui fixer des limites et lui proposer d'autres jeux en lui expliquant pourquoi. Sinon, l'enfant peut s'enliser dans le plaisir qu'il prend à manipuler sa mère. Cela l'empêchera d'avancer et de passer à autre chose.

Durant la période scolaire, à la maison, il y avait une règle à propos de la télévision, des jeux vidéo et de l'ordinateur. Du lundi au jeudi, il était interdit d'écouter la télévision, de jouer au Nintendo ou encore de clavarder à l'ordinateur. Cette règle a été en vigueur de la première année scolaire de ma fille jusqu'à sa quatrième secondaire, soit de six à seize ans. Évidemment, ma fille a protesté les premières semaines, prétextant qu'elle n'avait rien à faire en soirée après avoir complété ses leçons et ses devoirs. Je lui offrais alors un chiffon et je lui disais que la salle de bains avait justement besoin d'un bon nettoyage. La première fois, elle s'est exécutée avec plaisir : c'était amusant de laver la toilette. La deuxième fois, lorsque je lui ai à nouveau tendu un chiffon, elle m'a répondu : « Je pense que je vais appeler un ami et aller jouer. » Ses six années au primaire se sont ensuite bien déroulées. Ma fille avait de nombreux amis et jouait dehors, contrairement à d'autres qui étaient rivés à leur écran, de la fin des classes à l'heure du coucher.

Au secondaire, elle m'a demandé de permettre une exception à la règle pour pouvoir regarder l'émission *Occupation double* (une émission de téléréalité québécoise

Une discipline sans douleur

sur l'amour et la séduction). Elle m'a fait mille et une promesses, toutes aussi invraisemblables les unes que les autres et j'ai évidemment refusé. Je lui ai offert d'enregistrer son émission, afin de la regarder durant la fin de semaine, mais cela ne lui convenait pas, car elle tenait à en discuter avec ses amis le lendemain même de la diffusion. Elle a donc trouvé une solution à son problème : elle a décidé de se lever quinze minutes plus tôt le matin pour syntoniser la chaîne de radio où l'on commentait les principaux événements de l'émission. Conclusion : on a tort de considérer que les interdits briment un enfant. Au contraire, ils lui permettent de se structurer et de s'épanouir en sécurité.

Au moment où j'écris ces lignes, ma fille est en cinquième secondaire et j'ai décidé de ne plus appliquer cette règle. Croyez-vous qu'elle écoute davantage la télévision cette année ? Pas du tout. Même en ce qui concerne l'émission *Occupation double*, elle l'écoute si elle est disponible, mais cela ne fait pas partie de ses priorités.

Pour certains adultes, distinguer les « bonnes » limites des « mauvaises » n'est pas toujours aisé. Posez-vous les questions suivantes : « Cette règle est-elle indispensable à l'enfant ? La majorité des parents l'appliqueraient-ils comme moi ? » Par exemple, peut-on laisser un enfant se coucher à minuit, sachant qu'il sera mort de fatigue le lendemain ? La réponse est « non ». Peut-on lui laisser manger uniquement des bonbons toute la journée ? La réponse est encore « non ». Peut-on le laisser sortir en tee-shirt alors qu'il fait moins cinq ? Évidemment pas. Donc, tout parent a le devoir de répondre « non » à ces demandes de l'enfant.

LAISSER PLEURER

Une autre problématique vécue par plusieurs parents est l'imposition d'une heure de coucher. Prenons l'exemple d'un enfant en santé qui ne veut pas s'endormir et espère que ses parents viennent le chercher dans son lit ou encore celui qui réclame la permission de dormir dans le lit de ses parents. La question la plus fréquemment posée à son sujet est : peut-on le laisser pleurer ? La réponse est « oui ». Laissez-le pleurer jusqu'à ce qu'il s'endorme. Il faut lui imposer de dormir dans son lit, il n'y a pas de mal à cela et ses pleurs n'expriment que son mécontentement. Toutefois, il ne s'agit pas simplement de le mettre au lit et de le laisser hurler. Ses parents doivent lui expliquer ce qu'ils attendent de lui, même s'il est tout petit. S'il est un peu plus âgé, on peut lui expliquer que les papas et les mamans ne sont pas que des papas et des mamans, qu'ils sont aussi un couple ayant besoin de temps pour eux. Évidemment, il reviendra à la charge pour s'assurer de la solidité de l'interdit avant de renoncer à ses caprices et de passer à autre chose. Si les règles sont clairement expliquées à un enfant et si ses parents lui montrent qu'ils ne permettront pas de retour en arrière, la situation problématique ne durera jamais très longtemps.

Pourquoi les enfants ne veulent-ils jamais aller dormir ? Principalement parce que beaucoup d'enfants ne savent pas à quoi sert le sommeil et pensent donc que c'est du temps perdu. De fait, les enfants ne voient que bien rarement leurs parents dormir : ceux-ci sont généralement levés avant eux et couchés après eux. Ce moment « sans rien faire » peut sembler absurde si l'on ne sait pas qu'il est indispensable à l'organisme. Il faut donc leur expliquer les raisons du sommeil[*], telles que :

---

[*] LANGEVIN, Brigitte. *Comment aider mon enfant à mieux dormir*, Boucherville, Éditions de Mortagne, 2009, 208 pages.

- Grandir. « Tu grandis en dormant ! Ton corps se répare et se construit. Durant le sommeil, ton cerveau secrète une hormone de croissance qui t'aide à grandir. »

- Mémoriser. « Pas de bonne mémoire sans un bon sommeil ! Pendant le sommeil, tu ranges dans ta mémoire ce que tu as appris pendant la journée. »

- Récupérer. « Pendant que tu dors, tu permets un temps d'arrêt à ton corps, ton cerveau et ton esprit. »

- Garder le sourire. « Plus tu manques de sommeil, moins tu as bon caractère. »

- Préserver la santé. « Pendant la nuit, ton système immunitaire se fortifie afin de mieux te protéger des bactéries et des virus et tu as plus d'énergie pour te livrer à tes activités préférées. »

Toutefois, chez certains enfants, le refus de dormir est dû à une angoisse et il faut la décrypter. Souvent, c'est chez ses parents que se trouve la réponse : plus ces derniers sont anxieux, plus leurs enfants le sont.

« Il pleure parce qu'il est triste ? », demandent certains parents. « On dirait qu'il veut vraiment nous gâcher notre souper ! », affirment les autres. Pour un adulte, pleurer signifie déverser un trop-plein d'émotions, telles que la tristesse, la joie, la colère, etc. Si pleurer est généralement perçu négativement par les adultes, c'est que leurs raisons de pleurer sont bien différentes de celles des nourrissons. Chez ces derniers, nulle tristesse, nulle manipulation, nul esprit de vengeance : ce sont des bébés, ils ne connaissent rien du monde, comparés à nous. Ils n'ont pas vécu nos expériences.

Voici quelques significations possibles des pleurs d'un bébé bien-portant :

Significations possibles	Significations impossibles
J'ai faim.	Je suis fâché contre toi.
Je suis fatigué.	Je suis triste.
Cessez de revenir me voir, à la fin !	Je suis seul.
Il n'y a rien d'autre à voir ?	Je m'ennuie.
J'ai mal au ventre.	Je te déteste, lâche-moi.
Quelque chose me gêne.	J'ai décidé de t'en faire voir de toutes les couleurs.
J'ai trop chaud.	Tout le monde m'abandonne.
J'en ai assez ! Je veux dormir !	Je suis allergique à mon matelas.
Je veux être dans les bras de maman.	Si j'avais pu naître dans une autre famille !

Par ailleurs, les parents ne comprennent pas que les refus et les pleurs de l'enfant plus vieux sont uniquement dus à des désirs (être dans les bras de maman, être bercé par papa, faire la sieste dans la poussette ou dans la voiture pendant qu'elle roule, etc.) et aucunement à des besoins (dormir suffisamment et profondément dans un endroit rassurant). Les enfants veulent être l'objet exclusif de l'amour de leurs parents. Le travail des parents est de les ramener à la réalité. Les limites servent à cela et c'est une dimension essentielle de l'éducation. Expliquez-leur que vous n'êtes pas à leur service, qu'ils ne sont pas le centre du monde, que vous les aimez et que votre rôle est de prendre soin d'eux, non pas comme ils le désirent, mais comme ils en ont besoin. Les adultes perçoivent souvent les enfants comme des êtres « innocents ». Ils ne le sont pas.

RÉSISTER À L'ENVIE DE CÉDER

Certains parents cèdent à l'usure. Après avoir refusé cinq fois de donner un bonbon à l'enfant, ils finissent par craquer : « Bon ! D'accord pour cette fois, mais cette fois seulement ! » L'enfant ne comprend pas cette phrase. Pour vous, c'est une exception ; pour lui, c'est la preuve qu'il peut obtenir ce qu'il veut. Il se dit que si c'est vrai pour cette fois, cela le sera aussi demain. Ce type de situation fait en sorte que l'enfant négocie tout, tout le temps et qu'il finit toujours par l'emporter. Il est évident qu'il faudra aussi lui demander maintes et maintes fois d'aller se brosser les dents, d'aller se coucher, etc. Ces enfants n'ont pas intégré l'idée même de règle, car l'ensemble de leur éducation est flottant. Les enfants qui sont bien encadrés ne reviennent pas à la charge constamment pour tout et pour rien. Par ailleurs, si vous voulez leur inculquer une habitude (par exemple, mettre son linge sale dans le panier à linge) vous devez l'exiger chaque jour. Ne faites jamais d'exception.

Si vous constatez que c'est le problème que vous vivez en tant que parents, il y a moyen d'y remédier. Il faut d'abord vous interroger sur les raisons qui vous font toujours céder. En général, vous trouverez la réponse dans votre propre éducation ou dans la peur de faire souffrir l'enfant. Surtout, il faut alors lui expliquer pourquoi vous avez cédé, lui dire que vous vous êtes trompé et ensuite rectifier votre façon d'agir. Vous pouvez aussi mentionner à l'enfant que vous faire céder est peut-être agréable pour lui, mais que cela l'empêche d'accéder à des choses plus intéressantes. En effet, toute l'énergie qu'il dépense pour contester les limites et les transgresser, il ne peut l'utiliser pour avoir des idées nouvelles et s'amuser avec ses amis.

Si vous ne cédez plus, les éternelles négociations entre vous et votre enfant prendront fin. Je vous raconte une anecdote pour bien l'illustrer. Lors du lancement de mon premier livre, l'excitation était à son comble, c'était pour moi un grand moment. Ma fille et sa cousine étaient en charge des breuvages et des croustilles. Durant la soirée, nous avons manqué de boissons gazeuses, ma fille a offert d'aller en chercher à l'épicerie, elle et sa cousine ayant le goût de prendre l'air. Il était plus de 21 heures, le dépanneur était à cinq minutes de marche. Pour des jeunes de douze ou treize ans, être dehors semblait plus intéressant, mais pour leur sécurité et pour m'éviter des inquiétudes, j'ai décidé de refuser. Je lui ai donc dit de servir de l'eau puisque la soirée tirait à sa fin. Ma fille a avisé sa cousine de ma décision. Sa cousine a répondu : « Ben achale-là, elle va dire oui ! » Et ma fille de lui répondre : « Ben non, ça marche pas avec ma mère ! » Ce fut un des beaux moments de mon lancement de livre.

N'allez surtout pas croire que je n'ai jamais fait d'erreurs de jugement ! De fait, je me souviens d'un été où j'avais permis à ma fille de se coucher à la même heure que nous durant nos deux semaines de vacances. Comme nous allions tous dormir dans la même chambre, mon conjoint, ma fille et moi, il me semblait que c'était à propos. Elle avait environ onze ans.

Le premier soir des vacances, mon conjoint, qui n'était pas encore informé de notre arrangement, a avisé ma fille qu'il était l'heure d'aller au lit. Offensée, elle m'a regardé et m'a dit : « Maman, ce n'est pas ce qui était convenu ! » Mon conjoint, comprenant ce qui se passait, m'a regardée et m'a dit : « Nous aussi on est en vacances et j'aimerais bien passer du temps avec mon amoureuse ! » Oups ! J'avais pris cette décision sans tenir compte que j'étais non seulement une mère, mais aussi une femme en vacances avec son amoureux. J'ai donc expliqué à ma fille que je m'étais trompée, que je n'aurais pas dû prendre cette entente avec elle et que j'avais moi aussi besoin de moments avec mon amoureux.

Afin de réparer les pots cassés, mon conjoint et moi avons alors décidé qu'elle se coucherait seulement un soir sur deux à la même heure que nous. Elle a chialé un peu le premier soir, mais tout est rentré dans l'ordre pour le reste des vacances.

EXPRIMER SA COLÈRE

De nos jours, la croyance en une sorte de « parent zen » se répand, c'est-a-dire la croyance en un parent qui pourrait demeurer calme et « psychologiquement correct » en toutes circonstances, et ce, quoi qu'il arrive. Ce n'est pas réaliste ! On peut arriver à être plus calme si l'on comprend ce qui, au-delà des apparences, provoque notre énervement. Mais il faut garder à l'esprit que la perfection n'est pas de ce monde..

Par ailleurs, un parent qui voit son enfant essayer d'étrangler un chat et qui se précipite pour l'arrêter, lui permet, par son émotion même, de comprendre et de ressentir sur-le-champ la gravité de son geste. Si l'enfant voyait ce même parent lui dire calmement, « pédagogiquement » et sans bouger de son fauteuil : « Mais voyons, ce n'est pas bien ce que tu fais. Il ne faut pas faire mal au chat... » Que comprendrait-il ? Il s'imaginerait que l'adulte énonce une règle abstraite et vide, guère plus importante que celle qui lui interdit de mettre ses doigts dans son nez.

Une chose ne deviendra inacceptable pour un enfant que si elle l'est aussi pour ses parents. En effet, pour qu'il comprenne qu'un comportement n'est pas admissible, les paroles ne suffisent pas. Il faut que l'enfant sente que l'adulte refuse de tout son être ce comportement et qu'il lui est insupportable. Un recul, une crispation, un regard franchement désapprobateur ou inquiet peuvent remédier à un comportement inadmissible de l'enfant plus efficacement que ne le feraient de simples paroles.

Un parent n'est pas un manuel de morale monté sur deux pattes. C'est un être de chair et d'émotions. C'est aussi en se confrontant à ces émotions qu'un enfant se construit. Et c'est grâce à ces émotions que les siennes s'éveilleront. On n'apprend pas seulement les règles avec sa tête, on les apprend aussi avec son corps et avec sa sensibilité. À partir d'un certain âge, par exemple, un enfant peut comprendre la souffrance d'une personne âgée qui tombe parce qu'on l'a bousculée. Autrement, il ne pourrait jamais comprendre pourquoi on ne peut pas courir en tout sens dans un lieu public. Cela resterait abstrait pour lui.

La colère de l'adulte n'est donc pas à proscrire. On peut toujours expliquer à un enfant pourquoi on s'est mis en colère. En général, il n'en aura aucune idée mais, si on prend le temps de lui expliquer, il comprendra très bien.

Lorsque j'ai pris la décision de changer mon attitude et de faire preuve de discipline avec ma fille, il est évident que celle-ci m'a mise à l'épreuve plus d'une fois. Je me souviens très bien de cette ultime fois où elle avait décidé, à l'âge de huit ans, de ne pas aller à l'école un matin, car elle avait mal dormi.

Je lui ai alors expliqué que je comprenais très bien sa fatigue, mais que ce n'était pas une raison valable pour demeurer à la maison. J'ai continué en lui disant que j'allais expliquer la situation à son professeur et qu'il l'a laisserait sûrement déposer sa tête sur son pupitre si elle tombait de fatigue durant la journée. Je lui ai demandé par la suite de venir déjeuner et elle m'a répondu : « Non, maman, je ne vais pas à l'école ! » Puis, elle s'est recroquevillée, toujours en pyjama, dans un coin de la salle à manger. Inutile de vous dire que je sentais la colère monter en moi. J'ai donc monté le ton (de quelques crans) et je lui ai dit fermement d'aller s'habiller, car nous allions partir dans quelques instants pour l'école. Elle a encore refusé.

Je m'étais promis d'éviter de crier dans ce genre de situation. Pourtant, je l'ai avisée que si elle ne bougeait pas, j'allais hausser le ton davantage. Comme elle ne bougeait pas, j'ai mis des fruits et des vêtements dans son sac d'école et je lui ai dit d'une voix très forte : « Maintenant ça suffit ! Viens-t-en, nous partons pour l'école. » Elle n'a pas bougé d'un iota ! Sans un mot de plus, j'ai attrapé son manteau et je l'ai empoignée par la taille. Elle se débattait et hurlait. J'étais enflammée (vous auriez dû voir la scène !) mais je me maîtrisais encore. Je l'ai assise avec aplomb sur le siège arrière et j'ai démarré la voiture. Rendue à l'école, elle s'est mise à pleurer en me disant : « Je n'ai pas déjeuné et je ne suis pas habillée, tu ne peux pas me laisser à l'école! » Je lui ai alors remis son sac en lui disant d'un ton ferme que tout s'y trouvait et qu'elle devait maintenant aller s'habiller dans les toilettes.

Je n'avais pas cédé. La partie était gagnée pour cette journée... et pour tous les autres jours !

Après avoir écrit cette anecdote, il m'est arrivé de la relire alors même que ma fille était près de moi et je lui ai alors rappelé cet épisode de sa vie. Elle se souvenait de tout et nous en avons ri ensemble. Les enfants ont besoin de notre amour et leur fixer des limites est un geste d'amour !

Aujourd'hui, je sais que poser des limites n'est pas tout. Il faut aussi que l'adulte éprouve un sentiment de légitimité au moment de le faire. Et ce sentiment ne peut venir que de la conviction de transmettre une règle de vie en société qui soit pleinement justifiée. Ainsi, quand j'interdis à mon enfant de mettre à l'envers mon tiroir de vêtements, je sais que je ne le fais pas seulement pour mon bon plaisir ou parce que je tiens à mes petites affaires (même si j'ai le droit d'y tenir !), mais parce que c'est une question de respect. Toutefois, ce n'est pas parce que j'ai de l'autorité que l'enfant acceptera la limite. C'est important de le préciser.

Certains parents pensent que d'autres font mieux qu'eux et que ces derniers détiennent une autorité naturelle devant laquelle leur enfant s'incline. Or, ce n'est absolument pas le cas.

L'enfant doit apprendre les règles de la vie en société. C'est l'apprentissage de ces règles éthiques qui différencie les humains des animaux. Cependant, si vous vous apercevez que votre enfant n'a pas encore fait cet apprentissage, rappelez-vous qu'il n'est jamais trop tard pour commencer ! Mais voyez-y sérieusement dès maintenant !

LE LAISSER S'EXPRIMER

Il est fréquent d'observer que de nombreux parents souhaiteraient que leur enfant s'abstienne de pleurer, par exemple, lorsqu'il vit une frustration ou qu'il se blesse. Cependant, les enfants sont aussi des êtres de chair et d'émotions, pourquoi les empêcherions-nous de s'exprimer ? Par exemple, combien de fois voyons-nous un parent, mal à l'aise de voir pleurer son enfant en public, lui demander d'arrêter ses larmes ?

Dernièrement, je suis allée voir mon chiropraticien. Une maman et son garçon de quatre ans se trouvaient dans la salle d'attente. Celui-ci s'amusait, assis par terre. Lorsque le médecin l'a appelé, il s'est levé rapidement, a perdu l'équilibre et est tombé. Sa lèvre supérieure semblait légèrement fendue. Au moment même où il allait se mettre à pleurer,

Une discipline sans douleur

sa mère a levé son chandail, dégrafé son soutien-gorge et lui a donné le sein sans même prendre le temps de vérifier ce qu'il avait. Les autres patients et moi-même étions abasourdis ! Malheureusement, cette maman était persuadée que pleurer est négatif !

Certains parents bien intentionnés vont même jusqu'à remplacer rapidement un animal domestique mort ou disparu pour éviter à leur enfant de la tristesse et des pleurs. Quel genre d'adulte allons-nous créer en agissant de la sorte ?

Que vous soyez sensible ou non aux pleurs, vous devrez « faire avec » si vous avez un bébé. Tel sera votre lot pour au moins quelques années ! Plus rapidement vous saurez interpréter les pleurs de votre enfant, plus rapidement ils diminueront. En attendant, ne collez pas d'étiquettes négatives sur ses pleurs et rappelez-vous que ceux-ci ne signifient surtout pas que vous êtes une mère indigne !

Il arrive aussi que certains parents ne supportent tout simplement pas les pleurs de colère, de protestation, de tristesse ou de douleurs de leurs enfants parce qu'ils trouvent écho en eux. Ils ravivent leurs blessures d'enfance. En accourant aux moindres pleurs, ces parents tentent en quelque sorte d'apaiser leurs souffrances passées. En fait, ils projettent tout simplement leur histoire sur leur bébé. Voici quelques exemples de projections :

- La solitude vous angoisse et vous concluez que votre enfant se sent abandonné parce qu'il pleure un peu avant de s'endormir.

- Vous êtes hypocondriaque et, à la première larme, vous voyez déjà votre enfant hérissé de tubes et de tuyaux.

- Vous êtes soupe au lait et vous prêtez à votre bébé un tempérament colérique.

- Vous avez tendance à vous déprécier et considérez que votre petit manque d'assurance.

- Vous faites régulièrement de l'insomnie et, lorsque votre bébé met des heures à s'endormir le soir, vous le prenez en pitié ?

- Vous vous sentez coupable d'avoir repris le travail et, quand vous trouvez votre enfant en larmes à la garderie, vous vous dites qu'il s'est ennuyé de vous ?

Le remède est de nommer votre souffrance et, ensuite, de vous interdire de penser que votre enfant la partage chaque fois qu'il pousse un cri. Prenez plutôt le temps de vous demander : « Suis-je à l'unisson de mon bébé ou ma réaction est-elle suscitée par des émotions qui me sont propres ? »

Par ailleurs, certaines mamans donnent automatiquement le sein ou la tétine en réponse aux cris de leur bébé, tant elles craignent d'être de mauvaises mères. Distinguer ce qui vient de notre propre histoire de ce qui appartient à l'enfant permet d'entendre réellement ce qu'il demande, raconte ou affirme. Cette distinction vous évitera d'en faire un adulte qui avale ses émotions au lieu de les exprimer !

Parfois, on ne comprend pas les pleurs de son bébé. C'est normal. On n'est pas omniscient. Alors, nous pouvons lui dire que nous ne comprenons pas ses pleurs et reconnaître qu'il a sûrement une très bonne raison de pleurer parce qu'un petit enfant – et *a priori* un nouveau-né – fait corps avec les événements qu'il vit. On l'aidera beaucoup en lui nommant ce qui lui arrive, en lui témoignant notre sympathie, en reconnaissant qu'il traverse une difficulté, et ce, même s'il s'agit d'un nourrisson de trois semaines. Nommer une expérience l'humanise, lui donne un sens et aide à mobiliser les ressources intérieures nécessaires pour la surmonter. Et surmonter une épreuve, c'est gratifiant.

ÉCOUTER ET NOMMER

Lorsque nous sommes capables de comprendre les sentiments d'un enfant, de les accueillir et de l'aider à les nommer, nous l'aidons à mieux se sentir. Lorsque l'enfant se sent bien, il se comporte bien.

Lorsqu'il m'arrivait de raconter à une amie de confiance, les erreurs que j'avais commises dans l'éducation de ma fille, je me faisais continuellement dire : « Tu n'as pas à te sentir coupable, tu ne pouvais pas donner ce que tu n'avais pas ! » Pourtant, je vivais néanmoins un sentiment de culpabilité. Il en va de même lorsque quelqu'un vous dit : « Tu ne peux pas être fatiguée, tu arrives de vacances. » Vous vous sentez tout de même vraiment fatiguée ! Peut-on se débarrasser d'un sentiment parce que quelqu'un prétend que nous n'avons pas à nous sentir ainsi ? Bien sûr que non ! Non seulement nous restons avec ce sentiment mais, en plus, nous nous sentons incompris.

Parfois, en tant que parents, nous croyons mieux savoir que notre enfant ce qu'il ressent. Par exemple, lorsque notre enfant nous dit qu'il n'a pas faim et que nous lui répondons : « Tu dois avoir faim, tu n'as pas mangé depuis ce matin. » Nous commettons alors une erreur. Il vaut mieux lui dire : « Tu n'as pas faim malgré que tu n'aies pas mangé depuis ce matin. » Apprécions la nuance. Il se sentira alors compris, mais le plus important est qu'il apprendra à reconnaître en toute confiance son ressenti. Lorsque nous prétendons qu'il n'a pas raison de se sentir ainsi, il peut devenir confus et ne plus savoir reconnaître ce qu'il ressent. Voici d'autres exemples de l'importance de bien choisir ses mots :

- Si un enfant est en colère et nous frappe, évitons de lui dire : « Tu n'es pas gentil, va te calmer dans ta chambre. » Disons plutôt : « Tu m'as l'air très fâché, dis-le-moi avec des mots plutôt qu'en frappant. »

- Si l'enfant doit cesser une activité agréable et que cela le frustre, évitons de dire : « Tu n'es jamais content, cela fait pourtant longtemps qu'on est au parc. » Disons plutôt : « Tu es frustré de quitter le parc. Tu aurais aimé continuer à jouer. »

- Si un enfant de deux ans pleure tous les matins pour ne pas aller à la garderie, disons-lui simplement : « C'est dur d'avoir deux ans et de quitter papa et maman tous les jours pour la garderie. » Il se sentira compris, important et aimé, et acceptera plus facilement d'être séparé de vous pour la journée.

Par ailleurs, si nous souhaitons que nos enfants apprennent à satisfaire adéquatement leurs besoins, il faut d'abord les aider à les reconnaître. Voici donc quelques façons de les y aider :

- Si l'enfant est turbulent dans la voiture, nous pouvons lui dire : « Tu as besoin de t'exciter, mais c'est dangereux lorsque je conduis. Pour notre sécurité, j'ai besoin de tranquillité. J'arrêterai dès que ce sera possible pour que tu puisses courir quelque part. Serais-tu d'accord pour rester calme en attendant ? » La prochaine fois qu'il voudra s'exciter, il y a de fortes chances qu'il nous dise : « J'ai besoin de m'exciter, peut-on s'arrêter bientôt ? » Il aura appris à nommer son besoin.

Une discipline sans douleur

- Si un enfant nous réclame sans arrêt pendant la préparation d'un repas, nous pouvons lui dire : « Tu as besoin de me raconter quelque chose, mais je dois maintenant préparer le repas... Serais-tu d'accord pour attendre après le souper afin que je prenne tout mon temps pour t'écouter ? »

- Si un enfant tarde à ramasser ses jouets, nous pouvons lui dire : « J'ai besoin de ta collaboration pour ranger la maison. As-tu des idées de comment nous pourrions le faire en nous amusant ? »

- À un enfant d'âge scolaire, nous pouvons dire : « J'ai besoin de savoir où tu vas et quand tu rentreras. » Ou encore : « J'ai besoin d'être rassuré sur tes efforts en mathématiques. » Puisque nous sommes ses modèles, plus nous exprimons nos sentiments, nos émotions et nos besoins, plus il apprendra à le faire lui aussi.

- À un bébé qui s'impatiente, nous pouvons dire : « Ton biberon arrive. On dirait que tu es en colère qu'il ne soit pas prêt. »

ENCOURAGER ET COMPLIMENTER

Que faites-vous lorsqu'il arrive que votre enfant s'occupe tranquillement à jouer dans le salon sans déranger personne, qu'il mette son linge sale dans le panier à linge, qu'il se brosse les dents avant de se coucher, qu'il range son jouet lorsqu'il en a terminé, qu'il joue avec sa sœur une demi-heure sans se chamailler ou qu'il accroche sa veste à la patère en rentrant de l'école ? Si vous êtes comme 99 % des parents, la réponse est : rien. Vous ne dites rien, parce que vous trouvez tout cela normal. Parce que comme tous les êtres humains, vous êtes programmés pour voir ce qui ne va pas et ne pas voir ce qui va. Sachez, chers parents, que ces comportements, s'ils ne sont pas encouragés, risquent de disparaître !

Au primaire et même au secondaire, les amis de ma fille appréciaient encore plus venir à la maison lorsque j'y étais. Cela vexait un peu ma fille, et je m'en rendais bien compte. Un jour, je lui ai demandé pourquoi ses amis m'appréciaient tant et elle m'a répondu : « C'est parce que tu leur dis souvent des choses gentilles, leurs parents ne font pas ça. » En fait, tout ce que je faisais, c'était souligner leur bon comportement lorsqu'ils étaient chez moi ou encore m'intéresser à leurs réussites, scolaires et autres, lorsque j'en étais témoin.

Par exemple, lorsque je servais une collation et que chacun ramassait les miettes tombées sur la table, je m'exclamais avec admiration : « Wow ! C'est vraiment gentil de nettoyer la table, je l'apprécie beaucoup ! » Quand un petit ami me demandait s'il pouvait appeler sa mère pour dire où il était, je lui disais : « Wow ! Ta mère doit tellement être contente que tu l'appelles, je suis fière de toi ! »

Évidemment, la sincérité est importante. Un enfant sent d'autant plus la sincérité d'une remarque lorsque celle-ci est explicite. Par exemple : « Merci de m'avoir aidée à préparer la collation pour tes amis et toi. » Et non pas : « C'est gentil. » Avec un compliment explicite, l'enfant ne se sent pas seulement aimé, il se sent vu et reconnu.

Une remarque inattendue a aussi beaucoup de valeur. Par exemple, lorsque plusieurs amis se trouvaient à la maison en fin de journée, je lançais : « Merci d'avoir mis vos bicyclettes sur le gazon, comme ça l'entrée de garage n'est pas encombrée. »

Une discipline sans douleur

Par ailleurs, quand je rencontrais les parents des amis de Karelle, je n'hésitais jamais à leur dire combien respectueux et serviables étaient leur enfant. Je sentais alors l'enfant grandir d'un mètre tellement il était fier que je l'aie complimenté devant ses parents. Il en va de même pour nos enfants ! Par exemple, quand des amis ou des membres de la famille étaient venus souper et avaient admiré la table joliment décorée, je n'avais pas hésité à leur dire : « Ce n'est pas moi qu'il faut féliciter, c'est Karelle. C'est elle qui a confectionné ces petits bouquets de fleurs et qui a eu l'idée de les mettre au milieu. »

De plus, si vous voulez que votre enfant développe telle qualité ou telle compétence, comportez-vous comme s'il l'avait déjà ou comme si son acquisition ne lui poserait sûrement aucune difficulté. Par exemple, si vous voyez votre fils bousculer un enfant qui essayait maladroitement de se tenir sur ses deux jambes, dites-lui : « Je suis étonnée quand je te vois pousser quelqu'un. Toi qui es si gentil, comment est-ce possible ? » Vous constaterez qu'il aura l'air interloqué, comme s'il se disait : « C'est vrai que je suis gentil, même maman le pense. Je ne devrais pas la décevoir. » Si vous voulez un enfant gentil, dites-lui qu'il est gentil. Si vous voulez qu'il persévère dans ses cours de piano, dites-lui que vous savez qu'il ira loin. Si vous voulez que votre adolescent se montre digne de confiance, donnez-lui l'impression que vous l'en croyez déjà digne.

Il n'y a pas que des paroles qui peuvent encourager votre enfant ou le complimenter. Un sourire complice, un clin d'œil, un pouce levé, un « high-five » ou un petit mot sur son oreiller ou dans sa boîte à lunch sont autant de précieux encouragements.

Attention, complimenter n'est cependant pas flatter. Les compliments exagérés perdent leur crédibilité. Par exemple, dire à votre enfant qu'il est le plus bel enfant du monde passera peut-être s'il a trois ans, mais assurément pas s'il en a huit. Un tel compliment provoquera plutôt l'incrédulité de votre enfant, qui sera sûrement tenté de vous répondre que vous dites cela parce que vous êtes sa mère, ou la méfiance de votre adolescent, qui y verra une forme de manipulation... à peine déguisée !

Voici quelques exemples d'encouragements ou de compliments :

- J'admire la vitesse à laquelle tu t'es décidé.

- J'aime bien que tu aies mis plein de couleurs dans ton dessin.

- Je suis contente que tu aies pris soin de ton compas et que tous tes accessoires soient rangés dans leur boîte.

- C'est gentil d'avoir fait la vaisselle !

- Super, la manière dont tu as rangé ta chambre !

- Merci d'être souriante ce matin !

Enfin, il arrive un moment, vers l'adolescence, où le renforcement positif doit laisser la place à une reconnaissance des acquis. Par exemple : « Que penses-tu de ce bulletin ? » « Tu peux être fière de ce que tu as réalisé. Ce résultat, tu ne le dois qu'à toi-même. » L'enfant est content de lui ; le but principal d'un adolescent ne doit plus être de simplement contenter ses parents !

DIRE JE T'AIME

Si vous êtes nés dans les années 1960 ou 1970, vos parents étaient assez avares de mots d'amour à votre égard. Fort heureusement, la majorité d'entre nous avons malgré cela abreuvé nos enfants de « je t'aime ». Si vous faites partie des nouveaux parents (nés dans les années 1970 ou 1980), vous employez les mots d'amour encore plus facilement que les précédents. Certains d'entre vous les emploient même lorsqu'ils s'adressent à leurs parents. Attention, dire « je t'aime » trop souvent à ses enfants peut dénaturer le sentiment. De fait, quelque chose de répétitif et d'insistant finit toujours par perdre de sa valeur. À force d'être utilisées, les expressions finissent par s'user. De là l'importance de dire « je t'aime » avec son cœur et non de façon machinale.

Quelque temps après m'être reprise en main et avoir mis en place des stratégies éducatives saines et respectueuses, j'ai posé cette question à ma fille de huit ans : « Penses-tu que je t'aime ? » Elle m'a répondu par l'affirmative. Quelle bonne nouvelle après tout ce que je lui avais fait subir ! J'ai alors continué mon enquête en lui demandant comment elle se sentait aimée ? Quelles paroles et quels gestes lui faisaient sentir que je l'aimais et qu'elle comptait pour moi ? Je m'attendais à ce qu'elle me réponde que sont les « *je t'aime* » et les câlins que je lui prodiguais à profusion. Quelle ne fut pas ma surprise lorsqu'elle m'a répondu : « Quand tu restes avec moi pendant que je prends mon bain au lieu d'aller faire la vaisselle. » En fait, c'était lorsqu'il y avait un investissement de temps et d'attention de ma part. Cette phrase n'est pas tombée dans l'oreille d'une sourde, croyez-moi ! J'ai décidé de demeurer dans la salle de bains avec elle au moins trois soirs par semaine. C'était notre moment d'exclusivité, rien ne pouvait m'y soustraire, pas même le téléphone, la sonnerie de la porte ou un commentaire de mon amoureux. Elle me racontait alors ses joies, ses tristesses, ses peurs, ses inquiétudes, ses amours, ses difficultés scolaires, etc. Voilà comment elle aimait que je lui dise « je t'aime ». Même encore aujourd'hui, elle m'invite dans la salle de bains à l'occasion, tire le rideau de douche et pendant qu'elle se lave elle me raconte sa vie.

Les psychologues et orthopédagogues ont constaté que les comportements désagréables (mordre, taper, pousser, faire des crises et ne pas écouter les consignes) disparaissent assez rapidement, généralement en moins de deux semaines, lorsque les parents répondent plus adéquatement au besoin d'amour de leur enfant, notamment en lui consacrant plus de temps et en faisant en sorte qu'il se sente important et aimé. Or, nous n'avons rien de plus important que notre temps à offrir à ceux qu'on aime. Si on ne consacre pas un temps de qualité à chacun de nos enfants, soit vingt à trente minutes par jour d'exclusivité (sans télévision, sans jeux électroniques, sans vaisselle, sans journal, etc.), on ne leur offre que des mots. Et les mots sont parfois insuffisants pour dire l'amour.

PERSÉVÉRER AVEC LES ADOS

Les ados s'opposent à tout, c'est connu. Face à ce comportement, les parents ne savent pas toujours comment réagir. L'adolescence est pour eux une sorte d'épreuve de vérité, car les adolescents ont un véritable génie pour remettre en question les interdits et épuiser leurs parents. Leur peur : que leurs parents ne reconnaissent pas qu'ils ont grandi et ont gagné le droit à une certaine autonomie. Pour cette raison, ils contestent sans relâche leur autorité.

Il ne faut pas oublier que le devoir des parents est d'apprendre à leurs enfants à se passer progressivement d'eux. Les parents suivent leurs enfants de près, mais ils doivent lâcher prise lorsque ceux-ci atteignent l'adolescence. Il faut donc qu'ils réfléchissent aux limites qu'ils imposent. Il leur faut renoncer à celles qui n'ont plus de sens : les empêcher de s'habiller comme ils le souhaitent, exiger qu'ils portent les cheveux courts ou les obliger à mettre des bottes en hiver. Mais il importe d'en conserver, par exemple : dire chez qui l'on va quand on sort et ne pas rentrer pas à 3 h du matin. Ces limites-là, qui ont encore un sens, les adolescents ne les aiment pas non plus. Elles les font hurler, mais elles les rassurent néanmoins, car elles constituent pour eux des garde-fous indispensables.

Vers l'âge de quinze ou seize ans, ma fille m'a demandé de se coucher plus tard la fin de semaine. À cette époque, elle se couchait à 21 h du dimanche au jeudi et à 22 h 30 le vendredi et le samedi. Sa requête était de pouvoir se coucher à minuit le vendredi et le samedi. J'ai accepté en partie. J'ai alors rédigé une entente que nous avons signée : je lui permettais, un soir sur deux, soit le vendredi ou le samedi, à sa guise, de se coucher à minuit.

Quelques semaines plus tard, un samedi soir, vers 19 h, un copain l'a invitée à sortir avec des amis. Ce copain, que je ne connaissais pas, avait une voiture. J'ai demandé à ma fille de me le présenter à son arrivée à la maison. J'ai dit à ce jeune homme de dix-huit ans que ma fille m'était très précieuse et que je comptais sur lui pour conduire prudemment. Ensuite, je me suis tournée vers ma fille et je lui ai rappelé que, en vertu de l'entente que nous avions, elle devait être couchée à 22 h 30, car elle s'était couchée à minuit la veille. Après mes deux interventions, si ma fille avait eu des pistolets à la place des yeux, j'étais fusillée à mort ! Ils partirent ensuite.

Vers 22 h, le téléphone a sonné. J'étais alors confortablement installée au salon, dans une tenue de détente, et blottie contre mon conjoint. À l'autre bout du fil, ma fille m'a d'abord dit : « Maman, tu sais combien je t'aime ! » J'ai rapidement compris qu'elle voulait me demander de rentrer plus tard. Elle a ajouté : « Maman, nous sommes au cinéma avec les amis, est-ce que je peux rentrer plus tard ? Je te promets d'être trois fins de semaine de suite au lit pour 21 h. » Une promesse d'ivrogne, bien entendu !

Après une longue inspiration, je lui ai répondu : « L'entente conclue dit bien que tu n'as le droit de te coucher vers minuit qu'une seule soirée par fin de semaine. C'est donc non ! » Elle a répliqué : « Maman, tu ne peux pas me faire ça ! En plus, il ne peut pas venir me reconduire, il a déjà payé son billet et il y a tous les autres amis. Maman, c'est humiliant ! » Je lui ai répondu, toujours d'un ton calme mais ferme : « Tu le savais, c'était à toi d'agir en conséquence. » Je lui ai alors demandé à quel cinéma elle se trouvait, lui ai dit de sortir à l'extérieur et que j'y serais dans dix minutes. J'ai enfilé des vêtements et je suis allée la chercher. Elle ne m'a pas parlé durant le trajet. À 22 h 30, elle était au lit.

Bien sûr, je n'étais pas la mère la plus *in* en ville ce soir-là ! Mais qu'importe, mon rôle n'était pas de me faire aimer de ma fille, mais bien de faire respecter les règles établies.

Les enfants éduqués selon cette approche sont le plus souvent calmes et équilibrés. Ils perdent peu de temps à contester les règles. Toutefois, il est important que ces règles respectent leur évolution et n'aient pas un caractère immuable. En effet, à mesure que les enfants vieillissent et acquièrent de la maturité, les règles devraient être réajustées pour s'adapter à leurs nouveaux besoins d'encadrement.

Toutes règles mises en place au sein d'une famille devraient être respectées 99 fois sur 100. Ne dit-on pas que l'exception confirme la règle ? Cette petite latitude permet ainsi à l'enfant, lors de circonstances exceptionnelles, de faire valoir un point de vue différent et d'obtenir ainsi une permission spéciale. En outre, cette possibilité de négocier lui donnera confiance en sa capacité à faire valoir un point de vue et à influencer le cours des choses. Elle lui permettra de bâtir sa confiance en lui.

Dans la situation précédente, j'ai pourtant refusé à ma fille la permission de retarder son retour à la maison. Pourquoi n'ai-je pas fait exception à la règle ? Parce que j'ai considéré qu'elle me forçait la main, consciemment ou inconsciemment, en m'appelant à la dernière minute alors qu'elle ne pouvait plus être raccompagnée à la maison par son ami. Cette situation pouvait résulter d'un manque de prévoyance de sa part, mais également d'une certaine forme de manipulation. J'ai donc préféré maintenir la règle.

Par ailleurs, un enfant ou un ado qui engage une discussion parce qu'il croit qu'une règle n'a pas ou n'a plus sa place, mérite d'être entendu. Peut-être émettra-t-il un point de vue valable et ressentira-t-il finalement la fierté de s'entendre dire : « Tu as raison, je ne l'avais pas vu sous cet angle. »

Ainsi, lorsque j'ai décidé de recourir aux « conséquences logiques » et non aux punitions, il m'est arrivé à quelques reprises de me méprendre. Ma fille exprimait alors qu'elle ressentait que la supposée conséquence en fait était une punition. Toutes ces fois, je me suis remise en question. À plusieurs reprises, je suis revenue sur ma décision et je lui ai donné raison.

Voici une autre anecdote. Ma fille était alors âgée de treize ans. Elle m'avait dit que cela n'avait plus de sens de jouer uniquement dans la cour les soirs d'hiver. Pour moi, elle n'était encore qu'une petite fille et la possibilité de la surveiller en regardant par la fenêtre me rassurait. Je lui ai d'abord répondu que j'y réfléchirais. Puis, j'ai effectivement modifié la règle.

Ce style d'éducation, ferme mais souple, n'exclut pas le mouvement, le dynamisme ou l'adaptation. Chaque jour, le parent doit relever le défi d'inventer une discipline intelligente, laissant progressivement plus d'initiatives et de responsabilités à son enfant au fur et à mesure qu'il grandit.

En parlant de responsabilité, je vous fait part d'une autre anecdote. À ce moment-là, elle était âgée de seize ans et était en quatrième secondaire. Nous étions en janvier. À l'école, un voyage à New York se préparait pour le mois de mai. Je l'ai donc avisée que son passeport serait échu en avril et qu'il était de sa responsabilité de choisir le bon moment pour la prise de photo (c'est qu'elle est coquette !). De mon côté, j'allais me charger de remplir le formulaire et de le faire signer. J'ai ajouté qu'il fallait faire vite, car il faut un certain temps pour obtenir un nouveau passeport.

En février, sa photo n'avait pas encore été prise. Je lui ai rappelé que c'était sa responsabilité de la faire. Elle m'a répondu qu'elle avait encore du temps devant elle. Je lui ai dit que je n'en étais pas si sûre, car il fallait compter au moins six semaines pour l'obtention du passeport. Rien n'y fit.

Mars est arrivé et la photo n'était toujours pas prise ! Je lui ai rappelé que le gouvernement n'était pas à son service et que, lorsqu'elle serait enfin prête pour la photo, il serait peut-être trop tard et que, même si elle criait alors haut et fort son indignation, son passeport ne lui serait pas délivré plus rapidement. J'ai ajouté qu'il n'y aurait malheureusement pas de voyage sans un passeport !

La photo a finalement été prise à la mi-mars et les documents ont été postés aussitôt.

Début mai, le passeport ne nous avait toujours pas été envoyé. Le départ pour New York était prévu pour le 10 mai. Ma fille commençait à s'inquiéter, car elle craignait de ne pouvoir participer à ce voyage qui lui tenait particulièrement à cœur ! Elle en a parlé à son professeur qui m'a appelée en me disant que son certificat de naissance suffirait (à cette époque le passeport, quoique préférable, n'était pas encore obligatoire pour un voyage en autobus aux États-Unis). Or le seul certificat de naissance que je détenais était joint à la demande de passeport et ne me serait retourné qu'avec le passeport. Son professeur m'a donc informée que je pouvais en obtenir un autre en 48 heures, en me rendant directement au bureau de l'état civil. Croyez-vous que j'ai perdu une journée de travail pour m'en procurer un autre, compte tenu des circonstances ? Bien sûr que non ! Si je voulais qu'elle comprenne que ni ses parents ni la société ne sont à son service, il me fallait être ferme même si je risquais de perdre l'argent déboursé pour le voyage (350 $). Ma fille en a avisé le professeur. Figurez-vous donc qu'il m'a rappelée pour me dire qu'elle pourrait probablement voyager sans passeport et sans certificat de naissance, car il était rare, selon lui, que les douaniers demandent les passeports de tous les jeunes présents dans l'autobus. Ils se contentaient généralement d'en choisir quelques-uns au hasard. Je lui ai demandé ce qu'il adviendrait de ma fille si c'était elle qui était choisie au hasard... Il a observé un long silence et n'a plus insisté.

Finalement, son passeport est arrivé la veille de son départ. Ma fille a eu sa leçon, croyez-moi ! Pour ma part, j'étais fière de moi : je n'avais cédé ni à la pression du professeur ni à celle de ma fille !

Éduquer vos enfants n'est pas de tout repos. Il ne faut pas que vous relâchiez la discipline à l'adolescence, même si vous devez alors démontrer une certaine souplesse et une ouverture d'esprit. Vous trouverez dans le prochain chapitre des stratégies d'intervention qui vous aideront dans votre travail de parent, et ce, dès le jeune âge de vos enfants.

Chapitre 5

STRATÉGIES D'INTERVENTION

Dans le passé, à une époque pas si lointaine, lorsqu'un enfant questionnait la raison des interdits, il récoltait comme toute réponse : « Parce que c'est comme ça ! » Point à la ligne. L'adulte exigeait de l'enfant qu'il se soumette à son pouvoir, c'est-à-dire à la loi du plus fort, et non à des règles sensées. C'était à la fois violent et aliénant, car l'enfant ne pouvait ni comprendre le « pourquoi » d'une règle ni découvrir que l'adulte était lui aussi soumis à de telles règles.

De plus, les punitions ne sont pas une bonne manière de mettre un terme à un comportement répréhensible. Certains parents affirment que les punitions fonctionnent puisqu'elles mettent effectivement fin à une attitude fautive de l'enfant. Mais il convient de se méfier d'un tel résultat. À long terme, on constate le plus souvent une aggravation des problèmes de comportement au lieu d'une amélioration. Lorsqu'elle donne des résultats, la punition y parvient par la peur du châtiment et non par le désir de bien se comporter. La punition met d'ailleurs l'enfant dans un état de colère, d'humiliation et de détresse qui n'est pas le meilleur des ressentis pour apprendre.

Une discipline sans douleur

La punition sert en fait à défouler le parent et elle va donc souvent de pair avec les manifestations de colère : gronder, crier, menacer, frapper, etc. Même si la punition vise à réfréner un comportement, elle n'enseigne pas le comportement souhaité. La punition se reconnaît facilement car elle n'est pas du tout liée au comportement à sanctionner. En voici quelques exemples :

- Envoyer un enfant se coucher plus tôt parce qu'il a fait une crise.

- Priver son enfant de dessert parce qu'il n'a pas ramassé ses jouets.

- Confisquer un jouet parce qu'il a lambiné dans le bain.

- Priver un enfant de sortie avec ses copains parce qu'il n'a pas ramassé le linge sale dans sa chambre.

Dire « non » sans fessée, sans cris et sans marchandage est possible. Mais l'idée que l'on puisse y parvenir sans efforts est une idée fausse qui nuit aux parents. L'utilisation de la fessée, des cris ou du marchandage est une réaction d'impuissance. Si les parents apprennent une autre façon de réagir et s'ils comprennent que l'éducation n'est pas un jeu d'enfant, ils se sentiront moins impuissants et moins incapables. En fin de compte, tout le monde y gagnera.

Certaines écoles de pensée à la mode promettent de résoudre les difficultés et les conflits entre parents et enfants à l'aide d'une technique miraculeuse qui surpasserait toutes les autres. Cependant, dans les faits, aucune méthode ne saurait résoudre tous les problèmes de comportement ou régler toutes les situations. Chaque situation a ses particularités et chaque est enfant unique. Il est donc essentiel de

STRATÉGIES D'INTERVENTION

connaître plusieurs stratégies pour vaincre la résistance d'un enfant, pour l'emmener à se discipliner ou pour corriger une simple erreur.

N'oublions pas que l'enfant n'est pas un adulte miniature, il ne pense pas comme nous. Il obéit souvent à ses impulsions et sa raison ne peut le guider. Par exemple, si un bébé de quatorze mois fouille dans la poubelle, la première étape pour bien se faire comprendre, est de l'interpeller par son prénom, d'aller le chercher par la main, de se mettre à sa hauteur, de capter son regard, de lui faire les gros yeux, d'employer sa grosse voix et de lui expliquer la règle avec des mots simples : « *Les déchets c'est pas bon, on ne touche pas.* »

Les enfants méritent qu'on les traite comme des personnes à part entière, comme des êtres valables, même lorsqu'ils agissent mal. Notre objectif, en tant que parent, doit être de diriger l'enfant vers les comportements adéquats.

Enfin, avant de consulter l'éventail des stratégies, il faut savoir qu'une méthode qui a bien fonctionné avec un aîné peut ne pas obtenir le même succès dans une situation semblable avec un cadet. Que faire si cette technique s'avère inefficace avec un second enfant, malgré des essais répétés ? Blâmer l'enfant, baisser les bras ou s'obstiner mènera à une impasse. Il ne faut donc pas hésiter à varier les approches, à nommer les émotions de l'enfant et à lui dire ce qu'on attend de lui.

Chacune des stratégies suivantes est présentée en trois points : une définition, un but et des exemples d'application.

CONSÉQUENCE NATURELLE

Définition : Cette stratégie consiste à laisser l'enfant assumer les conséquences **naturelles** de ses actes sans tenter d'y remédier, en autant que sa sécurité ne soit pas compromise.

But : Discipliner tout en laissant l'enfant expérimenter, apprendre de ses erreurs et bâtir sa confiance en lui. Cela sans colère chez l'enfant ou le parent parce qu'il n'y a ainsi pas de conflit. De plus, l'enfant voit clairement pourquoi il devrait changer de comportement et c'est bénéfique pour lui. Il apprend de ses propres erreurs.

Exemples :

- Il s'est empiffré de bonbons. Conséquence naturelle : il fait une indigestion et ne pourra aller au cinéma en soirée avec ses parents. Les parents ne le chicanent pas, mais ils ne reportent pas cette sortie à une autre date pour l'accommoder. Ainsi, l'enfant gourmand apprend la leçon, sans autre discours.

- S'il tarde à se lever le matin, c'est qu'il est fatigué, non ? S'il a plus de six ans, il sera donc mis au lit plus tôt le soir pour récupérer. S'il a quatre ou cinq ans, il faudra qu'il respecte la sieste scrupuleusement. Plus question de le laisser faire un jeu calme durant cette période. Soyez certain qu'il cessera rapidement son petit manège !

- S'il refuse de manger parce qu'il n'aime pas ce qui est au menu, plutôt que de vous bagarrer pour trois haricots, laissez-le sortir de table sans les avoir mangés et laissez-le expérimenter la faim jusqu'au prochain repas.

STRATÉGIES D'INTERVENTION

CONSÉQUENCE LOGIQUE

Définition : Dans la stratégie de la conséquence **logique**, le parent impose à l'enfant une pénalité liée à son manquement ou à sa mauvaise conduite. Il doit nécessairement y avoir un lien entre le comportement répréhensible ou indésirable et la conséquence choisie.

But : Le même que celui énoncé pour les conséquences naturelles, c'est-à-dire éviter une lutte de pouvoir en laissant l'enfant assumer les conséquences de son propre comportement.

Exemples :

- Pour un enfant de deux ans qui renverse un verre de jus alors que vous l'aviez avisé de cesser de taper sur la table, la conséquence logique serait qu'il éponge lui-même son dégât. Pas de cris, pas de sermons, pas d'accusations.

- Pour un enfant de quatre ans qui se relève continuellement de son lit et sort de sa chambre une fois son rituel d'endormissement accompli, alors qu'il avait été formellement avisé de rester dans son lit, la conséquence logique serait qu'il perde le privilège de garder sa porte ouverte.

- Pour un enfant de six ans qui éclabousse le plancher lorsqu'il joue dans la baignoire, alors que vous lui aviez demandé de faire attention, la conséquence logique serait qu'il éponge.

- Pour un enfant de dix ans qui s'est fait voler son vélo parce qu'il a négligé de le rentrer dans le garage ? Si

Noël est dans six mois, la conséquence logique serait qu'il s'en passe d'ici là.

- À treize ans, s'il a pris l'habitude de claquer la porte de sa chambre chaque fois qu'il est contrarié ou de mauvaise humeur, informez-le que ce geste est inacceptable et que la conséquence logique serait que vous retireriez la porte de sa chambre pendant trois jours.

- À seize ans, s'il laisse son linge sale s'empiler dans un coin de sa chambre au lieu de l'apporter dans la salle de lavage, la conséquence logique serait qu'il aille à l'école avec du linge froissé qui n'est pas tout à fait net.

STRATÉGIES D'INTERVENTION

RENFORCEMENT POSITIF

Définition : Encourager, approuver, féliciter et complimenter les bons comportements d'un enfant.

But : Favoriser la confiance en soi chez l'enfant en lui signalant ses compétences ou qualités et encourager ses comportements positifs.

Exemples pour un enfant de 0 à 5 ans :

- Bravo, tu as fait vite pour te préparer ce matin !
- Je te félicite : tu as exprimé calmement ton désaccord à ta sœur quand elle a pris ton jouet.
- Tu parles bien, je suis fière de toi !
- J'apprécie que tu m'aides à mettre le couvert.
- Félicitations ! tu as géré ta colère et tu n'as pas fait de scènes aujourd'hui.

Exemples pour un enfant de 6 à 12 ans :

- Je te remercie d'avoir essuyé la vaisselle, cela m'a rendu service !
- Je suis contente que tu aies fait ton lit !
- Bravo, champion ! Je suis très content de ton bulletin !
- Je vois que l'on peut te faire confiance !
- Merci d'avoir pensé à m'appeler pour me dire où tu étais. Après cela, je n'étais plus inquiète.

Exemples pour un adolescent de 13 à 18 ans :

- Tu as du talent pour garder les enfants !
- Veux-tu me donner ton avis sur cette couleur ? Je trouve que tu as le sens de la décoration.
- Je trouve ta nouvelle amie bien sympathique.
- Je suis sûr que tu vas réussir. Lâche pas, tu es capable !
- Je te félicite de ne pas fumer. Tu prends bien soin de ta santé.

STRATÉGIES D'INTERVENTION

ADAPTER LE MILIEU

Définition : Cette stratégie consiste à modifier l'environnement de l'enfant. La réorganisation d'un espace ou d'une activité peut suffire à résoudre un problème donné.

But : Éliminer la conduite répréhensible ou la prévenir.

Exemples :

- À l'heure du coucher, rendez son milieu moins stimulant en y pratiquant des activités calmes et apaisantes, en tamisant les lumières ou en éteignant la télévision.

- Durant la journée, si un enfant s'ennuie, il commettra plus des bêtises et se querellera plus souvent. Aménagez son environnement de manière plus stimulante, de façon à lui offrir des activités intéressantes et variées.

- Si c'est possible, il serait intéressant d'aménager de façon fonctionnelle une cour arrière pour les tout-petits ou encore d'installer une salle de jeux pour les jeunes. Ils y dépenseront leur énergie en toute liberté. Également, vous pouvez désigner une pièce de la maison où les adolescents pourront rencontrer leurs copains et écouter leur musique (cela leur évitera de vagabonder et de flâner dans les centres commerciaux).

LE HORS-JEU

Définition : Il s'agit d'un isolement bref de l'enfant. Cette technique est connue sous plusieurs noms : hors-jeu, retrait, temps mort, arrêt d'agir et temps de réflexion.

But : Imposer un moment d'inaction, de manière à permettre à chacun de se ressaisir, de se calmer et, ensuite, de discuter calmement du problème.

Le hors-jeu consiste en quelques minutes relativement ennuyeuses où rien ne se passe. L'idéal est de chronométrer sa durée ; une sonnerie indiquera ainsi à l'enfant la fin de son retrait. Le parent ne doit pas lui parler durant le hors-jeu. Une bonne façon de déterminer la durée approximative du retrait est de compter une minute de hors-jeu par année de vie : trois minutes pour un enfant de trois ans, quatre minutes pour un enfant de quatre ans, et ainsi de suite...

Exemples :

- Si deux enfants de quatre ans se disputent un objet, séparez-les en les envoyant dans deux endroits différents. Lorsque la minuterie sonnera au bout de quatre minutes, demandez à chaque enfant d'expliquer le problème à tour de rôle. Accordez trente à soixante secondes à chacun pour exposer son point de vue. Rappelez-leur de chercher quel est le problème et non de chercher à qui revient la faute. Résumez ensuite le conflit et proposez-leur des solutions : utiliser une minuterie pour que chacun profite du jouet également, le laisser de côté pour un jeu qui se joue en équipe, etc. Invitez-les à chercher d'autres pistes de solution, puis à en sélectionner une et à l'appliquer.

STRATÉGIES D'INTERVENTION

Par ailleurs, cette stratégie s'avère très efficace lors de crises. Cependant, il faut l'appliquer aussi rapidement que possible, c'est-à-dire dès le début de la crise. La séquence à suivre est donc :

- Mettre l'enfant à l'écart (dans une salle de toilettes ou dans une voiture, par exemple, si vous êtes au centre commercial). Ne pas attendre d'être excédé avant d'agir. Commencez par nommer les émotions en jeu, par exemple : « Tu es fâché parce que j'ai refusé d'acheter des bonbons. » Ensuite, répétez fermement et calmement la consigne, dans ce cas-ci : « Calme-toi d'abord et nous retournerons au magasin ensuite. »

- Dès que l'enfant est calmé, lui expliquer la conduite attendue : « Quand tu m'accompagnes au supermarché, tu as le droit de choisir une boîte de céréales, mais c'est moi qui décide du reste. As-tu compris ? » Obtenez sa parole.

- Ramenez l'enfant au centre commercial le plus tôt possible (ou au lieu de la crise), afin de lui permettre d'intégrer rapidement le comportement souhaité. Juste avant de retourner magasiner, rappelez-lui la conduite à tenir et obtenez encore une fois son engagement.

1... 2... 3 !

Définition :   Cette stratégie consiste à compter jusqu'à trois pour obtenir qu'un enfant cesse un comportement négatif.

But :   Préserver le calme en évitant de discuter. L'enfant a moins de ressentiment et plus de bon temps à passer avec vous. Une pause après chaque chiffre est le secret de la réussite.

Exemples :

- Vous lui demandez d'arrêter de donner des coups de pied sous la table. S'il arrête tout va bien. Sinon, vous dites « 1 ». L'enfant arrête ? Très bien. Il continue ? Vous dites « 2 ». Il continue encore ? Vous terminez avec : « 3 ». Hors-jeu. Isolement bref sur une chaise. Si la situation nécessite une explication, donnez-la brièvement avant de commencer à compter.

- Ma fille avait quinze ans. Nous étions dans un supermarché bondé un jeudi soir. Elle m'a alors dit : « Maman je m'achète une gomme ! » Je lui ai répondu : « Non, tu sais très bien que tu ne peux pas en mâcher à cause des broches que tu portes dans la bouche. » Elle m'a redit : « Maman je m'achète une gomme. » Mon cœur s'est mis à battre plus rapidement et je me suis demandé ce que j'allais faire, elle avait tout de même quinze ans ! Spontanément, j'ai pris mon panier d'épicerie, je suis passée devant elle et j'ai dit, à voix haute et d'un ton ferme : « 1 ». Il y avait belle lurette que je n'avais pas fait cela. Elle a répété plus fort : « Je m'achète une gomme ! » J'ai continué mon chemin (lentement !) et j'ai dit, toujours d'une voix ferme :

« 2 ». Finalement, je l'ai entendue arriver derrière moi et dire « Tu veux jamais rien ! » À l'intérieur, j'étais fière de moi. Puisque j'avais utilisé cette technique depuis son jeune âge, celle-ci s'avérait encore efficace, même à l'adolescence !

LA DIVERSION

Définition : Cette stratégie consiste à présenter à l'enfant un ou plusieurs choix.

But : Détourner l'attention d'un enfant qui exige qu'un désir soit satisfait de façon immédiate.

Cette technique fait des merveilles, particulièrement auprès des tout-petits en pleine phase d'opposition. Un enfant aime prendre des décisions, donc offrez-lui un choix (même fictif) au lieu de lui imposer quelque chose.

Exemples :

- Vous lui dites habituellement : « Donne-moi la main pour traverser la rue... » Demandez-lui plutôt : « Veux-tu tenir ma main gauche ou ma main droite pour traverser la rue ? »

- Au lieu de lui imposer un chandail qu'il refuse, demandez-lui : « Préfères-tu porter ton chandail vert ou celui avec un Mickey Mouse ? » De nombreuses confrontations seront ainsi évitées.

- Un enfant exige avec impatience d'avoir des ciseaux pointus et refuse ceux à bouts ronds ? Annoncez alors : « Tiens ! C'est l'heure de ta collation. » Et comme par enchantement, il oubliera les ciseaux.

L'EXEMPLE

Définition : Cette stratégie consiste à montrer l'exemple à son enfant, à être un parent inspirant.

But : Amener votre enfant à vous imiter. Il est connu que la tendance naturelle des enfants est d'imiter ceux qu'ils aiment.

Exemples :

- Si vous voulez développer la persévérance de votre enfant, donnez l'exemple. Vous leur demandez d'être polis ? Alors soyez-le avec eux, c'est la moindre des choses. Un enfant de deux ans sera très sensible au fait que vous lui disiez « s'il te plaît », « merci » ou « excuse-moi ». Sans comptez que c'est le meilleur moyen pour qu'il apprenne à le dire lui-même.

- Si vous souhaitez que vos enfants soient honnêtes, vous devez l'être vous-même. Pour leur apprendre à tenir leurs promesses, vous ne devez surtout pas oublier celles que vous leur faites. Pour leur apprendre à admettre leurs erreurs et à les corriger, vous devez d'abord admettre les vôtres. Il n'y a pas de meilleur antidote à une attitude négative qu'un modèle positif.

- Vous pouvez difficilement exiger de votre enfant un comportement que vous n'avez pas. Si vous lui demandez de ranger sa chambre et que la vôtre est en désordre, il y a fort à parier qu'il vous le mettra sous le nez tôt ou tard.

Je vous raconte une dernière anecdote. J'étais en voiture avec ma fille. Elle avait environ neuf ans. Comme je vivais dans un petit patelin de 2 km^2 , j'avais la mauvaise habitude de ne pas attacher ma ceinture de sécurité lorsque je circulais dans les rues de mon quartier. Évidemment, ma fille était toujours attachée et elle ne se doutait aucunement que ce n'était pas toujours le cas pour moi. Alors que je circulais sur la rue principale, j'ai croisé une voiture de police en direction inverse. J'ai alors dit à voix haute : « Zut, j'ai pas bouclé ma ceinture de sécurité ! » Au même moment, la voiture de police a fait demi-tour, a allumé ses gyrophares et a fait retentir sa sirène ! Je me suis alors garée dans le stationnement d'une station-service espérant qu'elle poursuive son chemin. J'osais l'espérer ! Hélas, elle venue se stationner juste derrière moi. J'ai alors dit « bateau » à voix haute pour exprimer mon mécontentement ! Ne riez pas, c'est le patois que j'emploie au lieu de blasphémer, pour donner le bon exemple à ma fille ! Comprenant la situation, ma fille m'a dit : « Mais attache-toi maman, tu as encore le temps ! » Je lui ai répondu : « Ben non ! J'étais pas attachée. » J'avoue toutefois que l'idée m'était passée par la tête ! Lorsque le policier est arrivé à la hauteur de ma portière, il m'a demandé : « Savez-vous pourquoi je vous arrête ? » Je lui ai répondu : « Parce que je n'étais pas attachée. » Surpris de mon honnêteté, il m'a annoncé : « Étant donné que vous m'avez dit la vérité, je ne vous donnerai pas de contravention cette fois-ci, mais soyez prudente et prenez l'habitude de vous attacher dorénavant ! » Non seulement j'avais eu ma leçon, mais j'avais montré à ma fille que j'étais honnête et que ça allège parfois les conséquences de dire la vérité !

Donner l'exemple est plus qu'une stratégie parmi d'autres : c'est une nécessité.

Avec le temps et la pratique, vous parviendrez à mieux cerner chaque situation et à savoir rapidement quelle technique donnera le bon résultat. Donnez-vous du temps et, surtout, accordez-vous le droit à l'erreur. De plus, sachez que, selon certaines études, les enfants bien encadrés possèdent une meilleure estime de soi, sont plus courtois et acceptent mieux la critique que ceux qui sont élevés dans un milieu permissif. Cela récompensera maintes fois les efforts que vous aurez déployés à les encadrer.

Chapitre 6

POUR L'AVENIR DE NOS ENFANTS

Selon certains spécialistes, l'apprentissage des interdits se fait entre dix-huit mois et quatre ou cinq ans. C'est donc à cet âge que se fait la véritable prévention de la délinquance.

Au Moyen Âge, on croyait qu'une personne qui commettait des délits ou des meurtres était possédée par les démons. Aujourd'hui, on accuse plutôt des facteurs génétiques, la pauvreté, le chômage ou des dépendances diverses (drogue, alcool, etc.). Pourtant, la délinquance et la criminalité ne surviennent pas seulement chez les analphabètes ou les pauvres, mais également chez les nantis et les puissants.

ÉVITER LE CHEMIN DE LA DÉLINQUANCE

La maltraitance des enfants n'est pas inscrite dans notre patrimoine génétique : dans la nature, ce phénomène n'existe pas. A-t-on déjà vu un animal maltraiter son petit ? Non. C'est pourtant fréquent chez l'être humain. Depuis des milliers d'années, nous sommes programmés pour prodiguer aux nouveau-nés des soins, de l'attention et de la tendresse. Par ailleurs, nous sommes génétiquement conçus pour

Une discipline sans douleur

recevoir ces traitements positifs. Par conséquent, malgré une capacité d'adaptation hors du commun qui nous permet de faire face à l'adversité, il peut s'avérer difficile pour nous de surmonter les mauvais traitements sans en garder des séquelles.

Par mauvais traitements, j'entends la permissivité autant que la maltraitance : elles représentent deux extrêmes néfastes pour un enfant. Les parents qui se livrent au marchandage ou à la manipulation de leurs enfants leur transmettent des comportements malsains. Par ailleurs, cette nouvelle génération d'enfants explosifs, qui ne supportent pas les refus et qui y réagissent avec violence, m'inquiète tout autant que celle des parents qui usent de violence ou commettent des abus verbaux, ou encore que celle de ces autres parents qui se complaisent dans la non-intervention.

Les enfants qui ne connaissent que la violence ou que le laisser-aller tiennent ces attitudes pour normales. Ils ne savent pas que la relation avec leurs parents pourrait être bien différente. Plus tard, ils croiront que seules la violence et la force permettent de se faire entendre et de se faire respecter. Et cette croyance, ils l'ont acquise très tôt... de leurs parents. Les cas de maltraitance nous indiquent que l'âge des coliques (de 0 à 3 mois), la phase du non (de 2 à 3 ans) et la préadolescence (de 10 à 13 ans) sont trois périodes particulièrement à risque.

Heureusement, de nombreux enfants maltraités ou peu encadrés ne sont pas devenus des délinquants pour autant. Certains ont eu la chance de rencontrer des personnes secourables et lucides qui leur ont manifesté un intérêt sincère, leur ont accordé respect et sympathie, et les ont aidés à mieux accepter leur début de vie difficile. En guérissant de leur enfance, ces jeunes pourront peut-être éviter de mal agir avec leurs propres enfants.

Ignorer les attitudes inadéquates ou les conduites violentes de nos enfants, sous prétexte qu'il serait inutile de revenir en arrière, que le passé ne peut être changé, témoigne d'une attitude passive et défaitiste lourde de conséquences.

Lorsque j'ai frappé ma fille au visage, j'ai pris conscience qu'une violence inouïe m'habitait. J'en ai eu tellement peur que j'ai tenté de l'ignorer et de la nier. Combien d'autres adultes ont choisi d'occulter le souvenir des offenses et des coups, tant le souvenir de ceux qu'ils ont subis que celui de ceux qu'ils ont infligés ? Par ailleurs, certains prétendent que ces méthodes (les sévices corporels) leur ont été bénéfiques et ils les perpétuent auprès de leurs enfants.

Si j'avais continué à recourir à la violence pour exercer mon autorité, j'aurais détruit ma propre enfant, en dépit de mes meilleures intentions. En effet, j'aurais simplement considéré ces comportements répréhensibles comme étant tout à fait normaux et légitimes.

AVOIR OU NE PAS AVOIR D'ENFANTS

Le livre de Corinne Maier, intitulé *No Kid* ou *40 raisons pour ne pas avoir d'enfants*, en a secoué plus d'un. Ce livre choquant mais rempli de vérités relate que l'arrivée des enfants signale la fin des grasses matinées, du cinéma à l'improviste ou des sorties passées minuit et qu'elle annonce l'ère du « métro-boulot-marmot ». L'auteure affirme qu'avoir un enfant « tue le désir » et sonne le « glas du couple ». Elle mentionne également qu'un enfant coûte cher, gobant 20 à 30 % de votre revenu, en plus de vous astreindre à un horaire-marathon et de vous imposer les pires corvées.

L'auteur, dotée d'une plume assez incisive, en rajoute en écrivant que si vous rêvez de joyeux soupers en famille, vous êtes en fait promis à une amère désillusion :

Une discipline sans douleur

« Le dialogue parents-enfants, c'est le dîner de cons tous les jours. » Selon elle, vous pouvez également oublier les joyeux Noël sous la neige et vous préparer aux « engueulades sous le sapin ».

Si les sorties en famille sont un tel enfer, la corvée des devoirs une torture et la routine une prison, pourquoi diable a-t-elle eu des enfants ? Voici ce qu'elle répond : « On a des enfants pour des raisons égoïstes. Cela a été mon cas. Je n'ai pas de parents, ni frères ni sœurs. J'ai fait des enfants pour me sentir moins seule. »

Malgré la part de réalisme contenue dans les propos de Corinne Maier, évitons de jeter le bébé avec l'eau du bain ! Ce ne sont pas les enfants qu'il faut éliminer, mais les mauvaises méthodes éducatives.

En contrepartie, voici au moins 30 bonnes raisons[*] d'avoir des enfants :

1. Comprendre nos propres parents et le million d'inquiétudes qu'ils ont vécues.
2. Vivre la fierté de tous leurs exploits, petits et grands.
3. Donner la vie, participer à un mystère qui nous dépasse.
4. Donner et recevoir le plus grand amour qu'il y a sur cette terre.
5. Jouer notre rôle dans la grande chaîne de l'humanité.
6. Toucher une petite part d'immortalité à travers la vie de nos enfants.

---

[*] Plus de 80 raisons sont mentionnées sur le site www.mamanpourlavie.com

7. Assumer le défi de se surpasser... chaque jour.
8. Entendre de nos enfants les noms d'amour les plus doux : *Maman* ou *Papa*.
9. Avoir la plus belle des raisons de vivre.
10. Ressentir la confiance totale dans leurs yeux.
11. Pleurer avec notre enfant, rire avec lui, redécouvrir la vie à travers ses yeux.
12. Devenir encore plus conscient du sort de la planète.
13. Élargir notre compréhension de la vie et ouvrir notre cœur.
14. Devenir le héros d'au moins une personne... jusqu'à la préadolescence !
15. Élargir notre capacité à aimer, voire aimer d'un amour inconditionnel.
16. Apprécier davantage les petits moments d'intimité ou de solitude.
17. Entendre les « T'es belle Maman ! » Et aussi les « Je t'aime gros comme le ciel ! » Des baumes après une dure journée.
18. En tant que mère, vivre une expérience de communion et d'intimité avec notre enfant grâce à l'allaitement.
19. Apprendre à se faire confiance, se découvrir à travers ce nouveau rôle de parent.
20. Comprendre à quel point nos propres parents peuvent nous aimer.
21. Être totalement essentiel pour quelqu'un.

22. Renouer avec l'espoir d'améliorer le monde en transmettant nos plus belles valeurs.
23. Apprécier nos parents en reconnaissant le don de soi qu'implique le fait d'être un parent.
24. Nous redonner le sourire, même lorsque le monde semble s'écrouler autour de nous.
25. Léguer à nos enfants le meilleur de nous-mêmes et les aider à grandir en beauté.
26. Être fier et heureux d'exercer la plus importante responsabilité au monde, celle d'élever un petit être humain.
27. S'émerveiller devant le miracle qui s'opère de la conception à la naissance.
28. Pouvoir un peu changer le monde.
29. Accompagner un enfant dans son apprentissage de la vie, c'est suivre une psychothérapie quotidienne parce qu'on apprend beaucoup sur soi.
30. Avoir un enfant est le plus beau des voyages. On découvre chaque jour quelque chose de nouveau.

Amusez-vous à enrichir cette liste !

SAVOIR QU'IL N'EST JAMAIS TROP TARD

Si des règles adéquates sont mises en place pendant les premières années de l'enfance et que les enfants intègrent bien les interdits, leur adolescence se vivra beaucoup mieux pour tout le monde. Cependant, il ne faut pas se leurrer, les parents devront se réajuster constamment pour traverser ce cap où l'adolescent va continuellement tout remettre en question.

Les graves dérapages durant l'adolescence font écho aux écarts survenus lors de la petite enfance. Durant cette étape de l'enfance, on peut accomplir le gros du travail, établir les assises de la maison. Ensuite, peu importe ce qui pourra se produire, les bases seront saines et solides, tout ne s'effondre pas.

Certains parents se demandent s'il est trop tard pour mettre en place des règles ou encore pour modifier leur propre comportement envers leurs enfants. La réponse est « JAMAIS ». D'abord, vous n'avez pas tout raté puisque vous êtes un parent qui se questionne sur la justesse des valeurs qu'il transmet. C'est déjà un atout inestimable pour vos enfants. Et puis, il n'est jamais trop tard pour parler à l'enfant et lui expliquer qu'on s'est trompé, pour lui dire : « Je pensais faire pour le mieux mais je me suis trompé. J'ai compris, donc je redresse la barre. » Il va sans dire que le parent et l'enfant passeront alors sans doute par une période difficile.

RESSOURCES EN CAS DE CRISE

Des ressources gratuites sont disponibles pour les parents démunis dans certaines situations problématiques. En voici deux :

Éducation coup-de-fil

Service téléphonique bilingue, anonyme, confidentiel et gratuit de consultation pour les difficultés courantes des relations entre parents et enfants. Un intervenant d'expérience, possédant une formation professionnelle en travail social, psychologie ou psychoéducation vous répondra. Il vous aidera à trouver le « quoi faire » et le « comment faire ». Un parent, un adolescent, des amis peuvent appeler. Voici le numéro : 514 525-2573. Service offert de septembre à juin, du lundi au vendredi de 9 heures à 16 heures et les mercredi et jeudi de 18 h 30 à 21 h.

La ligne parents

Un service téléphonique bilingue uniquement pour les parents, gratuit, anonyme, confidentiel et accessible partout au Québec. Des professionnels, disponibles en tout temps, répondent à vos questions sur l'éducation, sur le développement des enfants, sur la gestion de crise ou de conflits. Voici le numéro : 514 288-5555 (Montréal) ou 1 800 361-5085 (extérieur).

Lorsqu'une crise familiale perdure ou s'aggrave et que la vie devient infernale, consulter un professionnel devient alors nécessaire. Il est important que les parents entreprennent d'abord la démarche. Les enfants pourront suivre par la suite.

Il faut saisir ce qui se passe au quotidien, c'est-à-dire découvrir comment la situation s'est installée et pourquoi. Également, il importe de comprendre comment cette situation trouve écho dans l'histoire de chacun des parents et savoir quelle éducation ils ont reçue. Il suffit souvent de quelques séances pour que les choses se remettent en place. Les rapports difficiles qu'un enfant entretient avec les limites n'est jamais imputable à lui seul. Il est lui-même le produit d'une situation familiale dans laquelle chacun joue un rôle.

Le directeur de la protection de la jeunesse (DPJ)

Bien que les parents soient les premiers responsables du bien-être de leur enfant, certaines difficultés peuvent les empêcher d'assumer leurs responsabilités. La Loi de la protection de la jeunesse (LPJ) s'applique aux enfants qui vivent des situations compromettant, ou pouvant compromettre, leur sécurité ou leur développement. Il s'agit d'enfants en grande difficulté qui ont besoin de protection.

Par ailleurs, la LPJ considère que la sécurité ou le développement d'un enfant sont compromis dans six situations[*], lorsqu'il y a entre autres de la négligence[**] et des troubles de comportements sérieux[***]. Par exemple, selon l'article 38b de la LPJ, voici quelques indices de négligence :

- Manque de stimulation de l'enfant sur les plans langagier, moteur, social ou intellectuel, compte tenu de son groupe d'âge.
- Absence d'une routine de vie stable.
- Absence d'encadrement de la part des parents.

Voici aussi quelques indices révélant des troubles de comportement sérieux (art. 38f) :

- L'enfant manifeste de l'agressivité et de la violence de façon fréquente et incontrôlable.
- Les parents présentent des limites personnelles (ex. : trop grande permissivité, inconstance ou rigidité).
- Les parents nient ou banalisent la situation.
- Les parents ont démissionné face aux comportements de leur enfant.

---

[*] Voir au www.msss.gouv.qc.ca/jeunes pour connaître les situations et les indices qui vous permettent de croire que la sécurité ou le développement d'un enfant sont, ou peuvent être, compromis.

[**] Tient compte des modifications apportées à la Loi sur la protection de la jeunesse qui sont entrées en vigueur le 9 juillet 2007.

[***] Id.

Une discipline sans douleur

Selon les indices énumérés ci-haut, lorsque vous soupçonnez qu'un enfant est victime de négligence, qu'il est en grande difficulté et a besoin de protection, le directeur de la protection de la jeunesse (DPJ) peut intervenir. Cependant, le DPJ peut intervenir pour assurer la protection et le bon développement de l'enfant **UNIQUEMENT** si la situation de celui-ci est signalée. Faire un signalement signifie communiquer avec le DPJ pour lui faire part d'une situation que vous considérez inquiétante et qui vous fait croire que l'enfant est en danger ou que son développement est compromis, compte tenu des confidences de l'enfant, des attitudes et des comportements manifestés par celui-ci ou par ses parents.

Il faut être vigilant si vous décidez d'enquêter auprès de cet enfant avant de faire votre signalement. Des adultes bien intentionnés finissent parfois par mettre des mots dans la bouche d'un enfant en le questionnant, par exemple en voulant savoir si sa mère lui donne à manger le soir. Un enfant qui n'aime pas le repas que sa mère lui sert parce qu'il comporte des légumes et non des frites peut très bien répondre que « non » et vous induire en erreur. En fait, il est préférable de laisser ce travail d'enquête aux professionnels.

Même si prendre la décision de signaler la situation d'un enfant peut générer son lot d'émotions, les voisins, les professeurs, les personnes œuvrant dans un milieu de garde **DOIVENT**, dans l'exercice de leurs fonctions, signaler au DPJ toutes les situations pouvant compromettre la sécurité ou le développement d'un enfant !

Il n'est pas nécessaire d'être absolument certain pour effectuer un signalement au DPJ. Lorsque vos observations vous donnent des motifs raisonnables de croire que la sécurité de l'enfant ou son développement sont ou peuvent être compromis, vous devez signaler, sans délai, la situation au DPJ. Il y a un DPJ dans chacune des régions du Québec. Il travaille au sein d'un centre jeunesse*.

Rappelez-vous que c'est la responsabilité de tout adulte d'intervenir et qu'il n'est jamais trop tard pour le faire !

---

* Association des centres jeunesse du Québec : www.acjq.qc.ca. En cas d'urgence, composez le 911.

CONCLUSION

Je ressens toujours beaucoup de tristesse quand des parents semblent malheureux et excédés à cause de leurs enfants, même lors d'activités qui devraient être agréables à tous : vacances, pique-nique, repas, etc.

Avoir un enfant a été l'une des choses les plus merveilleuses de ma vie. Je crois que tous les parents devraient le vivre ainsi. En sachant faire de nos enfants des adultes responsables, notre paternité ou notre maternité devient une expérience profondément enrichissante, et non pas une époque pénible de notre vie.

J'espère que ce livre redonnera à beaucoup de parents la joie et le plaisir d'avoir des enfants. Et par-dessus tout, je vous souhaite de connaître, en tant que parents conscients, la joie de retrouver l'enfance à travers vos enfants. Vous irez de découverte heureuse en découverte heureuse et passerez avec eux des moments uniques qui, je l'espère, resteront gravés à jamais dans votre mémoire.

A Mythic Romance

By Diana Wallace

Herculine: A Mythic Romance
Diana Wallace

Copyright © 2015 Diana Wallace

All rights reserved. No part of this book may be reproduced in any form whatsoever without permission in writing from the author, except by a reviewer, who may quote brief passages in critical articles or reviews. This is a work of fiction; any resemblance to actual people is entirely coincidental. While the broader historical framework of the book is factual, all the specific historical events described herein are entirely imaginary. All Sophia Danton's poems, and Herculine's translations of Pindar's Odes are by Diana Wallace.

ISBN: 9781515238324

Design and Layout by Diana Wallace using CreateSpace
Original cover artwork by Diana Wallace

Email: dianawallace14@gmail.com

http://dianawallacebooks.com

*In memory of my dad, in honor of my mom,
and in gratitude to all my loved ones.*

CONTENTS

Prelude.. 1
Theo, 1942 Paris... 2
Herculine, 1989 New York............................... 5
Sophia, 1936 Paris...17
The First Poem: Electra.............................. 23
Theo, 1943 New York............................... 39
The Second Poem: Medusa......................... 42
Clea, 1989 New York................................. 60
The Third Poem: Daphne......................... 70
Johanna, 1990 Paris................................... 94
The Fourth Poem: Persephone..................... 102
The Fifth Poem: Echo............................. 119
Sophia, 1937 Paris.................................. 130
The Sixth Poem: Galatea........................... 133
Hercule, 1990 Paris.................................. 149
The Seventh Poem: Ariadne....................... 161
Theo, 1978 New York............................ 181
The Eighth Poem: Penthesilea..................... 187
Hyla, 1990 Mexico................................ 199
The Ninth Poem: Psyche........................... 205
Sophia, 1941 Paris.................................. 225
The Tenth Poem: Cassandra....................... 231
Calypso, 1990 Mexico.............................. 256
The Eleventh Poem: Atalanta....................... 260
Theo, 1978 New York............................. 288
The Twelfth Poem: Eurydice....................... 291
Sophia, 1942 Paris.................................. 316
Herculine, 2000 Berkeley........................... 319

Prelude

Herculine is dreaming…so hungry for the sound of her father's voice, she hears him in her dreams. In dreams she sustains the connection between their minds that had been the place where they had met most closely. She is dreaming that she is reading his books. As she reads, she imagines him reading to her. She holds the books that he had held and can feel his touch within them: she can sense the strength of his strong, unwavering hands as he held each one, his long fingers carefully, rhythmically turning pages as he sifted through for just the right words to read out loud. She can hear his voice then, low and excited, or steady and fluid, depending on his affection for the passage he had chosen. Soon, in her waking life, she will go to his books: there she will be able to hear his voice inside her head, hear his inflections, his many distinctive intonations in her mind.

In the years after his death, she feels her father watching over her as she goes about her day, and as she does now, in her dream, while she sits in his library, in search of him. In some ways, she knows she has already become him, has taken on his role as her mother's protector, and shouldered his massive scholarly legacy onto her own slender frame. What she does not yet sense is that she has also successfully internalized the full force of his love for her—as he had hoped that she would—so that she would never be without him.

Standing in his study, deep in her dream, Herculine also watches herself – pale and serious, scanning the shelves, oblivious to the blue of the sky outside the tall windows, her brow furrowed with concern. She is surprised to find herself beautiful: poised and graceful, even with her ripped jeans, t-shirt, and haphazardly cropped hair. But her burnished curls catch the light, as do the soft planes of her face, in a way that emphasize the delicate melancholy cast of her features. Sulky and intent, she gazes at the seemingly endless spines of her father's books, and her dreaming mind is suddenly aware of her own androgynous resemblance to him as she imagines him in his youth, as he had often stood, similarly frowning in front of vast dusty shelves, searching through archives and manuscripts in the early days of his studies.

"Never speak of love in the past tense," Theo had told her, as he was dying. "Once we have known love, we go on loving, even after the one we love has died. If we deny this, we do ourselves a violence, and do the beloved an injustice. I will love you even after I am gone, and you must continue to love me—actively, in the present tense—for your own sake, not mine."

She had promised, through her tears, that of course she would; but she had been only a child then, and it would be many years before she understood the wisdom of his words, or thought to question how it was that he had come to such an understanding himself. When she wakes, it is always with tears in her eyes.

Theo
Paris, 1942

It was dark in the small room. The boy awoke to the sensation of being lifted from his bed by large gentle hands, his blanket still tucked close around him. Strong arms pressed him against the wide solid chest of a man who did not smell like his papa. This man smelled of earth and wet wool.

The smell was familiar, so the boy was not afraid. He opened his eyes and saw the man smiling at him sadly. It had been a long time since they had seen each other. The man's eyes were large and kindly crinkled at the edges. He was wearing a black cap and a heavy coat, and he pulled the boy's blanket up over his head like a hood to keep him warm.

The boy's mother came into the room, kissed the man on the cheek and then embraced her son, saying in French through her tears, "Shhhh, my darling. You must sleep. Remember Hercule? He is our friend. You must trust him and be very brave. I love you with all my heart, my little one. Always remember how much I love you." The boy nodded at her sleepily, wondering why mama was so sad, but when he turned to ask her, she was gone.

The man named Hercule slung a bag over his shoulder and then – curiously – rather than leaving through the door as the boy's mother had, he carried the boy out through the bedroom window and quietly down the fire escape into a side alley where a car was waiting for them. Still held close in the kind man's arms, the boy slept again as the car drove for many hours into the night. He awoke again only when the motion of the car had stopped. Blinking with confusion until he remembered the blurry events of leaving his home, he asked where his mama and papa were, and where were they going? The man lifted the boy out of the car and set him down on the grassy bank near a wide river. He said, "It is no longer safe for you to stay in Paris, little one. Your mama has asked me to take you to a safe place until she can come for you herself. For now, she and your papa will stay there."

Hercule turned away to give the driver a hearty embrace and the car drove off. The boy felt tears welling up in his eyes. How

long before he would see mama? Then he remembered that she had told him to be brave. After all, he was a big boy now – he had just turned five, hadn't he? He would do as mama had asked.

The man took the boy's hand and led him to the river. He opened his bag, which contained warm clothes for the boy and layered all of them over the boy's pajamas. Within minutes, the faint sound of muffled oars reached their ears, and a small rowboat approached them. The sky was still dark.

The man and the boy walked to the edge of the river and prepared to get into the boat, but the oarsman called out: "*Qu'est-ce que c'est?* What's this? Where's the third one? I'm supposed to be paid for three!" Hercule motioned to the man to keep quiet, and responded firmly that all the promised money would be waiting for him at the drop-off point. The man in the boat glowered at the boy, but motioned for them to climb aboard. He rowed them slowly across the river and downstream as daylight began to break.

"Faster," urged Hercule, "We must arrive before dawn," but the oarsman kept the same slow steady pace. They approached the opposite shore where this time a large truck was waiting for them, its motor idling noisily. The driver of the truck gave a handful of bank notes to the oarsman, who rowed away. The little boy heard him muttering to himself as he pulled away from the shore, cursing the war and winter and rich men's sons who could escape them both.

Hercule lifted the boy into the back of the truck and the driver covered them with blankets and burlap sacks. The driver murmured something in a language the boy did not understand, but Hercule said "*Merci*" and the driver closed the back doors of the truck, leaving them huddled together in the darkness.

Hercule held the boy close during the loud, bumpy, and uncomfortable drive. After several hours on the road, the boy awoke frightened and missing his mother. He asked Hercule why the man in the boat was so angry and would mama come meet them soon? Hercule looked at him with his sad smile and said, "No, little one. It's going to be just the two of us for a while. Your mother is staying in Paris. And we are going to America." The boy's eyes widened and he blinked his tears away: was it possible? Was it true? America? Would they take a big ship there? Yes, said Hercule, they would take a big ship tomorrow. But tonight they must sleep in this truck. He brought out some bread and cheese from his coat and fed the boy.

True to his word, they boarded a ship the next day – again, before dawn. The boy watched silently as more money and other

papers were exchanged, and they were led below decks to a small room where two other men were already sleeping. There was only one remaining berth, so the boy and his new guardian shared it all the way to New York, the man holding him safe and close, staving off the dread of the large rolling vessel that contained them, filled with sorrow for all they were leaving behind, and in wonder of the unknown life awaiting them.

Herculine
New York, August 1989

The morning after my twenty-first birthday I was standing in my father's library for the first time in my life. My head was pounding with a champagne hangover, and I had barely slept the night before.

Two hours earlier, a ringing phone had woken me up from a sleep that should have lasted until noon. When I heard the answering machine pick up, and a smooth male voice identify himself as my father's lawyer, I groaned and crawled over the deeply slumbering bodies of my lovers, Ben and Lucy, to pick up the phone.

"Um, hello?" I mumbled into the receiver.

"Ah yes, hello Miss Danton, good morning...and happy birthday."

It took me a few moments to register the rest of his words, but after I asked him to repeat himself, it became clear that this lawyer was calling to inform me that my father, who had died eleven years ago, had bequeathed his entire personal library to me on the day that I turned twenty-one.

I stood naked in the middle of my room in disbelief: when my dad died, there had been no mention of an inheritance that would come to me eleven years later. I had never expected to receive anything from him, and I was stunned that he had left me all his books. I was my father's only child, sure, but my mother had only been his mistress, his real wife had hated us, and I had been ten years old when he died. My father – Theodore Danton, former Professor of Classics at Columbia University – had been married to Johanna Danton, another professor, the whole time I was growing up, and they lived way uptown in a house I'd only ever seen from the street. There were many times over the past eleven years when I felt like I had barely known him.

Still, only two hours after receiving the lawyer's call, there I stood in my father's library, head spinning with fatigue, trying to comprehend through the hazy veil of last night's champagne in my veins that all of his books were suddenly mine. I was uncomfortably aware that my ripped jeans, tank top, and unruly mop of hair contrasted sharply with the elegant interior of the large, mahogany-

paneled room. I felt like I was dreaming…like somehow I'd been there before. But not only was this the first time I'd been in his library, I had never even set foot in his home. He had lived here with his wife for over twenty years, whenever he wasn't with me and my mom. Our apartment must have seemed so bohemian to him compared to this elegant place: mom's loft was filled with plants, friends' artwork, and eclectic chaos, while this home was, well – a formal mansion.

As I gazed at the countless shelves of books lining the walls, I remembered the nights that my dad would come over to visit us and read aloud to me before bed, his voice low and warm, turning the pages with his long, graceful fingers. He had died so long ago, and I had imagined this room filled with his books my whole life. Now here I was in his library, the place I had longed to share with him, but he was gone.

Standing in the cool silence of the room, I remembered how he would gather me up in his arms at night when I was still small, carrying me from the deeply cushioned window seat in my mom's loft where I had fallen asleep reading, over to my bed to tuck me in. On these nights I would wind myself tightly around him so that he couldn't leave, and he would humor me, dozing beside me until my breath became deep and steady, and he could gently extract himself from my slackened grip. In the morning he was never there. Honestly, it would probably have come as a shock to find him at the breakfast table, or in the bathroom, brushing his teeth or shaving, as I imagined other fathers did.

My throat began to thicken with emotion, so I pulled myself away from my memories and turned my attention to the task at hand. In a few days Johanna Danton would return from Paris to sell the mansion, so the lawyer had given me only one day to pack up my dad's vast library and I didn't know where to begin.

As I gazed in wonder at the hundreds of books in his collection – many of which seemed quite rare, I was drawn to the shelf of books that my father himself had written. They were set apart from the rest, close to his desk. I ran my fingers over the long row of gilt-embossed cloth spines, barely registering the list of titles: *Patriarch and Poet: the Legacy of Virgil; Hubris and Alienation: The Rise and Fall of Oedipus Rex; Sirens, Nymphs, and Mortals: Studies in Seduction; Anti-Odysseus: Understanding the Aeneas Archetype; Redefining Heroism: Reclaiming Hercules.* There were many more, but I paused at this last book, and extracted it from the rest. It was slim, bound in dark green

6

cloth, and—as I well knew—was the one volume in the entire collection that had been dedicated to me: his only public acknowledgment in print of the fact that he had a child. I knew that the dedication had caused a scandal at the time the book was published, but on this afternoon it produced only a small lump in my throat.

The page read simply, "For my daughter, Herculine Danton."

Seeing my name in print caused the usual cringe. My parents had explained to me often enough when I was a child, through my tears, why they had both blessed and cursed me with such an unwieldy, unfashionable first name: they wanted to give me the inner strength of Hercules, they said, because they knew that I would need it.

"As a woman in a man's world," my mother Clea said.

"As my daughter," said my father.

Both of them implying that I would have to be as strong and brave as twenty girls, just to live up to what they, and the rest of the world, expected of me. Right, I thought, with a pang of bitterness, as if being the love-child of a single mom and a married father wasn't enough. Haunted by those unwelcome old feelings, I stood in my father's library as if in a trance, wishing I could clear my head and heart.

Just as I was about to put the book down, sit on the floor, and surrender to my conflicting emotions, a breeze came through the tall open windows, causing me to notice the sky for the first time that day. Clear, cloudless, late summer light slanting through the branches heavy with leaves. And as I looked up, the breeze lifted the pages of the book I was holding, blowing them over, one by one, until the mid-section was exposed, marked by a slim stack of folded pale blue paper, tissue thin, the edges brown with age, stuck deep into the center crease of its pages.

I lifted them gingerly from their hiding place, and set the book on the glossy surface of my father's dark mahogany desk. Each sheet of paper was covered in spidery script. The first looked contained a title with a dedication, but after that the next twelve pages each contained one long poem. All of it was written in French.

I slid down the side of the desk and sank to my knees on the wine-colored carpet. I held the first page in my hands and read: *La Nouvelle Panthéon*, Sophia Danton, 1942. The sheet of paper was now shaking in my hands. The New Pantheon? What could that mean? I

7

knew that a pantheon was a gathering of gods, but *new* gods? And who was Sophia Danton? From the last name, she had to be a relative of mine, but my father had no living family that I knew of, and he had made a point of never speaking to me about his past.

All I knew was what my mom had told me. My dad had been smuggled out of France during the war as a child, and had been raised by a family friend in New York. When I was little, whenever I had asked my dad to tell me about his childhood or his parents, he had always become tense and changed the topic, explaining that it was too painful for him to think about. After a few tries I had stopped asking. Maybe these poems had something to do with his past... But why had he stored them away in the one book he had dedicated to me? Had he hoped that someday I would find them?

Puzzled and intrigued, I translated the dedication: *Pour Hercule, qui connait que l'amour ne meurt jamais*: "For Hercule, who knows that love never dies." Who was Hercule? The similarity of his name to my own was confusing. Was he another relative? I gently leafed through the rest of the pages. Each of the twelve poems bore the title of a different woman's name from classical Greek myths and legends: Electra, Medusa, Daphne, Persephone, Echo, Galatea, Ariadne, Penthesilea, Psyche, Cassandra, Atalanta, and Eurydice. Quite a cast of characters. What was this Sophia Danton up to? I leaned back against the desk and began to translate the first poem, which was entitled "Electra."

Whom could I have loved
if given the chance?
My brother, self-absorbed
and banished?
My father gone to war,
then murdered
by my mother's hand?
My mother?
None of these.
But it depends on how you define love.
I define it by pain.
The one who caused me the most pain,
the only one I ever really loved...
Iphigenia, my sister:
the virgin sacrifice
for good sailing wind.

Nobody knew what we shared.
The love of sisters,
innocent enough.
But our love was ravenous.
We were like lions,
hunter and prey,
prey and hunter.
When they came to take me to the altar,
You offered yourself instead to save me,
Leaving me here,
mad with grief, without you.

How strange, I thought. That's not the story of Electra; at least not any version that I'd ever read. In Aeschylus's *Oresteia*, Electra is merely the dutiful, grief-stricken daughter of Agamemnon and Clytemnestra. When Clytemnestra kills Agamemnon upon his return from the Trojan wars for sacrificing their younger daughter, Iphigenia, to the gods for fair sailing winds, Electra helps her brother Orestes avenge their father's death by plotting the murder of their mother Clytemnestra. Centuries later the term "Electra complex" was coined to describe women who were literally or symbolically too attached to their fathers. I grimaced; this was one complex I had been battling my whole life, even with my father *in absentia*. But Electra becoming lovers with Iphigenia? Electra recast as the intended virgin sacrifice, saved at the last minute by her sister? These were new twists on an already twisted plot.

Carefully tucking the poems back into my father's book, I began pacing the length of the room. Twelve women, twelve poems written for a man named Hercule who knew that love never dies. Twelve... Just like the twelve labors of Hercules... Coincidence? Maybe, but still... What was the first labor of Hercules again? I could never remember them all, let alone in order. I scanned the bookshelves, spotted my father's worn copy of Apollodorus's encyclopedia of Greek mythology, and looked up Hercules.

Born from the adulterous liaison of Zeus and the mortal Alcmena, Hercules was the constant target of Zeus's jealous wife Hera's wrath. After years of torment, Hercules consulted Apollo's oracle who told him that to appease Hera he must perform twelve heroic labors for King Eurystheus. The first labor he was to perform was to kill the Nemean lion that was terrorizing the land. What was that line in the poem I had just read? I turned back to read it again:

9

"…we were like lions…" Another coincidence? Probably not, with the entire collection dedicated to somebody named Hercule. I wondered if the rest of the poems contained similarly cryptic references to the other twelve labors… I'd have to check later. But now the question was: what did it all mean?

I took my father's book, the poems, and his copy of Apollodorus and placed them in my black canvas shoulder bag. My mind was racing with the mystery of my discovery, and as the the haze of my hangover lifted, I felt galvanized with excitement. I began filling empty crates with the books that seemed most important for me to keep. Even though Johanna Danton had moved out months ago, the lawyer had told me that it was stipulated in my dad's will that she couldn't sell the house until I had collected my legacy. She was "impatient to resolve this matter," he said, and I should "avoid inconveniencing her any further." In fact, I'd been inconveniencing her my whole life, and now was no exception.

My dad's books and his desk were all that remained in the empty house except for one solitary piece of furniture: the deep leather armchair that mom and I had given him for his birthday fifteen years ago. Apparently Johanna had left it for us when she moved to Paris, knowing that it had been our gift to him, and probably having resented its presence in her home for its entire duration there. I was grateful to her, even though I knew that she harbored only hatred for me. That had been clear throughout my four years as an undergraduate at Columbia, where Professor Johanna Danton of the French Department had made a point of avoiding me at all costs.

It had been with a mixture of trepidation and curiosity that mom and I had climbed the steps of my dad and Johanna's stately Riverside Drive home earlier that day. My heart was pounding so hard that I had even reached out to hold her hand. As she felt my grasp, my mom smiled bravely, and I asked her if she remembered the first time we had seen their house from the street, when I was just a little kid. She had taken me there only after I had begged her for days to see "where Daddy lives." After a long subway ride uptown, finally standing on the pavement across the street, looking somberly at the elegant old townhouse, I had asked her, "Why can't we go inside and see him, Mommy?"

She had replied evenly, "Because the Ice Queen would get angry, honey…"

10

That was all I had needed to stay away. The reference to Hans Christian Andersen's seductive villainess held a deeper threat than even my mother's sarcastic tone. After that, I rarely questioned the invisible barrier between my father's other life with his Ice Queen and the one he shared with us.

Now that barrier was gone.

Today we had finally entered the house, and after the large oak door had closed behind us, we moved in a daze through the empty rooms of the spacious mansion. My old feelings of loss and grief for my dad felt sharply new. Even though I was only ten years old when he died, my love for him was still strong and my memories of him were clear. In the summer of 1978, only a few weeks before my tenth birthday, he had been diagnosed with a brain tumor, admitted into the hospital, and died during surgery before we even knew he had been hospitalized. We never had a chance to say goodbye. His lawyers had called the following day to tell us he was dead, leaving us in shock and disbelief, opening up a void in our lives that had never really healed. Mom seemed to have moved on eventually, but there was still a place in my heart that I tried not to think about too often because it was still numb with his loss.

Surrounded by traces of his essence in the house he had lived in for over thirty years with his wife, the task of sorting through his vast library was made even more difficult by my consciousness of being in the space that he had occupied daily for years, whenever he was not with us.

Mom had tried to help me with the books at first, but after only a few minutes, she had lost her nerve and left the library abruptly, announcing, "I don't know if I can stand this, Herculine. We don't even have room for half of these books in our apartment. I think you should just pack a few boxes and donate the rest of the books to the university. Then we can get out of here."

I observed her for a moment as she walked away, watching as she played nervously with stray wisps of her auburn hair. When she turned back to face me, I could see that the graceful angles and curves of her face were drawn with concern, and her large gray eyes were serious. I hadn't expected to take all of the books, but now that I was finally in my dad's library, I wanted to stay here as long as possible. However, I didn't want my mom to have to stay and sort through hundreds of old books if she didn't want to. Books were *my* passion, not hers.

"I'll keep the ones I want separate," I said.

"How many?" she asked with an edge to her voice.

"I'm not sure yet," I replied cautiously. "Give me an hour or two to decide."

She nodded and offered to go out and get some food for us in the meantime; I knew that the fresh air and a brisk walk would help clear her head and heart – at least for a little while, and it would give me some time alone in my father's library, which is what I wanted more than anything else. She was still gone when I found the poems.

Moving quickly through the shelves, and rapidly filling my crates with books, I wondered if my mom might know who Sophia Danton was and decided to ask her as soon as she came back. If I finished packing the rest of the books quickly, there might be time to get to the university library before it closed. I wanted to see if I could learn more about the poems, and their author.

I realized that the majority of my father's library would be welcomed warmly by Columbia, and – true to the egalitarian spirit my mother had instilled in me – I also knew that I would have just as much access to his books there as in the privacy of my home. Our makeshift artist's loft wouldn't be my home much longer anyway: in a few days, I would be on my way to begin a Ph.D. program in Classics at Berkeley. Ben and Lucy weren't too thrilled about this, but I promised I would see them over winter break, and told them they were welcome to visit me any time in California.

I let my mind wander over moments from the nights I'd shared with them over the past few weeks as I packed up more books. Lucy was a tall, dark-haired beauty, and Ben's tousled brown curls and wire-rimmed glasses set off his earthy charm. They were witty and playful, passionate and creative, and the connection between them was more compelling than any other couple I'd known. About an hour later, I heard the front door open and close, followed by the sound of mom's boots against the floor. I wiped my hands on my jeans and walked out to the terrace where she was resting her slender dancer's body in a chaise next to an unopened bag from the market. She looked pale under the cool canopy of trees, and I knelt down beside her.

"Mom?" I murmured.

She stirred and opened her eyes, "Mmmm? Is everything all right?"

"Yeah, I'm done, so we can go; but I found something really interesting, and I'm wondering if you happen to know the name Sophia Danton?"

She sat up quickly and turned to look at me intently, "What? What did you find?"

Surprised by her shocked reaction, I underplayed my discovery, and nonchalantly turned away to open up the grocery bag. I pulled out an apple, and said, "Um, just some poems she wrote that were in one of Dad's books..."

I watched as she a deep breath. Then she spoke tentatively, "That was his mother's name, I think. He only mentioned her once to me, a long time ago. He wouldn't talk about her again when I asked. He would get angry when I mentioned her name, so I never brought it up again..." She seemed far away as she trailed off.

I was silent, my mind racing. Why had the mention of his mother's name made my dad angry? Why had my mom never mentioned Sophia to me before?

"How much do you know about her?" I asked.

Mom seemed hesitant, "Just that she died during the war, soon after your dad escaped. He never saw her again."

So this was why my dad didn't like talking about his past. But I was sure that he had left his mother's poems in that book for me to find, so it was time for me to learn his story, even if he wasn't around to tell it to me. I let mom rest on the terrace as I packed up the remaining boxes of books I had set aside for myself. Then I called dad's lawyer both to see if they had his mother's name on file –which they didn't – and to arrange for a moving van to bring the books I wanted down to our apartment in Greenwich Village the following day. The lawyer said the office would took care of the donation arrangements for the rest of the library to Columbia too.

Mom and I were solemn as we locked up the house, and I regretted that I would never again be able to spend a day in my father's study. My one afternoon there had been exciting, but far too brief. Standing on the sidewalk, I gave her a quick hug and turned away, not wanting her to see the tears welling up in my eyes. I waited as she hailed a cab back down to the Village, and then I walked over to Columbia in the balmy early evening air. I could feel sharp edges of excitement prickling my skin: as if in an effort to counteract my heart's numb sorrow, my brain was humming with curiosity about the poems and the shadowy figure of Sophia Danton. I may have left my dad's study behind, but I had brought a piece of him with me.

13

The comfort of this thought quickly gave way to a familiar irritation. Why did I have so few pieces of him? Why couldn't he have let me into his past, even if it was painful? Isn't that an important part of what it means to be a parent? Passing on the family history, being a role model of strength and resilience? Was it just that I had been too young? That couldn't have been the only reason. After all, he hadn't been willing to fully let my mom in either.

I knew that he had probably just wanted our time together to be focused on the present, not the past, but I was frustrated that the only connection to his life that he had given me while he was alive was his love of classical myths. In a strange way, the stories of all those gods and goddesses had been substituted in my imagination for the mystery of my own father's life story. As I approached the entrance to the university, I wondered: if my father had known that he was dying, would he have told me about the poems?

Once I was inside the vast, vaulted halls of Butler Library, glowing with gilt-edged marble and carved wood paneling, these musings fell away. I slipped into my favorite heightened mind state: the researcher's passion for the hunt. First I approached the computer terminals containing a catalogue of the library entire holdings, and I typed in the name "Danton, Sophia." Nothing came up. No mention of her as an author or a subject, and no entries in any encyclopedia. I tried again, and this time simply typed in the name "Danton." A long list flashed onto the screen, and I scanned it quickly: there were scores of other Dantons, each accompanied by a brief biographical blurb. I scrolled through entries for Armand, Charles, Florence, Henri, Jean-Paul, and then something caught my eye…"Julien Danton, Minister of Culture, 1940-44, born 1905-died 1946; m. Sophia, 1915-1943."

I realized that I had been holding my breath and exhaled sharply. There she was. But who was Julien Danton? My grandfather? And had Sophia Danton only lived one year after finishing the poems? Grabbing my bag and breaking into a sprint, I raced downstairs to the microfiche archive. Out of breath and impatient, I reached the counter in a rush and hurriedly requested the tape for the Paris newspaper *Le Monde* for the year 1943.

Two hours later, after poring over endless Obituary columns in tiny French print in search of the name "Danton," eyes aching with strain, I was about to give up, when a short entry on June 10, 1943 stopped me in my tracks. Haltingly, I translated:

Sophia Danton, wife of Julien Danton, respected Vichy government official. Cause of death: suicide. Mme. Danton was suspected of politically subversive activities and anti-Vichy actions. Mme. Danton, née Demetrius, the daughter of Céline Demetrius, formerly of the reputable auction house of Ebermann and Demetrius, dissolved in 1942 due to the untimely death of M. Ebermann and the emigration of Mme. Demetrius in 1936.

"Suicide?" I was so shocked that I barely registered the rest of the information. I had to re-read the entry several times to make sure there was no mistake. I was weary and shaken and my head was pounding once again, but not from a hangover this time. The library was closing in a few minutes, so I pressed the copy button on the machine and made myself a print of the page. I could devote more time to it later. After I tucked the photocopy into my notebook, I left the viewing booth, walked up the stairs entirely preoccupied, and felt my head clear as I stepped out of the library into the cool evening air. I walked for blocks to unravel the questions that were bursting inside me.

Had my father known that his mother had committed suicide? Could that have been why a mere mention of her name had made him angry? But wouldn't he have just been saddened? And what did it mean that his father, Julien, had been a Vichy official, but his mother was suspected of having been involved in "anti-Vichy" activities? Had my father's parents been on opposing sides of the war? Was that why he had been smuggled out of the country? Had his life, or his mother's life, been in danger? There was so much more I wanted to know, but I couldn't begin to think of how to find out.

With only a few days left before I had to leave for California, I knew there would be no more time for trips to the library...just packing and preparation for leaving. So each night I spent an hour or two with my grandmother's poems, translating them slowly from French into English. My first attempts were rudimentary, but I would work out their subtle nuances later. All that mattered was that I could see that a story was emerging from them, even if it was still cloudy.

On my last night in town, after a bittersweet farewell dinner party with mom and our closest friends, I went to say goodbye to Ben and Lucy, which turned out to be harder than I had expected. While we were in bed, when I told them I would miss them, Lucy teased me as she wrapped her thighs around me more tightly, "Come

on, Herculine. Don't worry…you'll be catnip for all those Berkeley girls… You'll see: you'll forget all about us in a matter of hours."

Ben looked at me a little wistfully, then he leaned down to kiss my shoulder and whispered, "All those Berkeley guys too…"

But I wasn't so sure. Would I fit in at Berkeley? I had never been one to make new friends easily. Brief lovers, yes; but lately I had been craving something more substantial and lasting. Would I discover it in California? There was only one way to find out.

On the morning of my departure, I felt weightless. My boxes of books were in temporary storage, and I had shipped my dad's leather chair off to Berkeley so that it would arrive by the time I had found a place to live. When I had asked my mom if I could take the chair with me, she had immediately agreed, adding that the sight of it was more than she could bear. It was hard for me to understand her sometimes; I knew that she had loved my dad deeply, but after he died, she'd had a steady stream of lovers, and never seemed to want to talk about him. As for me, any reminder of my dad was welcome. I had never had enough of him even while he was alive.

The poems are a part of him too, I thought. The longing to continue my research on Sophia Danton's poems once I was in Berkeley was pulling at me so hard I could barely concentrate on what to pack. Soon there was nothing left to do except say goodbye to my mom as a taxi pulled up to the curb to take me to the airport. Feeling as if my heart was already halfway to California, I gave her a quick kiss and a smile, handed my suitcase to the cab driver, and climbed inside. I closed my eyes and rested my head back against the cool vinyl seat, waiting for my journey to begin.

Sophia
Paris, 1936

The young woman walked briskly through the rain, the collar of her fine wool coat turned up against the cold wind, one gloved hand keeping her veil pulled down – firmly shielding her face from the weather, as well as from the curious gazes of passersby. It was late in the afternoon, and she was not in the best part of the city, but this is where the secret room was hidden, a rented basement apartment turned into a makeshift bistro. And it was there that she met Yvette whenever she could manage to get away from home.

Home. She shivered – and not from the cold rain whipping her slender frame. The lavish town house in the eighth arrondissement where she lived with her husband Julien had never felt like home. It was a prison, and he was a beast.

With her free hand she gently massaged her bruised shoulder as she hurried along the street. She couldn't bear to think about him now. Not when she was this close to seeing Yvette. Thoughts of her lover sped her on, and warmed her core with the promise of affection and passion that awaited her in the room above the bistro where they would spend a few stolen hours together before parting again, never knowing for how long.

She could see the building two blocks away and walked faster, her delicate leather boots splashing through the small puddles collecting between the cobblestones. When she reached the corner, she turned down an alley where a large doorman ushered her through an archway and down a flight of stone steps. He opened a thick wooden door after unlocking a formidable padlock and closed the door again behind her.

Sophia breathed deeply with relief as she entered the bistro: it was warm, lit by glowing lamps, and there was soft music playing on the phonograph in the corner. Several clusters of women were arranged throughout the room, drinking wine, talking, laughing, dancing, embracing. She barely noticed as an older woman took her coat and handed her a glass of wine. Because there was Yvette coming towards her with open arms.

She was safe now. She was home.

Yvette pulled Sophia close and embraced her, saying, "Cherie, it has been too long, how late can you stay this time?"

Sophia buried her face in Yvette's richly perfumed dark blonde hair and murmured, "I only have a few hours... Come, sit with me. I feel like I ran all the way here."

Yvette smiled, but Sophia was not exaggerating. She was flushed and out of breath. Yvette led her over to a table in a dimly lit corner of the room, and as Sophia took off her stylish *chapeau* and veil, her lustrous auburn curls tumbled down around her shoulders. Yvette gathered a handful of Sophia's hair and held it to her lips.

"I have missed every strand of you, Sophie," she said, her eyes large with desire.

Sophia responded, "And I have longed for you with every fiber of my being," which was true. She lived for these stolen afternoons. And before Yvette, she had lived for them with Françoise, and with Hélène before her. She had been living a secret life for years, even before her marriage to Julien.

Without breaking eye contact with Yvette, she took a long sip from her wine glass and felt the potent liquid warm her still shivering skin. She put her glass down on a small café table nearby and reached out her hands to Yvette, who – still gazing at her intently – silently drew off Sophia's gloves and held her hands in her own. In the next instant the two women were in each other's arms, more urgently than before, their mouths seeking communion in each other's lips, as their hearts sought salvation in each other's bodies. They pressed tightly together, their legs entwined beneath the table, their passion visible to all the other women in the room, who eyed them appreciatively.

Some of these women were former lovers of Sophia's and some had once been involved with Yvette. The *sapphiste* society in Paris often felt stiflingly small, riven with petty jealousies, but if there were betrayals, they stayed within the community – no one ever exposed another woman publicly. If she had, she would have been shunned and barred from the community. Occasionally eccentric or artistic women went public themselves, those luminaries who could afford to or who even thrived on the scandals, but for relatively ordinary married women like Sophia and Yvette, such exposure would have been disastrous. Yet, compared to Sophia, Yvette's situation was enviably free. Her husband had revealed to her his own preference for men soon after their marriage, and they amicably

18

frequented the deviant dens of their respective double lives while keeping up a fashionably elegant public front for all of Paris to see.

Sophia, by contrast, was practically fettered. Her husband, a stern, joyless government official, kept a close watch on her at all times, and there were even occasions when she was sure that she was being followed when she left the house. Today, for instance, the same large black car seemed to be gliding by her at each intersection, but she had ducked into a boutique with a back door several blocks from the bistro and had eluded them. Sophia tried to push all of these distracting thoughts away as she kissed Yvette, but she still made a mental note to use the back door of the same boutique on her way home, so that she would exit from the shop's front entrance, thus establishing her alibi in case the men in the car had been waiting for her to emerge.

Yvette sensed Sophia's distraction and pulled her up to her feet to dance. As they swayed to the melodic strains of a mellow jazz trio, Sophia rested her head on Yvette's shoulder and closed her eyes, enjoying the feeling of her lover's body pulsing to the music, the rhythm of their hearts augmented by the syncopation of the artists that seemed to be playing just for them. Jazz was the music of the marginalized, the fringe, the avant garde – and Sophia felt that its freedom called to her like no other music she had ever heard.

Freedom.

The reason she was here. The feeling she had when she was in a woman's arms. The true longing she felt whenever she was not here at the bistro, or at any of the other safe spaces for *sapphistes* in Paris. The misery she felt whenever she was in her husband's stifling, threatening presence. The desire to escape. But where could she go? She had nowhere to run permanently, so she took her freedom here, in small doses. How long she would be able to survive like this, she didn't know.

This thought tightened her throat and Sophia opened her eyes, as if she might see some opportunity, some large window to freedom that had suddenly opened, which she had never seen before. But instead, she saw a man staring at her from the shadows near the entrance to the bistro.

He was slightly built, wiry with lean, muscular strength. He had a tousled mop of dark curls and held his humble workman's cap in his hands. His clothes were shabby, but his eyes were alight with intelligence and warmth. She had seen him before. He came around to all the *sapphiste* haunts, supplying the women with cut-rate

cigarettes and silk stockings from the black market. Occasionally even she – who could afford to shop at the overpriced boutiques on the *Champs Elysées* – had bought stockings from him, not caring if they were stolen, thinking only of the money she saved that could be used for paying off her household servants not to inform on her whereabouts on the afternoons when she disappeared to meet Yvette.

The man in the shadows had always been cordial to her, and once had even bought her a glass of wine as she had sat alone at a table, waiting for Yvette to arrive. She couldn't remember his name... was it Henri? No, it had some mythological reference...Helios? She suppressed a smile and turned her face to hide in Yvette's neck. No, no...she remembered now. The man's name was Hercule. She remembered having thought that he was a bit small for such a large name. She turned back to look at him. Why was he still staring at her?

Seeing that she had noticed him, he beckoned to her and she stiffened in Yvette's arms. Yvette pulled back so that she could see Sophia's face.

"What's wrong?" she asked, worry in her eyes.

"That fellow over there," motioned Sophia with a nod of her head, "He just waved at me to come over and talk to him."

"Do you know him?" asked Yvette.

"He's the one who sells cheap stockings," Sophia murmured, "I've talked to him once or twice." She paused, then said, "Listen, stay here. I'll go find out what he wants and I'll be right back."

Yvette nodded, narrowing her eyes in suspicion as she gazed at the man by the door, and let her go.

Sophia walked over to Hercule with a question in her eyes, and before she could speak, he apologized for interrupting her dance.

"Forgive me," he said, "But I think you may be in danger, and I want to help you."

Sophia's expression changed to alarm as he continued.

"On my way here, I saw you walking near the river and noticed a large black car following you. You were smart and used that boutique as a cover," he smiled at her admiringly, "but the car is waiting on the street upstairs, and the two thugs inside are government men – I've seen them before."

Sophia stammered, "How – how do you know this? Who are you? Were you following me too?" She felt genuinely afraid.

"No, no, no," he assured her in apologetic tones, "I am on your side. I am a friend. Let me help you. There is another way out of this building, and I will distract them." He grinned with mischief like a boy, "There is a brothel nearby that they might like to visit for a while…"

Sophia looked at him carefully. He seemed sincere, and she needed to believe that he was a friend. Until he had said that he was "on her side," she hadn't realized that others had the same enemies she did. Thinking quickly, not wanting to sacrifice her precious time with Yvette upstairs, she asked, "How long can I stay?"

Hercule looked at her with seriousness in his face, finding it difficult to comprehend the risk she was willing to take for her liaison with her lover. He said, "I'll keep them away for an hour. When you are upstairs, use the fire escape at the end of the hallway; it lets you off in an alley the next street over. One of my friends will be there to help you. He'll have a cap like mine."

"Why are you doing this?" Sophia asked, trembling.

Hercule was silent for a moment, then said in a low voice, "I don't want you to get hurt."

Kindness, then She could accept that. How much did he know about her, Sophia wondered. Julien's government thugs in the car wouldn't dare harm her, even if they dragged her into their car and brought her back to her husband like a guilty truant child. No, it was Julien who would hurt her. Did Hercule know this too?

"Go," he said softly. "Make the most of your hour."

"Thank you," she said, and pressed his hand with her own.

She asked the hostess for her coat, then turned and walked with studied calm back to Yvette, where – without a word, she gathered her hat, purse, and gloves, and motioned to her lover to follow her upstairs.

Yvette smiled, "So soon? Wonderful!"

Sophia mustered a smile too. "Yes, come on," she said, "We have a whole hour. Let's savor every minute."

Just before she went through the door leading upstairs to the bedrooms, Sophia glanced back over her shoulder to thank Hercule once more. But he was gone.

'For centuries the scholarly community and popular culture together have reduced the figure of Hercules, or – as he is known by the Greeks – *Herakles*, to a parody of hyper-masculinity and heterosexual virility. We know him today as a mere muscle man, a fighting machine, the priapic conqueror of over one hundred wives and mistresses, and as the prodigious progenitor of a veritable tribe of descendents known as the *Heraclidae*. In fact, besides being flagrantly promiscuous, our bold hero was as bisexual as Achilles. Several sources claim that Hercules' young male lovers outnumbered the total of all of his wives and mistresses combined. Plutarch, in his *Eroticos*, maintains that Heracles' *eromenoi* (male lovers) were beyond counting. But the greatest of these loves was Hylas, the young Trojan prince who served him faithfully as an arms-bearer for years…"

Herculine Danton, *Mythic Truth*. University of California Berkeley Press; 1999.

The First Poem: Electra
Berkeley, 1989

By the end of my third week in Berkeley, the rush and excitement of starting graduate school and the challenge of finding a place to live had eclipsed any lingering reluctance to leave New York that I might have brought with me. After a week of new graduate student orientation in the mornings and hunting for a room to rent off-campus in the afternoons, I decided to move in with two other doctoral students a few blocks away from the University in a cozy craftsman-style house on Calpurnia Street. I had been lucky to find the well-situated rental, and even luckier to find my housemates, Hermàn and Anthea. Both were in their third year in the Comparative Literature department at the University, and I liked them from the start. They seemed to respect my solitary, bookish ways, yet had already made a point of including me in their social gatherings with other grad students. Every Saturday night, the house had some kind of party going on, but during the week it was as quiet as a cloister, and this arrangement worked perfectly for me.

I couldn't help but marvel at the beauty of my first Northern Californian autumn as I walked to school each day. Roses were still in bloom in early September, as were the oleander, datura, and magnolia trees. It seemed like every yard I passed was lined with thickly perfumed borders of lavender, rosemary, and sage. As soon as I reached campus, however, I found that I could barely pay attention during my classes or my part-time work-study job at the library – I was so absorbed by piecing together the mystery of Sophia Danton's poems. If my grandmother had indeed been involved in "politically subversive activities and anti-Vichy actions," as suggested by her obituary, I reasoned that researching the background of Vichy France and resistance activity during that era might help me to understand the poems, and perhaps my father's past too.

The Berkeley library yielded a rich cache of texts on both topics, and I spent many long afternoons soaking up new knowledge. Some days I read in the atrium in the library while I was on duty,

23

sometimes at home, but my favorite place to study in the afternoons was a little café close to campus where they made delicious chai lattés and the light filled the small room with an intimate glow. Some days I would read there for hours, sipping my tea, making notes, and gazing absentmindedly at the bright-eyed girl who worked behind the counter.

I learned that the Vichy regime had been established in France in 1940, by Marshal Phillipe Pétain, after the surrender of France to Nazi German forces. I was surprised to discover that while Pétain and his regime collaborated closely with Nazi Germany, Vichy was technically considered to have a neutral status in the war. I knew already that the French police had organized raids to capture and deport Jews, Gypsies, homosexuals, prostitutes, and communists from the country to concentration camps where most of them had died. However, I had not known that Pétain had also instituted a reactionary program called the "National Revolution," involving policies aimed at reviving the French "race" by raising the birth rate and improving athletic performance, modeling itself after the eugenics system practiced by the Nazis. I was relieved to learn that this French program was abandoned four years later when France was liberated by the Allied forces in 1944, and Charles de Gaulle restored the country to democracy.

This general background was useful, but I needed more specific information about the lives of women in Vichy France, and about the French Resistance too, if I was going to shed any light on Sophia Danton. One source I found, entitled *Femmes Fatales: the Women of the French Resistance*, explained that the roles that women had played in the Resistance were as dramatic and yet as understated as the roles women played in the tragedies of ancient Greece. They had been both heroines and central players in the strategies and operations of the movement, as well as shadowy marginal figures eclipsed by the more visible heroics of their male comrades.

The women of the French Underground served as crucial liaisons between operational cells across the besieged country. Skilled in codes and de-coding strategies, the female operatives were carriers and creators of many pivotal communiqués that determined the outcome of the movement's numerous small victories, including critical assassinations. Reading about these unknown heroines caused me to wonder if Sophia Danton's poems might not only shed light on her own dark past, but also possibly reveal valuable information about this vital moment in history.

Even though my head was preoccupied with thoughts of the poems and Vichy France, as I walked to campus one morning in early September I checked my watch and picked up my pace. I couldn't be late to my Archaic Greek Poetry class because I was already on trial with Professor Seidon.

Henry Seidon was the unofficial "king" of the Classics department. On the first day of class, while taking attendance, he had peered at me over his half-moon trifocal glasses (the eventual fate, I had noted grimly, of most classics scholars) and said to me coolly,

"Ah yes, Miss Danton. I knew your father well. *And his wife too.*"

I had been thrown off guard by the condescending tone in his voice. Unlike the faculty at Columbia, who had known whose child I was and had always treated me with respect, even in some cases, with explicit kindness, this Berkeley professor had a grudge against me that was utterly unexpected. Of course, I had known that my father's reputation would precede me whenever I moved in classicist circles, but it hadn't occurred to me that the Ice Queen also had colleagues who resented me on her behalf. Partially indignant and partially bemused, I wondered what this man could possibly have against me. Was he some old admirer of Johanna's who had been jilted when she married my dad? Or could he be one of her close friends and confidantes who knew how she really felt about me and my mom? Either way, taking Seidon's seminar was unavoidable; it was the foundation of the graduate program and I would have to surpass his prejudice against me with an impeccable performance in his class.

As I sat in my seat, waiting for Seidon to check off the other students' names to on his attendance list, my mind wandered back to the afternoon Latin lessons with my dad that I had loved and looked forward to when I was a child. He had taught me nursery rhymes and children's songs that he had lovingly translated for me, like "Twinkle, Twinkle Little Star." I could hear his voice in my head singing, *mica mica parva stella, mirror quondam sis tam bella, splendens eminus in illa, alba velut gemma caela.* I chuckled softly to myself at the memory, but my reverie was interrupted by Seidon's snide voice.

"Miss Danton? Would you care to join us, or at least be so kind as to share with us the source of your amusement?"

The assignment for the day had been to translate Pindar's first Nemean victory ode, in which Pindar retells the story of the infant Hercules who strangled two serpents sent by Zeus's angry wife

Hera to kill him in his cradle. I knew the passage well and had translated it twice with pleasure: first into an appropriately epic style of lofty ceremonial language, and second into more colloquial speech just for fun. But as I listened to the other students in the class go around the room reading their translations line-by-line, I became worried. My classmates had clearly struggled with the assignment; their translations were stiff, awkward, and in no recognizable style. When my turn came, I read from my notebook:

But as for me, I gladly return to the theme of Herakles, rousing an ancient story from among the great heights of his excellence, how when the son of Zeus suddenly came out of his mother's womb into the brilliant light, escaping her birth-pangs, he did not escape the notice of gold-throned Hera when he was placed in his saffron swaddling-clothes. But the queen of the gods, stung in her heart, immediately sent serpents. The doors opened, and they crept into the spacious inner-chamber, eager to coil their swift jaws around the child...

Professor Seidon interrupted me, "Miss Danton, your own translation please, *not* your father's."

I was struck silent with rage and surprise. I had never even seen my father's translations of Pindar; as far as I knew, he had never published any. How dare Seidon accuse me of presenting unoriginal work!

I responded to him with cold pride.

"Excuse me sir; I am not acquainted with my father's translations of Pindar. They must be unpublished. If you have a copy, I would be glad to see them. The translation I just read is my own work, and..."

Seidon interrupted me once again, "That will be enough, Miss Danton. See me after class. Next, please."

Baffled and humiliated, I wondered frantically: why had he thought that my work was my dad's ? Could my translations have resembled his so closely? My mind drifted off again as my classmates droned on. I remembered my dad telling me the stories of the twelve labors of Hercules at bedtime when I had been young. I could just hear his voice, *"...he did not escape the notice of gold-throned Hera when he was placed in his saffron swaddling-clothes. But the queen of the gods, stung in her heart..."* Wait: that was *my* translation! Or were those his words? I couldn't remember now, but my mind was swimming with the possibility that my father had been translating Pindar from memory for my bedtime stories. If he thas was true, and he had decided to

26

write them down afterwards, why had he never published them? And where could Seidon have read them?

Professor Seidon waited for me as the room cleared. When the last student left, he closed the door and spoke before I had the chance.

"Miss Danton," he said. "I want to believe you that the work was your own, but the resemblance to your father's original is simply too uncanny."

I was still too angry to respond, so I didn't.

He continued. "You are correct. Your father's translations of Pindar were never published. He and I were in graduate school together at Yale and studied Pindar in the same seminar. I still have the notes from our cram sessions and have used his translations in my teaching ever since. They are flawless."

He opened his briefcase and took out a manila folder containing a sheaf of yellowed papers, filled – unmistakably – with my father's handwriting. I reached for the papers instinctively. Seidon handed them to me gravely. I leafed through them, hungrily, looking for more personal traces of my father…and found them. There was the stanza I had translated, almost word for word. I looked up at Seidon, who was staring at me quizzically.

"How," he asked, "If you have never seen these translations, did yours approximate his so closely?"

I murmured, "He told me stories at night before bed all during my childhood."

Seidon sat down heavily at this news. "I had no idea, Miss Danton, that you and your father were so close. From what Johanna—I mean, Dr. Danton—told me, I thought you were barely a peripheral presence in their lives."

"Well," I said, "I was certainly a peripheral presence in *her* life, but my dad was over at our place several times a week, at least when I was little. Can I keep these? It would mean a lot to me."

Seidon nodded. "Certainly, though if you wouldn't mind carefully making copies of them at the department office for me so that I can continue to use them in my teaching…?" He looked at me somewhat sheepishly.

"Sure," I said. "Thanks. I'll have them for you at the next class."

As I walked out the door, Seidon said gruffly, "Miss Danton, I'm pleased to have you in the class. Your father would be proud of your ability."

I met his gaze evenly, said "Thank you," and left.

Head spinning with the import of my interaction with Seidon and the treasure of my father's youthful translations in my bag, I went to my work shift at the library and walked home four hours later in the golden afternoon light. Exultant, as if in my confrontation with Seidon's ego I had wrestled the Nemean lion itself to the ground, I felt brave enough to do just about anything. With a new sense of purpose, I walked quickly past the rows of cafés, copy shops, pubs and sushi bars that lined the streets surrounding the Berkeley campus.

Perhaps due to my heightened clarity of mind after Archaic Greek, perhaps due to the particular slant of the early autumn sunlight, I registered more of the many seasonal changes around me than usual. I noticed that a few pepper trees had already turned reddish gold and were filling the streets with their slender fallen leaves. The rest of the trees were still green: eucalyptus, bay and laurel, live oak and the occasional small grove of redwoods. There was a crisp, autumnal clarity in the air, and the angle of the sun lit up the city around me with an amber glow.

When I entered my favorite café, I also noticed immediately that the bright-eyed girl behind the espresso counter was no longer wearing her usual skimpy tank top and shorts but had switched to a pair of ripped brown corduroy pants and a greenish-gray sweater instead. The girl had a short mane of thick sun-bleached hair, cropped and spiky, yet softly beckoning to the touch. The delicate silver hoop pierced through her left eyebrow was set with a small green gemstone the same color as her eyes, catching the light in a distracting way.

I stood in line obediently, with the rest of the café's faithful customers, and wondered how many of them came to the café for its attractive wait staff. It was actually hard not to stare. The skin that showed through the holes in the counter girl's sweater was tanned, and when she left the counter briefly to clear some tables I could see that the lines of her thighs in the brown corduroys were lean and muscular. She had to be a cyclist or a runner. But it was her eyes that were her most mesmerizing feature: large, green, and deep-lidded, lazily cat-like when coolly observing a customer, but crackling with light and electricity when she laughed or smiled, as she seemed to do whenever I reached the front of the line.

In the several weeks I'd been in town, no one else had really caught my interest. There were beautiful, interesting people

28

everywhere, even one fairly good-looking guy in my Archaic Poetry class, and several grad students – male and female alike —who had made overtures to me when they came over to my housemates' parties, but nobody except this girl had turned my head and made me stare, wanting to know more.

"Hello, *chai latte*," Bright Eyes said teasingly when I reached the front of the line, calling me by the name of the drink I ordered every day.

"Hey there," I replied, trying to sound cool, but I blushed as I met her laughing eyes, and stammered, "Um, yeah, I *will* have a chai latte, as usual." She smiled, and was about to turn away to make my drink, when I decided to be brave and actually make contact. I blurted out, "So, uh – my name's Herculine. Is there, um, any chance that you'd like to join me for a glass of wine at the Bistro when you get off work tonight...?"

Bright Eyes looked at me in surprise, then turned away to fix my tea. My heart pounded with a force that was surely audible to the rest of the customers in line. Had I blown it? Was she annoyed now? I was in agony until she finally turned around, and I could see that her face was still serious, but her eyes were glowing. She handed me the drink and then held out her hand.

She said simply, "I'm Hyla. See you at five."

I took her hand and the softness of her skin combined with the strength of her grasp sent a current right through me. Our eyes were locked in a gaze that left me breathless. I quickly let go of her hand and placed two dollar bills on the counter, but she refused them, saying with a smile, "It's on me." Then she turned away, calling, "Next in line?" and I had no choice but to bow my head in acknowledgment of the gift, and move quietly away, heart still beating fast, out into the fading sun of a day that suddenly felt much more significant than it had ten minutes ago.

I sat down on a nearby bench in disbelief. People, even beautiful ones, didn't usually have this kind of effect on me. Leaning back, eyes closed, I raked my fingers through my disheveled curls. I took a few deep breaths to compose myself, soaked up the sun for a moment or two, then stood up again, hoisted my book bag onto my shoulder, drank some of the savory *chai*, and walked purposefully away from the café. Just because this girl made my heart race faster than I had known was physically possible didn't mean that she was going to turn out to be anything special. She'd be fun for a while,

like the rest, and that would be it. I liked my freedom. After all, I thought as I headed home, it was all I had ever known.

For the rest of the afternoon, I tried to read more about women in the Resistance, but I couldn't seem to focus my thoughts, which kept sliding back to Hyla and her catlike eyes. I finally put down my book, pulled myself out of the deep comfort of my father's leather chair, and went for a run to clear my head. Chuckling to myself at the sight of an elderly hippie couple dressed in flowing cotton robes getting into a BMW in front of a rambling old Julia Morgan style mansion, I noticed with amusement that there were Buddha statues on the front porch of three out of every five houses on the street. I wasn't in New York anymore; that was certain. But I liked Berkeley. It was like a sprawling Greenwich Village with more trees, and it was growing on me in other ways too.

My mind glided back to Hyla as I ran down another lushly gardened street, and I thought back to the last time I had slept with Ben and Lucy. They had been right: I had almost forgotten about them during these last few weeks, but now the memories flooded through me. My face felt hot and flushed as I remembered the fullness of Lucy's curves and the way Ben's hands had skillfully sculpted my body... And before them? There had been a long series of pretty faces and bodies, a few memorable names, but no one special. No one for more than a few nights.

I sighed and lost my stride, stopping by a large tree to stretch for a minute and prepare myself for the sprint back home. Then I ran as hard as I could, pushing everything out of my head except the awareness of my breathing and my feet hitting the pavement. Half an hour later, as I massaged my neck and shoulders in the shower, a small voice was clear in my head: maybe it was time for something different.

That night I met Hyla after she finished work and we walked together over to the Bistro on the corner. It reminded me of one of my favorite Greenwich Village restaurants: small and cozy, with exposed brick walls and plants hanging from the rafters, good jazz on the stereo, and an earthy atmosphere of muted cool. We sat at a candlelit table by the back wall and ordered two glasses of wine. Our conversation began easily, and soon we were weaving our way through the stories of our lives, past and present, as well as our future dreams. Hyla was working her way through graduate studies in film school at Berkeley, attending classes part-time. She wanted to be a documentary filmmaker, and was working on a project about the

lives of homeless women artists in the Bay Area. Mortified that I didn't even know that there *were* homeless women artists, I was awed by her project.

Hyla's life had been hard – brought up in foster homes, separated from her brother after their parents died, working her way first through a community college and then a state university, finally earning a scholarship for grad school at Berkeley. Now her day job was at the café, but her night job and undercover research was exotic dancing at a club in San Francisco on the weekends. When I raised my eyebrows in surprise, she explained.

"The money's pretty good, the other dancers are cool, and the clients aren't so bad. It's an upscale club so they take good care of us, and it's great material for my next film project." She shrugged, then added more invitingly, "You should come catch my act sometime…"

As I assured her that I would, I felt a shiver run up the back of my neck at the thought of her body barely clothed and doing anything that might be called "exotic." I looked at her thoughtfully for a moment then, cleared my throat, and – taking a chance – switched the subject, telling her about finding my grandmother's poems and researching the story behind them. As she listened, her eyes shone with interest.

"There's a film there," she said. "World War II, Paris, secret passion and danger, mysterious poems and codes… Maybe someday you'll write the script and I'll direct it?"

We clinked our glasses solemnly, toasting to the potential of much more between us than the distant possibility of working on a film project together. We finished our wine and talked for another hour; then I walked Hyla back to the café where her bicycle was waiting.

Before we said goodnight, my confidence bolstered by the intimacy of our conversation, I pulled Hyla close and held her in my arms. She smelled like sandalwood and clean sweat, coffee beans and cinnamon. My head was spinning. After a moment, she pulled away slightly and brushed the tip of her nose against mine. Then she moved her face closer, raised my chin with her fingertips and kissed me. I closed my eyes. Hyla's lips were warm, full, and even softer than I had imagined.

Our kiss was long and sensuous, and would have lasted several minutes longer, but Hyla leaned her head back, took a deep breath of the fragrant night air and said, looking at me with a smile

and the hint of a dare, "Let's go to your place. I don't have to be anywhere until my first morning class."

I smiled, placed my hands more firmly around her slender waist and pulled her close again. When we kissed this time, I felt an ache in my chest. I tried to ignore it by concentrating on the texture and scent of her hair. I ran my fingers through its thick silk and I found myself burying my face into its softness and inhaling her aroma even more deeply. I shivered with the force of unfamiliar emotion, and then she began kissing me with increasing intensity.

Many hours later, I awoke in my bed, only to find that Hyla was already gone, the sheets rumpled and the pillow still indented with the evidence that she had recently been there. I knew it hadn't been a dream. Sleepily, I padded out to the hallway in a t-shirt and shorts to see if either of my roommates had seen her leave. Hermàn was downstairs at the kitchen table.

He teased me, "Mmmm-mmm, I saw what *you* had for breakfast, honey. Half of Berkeley wishes they were you right now."

I ignored his innuendoes and sighed, "You saw her? What time did she leave?"

"You must have been out cold, *chica*," said Hermàn, "the whole *street* saw her leave. I think it made the morning headlines. I was just getting in from my run around 6:30 and she was walking out the back door. Details…I want details!"

"Not likely," I grumbled, "or I really *will* be on the morning headlines…"

Hermàn threatened to throw a piece of toast at me, so I ran back upstairs where I almost collided with Anthea coming out of the bathroom wrapped in a brightly colored towel.

"Sorry – are you okay?" I asked, with genuine concern.

Anthea laughed, "Girl, I wouldn't be surprised if you couldn't walk straight for *days* after all the action you had last night. Were you two in training for a marathon in there or *what?*"

Anthea's laughter followed me down the hallway as I stumbled wearily back to my room and I began to wonder if I had made the right decision to share housing after all. Though I was fiercely private by nature, I actually did appreciate my new friends' warmth and humor, and knew that I could count on them for anything, even if they were a little too interested in my sex life this morning. At least now I knew how thin the walls were.

For the next few weeks, I moved through each day in a haze of pheromone-induced distraction, barely concentrating on my

32

research, my schoolwork, or my library job at all. I spent all my free time with Hyla, except for when she was working late at the club in San Francisco or spending long nights in the video lab editing her film project. We went for long, ambling walks through Berkeley, eating whimsical picnics in parks and playgrounds, going to countless art house films together and spending hours in cafés discussing them afterwards with her friends. But several nights a week at least, we went out dancing. We explored every gay club and bar in Berkeley and San Francisco, as long as they had a dance floor. Sometimes we even went to straight dance clubs and raised a few eyebrows. When Hyla danced with me, she was unabashedly erotic in her movements, and our bodies were as well matched as dance partners as we were as lovers. Sometimes my feelings for Hyla went beyond words and sex, so dancing was a powerful form of communication for us too.

Even though we saw so much of each other, unlike other people I had been involved with, Hyla didn't smother me or demand more from me than I was willing to give. In fact, I could barely get enough of her. She was even a little distant at times, as if she had a secret that she never intended to share, and I liked that. Ironically, after having been accused by countless previous lovers as being infuriatingly "detached" and "aloof," I had the uncanny impression that dating Hyla was probably as close to dating myself as I would ever get.

There were times when we would hold each other close through the night, talking softly about our shared dreams. But sometimes she would pull away after only a few minutes and her mysterious veil would fall between us again. It made her endlessly intriguing, and it made me impatient for the times that we did connect closely, which were all the more precious because they were rare.

I had never felt insecure with a lover before, but whenever I would begin to wonder if Hyla shared the intensity of my new, unfamiliar feelings, she would do something wonderful, like pluck a tiny rosebud from a hedge and solemnly place it behind my ear, or hold my face tenderly in her hands and gaze at me in silence for a long suspended moment. I felt complete communion with her, and an unspoken level of understanding that I hadn't known before. Watching her face as a stream of emotions passed over it – desire, longing, fear, grief, gratitude, trust – I knew that her eyes were mirror images of my own.

After a month of immersion in each other's lives, as we were falling asleep one night, Hyla murmured, "So, Herculine, just curious, do you want this to be a monogamous relationship?"

I swallowed with some difficulty, then managed to say, "Um, I'm not sure. I'm actually a little new at this."

"Really?" teased Hyla. "You seem pretty experienced to me..."

"Uh...new to relationships, I mean," I answered carefully, panic rising in my chest. I stammered, "You know, um, I've dated and slept with a lot of people, but I've never actually been in a *relationship* with anyone." Let alone a monogamous one, I thought. I turned to look into Hyla's eyes, hoping that the fear flickering through my heart wouldn't show too clearly, "I really like you though. And there's no one else I'm interested in. Does that mean we're...?"

"In a relationship," Hyla smiled. "Yes, that's exactly what it means. Welcome to life beyond dating. I think you're going to enjoy it. And as for monogamy, personally I think it's over-rated, but if it's what you want, I'm willing. At least for a while." She pulled me close and gave me a kiss. I felt something kneel down inside me then, surrendering to wherever she was going to take me, with only a faint tremor of fear rising inside when I wondered what the journey would entail. I vaguely wondered if there had been more cause for the brevity of my previous affairs than I had been willing to admit. I hadn't even known there was armor around my heart until now, when I felt it crack.

One night in late September when Hyla was out working late, I forced myself to get back to my research on my grandmother's poems. There had been times when the lines from "Electra" had haunted me: *our love was ravenous, we were like lions, hunter and prey, prey and hunter.* I longed to understand more about the poem's cryptic meanings. I curled up in my dad's leather chair with the first book in the tall stack of histories of the French Resistance piled high by my bed. Although of little interest to others (I had been the first library patron to check it out in twenty years), I thought the book promised to be a juicy read indeed. Its title had drawn me in immediately: *Artists in Arms: or, How the Parisian Intelligentsia Won the War.* The author's theory was based on her discovery of several personal journals of Resistance members who had survived the war. She claimed that it was elaborate layers of artistic creativity that had enabled the Resistance (particularly several cells located in the heart

34

of Paris) to elude the watchful eye of the Vichy regime. Through their creative strategies, she claimed, Resistance agents had been able to establish a system of communication that was consistently successful and undetected.

After several hours of reading, just as I was beginning to nod off, a word on the page caught my attention and I jolted awake when I read the following passage:

...there was one operation called "Nemea": a code name used for a plan to assassinate a particularly powerful and deadly member of the Vichy government, Léonin Schiffer. The operation took place at night, when a storm system had been predicted to come through so heavily that it was used to cover up the power outage orchestrated by the underground to facilitate the murder. Schiffer was found strangled to death by a silk stocking laced with tiny shards of razor blades. He had been lightly drugged and the torque on the stocking had not been administered with great force. The consensus in government autopsy files was that the official had been seduced and killed by a woman, probably initially procured for sexual favors. But this Parisian Judith had given the "Léon sans merci" (as he was known) more than he had bargained for, justifiably without mercy, in retribution for all the Jews he had deported to camps and the resistance agents he had personally shot. This coup is considered by historians to be particularly inspired and creative because so few agents were deployed, none were captured, and the attempt was successful.

I realized that my hands were clenching the book. Artist assassins, women with deadly stockings, drugs, coded poems, and a leonine man killed for his war crimes. Could this be a clue to one level of my grandmother's mystery? Was the lion mentioned in "Electra" an allusion to the Nemean lion killed by Hercules? If so, could it also be a coded reference to this man named Léonin Schiffer (nicknamed the "lion without mercy") who had been killed by a resistance agent? Or was this all a coincidence?

And what about the rest of the poem? The taboo of incestuous sister-love, the willing self-sacrifice of the lover, and Electra's desolation after she is left behind... I opened my notebook with my translations in it and read the poem through again, pausing at the end:

The love of sisters,
innocent enough.
But our love was ravenous.

We were like lions,
hunter and prey,
prey and hunter.
When they came to take me to the altar,
You offered yourself instead to save me,
Leaving me here,
mad with grief, without you.

There was still more to this story, and it had to do with another woman. What kind of woman had my grandmother been? Had she loved women too? Was it this knowledge that had made my father angry at the mere mention of her name? I shivered. What on earth would he think of my own lifestyle? I shook my head to clear my mind of these pointless conjectures, and I remembered the books on the Vichy era that I had been combing through in the library for the past few weeks. I realized that I might just know where to find Sophia Danton after all.

The next morning, after a fitful night's sleep and waiting impatiently outside the library for the doors to open at 8 am, I ran past the security guard while flashing my student I.D., pushed through the turnstile, and sprinted up to the third floor where one small shelf held the book I needed: *Sapphic Salons in the City of Light: Dark Ladies of the Parisian Cultural Underground, 1900-1945*. The title had caught my eye during my initial research but since it wasn't explicitly related to the Resistance movement, I had filed it away in my head for future reference. I swiftly grabbed the book off the shelf, threw myself into the nearest comfortable chair and sat there reading until noon.

The book confirmed my suspicion that there were direct connections between the female operatives of the French Resistance and fashionable underground lesbian literati salons. Promiscuous, dramatic, and theatrical, the women in these privileged enclaves combined their passions for politics and the arts with their passions for each other, often with tempestuous results. Careers of budding writers and painters sabotaged by powerful jilted lovers were commonplace, as were laudanum addictions, and erotic triangles. Was it possible that my grandmother had frequented this admittedly incestuous and subterranean world as part of her Resistance activities?

The book also revealed that many of the salons had doubled as cells of Resistance activity and refuges for operatives whose

identities needed protection for more reasons than merely their penchants for social impropriety. One surviving member of a notorious Left Bank salon who was interviewed by the author told the story of a Resistance agent known only as "Eugénie," who was reported as having committed suicide due to political intrigue. She narrated:

Vichy spies occasionally infiltrated the salons, and Eugénie – caught in a web of romantic and political conflicts – took her life rather than endanger the life of her female lover, another Resistance operative. One of their underground colleagues was exposed as having Vichy affiliations and had threatened to kill Eugénie unless she divulged the names and identities of her allies. So she hung herself with one of her silk stockings, which we all thought was especially scandalous because silk was so hard to come by during the war, but she had also embedded tiny shards of razor blades tipped with arsenic in the stocking's seam. This was how we knew it was suicide.

This last comment stopped me in my tracks. The way "Eugenie" had killed herself resembled the method used during operation "Nemea" too closely to be mere coincidence. Had Léonin Schiffer's assassin been none other than "Eugénie," who had ultimately killed herself the same way? Or did all the female Resistance operatives at that time use this deadly signature mode of assassination? If it was "Eugénie," then she may have also been the basis for the figure of Iphigenia in my grandmother's "Electra" poem, sacrificing herself to save her lover, but aso leaving the lover behind to go mad with grief. Could Sophia herself have been Eugénie's lover? Or was her poem merely telling the tale of the dramatic lives of the women around her?

I emerged from the library puzzled, but not discouraged. I might not have completely "solved" the mystery of the first poem, but at least I had begun to sense the layers of meanings that it contained in context of the other twelve to come. I walked outside in the crisp afternoon light and leaned against a tree. I felt the weight of time passing and the multitude of brief, unknown lives of decades and centuries past. They were the force that upheld history and kept the world turning beneath my feet. I wished I could make time stop, slow down, or at least rewind, so that I could lift some of the weight of unknowing. The lives I had been reading about all morning and the night before had belonged to real, complex, passionate individuals and I wished I could have lived among them and known them all. The historians had done a better job of preserving their

memory than those living such secretive, dangerous lives could ever have hoped for, but I knew that I held a piece of their story that had not yet been told. And I was determined to know the rest.

Theo
New York, 1943

In the tiny apartment they shared on the lower east side of
Manhattan, it was impossible for six-year-old Theo not to notice that
something was wrong with his guardian. Usually so dapper and
energetic as he ran their little household and worked evenings down
at the docks loading the boats, Hercule had definitely not been
himself lately. Ever since a telegram had come for him three days
before, Hercule had been drinking more wine than usual, sleeping in
his chair at the kitchen table, neglecting to bathe or provide meals for
the two of them, and weeping whenever he saw Theo.

Young Theo had been wary and resourceful at first; he gave
Hercule a wide berth, and did his best to feed them both. He knew
how to boil eggs and there was cheese in the icebox, but he had to
take pocket money from Hercule's dresser and go alone to the corner
bakery to bring back a loaf of bread. After a few more days, when
there were no eggs left and Hercule was still in his oblivion, Theo
began to get frightened. One day, he climbed up onto Hercule's lap
at the table and put his arms around the older man's neck.

"Please, Hercule," he said. "Please tell me why you are so
sad."

Hercule held the boy so tightly that Theo was frightened at
first, but then Hercule took a deep breath, composed himself, got up
from the table, and walked into the bathroom. Theo followed and sat
on the edge of the tub while he watched Hercule bend over the sink
to splash cold water on his head and shoulders and rub his face
roughly with a towel. As Hercule shook his head, droplets of water
fell on Theo, which made the boy laugh. Hercule turned around to
look at him, and smiled for the first time in days. That was when
Theo knew everything would be all right. Hercule's smile became
sad, and Theo thought that he might even be fighting back tears as he
said,

"You look like your mama, do you know that? Do you
remember her face?"

"Yes, said Theo. "You have that pretty photograph of her in
your drawer and I look at it every day. Someday we will go back to

Paris and I will live with her and papa again, so I have to recognize her when I see her, right?"

Hercule's face grew so sorrowful that Theo was worried that he might have ruined everything. But Hercule mustered himself, knelt down and took both of the boy's hands in his own. He looked Theo in the eyes and said, "Theo, your mother loved you more than her own life. She longed for the day that you would come back and live with her again. But we will not be going back to Paris now. Your mama has died."

At this, Hercule choked and put his head in his hands. Theo sat blinking at him on the edge of the bathtub, and the room seemed to have suddenly chilled. Mama dead?

"And papa?" he asked fearfully, his eyes wide and face pale.

Hercule looked weary and averted his gaze, saying, "Your…your papa is in hiding, Theo. No one knows where he is."

"In hiding?" Theo felt panic rising in his small chest. "Hiding from who?"

"There is a war, *mon petit*, a very bad war, and your papa is on the wrong side. I'm sorry to have to tell you this. Any of this." Hercule grimaced as if he was in physical pain.

Theo gazed at him somberly, his heart racing. Now he understood why Hercule had been so sad these last few days. Hercule loved mama too. And papa was a bad man. Pieces of memories from his early childhood – before his departure from Paris – coursed through his head: tearful fights between his mother and father, usually ending with his mother curling up next to Theo and holding him through the night; the cold silences between his parents that would last for days, and the many times when Theo wouldn't see them at all but was attended to entirely by servants.

He felt tears well up in his eyes, and asked Hercule, "If mama is dead, do we have to stop loving her?"

Hercule looked up at Theo with wide, surprised eyes, and then he gently took the boy in his arms. "No, oh no, no, *mon cher,* we must always love her. You must know this from now on: love never dies, and we will love her for as long as we live."

After that night, Hercule pulled himself together and went back to his job down at the docks, resumed bathing and providing hearty meals for them both. He placed the photograph he had of Sophia on the mantelpiece in the living room instead of in the drawer by his bed. It was their shrine, he said, and as the days went on they

were strengthened by their shared devotion to the memory of the beautiful laughing woman in the frame.

"Hylas was a handsome young prince who accompanied Hercules on his many adventures and battles as his personal arms-bearer, and Hercules protected him fiercely. They were inseparable. When Jason asked Hercules to join the Argonauts in search of the golden fleece, he agreed only if he could bring Hylas along with him as his companion. One day, when the Argos was in port for the night and the crew was setting up camp on shore, Hercules and Hylas went off into the woods together in search of firewood. While Hercules was busy felling entire trees and breaking them up into kindling by hand, dreamy young Hylas wandered off into a clearing where he saw a beautiful pool and leaned over to take a drink. As he did so, a band of lovely naïads rose up from the water (at Hera's spiteful command) and beckoned Hylas into the pool to join them. When he resisted, their invitation turned to coercion as they pulled him into the water where he soon drowned. Some versions of the myth say that he did not die, but merely learned to love them and become one of them…Driven mad with grief over the loss of his beloved, Hercules screamed with anguish and destroyed the entire forest on the island. The Argonauts watched in horror as the brave hero wept for this lover like a broken-hearted schoolgirl. They had to force him back onto the ship when it was time to leave…"

Theodore Danton, *Redefining Heroism: Reclaiming Hercules.*
Columbia University Press; 1968.

The Second Poem: Medusa
Berkeley, September 1989

Late October in Berkeley wasn't like any autumn I had ever known. It was more like Indian Summer. Lazy golden days, the trees still green, not quite cold enough to wear a jacket during the day, and all around me flowers still in bloom. Between my late nights and lazy mornings with Hyla and my long hours of research on the poems, I barely felt like I was in graduate school, and sometimes I didn't quite make it to class, which was strange new behavior for me. But it all seemed fine, like a hazy dream that I moved through without quite recognizing myself, only occasionally remembering that this new life was the beginning of the academic future I had been working towards for years. Then I would apply myself to my studies with renewed commitment. It just never seemed to last very long.

Gazing at Hyla asleep in the late morning light one day during the last week of October, I felt the now familiar ache welling up in my chest as I contemplated the beauty of her face: a confusing combination of protectiveness, possessiveness, anxiety, and deep calm. Was this love? The more I came to know the enigmatic young woman beside me, the more I desired her, the closer I wanted to be to her, and yet there were times when she still seemed unreachable, unattainable, even more private than I am.

I had never met anyone who worked as hard as Hyla: long hours at the café, dancing at the club late into the night, attending film classes during the day, editing her video projects until dawn. When we were together, she often told me about the film theorists whose work she admired and of her visions for her future film projects. She wanted to tell the stories of women's lives on the margins of society: the sex workers, runaways, battered women and drug addicts she knew in San Francisco. I hadn't seen any of her work yet, but I was sure it would be powerful and brilliant. Just by watching the way her wide green eyes narrowed with sharp concentration when she shared her ideas with me, and hearing the shift in her voice from playful affection to a lower, more intense register of urgency when she spoke about her work, I could tell

passionate about her artistic vision. But until she either invited me to a screening or brought over a demo tape to show me, I would have to wait before I knew just how good her work really was.

Before meeting Hyla, the quest for knowledge and the pursuit of desire had been my two dominant, separate, and consistently unfulfilled drives. Now they were simply manageable thirsts that were being deeply quenched almost daily, because they were joined for the first time in my passion for and curiosity about Hyla. The line from *Antony and Cleopatra*, describing Cleopatra as making her consorts "hungry where most she satisfies," was often on my mind these days. Like the legendary Egytpian Queen, Hyla had a way of leaving me hungering and thirsting for her all too soon.

As I was gazing at her, Hyla stirred, stretched like a big cat, yawned, and smiled. She sleepily rolled over and turned her back to me, the small emerald set into her eyebrow ring catching the morning light with a flash. I pulled her close and spooned against her warmth. Hyla stirred again, turning towards me, gave me a quick kiss and raised herself up from the bed.

"It's an early morning for me today…" she stifled a yawn. "I've got a morning shift at the café. But I'll see you tomorrow, okay?"

Disappointed, I watched her pull on her jeans, t-shirt and sweater.

"How come I won't see you tonight?" I asked.

She sighed as she tied the laces of her running shoes, "I'm filling in for another girl at the club. But definitely tomorrow…!" One last kiss, and she was gone.

Feeling dejected, I lay in bed and ruminated. I still hadn't summoned the courage to go over to San Francisco to see Hyla dance. What was I afraid of? An unwelcome stream of images answered me…Hyla dancing, the men in the room ogling her as she danced "exotically" on stage with other women… These thoughts made my stomach tighten and clench with what I could only imagine must be jealousy: another unfamiliar emotion that I would have to learn to deal with. I remembered some of my previous lovers complaining to me of the jealous feelings I had aroused in them, and I'd had little sympathy for them then. But now I understood their torment: jealousy comes from scarcity, not only fear of infidelity. None of my lovers had ever felt like they had had enough of me or that I had been truly theirs, and I hadn't been. But now I pitied them with the empathy of a fellow sufferer.

43

A few hours later, I arrived at the library in a dark mood, and slammed books onto the returns cart with a vengeance. My supervisor, a stern but kind-hearted woman named Joyce who had run the circulation desk for thirty years, looked over at me sharply, and said,

"What did those books ever do to *you*?"

I blushed with shame; books were precious objects to me. What was I thinking? I was so embarrassed I couldn't even meet Joyce's gaze. I mumbled, "Sorry…just having a bad day…" and gently re-stacked the books with great care.

Seeing this, Joyce softened her tone and approached me, saying,

"Is everything okay, Herculine? You're usually so careful with the books…"

I sighed and managed a faint smile, assuring her that I would be fine soon. Then I turned and wheeled the cart into a corridor towards the stacks, relieved to have made a getaway without any further inquiries.

The hours passed slowly in the stacks. Each of the books that I had to re-shelve seemed heavier than usual. My mind wandered throughout the afternoon, and several times I realized that I had been standing with an open book in my hand, staring at pages with unseeing eyes. Finally I rubbed my temples, neck and shoulders and wheeled the cart back to the circulation desk. It was time for a break. I maneuvered past Joyce without incident, grabbed my bag and headed for the sunny atrium to eat a sandwich and think in peace. When I settled down in my favorite chair, I took my notebook out of my bag and turned to my translations of Sophia's poems. The second one, "Medusa," was even more cryptic than the first.

"Medusa" had been puzzling me for several days now. Its story departed too strangely from the original legend that I knew. In Ovid's *Metamorphoses*, Medusa was a beautiful mortal, a priestess of the goddess Athena. Medusa was so beautiful, in fact, that she was lusted after and raped by the ocean-god (and Athena's uncle) Poseidon. The angry goddess punished Medusa for defiling her temple by turning the girl into a hideous monster with snakes for hair, whose gaze turned men to stone with fear. Of course Athena did nothing to chastise Poseidon. This was an early yet classic case of "blaming the victim," but par for the course for Athena, who always seemed to be unfairly punishing mortal women and giving preferential treatment to men. In fact some critics attribute this

44

behavior to her origins – springing fully grown from the head of her father, Zeus. Forever taking the role of the "dutiful daughter," she was no friend to womankind. But in Sophia Danton's poem, this dark story took an unusual turn. I read over the haunting lines…

Once innocent, virginal, pure:
tempting to all, serving only one.
Beauty unmarred, unsurpassed:
My golden hair
A cloak of radiance.
She noticed. As did he:
rising from his watery depths
to sacrifice my virtue on her altar.
In her jealous rage,
she cursed and scarred me,
exiled and monstrous:
I turned fearful men to stone.
But you are not a man,
and you do not fear me.
Your heart is already made of stone.
You can still see my beauty
burning beneath the coils
of writhing serpents
wreathing my temples.
Cut off these curls
And others will grow in their place.
Each strand a hydra,
each tendril a poison arrow
racing towards its mark.
Come with me now, take shelter
behind this warrior's shield.
It was hers, but now it bears my sign.
I stole it for you: so steal away with me now
across the ocean
from these tired battlefields
and dying men with burning wounds.

I had already figured out that my grandmother's version of Medusa transformed her into a figure of power and revenge by fusing the Medusa story with the legend of another monster, the Hydra – which was the nine-headed creature Hercules had to kill in order to

45

fulfill his second labor. It was almost impossible to kill the Hydra however, because as soon as anyone cut off one of its nine heads, two more immediately grew back in its place. The only way to kill the beast, Hercules had discovered, was by cutting off each head and immediately cauterizing the bloody stumps, finally spearing the animal's breast with arrows dipped in its own poisonous blood. If Sophia had found power in this image, I thought, it had to be in her complex inversion and displacement of symbolism. Medusa's badge of shame, her snaky hair, turns into self-regenerating weapons that aim themselves against her enemies. But the cauterized stumps of Hercules' triumph over the Hydra are then transferred over to the war victims with their ""burning wounds." What did it all mean?

Beyond the densely cryptic mythic symbolism, this was also apparently another poem about love between women outside the law, but what did it have to do with the French Resistance? True, I mused, Paris was a literal "battlefield" for the members of the underground, but why did the two women in the poem think they could escape? From my research, I knew that it had been all but impossible to get out of Vichy France during the occupation. The connection with World War II had to be here somewhere. I gathered up my belongings and headed back to the circulation desk. But before my work shift ended, I hunted down a few more books about the Resistance, hoping that one of them might contain a clue to the enigmatic poem's meaning.

On my way to my Archaic Greek Poetry seminar, I felt my shoulders tighten as I hurried up the stairs. The class was held in the same wing of the library, several floors up and I slipped through the door of the classroom just as Professor Seidon was beginning his lecture on Pindar's *Olympian Odes*. He looked at me disapprovingly over the rim of his half moon glasses and said,

"Miss Danton, I had thought that you would at least have had the courtesy to arrive on time today when we are discussing the pivotal role your legendary namesake played in the founding of the Olympic festivals."

I lied as I took my seat, "Sorry Professor, I just couldn't rip myself away from those fascinating alternate translations you assigned for optional reserve reading..."

He nodded favorably in my direction, but I saw several of my classmates silently snickering and rolling their eyes. The optional reserve reading was notoriously dull and we had all stopped trying to read it after the second week of the semester.

The rest of class passed quickly. After hearing sections from all of our translations, Seidon gave us a pop reverse translation quiz and let us out early. Just as I was leaving the room, two of the other students rushed after me in the hallway, saying, "Hey Herculine, wait up!"

When I stopped and turned around to see what they wanted, they surprised me by voicing their appreciation for my cheeky behavior in class. One of students was Linus, the handsome, lanky fellow I had noticed before, and the other was Phoebe, a pretty woman in a leather mini skirt who always sat next to him. As Linus approached me, he witheringly mimicked the tone of our professor, looking over the top of his retro horn-rimmed glasses at me,

"*Excuse me*, Miss Danton," he whined, "You might have had the courtesy to be less witty at my expense today, hmmm?"

When I burst out laughing, Phoebe smiled at me and said, "We think you're really great. This seminar would be the most boring circle of hell if you weren't there to spice things up!"

Linus switched into his normal voice to concur, "Yeah, but I can't believe how rude Seidon was to you today! What did you ever do to get on his dark side, anyway?"

Phoebe poked Linus in the ribs and said, "It's just her name, stupid. He's jealous. Anyone knows that. He clearly has classical name envy."

Linus rolled his eyes and said, "Well, you would know, Apollonia, you share Herculine's pain…"

I looked questioningly at Phoebe – had I mistaken her name for someone else's in class?

But Phoebe just groaned, hoisted her book bag onto her shoulder impatiently, and said "Yeah, it's true: Apollonia's my middle name…my parents were big beatniks: into Nietzsche and Sartre and black turtlenecks. My brother's got it worse: his name is Dionysius. But he goes by Dion. He's down at UCLA, finishing his MFA in Drama." Then her face broke into a mischievous smile.

She said, "Hey, Herculine, do you want to meet us tonight at the Bistro for Linus's show?"

Linus looked startled and his eyes darted quickly from Phoebe to me and back again, then, trying to sound nonchalant but clearly quite pleased, he said, "Yeah, that'd be great…come on down, I start at ten."

"What kind of show?" I asked.

"Oh, you know," he said casually. "It's kind of a spoken word, acoustic/electric somatic intervention…"

Genuinely puzzled, I asked, "Do you mean, um, performance art?"

He looked at me as if I'd just stepped out of a backwoods swamp and replied coolly, "Is that what they're still calling it in New York?"

I laughed, "How did you know I'm from New York?"

They exchanged glances, then Phoebe said, "We know Hermàn and Anthea, of course. They told us all about you. Hey, if you want to bring them along tonight, we need as many warm bodies there as possible!"

Linus looked askance, paused for a minute, and then said "Oh sure…" with an offhand shrug.

Phoebe playfully swatted Linus on his backside as they turned to leave the library and said with a grin, "See you later!"

They were an interesting pair. And there had definitely been some flirtation in Phoebe's invitation. Suddenly I wished that Hyla could go with me to the show too. My thoughts longed to slide back to her, but I pushed them away and concentrated on finding a few more books in the library instead. I wanted to hurry home so that I could get some work done before my new social obligation tore me away from the night of research I had been looking forward to all day. However, a half hour later when I walked into the house, I saw that Hermàn and Anthea had already started their weekend partying at the kitchen table with several friends, a pitcher of homemade sangria and two large bowls of guacamole and chips.

At first I tried to sneak past the kitchen, in the hopes of heading upstairs to my room unnoticed. But then I paused, veered back, and said, "Hey there…Any chance you'd like to go with me to the Bistro later tonight to see that guy Linus do his 'somatic intervention' act?"

Hermàn rolled his eyes, and there was a murmur among their friends, but Anthea responded in a teasing tone, "Sure, we'd *love* to go. Did you know that Linus and Hermàn used to be an item?"

Somehow I wasn't surprised; it explained Linus' reaction earlier and it made him even more intriguing to me.

Hermàn snorted, but Anthea kicked him under the table and said, "We'll be ready to go at nine. Now come on in and join the party!"

48

"Oh, er, well…" I stammered, edging back towards the stairs. "The show, um, doesn't start until ten, so until about nine thirty I was thinking that maybe I'd…"

Hermàn and Anthea loudly finished my sentence for me in unison: "*Get some work done??*" The whole table of grad students laughed, and Hermàn said, "Yeah, we could've guessed…"

"Ha-ha, great; very funny," I grumbled as I climbed the stairs. In mock indignation I yelled over my shoulder, "Sometimes I wonder how much *more* work I'd get done if I lived *alone!*" More ripples of friendly laughter flowed behind me. But I felt pleased that my friends would be joining me later. The whole Berkeley grad student social scene was still a bit daunting to me, and having Hermàn and Anthea by my side was a comforting thought.

Upstairs in my room, I settled into my dad's deep leather reading chair and unpacked my book bag. For the past three weeks, I had been wading through hundreds of pages of historical data from World War II, sociological analyses of the power dynamics in Resistance cells, treatises on the *natalité* movement concocted by Vichy social visionaries that sought to return women to childbearing domestic servants, and biographies of leading figures in the Vichy government. I had filled two legal pads with notes, and finally this evening, with visible relief, I turned to the last book in my stack for the week. I had saved the book with the most promising title as my reward for days of diligent effort: *Double Agents in the Dark: Resistance, Reconnaissance, and Revenge*—a study of the members of the Resistance who had played dual roles during the war.

Vichy France had been a dangerous time for everyone, I knew, but it's never safe to be a double agent, especially if you're a woman. I scanned the book for stories of female spies who risked their lives to help the cause of the Resistance. There were accounts of several women who had posed as collaborators with the Germans in order to gain valuable inside information. When they were discovered, they were tortured and raped, then shot. But there was one woman who had apparently made it out alive. Her name was Madelcine Sousa, and her detailed account of her life had survived the war. Madeleine lived into her seventies, long enough to tell her story to scholars at the Sorbonne, who had transcribed her memoirs in the university's archive of Resistance documentation. She narrated:

For several months during the summer of 1940, I was working undercover in the house of a Vichy general as a nanny for his children, gathering information for the Resistance. Ironically, the Vichy government placed me in that job as a cover for the spying I was supposedly doing for them. But instead of infiltrating Resistance cells and assisting Vichy raids, the few bogus leads I had given the Germans had led to carefully orchestrated fiascos, resulting more often than not in fatal ambushes of the Vichy forces. Neither the general nor his German wife was aware of my covert ties to either camp. In fact, they treated me quite badly as their employee. The wife was always giving me menial tasks outside my duties as a governess and the general made aggressive sexual advances to me whenever his wife was not in the room. I fought him off as well as I could, but one night his wife heard my muffled screams and discovered her husband attempting to rape me in the pantry. After he denied everything and claimed that I had thrown myself at him, she called the Vichy police, threw me out into the street, denounced me as a collabo and fired me, disgracing me publicly. The penalty for a French woman having sex with a German man (known as "collaboration horizontale") was to have her head shaved and to be paraded through the streets, mocked by onlookers and often pelted with rotten fruit. I endured all of these humiliations too, accepting the ostracism of my neighbors willingly, since it was actually an excellent cover for my real activities as an undercover Resistance spy.

A close friend of mine from the underground briefly replaced me as a nanny in the general's household and one night not only managed to fatally poison the general but also to steal enough money and jewels from his wife in order to sell them for a fake passport for me to leave France. Once I was safely out of the country, I was able to accomplish even more for the Resistance: raising money and collecting supplies, gathering information, training others as spies and sending them back to France to help the struggling underground movement.

While I was reading this narrative, I could barely breathe. Madeleine Sousa's narrative was the story of my grandmother's "Medusa" transposed to the modern horrors of world war politics. True to the poem's paradoxical transference of images, once the enemy blamed the victim and shaved off the heroine's hair, she escaped under the cover of a friend's stolen shield (the passport), and more spies sprung from the one who had allegedly been cut down, just like the hydra. Each form of help she sent back to aid the Resistance (money, information, supplies, more agents) were like the poem's proverbial poisoned arrows, dipped in the monster's own blood: the best and only way to kill it. It felt like a fit, but I couldn't be sure...

Trembling, I set the book aside and began to write feverishly in my notebook. The reality of these women's lives, as told by Sousa, raised to mythic proportions in my grandmother's poem, filled me with wonder and despair. The courage they had, the endurance and ingenuity, and their commitment to serving a cause greater than themselves. What were they fighting so hard to protect? The enlightenment values that still fueled the abiding sense of French identity? Liberty, equality, and brotherhood. The battle cry of the French Revolution: *Liberté, egalité, fraternité.* I wondered if I could have done the same in their place. What would I fight for, risk my life for, and not only once, but daily, for years? Nothing in my brief, relatively protected life experience could provide me with an answer. I questioned whether it was possible to know what one might risk one's life to protect until it was actually threatened. Before the German invasion, the women in Paris whose lives I was uncovering were most likely carefree and unconcerned with defending their right to freedom, equality, and – in their case – sisterhood. What Madeleine's friend had done for her was the act of a true sister. But several questions remained: who was the close friend who had covered for Madeleine, and how had Sophia Danton known about it – had she played a role too?

I uncurled my stiff body from my dad's chair and stretched slowly, then shook my arms and legs to get out all the tension from my limbs. I paced around my room restlessly, and opened the window, hoping that a blast of cold night air would clear my head. I leaned against the wide windowsill, breathing deeply, the sweat finally drying from my palms. My mind was still in Paris, in the deep winter darkness of a blacked-out city in wartime. I imagined myself wrapped in a thin wool coat over a thinner wool dress and cotton stockings – no slacks for women then – huddled into my own body for warmth as I hurried down the street, hoping to go unseen as I ducked into a doorway where muffled voices and anxious hands exchanged stolen jewelry for forged passports.

I put my head in my hands, rubbing my temples to erase this unwanted vision, but it wouldn't go away. So I shut the window and walked down the hallway to the bathroom, my entire body now craving warmth after the chilling scene I had just imagined. I ran the water in the tub until it was steaming and then took a long, hot bath. As I ran my hands over my body, kneading my sore muscles, I thought of Hyla's hands earlier that day, and I felt my neck and

51

shoulders relax for the first time in hours. I smiled; but then I remembered that tonight Hyla would be at the club, not with me.

With that thought, I lost interest in the bath, and glumly stepped out of the tub, toweled myself dry, and raked my fingers through my curls. Well, I thought, just because I'm not with Hyla doesn't mean I can't have a good time. I rarely looked into the mirror, but I caught my reflection through the drying steam, and it pleased me, objectively and aesthetically. The sharp lines of my nose, chin, and cheekbones inherited from my father contrasted with the soft curve of my lips and eyes from my mother, all of which was framed by the critical arch of my eyebrows and the rebellious disarray of my hair. I raised my head defiantly and decided to dress for the evening's adventure in the snug black jeans that Hyla had given me, a skimpy green tank top, and my "better" pair of black leather boots. Overall, a considerably more stylish ensemble than my usual rumpled fare, and I was pleased with my rakish reflection in the mirror. On my way into the kitchen to get Hermàn and Anthea, I grabbed my leather coat from the banister for a finishing touch.

"Ready?" I called.

"Oh yeah, we're *ready*," drawled Anthea, as she appeared in the kitchen doorway, resplendent in dark red satin bellbottoms and a long blue velvet coat trimmed with fake blue fur, her short dreadlocks sprinkled with iridescent sparkles. Hermàn stood beside her wearing what I had come to know as his "club" outfit: leather chaps over strategically ripped and faded jeans, a black mesh muscle shirt and a tuxedo jacket, "For a little Cole Porter effect," he told me.

"Damn," I said, and I let out a low wolf whistle. "Look at the two of *you*!"

Anthea swept past me and said, over her shoulder, "You never know *where* we're gonna end up tonight, girl. *Any*thing can happen in Berkeley!" They laughed, and stepped out into the night, where the fresh cold air made me feel, indeed, that anything could happen.

There was a standing-room-only crowd at the Bistro, but since Phoebe was Linus's one-woman road crew, she had arrived early and saved seats at a table in front for us. We just had time to order a bottle of wine and pour four glasses before the lights suddenly went out, leaving the Bistro illuminated only by the small flickering candles on the tables. Just as suddenly, a single forty-watt bulb hanging from the ceiling at the front of the room came to life. In the small pool of light was Linus, eyes closed, dressed entirely in

52

black, and sitting on a metal stool as if he were in an interrogation chamber.

As my eyes adjusted to the light, I could see that he was holding a black electric guitar and that it was connected to a series of amplifiers and effects boxes on the floor. On a small metal table next to him was a computer connected to several small projectors pointed in different directions. He turned towards the computer, pressed a key, and looked at the audience for the first time, as waves of color and light surged through the room. Then Linus began playing his guitar. Slow, rhythmic, repeating chord patterns made spirals and webs of sound around my head. The tonality was haunting, almost Middle Eastern, yet familiar, and filled with angst and longing. The projectors were simultaneously pouring mandalas of swirling color over the walls, the ceiling, and the audience. And then Linus began to murmur over the music into the delicate microphone headset he wore, slurring his words provocatively, creating yet another layer of sonic texture, with only the occasional isolated recognizable word, which I realized after a few minutes were entirely in Greek. I figured out that Linus was reciting, by memory, smooth streams of the fragments of Sappho's poetry. I regarded my intriguing classmate with new respect.

Still murmuring hypnotically, Linus reached his foot over to one of the effects boxes on the floor with his foot and pressed it. He then placed his guitar on a stand behind him and miraculously, or so it seemed to me, the music continued to play. I looked at Phoebe questioningly.

"Everything he's been playing is now on a recorded loop," she whispered.

I whispered back to Phoebe with no small amount of disbelief, "He's amazing!"
Phoebe smiled with pride, and whispered back, "I wouldn't have stuck around if he wasn't!"

Light dawned on me and I said, "Oh, so you two are...?"

Phoebe just nodded and motioned with her head for me to look back at the stage. Linus was taking off his shirt and beginning to dance.

"Oh Lord," said Hermàn, with the jaded detachment of someone who had seen Linus perform many times, "Here we go..."

Linus hit another effects box with his foot and the music sped up. He pressed a key on the computer and the colors began to move faster too. Linus was dancing like no one I had ever seen

53

before: wild yet contained, graceful yet raw, his pale skin contrasting sharply against his black pants and hair. Now murmuring the names of Sappho's lovers into the microphone ("Dica... Atthis... Cypris... Cytherea..."), Linus appeared to have reached a trance state, but he was lucid enough to hit one last effects box on the floor. The music was joined by a pulsing beat, and people standing at the back and along the sides of the club began to dance too. The windows of the Bistro steamed up and people started pushing their tables against the walls. Soon everyone was dancing and a few had even taken off their shirts.

Suddenly I realized that Linus, *sans* headset, was dancing right in front of me. I turned and saw Phoebe move in behind me. I felt Phoebe's hands on my hips as Linus held my waist and the three of us gyrated together to the beat. I hadn't been in a situation like this since the summer with Ben and Lucy, and it felt good. Too good. Phoebe was kissing the back of my neck while Linus was tugging my tank top off my left shoulder. All I wanted was to lean back and surrender to this skillful couple's maneuvers, but the thought of Hyla held me back.

"Um, I have a girlfriend...?" I said to the air, my head resting on Phoebe's shoulder behind me, eyes closed and breath ragged, hoping they would hear.

"Cool," mumbled Linus, his lips against my ear, "Where is she?"

"Yeah," said Phoebe, slipping her hands into the waistband of my jeans, "Would she like to join us?"

An inspiration swiftly hit me: I stood up straight, swung around to face them both and said, raising one eyebrow with a hint of a dare in my voice: "Would you like to meet her?" When they smiled, I said, "Then come with me..."

Linus hurriedly arranged with the owner of the Bistro for his gear to be carefully stowed and locked up in the back room for him to pick up the next day. With his music still pounding and swirling behind us, Linus, Phoebe and I left the raging party as Hermàn, Anthea, and the rest of the crowd danced feverishly on. We piled into Linus's battered Volvo station wagon, and went speeding over the Bay Bridge to San Francisco, with the windows rolled down, laughing into the night.

Twenty minutes later, we pulled up to a sleek glass building in the downtown business district. There was no sign over the

54

entrance, just a street number carved into the granite face of the building, but Linus said, "Yeah, this is it: the Palladium Club." "How can you tell?" I asked.

He avoided my gaze and just murmured something about the place being "legendary."

Perplexed, I tumbled out of his car and onto the sidewalk as a valet stepped out of the doorway, took Linus's car keys and drove away. I certainly hadn't expected anything quite this upscale and looked around in wonder. In a way, I was relieved that it wasn't a seedier place, and I was right behind Phoebe as she pushed against the glass door that opened onto a long, mirrored, yet dimly lit hallway. A small flight of carpeted stairs led to another entranceway, above which the words "Palladium Club" were inscribed in a large rectangular plaque of brushed stainless steel. As we approached this next doorway, the sounds of dance music could be heard, but before we could open the door, it opened for us, and a large dark-skinned man in a wine-colored suit blocked our way.

In a deep, resonant voice, he said, "Good evening…Are you members?"
I stepped forward and said, "No, but we're friends of one of the dancers."

Unimpressed, he said, "Really." After scrutinizing us for a moment, he asked, "Which one?"

"Hyla," I said.

"Hmmph," he snorted, "What can I do for you?"

"Well," I replied, "We came to see her dance…"

"*Well*," he mimicked me, "Admission is $150 each. If you're over 21."

I gasped and stepped back to where my friends were standing. "Hyla never told me it was that expensive!" I whispered to them.

Phoebe pushed me gently to the side, handed Linus her jacket, pulled off her black tank top to reveal a red satin bustier beneath it, and walked purposefully up to the bouncer with a tantalizing smile.

"We're all over 21, mister," she cooed, "but we don't have that kind of money… Couldn't you just let us in to see our friend dance and then we promise to leave?"

The man appraised Phoebe's curves, and said, "I'd like to see *you* dance sometime, baby…" Then he turned back to me and Linus, frowning, but his eyes twinkled, and he said, "All right, all right,

55

twenty bucks each; but you stand at the back of the room and leave when she's done." Our faces lit up even though he glowered at us, "And if you don't, I'll come and *make* you leave."

We rummaged through our pockets and collectively managed to scrape together our revised admission fee. The man in the suit then checked our I.D.s and led us through the plushly carpeted club, weaving through tables where scantily clad dancers and cocktail waitresses worked the floor. He deposited us in a corner at the back of the room, facing a distant stage where two female dancers in matching sequined g-strings were grinding against each other to loud electronic music.

"You all got lucky tonight," he said, gazing back at Phoebe admiringly before he left us there. "Now be good!"

We looked at each other with disbelief, and Phoebe finally broke the silence, laughing and saying to me, "Honey, I don't know who this chick Hyla is, but man – I can't wait to see her dance: it better be worth all our trouble!"

I assured her with a smile. Knowing Hyla, it would be more than any of us had bargained for.

Curious, I scanned the room: the other patrons were all male, most of them wearing elegant business suits, some dressed more casually but with equal sophistication. On the other hand, the female staff members were dressed like exotic, colorful gems that glittered against the cool grey décor and the muted hues of the clientele. Were they dancers too? I felt like I couldn't be sure of anything here. I had never seen anything like this before and was having a hard time reconciling this world with the woman I had been holding in my arms earlier that day.

I was feeling impatient to see Hyla dance, but the first set of dancers seemed to go on forever. After ten or fifteen minutes their gyrations started to seem monotonous to me, but apparently not to Linus and Phoebe, who were discretely imitating the women's movements behind me as they stood against the back wall of the club. Soon Linus slipped his hands around my hips and pulled me up against him and Phoebe began nuzzling my shoulder; I felt my body flush with arousal. I might have surrendered to their attentions, but the dancers finally left the stage, the lights went down and the music changed abruptly. For a moment the stage was dark and the club was silent. A single spot light came on, a complex rhythm began to play, a faintly eastern melody soon joined in, then layers of hypnotic electronic sound slowly began to build over synthesized guitar

patterns that were strangely familiar. Both Phoebe and I turned to look inquiringly at Linus.

Phoebe said, "Hey! Isn't this *your* music?"

Linus looked confused and said, "Weird, yeah: it definitely is my stuff. I guess somebody here got a hold of one of my tapes when I was selling them after a show or something..."

Our attention was soon drawn back to the stage where Hyla had entered, body gleaming with a luminous sheen of silvery oil, wearing only a slender emerald sequin studded g-string and – to my surprise – a long, flowing, platinum blonde wig interwoven with delicate strands of silver and metallic green. A silver pole descended from the ceiling above the stage and four tall, mirrored panels swiveled out to face the room and reflect her image from behind. Linus's music continued to weave its magic on the audience as Hyla began to dance, sinuously and seductively, luring every onlooker into her spell. I looked around and saw that conversation had stopped at the other tables in the club. Hyla was mesmerizing everyone in the room.

She was dancing against and around the pole as if she were in an ancient yet futuristic pagan phallic-worship ritual. The mirrors caught every angle of her lean curves and turned her into an abstract work of art, refracted four-fold. I looked around again; my friends and the men in the club were motionless and speechless, turned to stone, just as if they had seen Medusa herself. I had mentioned the poem I was currently working on to Hyla a few weeks ago, but it hadn't seemed to make much of an impression on her. Watching her now, I knew that she had been listening more closely than I realized. She was the embodiment of Medusa. At least, an extremely erotic fantasy version of her.

As the music changed tempo, Hyla looked down into the audience, smiled, licked her lips slowly, and moved towards the edge of the stage. She knelt and vaulted down onto the floor, approached a table where four men sat, staring at her in wonder. She chose a man with elegant silver hair and gracefully straddled his legs with her own. She proceeded to give the man the most "exotic" lap dance that I had ever seen. Everyone in the club watched with open mouths and wide eyes as Hyla pulled the man up from his chair and rubbed her silver-slicked body up and down against his black suit until he was covered in silver too, and trembling. Then she abruptly pushed him, gasping, back into his chair and she swung herself onto the stage to finish her act, which culminated in the mirrors closing in around her as she

57

climbed up the pole and tore off her g-string, flinging it with expert aim into the lap of the man she had danced for. And then the room went dark and a surge of applause exploded in the room.

"So that's your girlfriend?" Linus asked appreciatively.

"Hot stuff," said Phoebe. "Does she treat you that good at home too?"

Amazed by what I had just seen, I couldn't speak. So *this* is what my girlfriend did for a living? Linus and Phoebe could see that I was shaken up and they suggested that we go back to the party in Berkeley and resume where we had left off. I nodded numbly, but as we began to edge our way towards the door, Hyla emerged from back stage in a skimpy black dress, without the wig. Her tawny blonde hair – usually so thick and spiky – was slicked back so that her head gleamed as if it were bare. Startled, we all stood frozen in our steps. Hyla looked like a *collabo*: head shaved of her Medusa-like tresses, defiantly denuded.

"What's wrong?" Phoebe asked, seeing the alarmed look on my face. I looked away from Hyla, who hadn't seen us, and raked my hands through my own hair, shaking my head to chase away the image of Hyla humiliated in the streets of wartime Paris.

I managed to murmur, "Nothing, nothing…I, I just thought that she was dancing on weekends to earn money for grad school. I never thought it was like this…"

As I spoke, I turned and saw Linus staring in amazement at Hyla. "Um, I, um," he stammered. "You know, I think I know how they – I mean, she—got my music. I think we, uh… 'met' a year or two ago." He turned to me with an apologetic look on his face and said, "I didn't know that you meant *this* Hyla. I didn't recognize her with the wig onstage…I didn't even know her name *was* Hyla!"

Phoebe laughed, and whispered in my ear: "They must have had a one night stand after one of his shows last year. He probably gave her one of his tapes too…"

"Oh, okay, it's cool…" I stammered, mind reeling. Linus and Hyla? Everything suddenly felt very confusing. I needed to sit down and clear my head, but as I started to lower myself into a chair, I saw the bouncer eyeing us suspiciously and stopped. I put my leather jacket back on instead and said, "I'm ready to get out of here anyway…"

As the words left my lips, I saw Hyla walk over to the bar where the manager introduced her to the silver haired man she had danced for, who I could see now looked faintly European. I watched,

58

dumbstruck, as Hyla led him behind a curtain into a back room with a smile on her face that looked like a cold, brittle mask.

I lunged forward. Where was she going? What went on in that back room? I knew I had to stop her. It was so wrong, so different from what I had expected when I imagined my lover's "night job" that every fiber in my being revolted against the thought of Hyla dancing privately, seductively, intimately, and perhaps even doing more than dancing, with multiple male clients several nights a week for the past two months we had been together. Why had she never told me what she really did at the club? As I rushed to prevent Hyla from going into the back room, my friends grabbed me over my protestations, and restrained me. The bouncer was now moving towards us menacingly.

"Come on," said Linus. "We're taking you home."

"Wait—no—I have to stop her!" I insisted through clenched teeth.

Pheobe held me back, as I struggled to free myself, and said, a little impatiently, "Look, you don't think she earns enough money to get through Berkeley just by dancing and working at that café, do you?" She looked around the room and I followed her gaze. Men throughout the club were staring at Hyla as she walked away.

Phoebe continued, "Honey, listen: after they finish dancing, it's time to go earn the real money. I know another girl who's a dancer and she told me that a private lap dance costs fifty bucks or more for each song. After your girlfriend's act tonight and that sexy little scene with that guy, I bet some of these men will spring for at least six songs. So, that's her reality. Deal with it. Or not." She paused and looked at Linus, who nodded encouragingly. "You know, you could take *us* home with you tonight instead…"

When I awoke the next morning tangled in a disarray of blankets, pillows, and clothing, wedged snugly between Linus and Phoebe's warm naked limbs, I only dimly remembered the drive back to Berkeley, my friends' efforts to cheer me with wine, music, and dancing in the kitchen, and then the giggling striptease up the stairway. The rest I remembered perfectly. Linus and Phoebe had reminded me of the joys of pure, disinterested lust. This morning I wasn't thinking about love. I was hurt and angry, but enjoying how good it felt to be free.

59

Clea
New York, December 1989

The morning light slanted through the vaulted windows filling the dance studio with early winter warmth as Clea unlocked the door and walked in. As she entered the studio she deeply breathed in the air, which still held traces of cigarette smoke, perfume, and sweat from the previous night's rehearsal. She set her leather coat and dance gear bag on the floor near the musical instruments in the corner then kicked off her leather boots. Their high heels struck the wall with a satisfying percussive echo. Her musicians would be back later to rehearse before this evening's show, but not for hours...not until after dark. She had all the time in the world.

Clea walked over to the thermostat at the opposite end of the studio and as she moved, she watched herself in the long row of mirrors flanking the walls below the windows. She liked what she saw. She usually did. Her long legs encased in snug faded jeans moved with supple strength, their allure accentuated by the slight sway of her slender hips. As she walked, she loosened her long auburn hair from its French knot and enjoyed watching it fall around her shoulders. Now in her mid-forties, her beauty had barely altered—if anything, it had simply matured – and she knew that if she wanted to, she could still play ingénues.

Clea was wearing the green hand-woven shawl that Herculine had sent her from a women's craft collective in Berkeley for her birthday the previous week. She stroked the shawl absently, thinking of her daughter and wishing she would call more often. She missed Herculine with a sharp ache at certain times of day, like now. They had shared over twenty years of bustling, affectionate mornings before going off to their separate worlds. Clea to her rehearsals and classes; Herculine to school. Now she was three thousand miles away in California, and mornings were too quiet without her. The years had gone by too fast, but for a single mother and only child, the loss was particularly sharp.

New York had been their city: its topography saturated with memories and meaning for them both. Clea had only lived in the city

a few years before Herculine was born, so they had explored and claimed its riches together. Images coursed through Clea's head as she leaned up against the wall in a pool of sunlight.

She remembered the day she had been "discovered" at eighteen by a photographer at an automat during her lunch break downtown with the other receptionists. He had asked her if she would pose for him, and gave her his card. He offered her more money for a two-hour photo session than she usually made in a week, and promised that she could keep her clothes on. He kept his word, and didn't even try to seduce her until after he'd helped her land her first modeling job, which led to acting classes at night and then her first semi-professional acting role, as Hermia in some NYU graduate student's production of *A Midsummer Night's Dream*. Her reviews had been strong, so she applied for her equity card, got an agent, and soon had her pick of off-Broadway romantic leads for the next ten years. But after a few decades on the circuit, she had wearied of the frenzied pace of auditions, rehearsals, and performances, so it was with some relief that she left the theater world behind her when she became pregnant with Herculine. She lived such a simple, bohemian existence that after Herculine was born Theo supported them both comfortably until she was ready to work again and Herculine was old enough to go to school. By this time, dance and performance art were the avenues of self-expression she had craved.

At night she had her art world, but by day, her life had been focused around her daughter. She could still see little Herculine as a small girl climbing on the Hans Christian Anderson and Alice in Wonderland statues in Central Park, or eating roasted chestnuts from a pushcart vendor out of a small paper bag in mittened hands in Washington Square. When Herculine was in elementary school, Clea would take her to the Museum of Natural History on rainy days to see their old friends the big blue whale and the dinosaurs, afterwards snuggling up together in the dark while they took in a galaxy show at the Planetarium. They'd had springtime bike rides through the cherry-blossom laden hills of Central Park, where only a few months before they had been sledding in the snow. When Herculine was a teenager, Clea balanced her studious daughter's countless weekends in the Public Library with a steady stream of off-Broadway shows and dance performances in the evenings—usually featuring at least one of Clea's friends. Yes, she had done her best, and Herculine seemed to have survived just fine.

61

Or had she? She was such a secretive kid sometimes. Always off in a corner with some book, never volunteering information, and responding so somberly when asked a question. Her daughter seemed uncannily centered and stable compared to all Clea's dramatic friends, but she did get noticeably moody whenever Clea brought home a new lover for her to meet. She was never rude or critical, just sulky and evasive: behavior that was perfectly normal, Clea was certain, for an only child who had her mother's undivided attention most of the time. But after a perfunctory handshake with the new man and a cool nod to her mother, Herculine would disappear to her room and the refuge of her headphones and books. As if in retribution for Clea's blithe promiscuity, Herculine had never brought home anyone "significant." There had been several "best friends" in childhood, but adolescence seemed to turn Herculine even further inwards. During her high school years, Clea was certain that her daughter was having sexual experiences – and then throughout her four years at Columbia there were many nights when she did not come home until dawn. She'd walk in quietly, go to her mother's bedroom and give her a kiss on the cheek and then close her own door and sleep until noon. She divulged nothing, and Clea did not pry. She had raised Herculine to be an independent spirit and she both respected her daughter's privacy and trusted her judgment. But she was curious.

One night, during Herculine's college years at Columbia, Clea had gone out dancing with some of her cast and crew at a gay club down in SoHo after a show. After getting a glass of wine at the bar, she leaned against a wall and surveyed the room, enjoying all the beautiful boys and tough women going through the motions of their own dances, mating rituals, and dramas. At one point, as she looked across the room, she had to shake her head, blink, and look again in disbelief: there, sitting in a dimly lit lounge area flanked by an androgynously handsome young man with long blonde hair and an equally striking dark-haired young woman in a red mini-dress, was Herculine, distinguished by her disheveled mop of auburn curls and tattered blue jeans. Clea peered closer and saw that her daughter had entwined her lithe frame with the bodies of both of her companions and was languidly soul-kissing each of them in turn. Clea, heart pounding with a range of conflicted feelings – shock, relief, and fascination – retreated to the shadows at the other end of the club and was soon thrilled when she saw her daughter rise and walk to the dance floor with her friends.

Clea had watched as Herculine began to move with a dancer's grace, engaging her partners in a sensuously mesmerizing *pas de trois* that pulsated to the electronic trance beat of the dance floor music. Waves of memories passed through Clea's mind: baby Herculine in her arms as she and Theo danced slowly by candlelight in their tiny loft…Herculine as a toddler, then as a little girl, laughing and dancing with her and Theo, holding onto their legs, dancing with, between, and around them. It had been well over a decade since they had all danced together, but it seemed as if Herculine had successfully transferred her two deepest primary attachments to more age-appropriate objects of desire. Wistfully, Clea thought of her own erotic adventures when she was Herculine's age and was glad to see that her daughter was embracing a passionate existence all her own. As she recovered some of her poise, Clea realized that other patrons of the club were watching the young threesome too. Ever the artistic opportunist, she waved over two of her newest dancer friends and without revealing her daughter's identity, urged them to watch the trio dance so that in their rehearsal session the following day they could incorporate some of the trio's moves into the new piece they were currently working on.

Clea had never told Herculine about that night, but it had subtly shifted the parameters of their relationship. Afterwards, it seemed that when she looked at Herculine, Clea saw a little more of herself in her daughter, and that was comforting somehow. Herculine had always been such a bookish girl, and it had been years since she had talked to her mother about the ideas that were filling her head. All too often she had wished that Theo was still alive so that he could meet Herculine in her intellectual realm and share his own passion for knowledge with her.

"Ah, Theo…" she sighed aloud. Clea, lost in her reverie, now sitting cross-legged on the floor with her back resting against the wall, waiting for the studio to heat up a little more before she changed into her gear, allowed herself the luxury of missing him. Even though he had not been her only lover while he was alive, he was the only man who had been an intimate partner in her life. She remembered the night he had shown up at her dressing room door as a shy admirer with white roses and his most recent book—*Sophocles and his Tragic Muse*—under his arm. She was only twenty-three when they met, and she had been playing Isabella in Shakespeare's *Measure for Measure*. When she had looked at him that night, she had seen a distinguished, handsome, slightly younger version of her own father,

63

which made his presence feel safe and familiar, and she let him into her dressing room. Within a few weeks, she had let him into her life.

It was a loving and discreet affair, filled for her with a sense of security and devotion without obligation that suited both her need for a man's love, as well as her more progressive sensibilities. Without yet having the vocabulary or political consciousness to accompany it, Clea knew that she was already possessed of a nascent feminism at that time. She may have experienced it only as a fierce desire for independence, but it set her apart from other young women her age. And yet, one night only two years into her relationship with Theo, when Clea's diaphragm tore and she had become unexpectedly pregnant, she embraced the idea of raising a child. When Herculine was born, Clea was determined that her daughter would grow up free: free from convention, from dependence on men and their institutions, and from the constraints of femininity that Clea felt had too narrowly shaped her own life.

When feminism had finally found her in the late 1970's, Clea rode the wave high. She formed a women's political theater collective and branched out into modern dance and contact improvisation. She took courses at NYU and held consciousness raising groups and political action committees in her home while little Herculine looked on. Theo had encouraged her in all of these ventures, sensing correctly that the self-knowledge Clea was gaining would bring the two of them closer. Her mind was filled with ideas, where before there had only been memorized lines. She shared what she learned with him, tested her budding critical ability on him, and in him found a truer ally and supporter than any other lover she had during those years of "free love" and experimentation.

Theo had stood by Clea throughout all the turbulent changes in her life during those ten years, supporting her and Herculine comfortably when she couldn't make ends meet, while giving her the space she needed to feel the freedom she continually craved. She had never asked him to leave his wife, and he had never offered. There were times when their arrangement had enraged her, but a combination of pride and fierce attachment to her freedom had helped her through and convinced her that she had the best of both worlds. He had been a loving father to Herculine, and – she had to admit – he was the only man she had ever truly loved.

Clea drew a fine distinction between loving someone and being "in love." For her, being "in love" was the heady, obsessive, lust-filled passion of an exciting romance that usually lasted a few

64

months at most – as had most of her affairs. But with Theo, their early passion and desire had given way to a deep kinship and trusting intimacy that had moved beyond the body and heart to a place that she could only identify as her soul, even though she didn't believe in such things. They had enjoyed that most rare and precious of human relationships: lovers who were also friends, both of them implicitly knowing that without ever owning each other or feeling in any way trapped by their connection, that they were committed to each other by choice for life. *Right*, she thought; *until one of them died.*

"Damn you, Theo," Clea said aloud in the large empty room, as she angrily got up from the floor and began stomping around, generating her own body heat. It was time to warm up for real. Ramon would be here any minute.

Clea flushed a little as she thought of Ramon and began to change out of her street clothes. What would Theo have thought of him? He would have smiled knowingly when he saw them dance together and kept his distance for a month or so until the flames started to die down, and then he'd have been back – just in time for Clea to complain to him about the younger man's limitations, his callowness, his ignorance. It happened every time. And every time she was so grateful to Theo for taking her into his arms, his own body still youthfully lean and filled with passion for her. She could still remember the last time they made love, even though neither of them had known that it would be their last night together. They had held each other silently for a long time afterwards, simply savoring the familiar warmth of each other's bodies, and Clea remembered marveling at the way their intimacy continued to deepen over the years. She hadn't felt anything even remotely close with a man since then.

Clea wiped a few hot tears away from her eyes. She roughly pulled off her jeans and hurled them into the corner. Sometimes she was so angry at him for dying that she wished she could forget him. She had tried to wipe out the memory of his touch, his loving face, and his body, with many young lovers already, but she hadn't forgotten anything. She wished she had someone she could talk to about Theo, what he had meant to her and how he had filled her world with his wisdom and quiet warmth. But there was no one besides Herculine who would understand. And yet when Herculine had pressed her for information about her father's past before she left for Berkeley, Clea hadn't told her everything she knew. There was one memory that she had promised she would never tell.

Early in her relationship with Theo, several years before Herculine was born, he had taken her with him to Brooklyn one day to visit someone he had known as a child. When it came to his past, Theo was unflinchingly secretive. Clea had often wondered about his childhood, raised by strangers in a foreign country, having to learn a new language without really understanding what had happened to his mother and father. But whenever she asked him about it, he brusquely evaded her and eventually she stopped asking. She had moved closer to him in the cab and put her hand in his protectively. The cab drove through a poor neighborhood of Brooklyn and stopped in front of an old dilapidated brownstone. They walked into the dark lobby and up two flights of shabby stairs. Clea had been surprised when Theo produced a key to one of the apartment doors. He knocked before opening, and called out softly, "*Hercule? Tu-es là? C'est moi, Théo…*" and he added, looking back at her with a smile, "*Et une amie qui s'appelle Clea…*"

She hesitantly followed him into the small apartment that smelled strongly but not unpleasantly of onion soup. The shades were drawn, and there was an elderly man sitting in a large armchair in a corner. He rose unsteadily with the help of a cane to greet them, but his eyes were twinkling, and his smile was warm and genuine. Theo embraced his old friend with both arms, and gave him a fervent kiss on each cheek. Hercule returned the embrace and the kisses as Clea shyly looked on. When Hercule noticed her, he ran his left hand through his sparse grey curls and winked at her. She laughed and he hobbled towards her, smiling, and embraced her while he kissed both her cheeks. They lunched on onion soup, bread, and cheese, and the two men conversed in French while she sat on an old green sofa and drank a glass of the red wine that Theo had brought along.

Occasionally Theo translated their small talk for her, but mostly she just sat back and watched them, taking in the evident affection between the two men without understanding a word. At one point, Clea got up to use the restroom, and after Theo pointed her vaguely down the hallway off the kitchen, she wandered through the apartment and ended up in Hercule's bedroom. A framed photograph on his nightstand immediately caught her eye: the image was faded and cracked, but still clear. A man and woman sat in a café, smoking and smiling, glasses of wine and the remnants of a meal on the table between them. The man was clearly a young Hercule—Clea recognized his twinkling eyes and kind smile beneath a thick head of curly dark hair. But it was the woman's face that

caused her to catch her breath: she could have been Theo's twin sister. Here was the same intelligent face, large dark eyes, long aristocratic nose, full lips, and strong chin as those of the man she loved. Could she be a relation? Clea lost track of how long she had spent looking at the photograph, until she heard Theo's voice calling her from the next room.

"One minute!" she called back, "I'll be right out!" And she hurried into the bathroom, which, as it turned out, was only accessible through the bedroom.

When they left, Theo held her arm tightly as he hailed a taxi to take them back to the city.

Clea asked him, "How do you know Hercule? Was he the one who took care of you when you were young?"

Theo had paused for a long time before answering her. Once they were inside the cab, he turned to her and said, "All I can tell you is that he is the man to whom I owe my life," and then closed his eyes, rested his head back against the seat of the cab and sat in silence for the rest of the drive, still holding tightly onto her arm.

Theo had never asked her to accompany him to Brooklyn again. In the whirlwind of her life, she had only occasionally thought of Hercule and the woman in the photograph. She hadn't remembered to ask Theo about him until one evening several years later, when little Herculine had begun crying about her name and she had seen Theo wince almost imperceptibly. Later that night in Theo's arms, she asked him,

"Darling, whatever happened to Hercule?"

He turned to look at her, and said, "I wasn't sure if you remembered him." He paused, then continued, "He went back to Paris many years ago."

Clea asked, "Does he know that we named our daughter after him?"

Theo said quietly, "I wasn't sure if you realized that we had. But no, he doesn't. Someday I will tell him, and Herculine too. Just not yet. The past is sometimes a story that is too painful to tell."

Gazing at him thoughtfully, Clea said, "Maybe that's why you like myths so much. There's always a reason for all the pain."

Theo gazed at her for a long time, held her closer, and kissed her hair, "Maybe yes, my dear. I think you may be quite right…"

And that was all Clea remembered. She had wanted to ask him more about the connection between their daughter's name and the old man, and if he knew who the woman in the photograph was.

67

She had often wanted to tell Herculine the true source of her name, but while Theo was alive she had honored his request that Herculine should not know about her elderly namesake, hoping that one day he would tell her himself. But he had died before he had the chance, and she wouldn't know what to tell Herculine about Hercule even if she had wanted to. Theo had associated Hercule with the memory of his painful past, so she had never questioned or probed any further.

Emerging from her memories, Clea stood in front of the mirror in her studio with bare legs and feet and slowly unwound the green shawl from around her torso. She pulled the wine-colored sweater she had on underneath up over her head and stood entirely naked in a pool of morning sunlight, gazing at her own reflection. Her auburn curls flowed freely past her shoulders, and she was pleased to see that the skin around her eyes, her long neck, and high cheekbones was still relatively smooth and clear. She examined her body as she pulled on her dance gear – cropped black tights and a leotard – then she moved through some preliminary stretches, a series of *plieés* and *porte des bras*, proudly noting the firmness of her skin and muscles. At forty-six, she was still flexible, strong, and relatively uninjured; there was occasionally some soreness in the mornings after a performance, but she had been spared most of the agonies of torn tendons and knee surgery endured by so many of her younger colleagues. Lately she had occasionally been surprised by a sudden tightness in her chest during strenuous performances, but had resolved to add more breathing exercises to her daily yoga practice.

Clea walked over to the *barre* and began her sequence of *arabesques*, meditatively approaching the state she loved best: total absorption in her body's every movement, unselfconscious immersion in the motion of muscles and skin through space. Only sex and dance took her to this place. Years ago she had given up acting because it had kept her too much in her head. Performance art and modern dance had called to her as her true art forms and every time she thought she had pushed herself to the edge of her ability, whole new possibilities for self-expression and artistic meaning would open up to her. Today in rehearsal, she was planning to try out a new idea for a dance sequence with Ramon based on one of the myths Theo used to tell her about: the story of Echo and Narcissus.

She imagined filling the studio with large panels of mirrors and glass hanging from the ceiling on cables. Then she and Ramon would dance in and around them, enacting a new version of the story

in which Clea would play Narcissus, and Ramon would be her Echo. Through dance, the two lovers would triumph over self-absorption and self-abnegation and finally unite after millennia of thwarted desire. As Clea moved to the center of the studio again to practice turns, she felt a sharp jolt in her right shoulder that quickly shot down her right arm. She stopped short, her jaw aching, afraid to breathe. A wave of nausea and dizziness passed over her and suddenly she was shivering. A cold sweat broke out along her spine and her chest contracted in a spasm of pain. "What the hell is happening?" she thought, as she sank to the floor, cradling her tingling arm against her breast. She crawled over to where her clothes were and covered herself with the green shawl.

"I should call Herculine," she thought, as she huddled, shivering against the wall. And that is where Ramon found her, barely conscious, when he finally arrived, twenty minutes later.

The Third Poem: Daphne
New York, December 1989

The view from my window seat on the red-eye flight to New York was a calm black void, interrupted only by a small flashing blue light perched on the wing. A hopeful talisman, I thought. A small brave torch leading me home.

The call from Ramon had awakened me late that morning from a deep, fitful sleep. There was a telephone ringing somewhere in my dream, but I couldn't find it, and I panicked, terrified that the caller would hang up before I could answer. The caller in my dream had been Hyla, whose voice I hadn't heard in weeks. And just as I dreamt that I uncovered the phone from under a pile of books and brought it to my ear, I opened my eyes to the sight of Anthea's concerned face as she gently shook my shoulder to wake me.

"Hey honey, it's for you. Something's happened to your mom."

Standing in the kitchen a few moments later, shivering in my bare feet, t-shirt, and pajama pants in the late-November morning chill, I listened in shock as Ramon related the previous morning's events. He had found my mom unconscious in her studio and immediately called an ambulance and administered CPR until help arrived. She was now stable in Lenox Hill Hospital's Intensive Care unit, and Ramon gave me the name and number of a doctor who would verify to the airline that I needed to fly home on a medical emergency. It was only after Ramon had finished giving me all the information that I snapped out of my daze and realized that I needed to get a pen to write it all down. Ramon's voice was kind as he patiently recited the information again. I wrote slowly, with a shaking hand, and thanked him. He said he'd be at the hospital all day and night and would see me there when I arrived.

I had never met Ramon, or even heard mom mention him before, but I was not surprised that he would be so attentive to my mother's needs. Mom's friends and lovers were all devoted to her. By the time I arrived, she would undoubtedly be surrounded by her loving tribe: the room filled with music, food, and flowers. Or did

they not allow this in Intensive Care? I didn't know, nor did I fully comprehend my ability to calmly hang up the phone with Ramon, look up the airline in the phone book, go upstairs to get my credit card, pull on jeans and a sweater, throw my books and some clothes into a small bag, go back downstairs to book a flight to New York, and call a cab. When the taxi pulled up to the house in the rain ten minutes later, I gave Anthea a quick hug and sprinted out the door. The fact that I was leaving twelve hours before my flight was scheduled to depart was the only indication that I was in a state of utter panic.

Once I arrived at the airport, I found a payphone and called the library and the Classics department to let them know what was going on. The head of graduate studies assured me that it should be no problem to set up an emergency contingency plan for me to finish my course work while I was in New York, and if taking Incompletes proved necessary, all leniency would be given for finishing them up before the new semester began in mid January. At the library office, Joyce had barely even grumbled about having to find coverage for my shifts; her voice was so kind as she wished my mom a swift and complete recovery that I could barely thank her.

Reassured about school and exhausted from shock, I promptly curled up and slept on an uncomfortable plastic chair in the airport until noon. Upon waking, I walked around the terminal in a surreal trance for a few hours, ate a tasteless overpriced meal, numbly watched TV on the muted monitors suspended from the ceiling, leafed through countless glossy magazines at newsstands, and finally surrendered to my emotions as I stared out the tall windows facing the runway at sunset. Tears streamed down my face, and I felt helpless in the presence of a depth of grief and fear that I had not known I was capable of. It was just too close to what had happened when my dad had died and brought back my childhood shock at the fact that one day he could be laughing and healthy, and the next day he could be gone forever. My mother had been fine when I left. We had just talked a few days ago and she had sounded breezy and lighthearted as usual. Lighthearted. Bad choice of metaphor. Her heart was light…would it make it through this test?

I trembled and bit my lower lip, trying to control my body's release of hours of pent-up tension, but then I realized that my feelings for my mom were not the only source of my anguish. I was suddenly missing my father too with the force of a kick to my abdomen. I doubled over with pain, resting my face on the knees of

my jeans, crying for the hole in the center of my life that he had left, which had become even deeper after my heartbreak over Hyla, and was now reaching epic proportions. I didn't think I could bear it if anything awful happened to my mother too. It was just too much, too soon. My tears left large wet stains in the denim so that it looked as if I had been kneeling in puddles of rain. If I had wanted to I could have. The Bay Area had been soaked for days.

My first experience of a Northern California winter rainy season had seemed unfairly symbolic. The grey skies, cold wind, and stormy clouds had mirrored the landscape of my heart following my disillusionment and break-up with Hyla. The rain followed me; it literally seemed to lay in wait, abating just long enough to ambush me when I thought it had let up. Sometimes I would look out the window in class and see that the skies had cleared, but as soon as I stepped outside, the deluge began anew. My world was sodden, saturated with sorrow and confusion, with only the occasional refuge in bottles of wine and the warmth of Linus and Phoebe's embraces. They didn't ask me any questions, and I received their attentions gratefully. I had tried to forget the night at the Palladium Club, and my scene with Hyla the following evening, but it was still too raw, the wound too fresh.

I remembered all too clearly the euphoria of the morning before that fateful night, and how close I had been to giving myself over to love for the first time in my life. A shudder passed through me, as I recalled the bitter words Hyla and I had exchanged less than thirty-six hours later. Hyla had called me several times the next day, but I had asked Anthea to tell her that I was unavailable. I hadn't felt ready to talk to Hyla yet; my thoughts and emotions about what I had seen at the Palladium Club were still unclear, and I was afraid of saying something hurtful that I might regret later. My rage had been soothed to some degree by Linus and Phoebe, but I was still confused and shocked that Hyla had neglected to tell me that her job at the club entailed privately entertaining male clients. Even though we had never settled the monogamy question, this seemed like a breach, or at least a deceptive evasion.

When Hyla called the fourth time, Anthea must have implied that even though I was unavailable, I was still at home, because Hyla showed up at the door twenty minutes later, and ran upstairs to find out what was going on.

I almost didn't let her into my room when she knocked. I was too angry to even say "hello," so I just sat down as far away from

her as possible across the room in my dad's leather armchair, my legs folded up against my chest in a protective pose, as she stood uneasily in the doorway.

"What's wrong?" she asked. "Why haven't you been answering my calls?" Her face was stricken with concern.

"I saw your act last night," I said quietly.

"Really..." she said, warily. "Why didn't you let me know you were there?"

"I was about to," I said, with an edge in my voice, "but you went off with some guy to a back room before I had a chance."

"Oh..." said Hyla. "So you're angry at me."

"Why didn't you tell me?"

"Tell you what? That you're so naïve?"

I felt like she had slapped me.

"No," I said, my teeth gritted with the effort to stay civil, "Why didn't you tell me that you're practically a sex worker, and not just an 'exotic dancer'?"

"They're usually the same thing, babe; I thought you knew," said Hyla dryly. "And besides, would you have minded any less if I had told you from the start?"

I pondered this question. *Would I have?*

"No," I said, after a moment, "I don't think I would have minded as much. You would have been open with me about what you do, we would have discussed it, and I'm pretty sure that I could have handled anything you had told me. I mean, you're not having sex with, uh, your 'clients'... Are you?"

Hyla shook her head, looking impatient, "No, of course not. They're not even allowed to touch me."

Relieved, I continued, "So no, I wouldn't have minded as much. What scares me, and makes me angry, is that you kept it from me. It feels like a deception."

Hyla looked thoughtful. She leaned against one side of the doorway and gazed meditatively at me with her large green eyes, then said, "I think I was afraid that you would judge me, and that you might not want to date me if you knew."

I wasn't surprised by this; I had been accused of being judgmental before by other lovers, friends, and even my mom. As soon as anyone got close to me they seemed to fear my judgment. But Hyla? She seemed so confident and secure.

I said, "I'm not judging you. But even if I was, isn't that a risk you have to take in a relationship? I mean, I don't know much about

73

love, but I do know about trust, and right now I guess I'm not sure if I can trust you."

"Love?" exclaimed Hyla, with a short harsh laugh.

"Yeah, *love*, Hyla. I thought I loved you. And I trusted you too. But if you lie to me about this – okay, I know, it was just a lie of omission – what else would you lie about to me if you fear my judgment so much? What else should I know that I don't?"

Hyla looked angry now, and her eyes filled with tears. She stood up straight, poised either for a fight or flight, and said, "You want too much Herculine. I really like you, you know? I thought you were cool and that we were onto something here, but you're way too critical for me, way too demanding. My life is complicated. You could never have known everything about me. No one does. And now you never will."

With that, she gave me a look of combined love and torment, then turned and ran down the stairs and out the front door.

I could hear Hyla's boots hit the pavement and the whir of her bicycle wheels as she rode away. I sat in my chair without moving for an hour, still shaken by our conversation and the events of the past twenty-four hours. *She loves me*, I thought to myself. *I know she does.* It can't be over. It just can't. I stayed curled up in my father's chair staring out at the dark sky for an hour.

Later that night, Linus and Phoebe had showed up to check on me and ended up staying for almost a week, during which I had no word from Hyla, and no urge to contact her either. I just felt numb, and lost. In an effort to distract me from my confusion and misery, Linus left one of his guitars in my room and was teaching me how to play. Soon I was diverted from dwelling on my broken heart by more than my new friends' amorous attentions and music lessons: as the semester ended, my schoolwork seemed to triple. Thirty-page seminar papers were due in two of my classes, as well as a translation of Pindar's entire first *Pythian Ode* for my Archaic Greek Poetry course. I worked feverishly, neglecting my analysis of my grandmother's poems as well as my research on the Resistance. I spent long hours in the library each night, poring over my translation and writing papers for my Literary Theory and Feminist Methodologies seminars. Throughout it all, visions of Hyla dancing, her body's undulations refracted in multiple mirrors, her anguished face framed in my doorway, haunted the corners of my concentration.

I had just managed to turn in the two seminar papers the day before Ramon's call, and my translation was almost finished. I had another day before it was due and planned to FedEx it in to Professor Seidon's office in the Classics department as soon as it was done. I vaguely wondered how Linus and Phoebe's translations were going and then realized that I hadn't even thought to call and tell them that I was leaving for New York. Hopefully Anthea or Hermàn would explain everything to them the next time they dropped by. During this past week, we had all been so busy that I had barely seen them at all.

I sighed. I had stopped crying, but felt raw and depleted. Wishing there was something I could lose myself in while I waited out the remaining few hours for my flight, I turned reluctantly to my grandmother's poems. I had been avoiding them as carefully as I had been avoiding running into Hyla. But just because the first two poems had become entangled with my personal life, I rationalized, that didn't necessarily mean that the third one would too. This one was new territory. It was time to take the plunge. I opened my bag and took out my notebook. I turned to the third poem in my series of translations, the one called "Daphne," and read through it once again:

I have been running my whole life.
Every man a hunter:
My beauty their prey,
My body their prize.
But I ran like the wind.
Like water I slipped through their snares.
They barely even saw me; never caught me.
Until the tireless one,
Eyes burning like the sun.
He hunted me for years,
Tracked and chased me without rest.
I ran from him until I ran out of breath:
Parched and weary,
A clear spring beckoned me to drink.
He almost caught me then:
I felt his clutch begin to tear my skin.
I called out to you for help –
Brother, father, stranger – and you
Caught me in your arms instead:

You could see what other men could not:
The glint of moonlight in my eyes,
The only trace of my flight.
Before he could trap me,
You transformed me to my core.
Your soul was rich soil:
For the first time, my flying feet took root.
My new branches sheltered you,
The kiss of my leaves upon your brow
Became the emblem of your skill.
He no longer knew me;
He turned away from me, and I was free:
Your captive, until you freed me once again.
You knew the life of the cursed and hunted,
So you showed me the path to trust:
Led me back to my sisters.
By day, we share a sacred virgin grove;
By night, we run like the wind,
For the hunters still ride.
We are sleek:
Like Diana's sacred hinds
Silver with moonlight
As we race the breeze,
And win.

I wearily rubbed my temples. This one was seriously strange. My grandmother had based her poem on the Ovidian myth of the beautiful wood nymph Daphne and her transformation into a laurel tree while running from Apollo's rapacious advances. Then she combined it with the legend of Hercules' third labor: capturing the Cernyian Hind, one of the sacred female deer belonging to the virgin huntress goddess Diana. According to Apollodorus' version of the story, which I had consulted when I did the translation, Hercules could only see the lightning-swift hind when the moonlight glinted on her antlers as she ran past him, and he caught her while she was wearily drinking at a spring after a year of his ceaseless pursuit. Over the course of this year, Hercules grew to respect and admire the hind, so when it was time to turn her over to King Eurystheus in fulfillment of his task, he said to the King, who intended to cage the magical animal as a trophy, "I have captured the hind for you, thus

completing my third labor; but if you want to keep her, you must take her to the cage yourself."

Hercules then let go of the hind, which eluded the King's grasp, and instantly vanished, racing back to Diana's protection.

Hercules said to the King, "Too bad; you were too slow," and left.

I had always liked that part of the story.

Despite the strangeness of the juxtaposition, I could see many important themes shared by the two stories: pursuit, entrapment, greed, desire, and even transformation. Hercules did after all, change from hunter to ally, just as Daphne changed from a nymph into a laurel tree, forever bearing the leaves that Apollo would thereafter use to crown a poet's brow. But what was my grandmother up to this time? Where was the connection to the French Resistance? I realized that I would have to wait to find out until I made sure my mom was in stable condition and I had a chance to get to the library at Columbia. In the meantime, my plane was finally boarding.

During the flight, I alternated between dozing off, re-reading the "Daphne" poem, and staring out the window at the brave little blue light. Occasionally I awoke to find that the small airplane pillow I was resting against was wet with tears, but I did not remember crying. My dreams were filled with moonlight and rustling leaves, the sound of hooves and the fear of pursuit.

After six hours of cramped and restless sleep, I was jolted awake by the thud of the airplane's wheels hitting the runway, and I squinted with disorientation as sunlight flooded the cabin. Dehydrated and exhausted, I stumbled through the airport to the subway, catching the Blue line train into the heart of New York. It seemed like an endless ride, accompanied by a brutal headache that was only made worse by the overpowering urban smells and unabashed stares of my companions in the subway car. No one used to stare at me in New York when I lived there. Why were they staring at me now? I discreetly checked myself to make sure that my fly was zipped up and that there were no unsightly stains on my clothing.

Once the train stopped at 80th Street, I emerged gratefully into the bracing cold air and pulled the collar of my leather coat up around my neck. I trudged through the gray slush on the sidewalks, melting under the faint glare of the pale sun, and made my way through the bustling city streets to the hospital. A nurse told me that my mom had been moved from Intensive Care, which was a good sign, and gave me directions to her new room. I steeled myself as I

rode the elevator up to the Cardiac Wing. Coming to the hospital made me think too sharply of my father and filled me with a surge of grief. Whenever I thought of my dad lately, a lump rose in my throat that was so painful I could barely breathe. I tried to relax and pull myself together before I saw my mother, so when the elevator stopped, I ducked into a bathroom off the corridor. I was surprised and annoyed when I saw my tear-streaked face. No wonder people had been staring at me. I plunged my entire head under the curved, elongated faucet poised over the handicap-accessible sink. The hot water coursing over my scalp felt wonderful.

I shook my curls free of excess water, patted my face gently with paper towels, hoisted my bag on my shoulder with renewed courage, and strode out of the bathroom down the hallway to find my mother. As I had predicted, there was a large group of theatrical looking people gathered in a nearby lounge. They turned to stare at me as I passed and entered my mom's room without knocking. Her room was empty except for a dark, handsome young man by the window who I assumed was Ramon. Mom looked like she was sleeping, and she was attached to so many tubes and humming machines that I was suddenly frightened and stood motionless in the doorway. Ramon's face brightened when he saw me, and he strode around the bed to greet me.

I shakily held out my hand to thank Ramon for saving my mother's life, but when he took my hand he pulled me close to him in a long, strong embrace. Surprised, I felt myself relax, finally, in Ramon's arms. I dropped my bag on the floor and rested my head on his shoulder, eyes closed, breathing deeply. He smelled good, like new leather and clean linen. After almost twenty-four hours of traveling through what seemed like seven levels of purgatory, I allowed myself to feel, even briefly, that I was home. I pulled away slightly and looked into Ramon's eyes questioningly.

He smiled and said, "She's going to pull through."

As if roused by the sound of her lover's voice, my mother's eyes opened slowly and struggled to focus on me.

"Mom?" I said softly, "It's me, Herculine." The panicked look on her face quickly faded into visible joy.

"Oh darling," she said to me, and weakly held out her hand.

I moved towards her, shaken by her pallor and the tubes connected to her arm, the wires monitoring her heart, and the thin blue cotton gown sheathing her body. I took her hand and leaned in to kiss her on the cheek. She then reached up to softly tousle my

78

curls, and at her touch I bent lower and burrowed my face into the familiar space where her neck met the hollow of her shoulder. I hadn't felt moved to do this in years, but now I wanted to stay and never leave. As we had done every night before bedtime during my childhood, mom and I breathed together deeply in this position for several minutes, until we were both smiling and the thousands of miles and several months that had separated us melted away.

I looked up into her eyes and said, "How soon can I get you out of here?"

She smiled and said, "Soon, baby. Ramon knows…in the next few days."

"A few days?" I groaned. "Can I get a cot in here and stay with you?"

"Stay at the loft while you're here, sweetheart," my mom said. "I know you'll come visit me every day…"

I grumbled that I would stay here at the hospital that night, cot or no cot, unless they threw me out. Mom sighed and patted my hand, saying, "Do what you want to, darling. I'm just glad you're here. Have you eaten anything?"

At her words, I realized that I was both ravenous and exhausted. I sat down heavily in the chair nearest the bed. As usual, mom had read my face and mood transparently. She waved to a cluster of her friends hovering by the open door. Several of them approached the bed hurriedly, faces expectant with the desire to please my mom, who asked them to bring me some nourishing food and drink. I did not interfere. I was grateful to benefit from my mother's generosity, as well as that of her minions, and the room was glowing with energy now that she was animated again.

Ramon leaned down and whispered in my ear, "You've brought her back to life, *chica*; she hasn't been this much herself since she's been here."

He sounded confident that he knew her "true self," and I would have usually sneered at such hubris, but he was so sincere that I suppressed my scorn. My mother's lovers all thought they "really knew" my mom. I knew better. But I was grateful for Ramon's devotion and spared him my post-adolescent cynicism. I smiled wryly at him instead: if he only knew what he was missing.

Mom and I talked quietly for half an hour about what had happened; the heart attack had been serious enough to warrant the insertion of stents into two of her major arteries, but the doctors

79

were optimistic that after cardiac rehab she could make an almost full recovery.

I raised my eyebrows, "Almost?" I asked. Mom looked down at her hands resting on the bed.

"Yes…it seems that I may not be able to keep dancing professionally." Seeing the disbelief on my face, she added, "I can still run the studio, and choreograph for my dancers…" She trailed off, then looked at me with a twinkle in her eyes, "Who knows? Maybe I'll go back to acting." She laughed weakly and turned away, suddenly seeming weary.

Ramon moved closer and said, "Let her rest." I bristled at having him tell me what to do, but saw my mother's fatigue and moved away reluctantly.

Just then, the group of dancers bringing food arrived. All the people in the room gathered at the small table by the door, enthusiastically preparing to eat, but the on-duty nurse came in at that moment and shooed them out into the waiting room for their brunch party. I didn't want to leave, but mom was sleeping again, and my hunger drew me into the hallway. One of the dancers beckoned me over to the food table.

"Hi, um, I wasn't sure what you'd want, so I got you a *chai latté*. It's my favorite – I hope you like it," she said, shyly holding out a steaming paper cup. "My name is Lyra… You look so much like your mom…oh, um, sorry. I bet everyone tells you that."

The girl seemed really nervous as I took the aromatic cup of tea from her, so I managed a forced laugh in an attempt to put her at ease.

"No," I said, "Usually people don't think I look like her at all. I actually look more like my dad."

"Oh," said Lyra, with wide blue eyes, "Is he a dancer too?"

At this I really laughed. "Oh no…definitely not a dancer. And he died a long time ago."

Lyra looked stricken, and mumbled, "Oh gosh, I'm sorry…"

"It's okay," I said, feeling sorry if I had made her uncomfortable, "You didn't know… See you later, and hey – thanks for the tea. It's my favorite too."

I flashed her a smile as I turned away and walked down the hall with a croissant in one hand and my *chai* in the other. And as I moved down the hallway, a dim memory of my mom and dad dancing together in mom's old apartment flashed through my mind. I could hear the bossa nova beat of "The Girl from Ipanema" lilting

80

over the scratchy vinyl of the record album on mom's old turntable and realized that I couldn't have been more than four or five years old at the time. He had held her with graceful strength, and her body had bent willingly in his arms as they glided around the room. Mom's eyes had been closed and her head was tilted back, a dreamy smile on her face. Maybe he had been a good dancer after all.

Once I reached the row of tall windows at the end of the hallway, I leaned against the wall and stared out at New York in the cold mid-morning light. Now that I was bolstered by food and warm drink, and reassured by mom's positive spirits, a craving for fresh air was pulling me towards the elevators. I ducked behind a group of nurses and made my way out the doors without being noticed by the happily brunching dancers in the lounge.

Back out on the street, I felt energized by being in New York. The city was waking up, people were bustling on the street, and I struck off uptown towards Columbia. It was good to feel the solid force of my boots against pavement. The walk was long and I knew it would clear my head. By the time I reached campus there was music in my head – one of Linus's songs – and my heart felt lighter than it had in weeks.

Entering Butler Library was yet another form of coming home. The vaulted ceilings and glowing wood beckoned to my mind in a way that eclipsed the regal marble chill of Berkeley's Doe Library. After a quick check of the computer catalogue, I found my way through the stacks to books about the Resistance. A few titles caught my eye: *The Hunters and the Hunted: French Jews, Vichy, and the Resistance; Poets or Patriarchs: Propaganda and the French Government from 1938-45*, along with several others. I read for a few hours, then used my alumna privileges to check them out for a week, not even knowing how long I would be in New York. Mom might need me around for a few days or a month – either way, I was ready to stay and realized that a break from the drama of my life in Berkeley was just what I needed. I'd give Ben and Lucy a call as soon as I was done with my research this evening as an extra treat. Things were starting to look up…

After an affectionate glance back over my shoulder at the library, I ran down the long stone steps and out to the curb to catch a cab back to the hospital. When I arrived, mom was sitting up in bed, and the color had returned to her face. She smiled broadly when I stepped in and Ramon, who apparently never left her side, smiled too and beckoned me over to the bed.

"The doctors say I can go home tomorrow," Mom said proudly. "My vital signs are stabilized and my blood levels are normal..." here she looked up at Ramon and then questioningly at me. "The only catch is that I need someone to take care of me for a few weeks. How long can you stay, Herculine?"

"I'm all yours," I said with a grin, knowing that once I sent in my finished translation, I was done with finals and on winter break for the rest of December and half of January.

Mom relaxed with a smile against her pillows, then said, "Thank you, sweetheart; it would be a great help to me, and of course Ramon can take over when you need a break...maybe the two of you could even work out a schedule so you don't get sick of me."

Ramon winked at me; it was clear that he wasn't planning to ever get sick of her. What he didn't know is that she was usually the one to tire of her lovers first.

She continued, "I know you want to spend the night here with me, Herculine; but I'd really rather that you took some time to yourself back at the loft before you're on duty full time. I know you, darling, and you'll thank me for this later."

I smiled sheepishly; mom was right. Even though I had been prepared to muscle it out with several large orderlies if they had tried to prevent me from rolling in a cot, it would be good to have some time to myself before she came home from the hospital. Maybe I would even invite Ben and Lucy to come over...

"Okay, you're right," I admitted. "I'll be back in the morning to bring you home."

"Did you remember your key?" She asked, then chuckled at my stricken look – in my hasty departure, I hadn't remembered anything as practical as keys. "Don't worry, sweetheart; Ramon's got one for you."

Ramon handed me a slim silver keychain with a set of keys. I put them in my pocket and as Mom leaned forward for a kiss, I embraced her gently, nodded to Ramon, and left.

I took the subway down to the Village and when I emerged onto Spring Street, I wished it really was spring and that I could stroll around my old favorite neighborhoods for a while. It was only late afternoon, but the winter evening was falling quickly, as was the temperature, so I hurried up to mom's loft, planning to call Lucy and Ben and then venture out into the night with them after a warm bath and dinner.

Mom had redecorated her apartment after I had left for Berkeley, so when I opened the door, I couldn't help but let out a low whistle of appreciation. I had always loved the high windows with their deeply inset cushioned seats, as well as the large colorful sofas that were strewn with pillows and afghans, but there was new exciting art featured on ingenious stands and easels scattered around the space, new wooden bookcases filled with the books I had kept from my dad's study, and several large luxuriant plants flourishing in each corner. I dropped my shoulder bag on the familiar centerpiece of the room: her long wooden table that she'd had for years, the site of many a late night dinner party, brunch feast and planning session. I had written countless term papers at that table and was filled with affectionate nostalgia for it as I walked into her spacious kitchen to find some food.

A large ceramic bowl filled with a colorful pasta primavera awaited me in the tall stainless steel fridge; I added some olive oil to one of mom's elegant copper bottom skillets and warmed up a heaping serving for myself on the stove. As I stirred the pasta, I called Lucy's house and Ben answered,

"Herculine! Great to hear from you...are you back in town?"

"Hey Ben," I said, feeling a little shy...there was only one reason I was calling, and he knew it. "Yeah, I'm back for a few weeks and wondered if you and Luce might want to get together later? I've missed you guys, and it would be great to see you..." Had I missed them? I hadn't realized it until now.

Ben's voice was apologetic, "Damn, I *wish* we could see you tonight, but we're on our way to hear a friend's jazz trio...want to join us?"

"Mmmm," I said, thinking that all I really wanted to join was their bodies, not just their company. "Another time, definitely."

"Well, hey – how about tomorrow night? Come on over for a home-cooked meal and stay for a while..."

That was more like it. I could just see Ben's brown eyes twinkling from the warm suggestiveness in his voice. "Sounds perfect," I said. "Just what I was hoping you'd say." We both laughed and made plans to meet the following evening.

Something to look forward to. Ben and Lucy were so different from Linus and Phoebe. They were a few years older, a little less athletic in bed, but being with them would be comforting and familiar, and I was looking forward to seeing them again. In the meantime, I had a precious night to myself. I poured a full glass of

Valpolicella and curled up in mom's old deep brown leather sofa with one of the books I had found in the library that afternoon: *Their Sisters' Keepers: Communities of Women in Vichy France.* While reading it, I learned that during the war, the shortage of men in France was a severe hardship for many families and women often banded together in quasi-socialist communal kitchens and laundries to help each other through hard times. Some of them even went so far as to live together communally, for warmth in the winter, to save on rent, or the cost of wood and oil, but mostly for adult companionship.

The situation became more interesting when groups of women just started living together even without families to support. They started small cottage industries and supplied much-needed services to their larger communities: food, clothing, and soap production; childcare, laundry, and minor healthcare. Even more unusual were the unorthodox nocturnal activities of these female collectives. Several of them formed vigilante safety squads to accompany working women home from their jobs in the evening. The streets, particularly in Paris, were not safe for women walking alone at night, so the women in the collectives spread the news of their safety squads by word of mouth and the response was overwhelming. The image of the dark streets of Paris, just before curfew, illuminated by the torches of small bands of brave women escorting each other home accompanied me as I drifted off into a deep sleep on the comfortable couch.

I dreamed that I was running through an endless forest, following a trail of lights that flickered through the trees. I was being chased, but I was also in pursuit of someone fleeing ahead of me. Occasionally I saw a flash of bare legs in the moonlight, but my quarry ran silently, while I was panting with exertion. All at once, the forest opened up into a clearing where a band of women in short white tunics stood around a shimmering pool of water. Torches were mounted around the edge of the circle, and the women – all beautiful, strong, and severe – looked at me expectantly. The leader of the group, who I realized looked exactly like my father's widow Johanna, was sheltering a panting young woman in her arms. The young woman turned around to gaze at me mournfully. It was Hyla. As I started towards her, I was immediately restrained by several women nearest to me. Johanna looked at me sharply and said, "Join the circle, Hercule. You have accomplished your task. Sophia is here, and she is safe." Why had she called me "Hercule," I wondered vaguely, as I watched as the women change their formation into a

84

defensive arc protecting Johanna and Hyla, facing out towards the forest. I joined them instinctively. A woman who looked like Phoebe handed me a quiver of arrows and a bow.

"You'll be needing this soon," she whispered, just as a man came crashing through the trees and stumbled into the clearing.

He looked around, bewildered, and sank to his knees. The arc of women opened slightly and Johanna stepped through alone, her bow and arrow drawn. The arc closed behind her, still protecting Hyla.

Johanna said to the man, "You have desecrated the body of one of our sisters. You have forfeited your life."

The man turned towards me and said, "Save me, Hercule!"

But I drew my bow along with the rest of the women, and said, "You will never harm her again."

As if this was a sign to the rest, all the women let arrows fly at the same moment and the intruder fell to the ground.

I awoke with a start and fumbled in the dark for my notebook and pen. Who was the man I had just killed? Why had he and Johanna both called me "Hercule"? Quickly, I wrote down the entire dream before I could forget it, and when I was done I read it over. In my fatigue, I realized that my dream world had continued working while I had slept: here was not only the connection between the "Daphne" poem and the women's safety collectives of the French resistance, but a possible key to my grandmother's role in the story. Had she too been protected by her sisters in the underground movement when hunted by a man? The man in the dream was vaguely familiar, but no one I had recognized. Seeing Hyla had been difficult enough, but at least it seemed as if I had been protecting her, not persecuting her. It had been reassuring to see Phoebe there as my ally, and disconcerting for Johanna to be the leader of the collective. Perhaps the real Johanna might know something about Sophia and her poems, or even her life? For the first time since finding out about the existence of the Ice Queen when I was a little girl, I actually felt a desire to contact my father's widow.

I had been only five years old when my dad thought it was time to explain the real reason why he could rarely spend the night at our apartment. Up until that point, I had been appeased by the explanation that "Daddy lives far away." But then my dad told me that while it was true that he lived uptown, he was also married to and lived with another woman named Johanna, who was a very nice person, so he had to spend time with her too.

85

"But why don't you come live with *us* and just visit *her*?" I had asked, bewildered.

"I don't want to cause Johanna any more sadness," he said somberly.

"Well, then can we go visit her sometime to make her happy?" I asked innocently.

He smiled. "I'm afraid not, sweetheart," he said ruefully, " though I am hopeful that you two will meet someday."

Of course, I was not content with this deferral of my curiosity and I pestered my mom about it daily until she gave in.

"Okay, kiddo, you want to see the Ice Queen? Let's go!"

It was a cold winter's day and mom bundled us both on a bus up to Riverside Drive. Once we were there, we bought a bag of roasted chestnuts from a pushcart vendor and sat on a bench across the street from Dad and Johanna's house. After a cold, fidgety hour, a tall, pale, blonde woman in a long white wool coat emerged from a cab in front of the house. She quickly glanced over at us – a rag-tag pair on the bench eyeing her hungrily as we nibbled on our chestnuts. Her face changed to an expression of alarm and she quickly turned away. With several long-legged strides, she disappeared through the front gate and into the house.

Mom snorted, "Well, that was her, baby; good thing she didn't catch you or she'd take you away to her ice castle!"

I remember being quiet for a few moments, then asking, "Is that where Daddy lives?"

Mom was more thoughtful at this, and said, "That's just where he sleeps, honey. In his heart, he lives with us."

As I replayed this old memory, I dropped back against the pillows on my mom's couch and closed my eyes. Exhausted from my dream and note-taking, the vision of Hyla staring at me sorrowfully from Johanna's protective embrace would not subside. So I wrapped my arms around a large velvet pillow and quietly cried myself back to sleep.

I awoke early the next morning with a stiff neck from sleeping on the couch and a hazy memory of torches lighting a forest grove. I looked over at the coffee table and saw the notes I had made in the middle of the night. As soon as I re-read them I could instantly project myself back into the dream. I had been so concerned about my mother that I hadn't consciously thought about Hyla since I had arrived in New York, so my dream had served as an uncanny return of the repressed. It had been a lucky trick of my unconscious

86

to make the connection between the "Daphne" poem and the women's safety collectives, but it had been a double-edged gift as well: against my waking will, my grandmother's third poem was now associated symbolically with Hyla along with the others. *Damn.* And yet in the hazy morning light, the memory of the real Hyla felt distant: the traces of another, much less substantial reality that seemed like something I had also dreamed here on my mother's couch without ever having left New York.

Thinking about my life in Berkeley caused me to remember my Archaic Poetry translation that I still had to finish and send in. Immediately that other reality took on a tangible substance. I sighed. After splashing my face with water and drinking a quick glass of orange juice, I went over to my small pile of belongings lumped unceremoniously on the kitchen table the previous night, rifled through my bag for my classics notebook and set to work. I scanned over my completed translation of the introduction to the Ode:

> *Golden lyre, the prize possession of Apollo and the*
> *violet-haired Muses, the dancers listen to you alone.*
> *You initiate all glorious festivals; the singers obey only*
> *your notes when you lead the chorus and preludes with*
> *your quivering strings...*

Aided by the perspective of several days since I had last worked on it, I read the words I had written for what felt like the first time. Their poetry unexpectedly brought back memories of Linus. I could see his long fingers moving over the quivering strings of his guitar, over my own body, and over Phoebe's trembling curves as well. I closed my eyes in a reverie, vividly remembering our last night together. We had all been so tired from studying, our triadic ménage had been slow and graceful, practically balletic, increasing in intensity as our bodies moved from arousal to wakefulness, to expertly choreographed climax. I shook my head to clear the image and continued:

> *You quench even the everlasting fire of the thunderbolt,*
> *the scepter of Zeus. The king of birds, the eagle, sleeps*
> *upon it, relaxing his swift wings on either side; and you*
> *pour down a dark mist over his curved head, a sweet seal*
> *on his eyelids. Slumbering, he ripples his liquid back,*
> *under the spell of your pulsing notes.*

It seemed that I could not escape the associations with Linus. Only now he was like Zeus's eagle, his liquid back rippling under my touch, the sweet seal on his eyelids the expression of blissful release on his face before he drifted into satiated sleep. That was enough; I got the point. I roamed around my mother's vast loft looking for the cordless telephone. When I found it underneath an afghan, I dialed Linus's number, completely forgetting that it was three hours earlier on the west coast.

His sleepy voice answered, "Hmmmm? Hullo?"

I felt an inexplicable ache in my chest and managed to say, "Hey Linus. How are you? Sorry to call so early..."

He cleared his throat, "Herculine? What's wrong? You sound really small and far away."

I smiled at this. "Um, nothing's really wrong. I had to go to New York 'cause my mom's in the hospital but she's okay now." Here my throat caught again and I realized that more was at stake in making this call than I had known.

Linus heard this and soothed me with his voice, "Hey, it's fine... How's she doing? Will she be all right?"

I managed to say, "Yeah...yeah, she's coming home today. Thanks. Um, how's Phoebe?"

Linus yawned and said lazily, "Well, I actually haven't seen her in a few days... She went down to L.A. to visit her brother when she finished her exams. Too bad you're not here. We could be having a good time..."

The innuendo in his voice sent a tremor through my body. "Yeah," I said, "I kinda wish you were here right now too..." Luckily I knew I would be with Ben and Lucy later.

There was a pause, then Linus cleared his throat, and said, "Me too, Herculine. But it sounds like you need to be there and take care of your mom now. You'll be back soon though, right? I'll be waiting for you." He yawned, then continued, "So, how's your translation coming along?"

I sighed, ran my fingers through my tangled curls, and said, "Oh, it's almost done. But hey – that's why I'm calling you. I was going over the Intro of the first *Ode* and it kept making me think of you!"

Linus laughed too: "No way, that's so weird...because I'm working on the ninth *Ode* and there was this section that made me think of *you*. Here, check it out!"

88

There was a rustling of papers, then Linus returned and read aloud to me:

She did not care for long afternoons spent at the loom,
nor for the delights of luncheons with her minions; instead, fighting with
bronze javelins and with a sword, she killed
wild beasts, providing great restful peace for her father's
cattle; but as for her sweet bed-fellow, sleep, she spent only
a little of it on her eyelids as it fell on them towards dawn.

Linus chuckled when he ended, and I smiled and teased him, "Okay…what in the world reminded you of me in that passage?"

He said, "Oh, something about killing wild beasts in the name of the father and not needing much sleep. You know, like the other night…"

"Ah," I said wryly, "I'm glad that we both found profound ways to make our work relevant to our lives."

"Sure," quipped Linus, now sounding quite awake, "What good would Pindar be without the erotics of his poetics?"

I laughed out loud at this and said gently, "Good to hear your voice, Linus. I'll be in touch. When you see Phoebe, tell her I say 'hi.'"

"Okay," said Linus, "Will do. Take care of yourself as well as your mom, okay?"

"Okay," I said, "You too."

I hung up, relieved that the lump in my throat had gone and the conversation had ended lightly, and I was able to concentrate on my translation with undivided attention for the next hour and a half – long enough to put the finishing touches on it before I was ready to send it off. Just in time to take a quick shower and head over to the FedEx office before I had to be back at the hospital to pick up my mom.

When I arrived, Ramon was already there, and mom was in a wheelchair, almost ready to leave. She smiled when she saw me and looked as excited as a little girl going to a party.

"How are you, darling?" she asked, "Did you have a good night?"

I couldn't answer her though; I was too horrified by the sight of her in a wheelchair.

She admonished me, "Just wipe that pitying look off your face, Herculine. I'll be out of this thing as soon as we cross the

threshold of the building. They're making me ride in it for legal reasons, but I'll be doing pirouettes from the curb to the cab."

Meekly I followed the small procession of nurses and friends outside to the sidewalk, where mom arose from the wheelchair unassisted, and looking slightly paler than she had a moment ago, curtsied deeply to the hospital staff. Then, taking Ramon's arm, she walked gracefully to the open door of the taxi, turning around to wave gratefully to her friends before she stepped in. Not quite pirouettes, but pretty darn good after three days in the cardiac ward.

Once we were all back in the loft, Ramon thoughtfully left me alone with mom while he went out for "provisions." Reclining on the same couch that had served me as an impromptu bed the previous night, mom wrapped herself in an emerald green afghan and pressed me for details of the several months I'd been away. I curled up by her feet on one end of the couch and tucked my toes under her warm thighs, as I had often done as a child. Something about the intimacy of our position and the quiet warmth of the loft on this cold winter morning enabled me to open up more than usual. I told her about Anthea and Hermàn, our house, my job at the library, and I even talked briefly about the progress I had made on my grandmother's poems.

"Actually," I said tentatively, "I was thinking about contacting Johanna to see if she knew anything about them."

Mom looked surprised, and asked, "Really?" then she quickly composed her voice to sound bored as she continued, "Well, good luck, darling. Do you really think she'd tell you if she knew anything?"

I scowled and said darkly, "I'll just have to make it interesting for her, won't I?"

I pushed myself off the couch and went over to the sink where I filled the stainless steel kettle with water and called over my shoulder to my mom, "Want some tea? I'm supposed to be taking care of you, right?"

She purred, "Mmmm. I like the sound of that. Tea would be lovely. So would a nap." She settled herself against the pillows and closed her eyes. When I heard her breath deepen, I poured only one cup for myself.

Ramon let himself into the apartment soon afterwards and nodded approvingly when he saw that she was sleeping.

I whispered to him, "Is it okay if I go out for a while?"

He shooed me silently towards the door and winked. I grinned, grabbed my bag and headed for the subway up to Columbia. On the train, I took out the book that had absorbed me the night before and continued reading. I learned that the Parisian women's collectives often transitioned smoothly into support networks for Resistance cells, some becoming centers of underground activity themselves. At the 116th street stop for Columbia, I emerged from my own relatively safe underground world into the cold grey afternoon, heading straight for the French Department.

When I entered the office I saw Irene, the elderly administrative assistant at the front desk, who harbored a time-honored loyalty to Johanna. I tensed involuntarily, remembering the snide tone and disapproving looks that Irene had subjected me to over the years. However, I managed to greet her politely and ask if she would give me the forwarding address for Professor Johanna Danton in Paris.

Irene looked at me suspiciously and said, "If you have something to send her, just leave it with me."

I didn't like this idea one bit and trusted Irene even less, but I had no choice. I sat in a chair in the corner and wrote out a letter on the spot.

Dear Professor Danton,

I would not presume to contact you if it were not important. When in the process of moving my father's books from his library, I discovered a manuscript of poems written by his mother, Sophia Danton. After translating the poems and completing several months of research on the historical period during which they were written, I think that these poems may contain valuable traces of a counter-history of the French Resistance movement that would be of interest to a scholar of this period. Would you happen to know anything about these poems or about Sophia Danton? Any information you have would be welcome. I look forward to hearing from you.

Respectfully yours, Herculine Danton

I folded the letter, asked Irene for an envelope, wrote out my return address and "To: Professor Johanna Danton" on the front before licking the flap shut. Irene accepted the envelope from me with as

much distaste as if it contained a deadly virus and dropped it into her "In" box.

"Um," I ventured, "How soon do you plan to mail it?"

Irene responded with an acid smile, "Don't worry, she'll get it eventually..." and then she turned her attention to her ancient computer monitor, effectively dismissing me.

Despite Irene's sour reception and the lingering worry that my letter might either be tampered with or never mailed, my heart was racing with the excitement of my decision. I knew that Johanna, as a scholar of *fin de siècle* Paris would immediately be intrigued by the poems. While I waited for a reply, I decided to get back to work on the poems and make as much progress on interpreting them as possible before I began negotiating with Johanna. She was a formidable woman and the risk I had just taken by contacting her could either turn out very well, or very badly indeed.

But first it was time to see Ben and Lucy. The poems could wait one more night.

"Hercules – whose Greek name, *Herakles*, ironically means "Glory to Hera" in honor of his greatest enemy, his father's jealous wife – was never Hera's enemy. He respected her far too much because he – more than any other mortal or god – knew the power of her wrath and the depth of her fury. Hercules knew he had to pacify Hera in order to end the strife she had caused him since birth. In many ways, it could be said that Hercules lived his life and completed his labors entirely in honor of Hera, both fulfilling his name and redeeming his father's adultery with the alluring mortal Alcemene, Hercules' mother..."

Theodore Danton, *Redefining Heroism: Reclaiming Hercules. Columbia University Press; 1968.*

Johanna
Paris, January 1990

Pale winter sunlight filtered through the cream-colored chiffon draperies still drawn against the morning's onset. Behind their gauzy suffusion, tall glass-paned doors led out to a balcony overlooking the Place des Vosges. Johanna was sitting in bed, a quilted silk duvet draped over her while she sipped a *café au lait* and read the morning paper. Delicate rimless reading glasses perched on her nose, and her short silver-blond hair glowed under her lamp. A thick white chenille robe encased her in its warmth, but the chill of the morning had not yet been subdued by the antiquated radiators in her large apartment. She pursed her lips at the thought of what it would cost to install a modern heating system in the vast duplex. No doubt it would have to be done throughout the entire building, and her neighbors could barely agree upon which contractor should be hired to fix the 18th century ornamental fountain in the courtyard that had been broken for three months. Johanna sighed. Winter in Paris was dreary this year.

She put the paper down, closed her eyes, and allowed herself the luxury of thinking back to her last winter in New York with Theo, before they knew he was dying. They would awaken each morning in their separate bedrooms, meet in the hallway and embrace fondly, then part briefly: she to her brisk morning walk along Riverside Drive, regardless of the weather; he to his daily calisthenics. When they rejoined in the kitchen an hour later for coffee and toast, they were both refreshed and eager to discuss the day ahead. Sharing the morning paper, they had also shared news of their departments at the university, as well as any research-related concerns that had arisen for either of them. After breakfast, Johanna would shower and change into her professional clothes. One wall of her closet was filled with exquisitely tailored suits in cashmere, wool crepe, and heavy silk for fall and winter. The other wall contained linen and lighter silk outfits for spring and summer. After she changed, she would call a cab and go into work. But it was never really "work." Whether spending hours researching and writing her latest article or draft of her next book, or teaching any number of her formidable seminars, Johanna's work had been her passion.

That's what is missing now, she mused, *passion*. Then she chided herself. Her retirement had simply made her lazy and depressed. It was time to get back to work, back to a passionate routine of scholarship and analytical productivity. She closed her eyes and lay back against the pillows as a wave of fatigue passed through her. That was all very fine, but there was simply nothing, no project at all that interested or inspired her. Since Theo had died, scholarship had seemed empty; academia seemed a meaningless pursuit.

Tears gathered in the corners of her eyes and she felt the familiar tightness in her throat, felt her whole body tense in resistance to the grief she knew was collecting in a deep well within her, but which would remain firmly sealed – as long as she had the power to keep it that way. "Depression was for cowards" was what she and Theo had always claimed, thinking they were safe in their shared fortress of courage and analytical strength. But ever since he was gone, she often felt afraid. The void that had been chasing her since childhood seemed to be getting nearer every day. Death in the abstract was easy to theorize about, but in reality—she now discovered—the thought of its imminence was paralyzing. She felt chagrin and regret for all the times she had accused others of cowardice during their spells of grieving or depression. She recognized the symptoms in herself now: listlessness, fatigue, indifference, despair. She wiped away the few tears that had escaped her vigilance and forced herself to get out of bed.

Just as she was pulling back the draperies, a quiet knock on the door interrupted her. Johanna said, "Entrée" and her new *domestique* entered timidly to take away the coffee tray. As the girl came in she handed Johanna the morning mail. There were quite a few letters: several invitations to give keynote addresses at various conferences in Berlin, Vienna, and Prague; a request for permission from a publisher to cite one of her books; household bills; and a letter from the French department at Columbia. Mechanically, she opened each one and either wrote out cheques or polite "decline to accept" notes. Only the publisher was given permission to quote her. Wearily, she turned to the letter from her department. What could they possibly want from her now?

But the letter itself was not from her department; only the envelope. The letter inside was handwritten in an unfamiliar script. Johanna scanned quickly to the end of the note and stopped cold. It was from the girl. Damn. She had tried so hard to forget about her,

to deny the fact of her existence. Damn her. Damn Theo. And that unspeakable actress. All of them. What the hell could she be writing about? Johanna paced the room angrily for a few minutes, then she composed herself, stood by the window, picked up the letter again and began to read. As she took in the full meaning of Herculine's note, Johanna slowly sank onto the antique chaise lounge by the window, her hand to her mouth in disbelief. The poems. The girl had found Sophia's poems. Theo had mentioned them to her years ago, but had never shown them to her. She had scoured his papers and personal effects to find them after he died and had given up, empty-handed. That girl couldn't possibly understand their significance to her father's life, to the historical era in which they were written. She couldn't have known anything about Sophia and Hercule, or could she?

Johanna felt weak with the weight of this discovery. She was filled with anger that anyone else should have those poems in their possession beside herself, but she was also pulsing with trembling excitement: they were almost, finally, hers. The girl would give them to her. She knew it. But she sensed that Herculine was also sly, so she would have to be firm, and covert. Lead her into handing them over with the promise of something she wanted. And that was easy: the girl wanted the same thing they all did. All the women Theo had left behind just wanted more of him. Some shred or trace or scent of him.

Only Johanna wanted something else too. The poems were probably the most important literary artifact of the French Resistance written by a woman, and she was confident that she was the only scholar who was in a position, both in terms of reputation and expertise, to reveal them in their true significance to the world. Not just to a dusty handful of scholars at conferences, or pale scribbling graduate students immured in library stacks in France and the U.S. These poems were of global importance. Historians, literary scholars, poets, feminists, even those self-insulating classicists would take an interest in Sophia's work. Well, if all that Theo had told her about them were true. Twelve poems re-writing the stories of twelve tragic classical heroines but also serving as coded narratives preserving the experiences of Sophia Danton's activity in the Resistance. These were stories that would contribute invaluably to the landscape of poetics and history, and Johanna was damned if that girl would stand in her way.

Standing at the window, gazing down at the street, Johanna remembered the first time she had met Herculine. She had formally summoned the girl to her office during Herculine's first week as an undergraduate at Columbia. Initially, she'd had to stifle her shock at the girl's uncanny resemblance to Theo: here was the same quizzical, guarded, intelligent face, yet softened by feminine delicacy and youthful beauty. She even had his burnished coppery curls. Johanna had noted with contempt the girl's black dungarees, pullover, shoulder bag, and leather jacket; she looked like an intellectual hoodlum who needed a haircut and a wash. Johanna sighed. That was what all her students looked like these days. She didn't know why she had thought this one would be any different. Perhaps she had thought Theo would have influenced her more, even though she must have been quite young when he died. Hopefully he'd had better luck with her mind than her comportment.

Even though Herculine had proven to be a reasonable creature by the end, Johanna had found their confrontation more difficult than she had anticipated. Her own carefully prepared speech had unraveled disgracefully, and the girl's insolent stare had not helped.

Johanna had called the girl to her office because she had a simple request to make of her: that, if asked, during her four years at Columbia, Herculine was not to admit that Theodore Danton was her father. "A distant relation" was Johanna's suggested reply to the hypothetical query, which was not entirely untrue, and besides, those who needed to know the truth already did know, and would never ask. Those who did not need to know would be the only ones who would be indiscreet enough to pry. Four years of courtesy to her in this manner would hardly be too much to ask in exchange for the past eighteen years of tolerance, was it?

"No," Herculine had said. "It's not too much to ask. You just want to keep up appearances; fine. I don't blame you. I asked Mom what she thought I should do, and she said I should just use my best judgment. I had pretty much just decided not to take any classes from you and hope for the best, but you're right. I'd rather avoid gossip and make it through this place on my own name, not his. Or yours."

And so she had. Their paths had rarely crossed over the next four years, and Johanna had done her best to keep the girl far from her mind, though a nagging memory of a conversation she'd had with Theo before he died continued to haunt her. The day of his

97

diagnosis, before he had consented to return to the hospital for tests, he had made an unexpected request.

"I'm afraid I have a favor to ask of you, my dear," he said.

She had been startled by his apologetic tone and reassured him, "Anything, darling; you know I would do anything for you..."

"Yes, well," he said, tentatively, "And I am grateful to you for that..."

At her questioning gaze, he continued, "It's about Herculine."

Johanna had felt her body stiffen and her jaw clench, hearing his illegitimate daughter's name.

He had said, in a rush of words, with an imploring gaze, "I want you to help her. To be open to her if she comes to you for help when I'm gone. No, I'm not sure exactly what kind of help – not financial assistance, certainly – but with questions, perhaps, about my life. There is so much that you know that I have still not been able to tell her. She is still too young to understand. She may never need to know. But someday, should she approach you, I beg you to receive her. That's all."

Struggling with her emotions – rage at his request, and grief at its necessity – Johanna had lifted her eyes to meet his once more and silently clasped his hand with her own, solemnly nodding her assent. When he had died, she had her lawyers contact the girl, ensuring that their paths would not meet during the aftermath of memorial services. But now Herculine had come to her for help, as Theo had predicted, and she would both fulfill her promise to him and get something she wanted out of it too.

Johanna paced the length of her room. She felt more excited and alive than she had in months. Her mind was racing. She could get on a plane to New York that afternoon. She could show up there and demand the poems from the girl, threaten a lawsuit if necessary. She could...she could... With a deep sigh, Johanna sat down heavily on her chaise and fell back against the pillows. She closed her eyes again. This time the tears flowed without restraint. She couldn't bear to go back to New York without Theo. It had been their city, and would always be.

Their marriage had been a true meeting of equals. They had been loving, and close, but never passionate. At first, they had attempted to bring sex into their intimacy, but it was awkward, unsatisfying for them both, and since Johanna was firm in her resolve not to have children, they abandoned their attempts with some relief,

98

agreeing to a union of souls and minds, rather than bodies. They were like brother and sister, healing the sense of orphaned-ness that they had both carried within them since the war.

Johanna's family, the Gottsteins, were rich German Jews, but blond and blue-eyed, and they had been assimilated into the elite social circles of Berlin for generations. When the war started, they were certain they would be immune from the pogroms; with friends in so many powerful places, they were sure to be protected. But as other Jewish girls and teachers began to disappear from the exclusive private school that her older sister attended, so did the family's powerful friends. It was only at the last possible moment before an imminent raid on the family's mansion that a loyal servant informed Johanna's father that they must flee. Reduced to impoverished refugees, the Gottsteins used the remainder of their fortune to buy the forged documents that allowed their escape. Their Aryan looks served them well one last time as they made it across the border posing as Swedes. Johanna had been only three years old at the time, but she remembered living in Switzerland during the war, then France, watching as her father slowly built up their fortune again. Despite their resilience, on a deeper level, the experience had devastated them all. Several years after their escape, Johanna herself had narrowly missed a brush with polio, and her only sister had died from the disease; soon afterwards, her parents had died too. Their deaths had crushed Johanna's heart, and until she had met Theo she had never let herself love anyone else, for fear of experiencing that level of pain again.

Over the years of their celibate partnership, Johanna assumed that Theo occasionally had affairs, so when he came to her with the news of Clea, she felt no surprise. She had even responded to his news with equanimity: it was to be expected, she said, and thanked him for informing her, requiring only that Clea not be a guest in their home upon any occasion. But two years later, when Herculine was born and Theo presented Johanna with his intention to acknowledge Clea's daughter as his legitimate heir, Johanna had been furious.

She had looked at him with pain and dignity and said, very quietly, "How vulgar," then turned and left the room. They didn't speak for months. Under a mask of icy disdain, she hid her terror that he would leave her. But soon it became apparent that he didn't want a scandal or divorce and that he continued to care for her as before, so she had resigned herself. Such arrangements, separate

bedrooms and all the discretion that went with them, were very common in France, after all.

And so she had begun her solitary travels, accepting for the first time all the offers of appearances at international conferences and symposia. A new world opened up to her in the cosmopolitan academic centers of Europe: a circle of scholars, poets, artists, and writers – as well as the rich, powerful, educated men and women who loved and supported them: gallery owners, publishers, museum trustees – the literati of the European art world. She met them at the elegant parties for book releases, art openings, auctions, and benefits for cultural causes they all believed in. These were the men and women she began to travel with, and with whom she began to allow herself to experience the first tastes of desire. For Johanna these were exciting but restless years. She felt as if she was always searching for someone or something as she circulated among her new friends and occasional lovers. She never told Theo about her adventures while she was traveling, and was certain that he had no idea of her double life.

When he told her that he was dying, she felt like she was hearing his voice from the end of a long corridor. He was finally leaving her. She had always known that he would. She retreated from him almost entirely then; attending to his every need with devotion, but shut down inside, grieving a loss decades older than his imminent death. Perhaps he had sensed her longing for family underneath the quality of her detachment from him, she wasn't sure, but when he tactfully suggested that when she inherited their home after he died, she should sell it upon her retirement and then establish herself in Paris so that she could be near Hercule, she agreed, knowing it would be both the beginning of a new life, and a reclaiming of her past.

Since she'd come back to France, feeling the void of Theo's death like a gap in the atmosphere around and inside her, she had reclaimed very little. A taste for thick *café au lait* in the morning, perhaps, and a glass of good sherry in the evening. She smiled wryly, hearing Theo's voice in her head, "Now darling, is this a life? What of the world of ideas? You must do more, while you can. For me." Well, now she could. Nothing had excited her as much in years as the possibility of working on these poems. She might not be able to bear a trip to New York, but she could strategize from Paris. Make the poems come to her. Even if that girl had to bring them herself.

Johanna wrote to Herculine immediately and rang for the *domestique*, hurrying her out to the post office to send the letter express. Once the girl was gone, Johanna walked through the spacious apartment to the room she called her office and combed through her files. Satisfied, she sat down at her desk and opened a leather-bound dossier of the papers Theo had entrusted her with after his death. One or two letters his mother had written, some of his own early poetry, and several precious photographs of him as a boy and as a young man. But the photograph she separated from the rest was not of Theo. It was of Hercule and Sophia, in a small leather frame cracking from age. She had found this photograph in Theo's desk. She knew that Hercule had given it to him before he moved back to Paris. But what she didn't know was if Theo had ever discovered its secret, as she had.

When she first found the photo, she had taken it out of its frame in order to see if the leather could be repaired. Upon removing the photograph, she had been surprised when two separate prints slid out from behind the glass, the second snugly hidden behind the first. In the top photo Hercule and Sophia were walking arm in arm, as friends or comrades would have, along a wide Parisian boulevard. In the second photograph, however, they were in full embrace. They were holding each other's faces in an intimate kiss, their bodies pressed up against each other with all the force of a desperate love. Johanna could stare at this photograph endlessly. Who had taken it? How could they have risked being seen like this? They were living in defiance of the destruction of their culture, their lives, and their love, risking everything to be together during the occupation. But one photograph like this could have destroyed everything. Sophia, of course, was married to another man the whole time. Julien Danton, the traitor and collaborator. Most likely the man who had exposed his own wife's resistance activities before she killed herself. Julien and Sophia were both dead, and Theo was too, but thankfully Hercule had survived.

Pensively, Johanna reached for the telephone and dialed a number she knew by heart. When a pleasant voice answered, "Maison de Convalesance," Johanna told the concierge of the nursing home to let the head nurse know that she would be paying a visit to Monsieur Hercule later that afternoon. Johanna hung up the phone, already planning her next move in her design to lure Herculine into giving her the poems, and smiled.

The Fourth Poem: Persephone
New York, December 1990

The winter days passed slowly, mostly in quiet comfort. My mom's recovery was steady, yet punctuated by occasional outbursts of frustration and moodiness as she adjusted to the new limitations of her body. Ramon and I learned to deflect her volatile emotions with a combination of wry humor and patience. We soon established a smooth routine of taking turns shopping for and preparing meals, escorting mom to rehab, and planning the small social gatherings that kept her spirits up. When he wasn't on duty, Ramon was either at dance classes or rehearsals, and when I had time to myself, I was at the library during the day, and with Ben and Lucy at night.

They had welcomed me back into their arms and their bed with warmth and fervor, and I sensed that they were newly inspired by my presence. They wanted to hear all about my adventures while I'd been gone, so I not only told them about Linus and Phoebe, but also about Hyla, who had stolen my heart.

It was hard to talk about her at first, but Ben's caring eyes and Lucy's soft arm around me helped me say what I hadn't yet expressed to anyone else. I was still in love with Hyla and missed her with every cell of my being. They listened avidly to the story of our few months together, and when I was finished describing the night at the Palladium Club, they were silent with compassion.

"I wouldn't have known what to do," Lucy said.

"I see what you mean by betrayal," Ben murmured. "I wouldn't have been comfortable with that lie of omission either."

"But if you still love her," Lucy mused, "You're going to have to try to fix things, right?"

"I'm not ready yet," I said, not realizing this was true until I had spoken the words. "But hopefully when I go back in January we can figure it all out."

I felt peaceful then, and relaxed back onto their pillows. I knew what I would have to do eventually, but in the meantime – as I spent my days helping my mom through her convalescence—Lucy and Ben's bed seemed like the perfect place for my own recovery.

My research on the poems was also progressing smoothly and my understanding of the confluence of political, social, and individual

forces during the occupation of France was deepening each day. Lately I had been reading books by World War II historians on the traffic of fugitives across national borders, the artwork by French painters that was exchanged for false passports and safe passage, as well as the age-old transactions of flesh for favors of every imaginable kind. Women's bodies were a valuable currency in wartime, and the greater the danger, the higher the price. Prominent French citizens had been known to marry off their daughters to German officials in exchange for safe passage out of the country for the rest of their family members. I wondered if there might be a hint of this kind of arrangement in the "Daphne" poem, and wished I knew how much of my grandmother's history was contained in its lines.

My days may have taken on an easy routine, but my nights – whether I was in Lucy and Ben's bed or my own—were often long and filled with tortured dreams. Hyla was always running, pursued, and I was never quite able to catch her or save her… Soon I turned to my old habits to keep the night's demons at bay. I went out to the clubs I used to frequent when I was in college, sometimes alone, occasionally with Lucy and Ben or a group of my mother's dancer friends after their soirées at the loft dispersed. Sweet, blonde, blue-eyed Lyra often attended these gatherings and seemed to understand that I didn't want to talk about whatever was weighing on my mind; so we'd go out dancing for hours, until our bodies glistened with sweat. One night Lyra stripped down to her small black lace brassiere on the dance floor and as soon as I saw her gleaming pale bare torso, I knew that I wanted her. Whether Lyra would help heal my grief over Hyla, or simply serve as a pleasant distraction from my pain, I didn't care. The first night I spent in Lyra's bed I slept in perfect dreamless sleep and awoke more deeply rested than I had been in weeks.

And so it went on. Days at the library, nights out dancing with Lyra and her friends, or cushioned in the comforting warmth of Ben and Lucy's arms. I felt calm, as if I was just keeping ahead of a gathering storm waiting to consume me as soon as I broke my rhythm. About two weeks into my winter refuge, I came home from the library one day to find my mom waiting for me, bright-eyed with anticipation, announcing in a teasing, sing-song voice,

"You've got a letter…" she was waving a slim blue rectangle of air mail stationery in her hand.

I dropped my bag by the door and casually went over to the stove to make some tea. "Want some?" I asked her, trying to sound nonchalant.

Her face fell with childish disappointment. She pouted, "Tea? At a time like this? Aren't you even curious who it's from?"

I smiled, then lunged onto the couch where mom was now playfully hiding the envelope under her afghan, saying, "No, no, you don't care, you don't really want it…"

I laughed and poked her, "Okay, I *do* care, I *do* want it, come on…"

She held the letter over her head, and I swiftly caught it and examined it closely: the return address was Johanna's in Paris. I tore it open in one quick motion. The envelope fell to the floor as I read:

Herculine,
I have information that would interest you. Please send me the
manuscript at once. Theodore mentioned these poems to me many years
ago. Did he tell you about Hercule?
Cordially, Johanna

Incredulous, I read through the short note several times then looked at my mother.

"So," I said, "who is Hercule?"

She closed her eyes and leaned back on the pillows with a sigh.

Concerned, I knelt on the floor by my mother's side, "What's wrong, mom? Why did the name Hercule upset you?" I took a deep breath and continued, "I need to know. Anything you can tell me. Please."

Mom turned to look at me. "I only met him once," she said. "Before you were born. Your father had known him since he was a little boy in Paris." Her eyes looked far away as she told me the story of her trip to Brooklyn with Theo almost twenty-five years earlier.

When she was finished, all I could manage to ask was, "Where was the apartment? Can you remember?"

She responded sadly, "Oh sweetheart, no…it was so long ago. And he moved back to France many years ago I think."

I sat up, asking, "What? How long ago?"

Mom looked away, murmuring, "Does it matter?"

I gripped her arm saying, "Yes, it matters. Why have you never told me about him? Why didn't you say anything when I first

104

showed you the poems? They're *dedicated* to him! He was clearly an important person in Dad's life and it's entirely possible that he's responsible for my crazy name, and…"

Mom cut me off, lifted my hand from her arm and held it tightly in her own. Then, holding my gaze steadily she responded, "Yes, he is partially responsible for your beautiful name. But your father asked me not to tell you about him, and I respected this request until now. His pain about his past and the war was something that I never questioned."

I sighed and turned away, holding my head in my hands as I sat on the floor, elbows resting on my upbent knees, my back against the soft leather sofa. I raked my fingers through my unruly hair and rubbed my temples. Once again, I felt as though I was throwing myself against the brick wall of my father's irrational secrecy.

"This changes everything," I said quietly, and turned to face my mother. "This is more important to me right now than you can even imagine. Please try to remember if there is anything else you know about him!"

But she just shook her head. "That's all, I swear. I'm sorry that I kept it from you all these years and that you think it's so important now."

I gazed at her and tried to convey the urgency of my request, "Hercule may be the key to finding out what those poems really mean. They're all framed in the symbolism and structure of the twelve labors of Hercules, and for the first time, I may have figured out *why*." I proceeded to tell my mother of all my discoveries so far.

When I was finished, mom exhaled deeply, "Honey, you're really on to something aren't you? Is it possible that your grandmother was actually involved in the Resistance?"

I looked somber, "Well, if she wasn't, she certainly knew a lot of people who were; so if Hercule was part of it too, he would probably know the stories behind the poems. Do you think he's still alive? Do you think I can find him?"

She said tightly, "I think those are questions for the Ice Queen, darling. Not me."

I paused for a moment then asked, "Have you ever been to Paris, mom?"

Visibly shifting her mood from annoyance to pleasure, she lit up at this question. "Only once with your father, before you were born, sweetheart. Why?"

"Well," I said, "You better work hard on your cardio rehab, because we may have a little adventure in store for us!" I squeezed my mom's foot beneath the afghan and said with mock formality, "And now you'll have to excuse me" – I bowed and turned to leave the room, brandishing Johanna's letter in the air – "for I have a *very* important letter to write!"

Mom leaned back against the pillows and closed her eyes; such lighthearted banter was unusual for us, and I had the feeling it was a rare treat for her. She was always trying to get closer to me, and I let her in as much as I could, but sometimes she just wanted too much. To be my friend, and not my mom. But I didn't begrudge her today; she just seemed too frail. As her breath deepened on the couch, I could imagine her visions of Paris in springtime, with my dad's warm laughter enveloping her in his familiar, protective presence, as she eased into the deep dreams of her afternoon nap. There were times that I was jealous of how much more my mom had been able to know and savor my dad, and I couldn't believe she had been keeping her meeting with Hercule a secret from me all these years. But my jealousy and surprise was muted by my concern for her health and my own building excitement over the poems.

While mom slept, I quickly composed a response to Johanna. Sending her the manuscript of the poems was out of the question. I knew better than to give her everything she asked for up front; once she had it, she could claim the discovery as her own. No…just one poem would be enough to whet her appetite and keep her wanting more. But there would have to be an equal exchange of information. Johanna had knowledge that could change the way I understood not only the poems, but my grandmother's life, and that meant more, ultimately, than any academic conquest. My letter was brief but painstakingly crafted:

Dear Johanna,
Thank you for responding to my first letter. I am glad to hear that you are interested in the poems. I am enclosing a copy of one for you now. I will send another to you if you will answer a few questions for me. I only know a little bit about Hercule but would like to know more. Who was he? What was his connection to my grandmother and my father? Is he still alive? Please tell me all you know.
Respectfully, Herculine

The question now was, which poem should I send? I took out my translation notebook and shuffled through the pages. The first three poems already seemed so deeply inscribed with my own personal significance that I couldn't bear to submit one of them to Johanna's scrutiny. The next poem in the sequence, however, the one entitled "Persephone," seemed like a good choice. I hadn't read it through since my first pass at the translations several months earlier. I remembered that there was a word in it that had tripped me up and I was curious to see if its meaning, then inscrutable, was any easier to grasp now. I read over it again:

I sat and watched the raging beast
Lay waste to the lands above:
Agent of my mother's wrath,
Her vengeance for the broken bargain
She struck with my cruel husband.
Lord of death and sorrow:
He owned me, and she is free.
He promised her I would visit,
But I never did.
My wedding gown stained with blood:
Deep pomegranate red.
It was winter in my heart all year long,
And she, who sold me into darkness,
Is now alone and raging,
Though she is safe, and far away,
In the land of the sun.
In her fury, she sent this beast:
Le Sanglier, the bloody one.
She said she'd rather have me dead
Than imprisoned here in hell.
But I think she is afraid
Of the story I might tell.
Before he could kill me,
You saved me.
We trapped him together
On a winter's night.
My snowdrifts chilled his flesh,
My icicles pierced his breast.
You wrestled him to the ground:
red blood stained the white snow.

107

You freed me then,
Brought me back to summer,
And in doing so, you gave me Life.

"Le Sanglier." That was it: I remembered now. Literally, it was the French word for a wild boar, which made perfect sense since this was the fourth poem and the fourth labor of Hercules was to capture the Erymanthian Boar that was destroying the land around the King's realm. The boar had been sent by Hera, the queen of the gods, who was still nursing her old grudge against Hercules. The boar was huge and vicious and almost killed Hercules, but, thanks to the advice of a wise centaur, he finally trapped it in a snow bank and was able to subdue it. "Red blood stained the white snow" indeed. Unfortunately, this was also an image that was all too common in WWII. The sight of bloodstained snow during wartime usually signified impromptu Nazi executions of Jews and those who hid them in the long, hungry winters. But in this instance, Sophia Danton seemed to imply that at least once the blood that had been shed was that of the enemy. But who was "Le Sanglier"? He seemed like a mercenary figure, a hired gun without loyalties to either side. Still, was sending an assassin to murder one's daughter the best solution to the unwanted marriage between this modern version of Persephone and Hades?

The twist Sophia had added to the traditional Persephone myth was disturbing: here it was Persephone's mother – the Demeter figure – who had sold her daughter off to enable her own escape to "the land of the sun" (a far cry from the perpetual "winter" of wartime Vichy France) as opposed to the raging goddess of classical myth who grieved her daughter's abduction by the Lord of the underworld. I mused over the appalling nature of this betrayal: a mother trading her daughter's body for her own freedom. I knew that war forced people to make terrible decisions, but the poem led me to believe that this modern Ceres felt more anger than regret about her bargain. Had she really wanted "Le Sanglier" to murder her own daughter because of incriminating evidence? What exactly had gone wrong with the bargain with her daughter's husband? Hadn't the Ceres figure in the poem realized that she would never see her daughter again?

My questions about the poem had to do with the unnamed "you" to whom the poem was addressed. Like the "Daphne" poem, this male protector/savior figure who was symbolically cast in the

role of Hercules seemed to be an increasingly likely candidate for the mysterious Hercule himself. And, as in the "Daphne" poem, "Persephone" also represented a triangulated power struggle between two men and a woman. Each time, Hercule(s) rescued the heroine from the man who oppressed her. But in this poem the relationship between the heroine and her savior was more explicit: they worked together to kill "Le Sanglier," and then he not only released her from the prison of her marriage, he also gave her "Life." I couldn't help but wonder about the nature of my grandmother's relationship to Hercule, and to her own husband, who – after all, had been a Vichy official.

I copied out the "Persephone" poem and added a postscript to my letter to Johanna: "*p.s. I'm also curious about Sophia Danton's husband, my grandfather. What was his involvement with Vichy? Is he alive? Again, please tell me all you know.*" In all of my conversations with my father, he had never mentioned his own father. When I had asked him once when I was very young, he had smiled sadly and told me that he didn't remember his father. He had stayed behind in Paris while my dad had been smuggled out as a little boy. I had thought this was unbearably sad at the time, but now I had a strong hunch that there was more to the shadowy figure of my grandfather than my father had been willing to tell me.

Feeling elated from my progress on the poems, as soon as I heard Ramon return from his errands I grabbed my coat and ran out the door in the hopes of making it to the post office before it closed. I got there just in time. So it was with a more carefree lilt in my step and uncharacteristically conversational charm that I picked up Lyra at the dance studio across town. Usually we just met up at a club or at her apartment, and sex had been our dominant form of communication.

"Hungry?" I asked her, leaning against the doorway of the women's dressing room.

"Really?" asked Lyra, bewildered: "You mean we might actually talk and eat and do normal stuff for a change?"

I grabbed her around her slender waist, pulled her close, and whispered in her ear with mock bravado, "*Normal* stuff? Oh honey, it'll never be normal when you're with *me*…"

Lyra looked startled and delighted, blushed deeply, and said, "Okay, um, cool…let's go get some crepes at this place I like around the corner!"

I spun Lyra around with one hand and exclaimed with pleasure in my best French, "*Crepes? Parfait! La cuisine de la belle France: c'est exactement mon gout preferable ce soir!*"

"Huh?" said Lyra, but I just laughed as we went off into the night. I wasn't in love with Lyra, but she had been generous and undemanding with me and my moody needs for a few weeks now. A whole new intimacy seemed to open up between us that night, and the next morning, when we parted ways it was with affection and warmth.

Later that afternoon, after hours of research at the University library, I returned to my mom's loft empty-handed and discouraged. I had tried every database I could think of, had scoured countless lists of code names for agents in World War II, and checked the indexes of at least twenty books on Vichy France without turning up a single reference to wild boars or "Le Sanglier."

My mom was standing in the kitchen and noticed my glum mood immediately. She offered me a glass of wine and said, "Cheer up, Herculine. It can't be that bad, can it? I hear that you and young Lyra are having quite a good time…"

I rolled my eyes upon hearing that I was now a gossip topic among my mother's friends. I had known that it was only a matter of time, but even so, the news caused me to cringe. I preferred that my mother know as little about my private life as possible. But I still accepted the glass of wine.

Mom continued, "Well, this should lift your spirits anyway…" She gestured towards a medium-sized box by the door, "It arrived a few hours ago."

I put down my glass, walked back over to the door, picked up the box and saw that it was from Anthea. Puzzled, I sat down and opened the package. Inside was a small padded mailing envelope with a Mexican postmark containing a videotape with a letter taped to it; there was also an object that seemed like a large record album, hastily wrapped in brown paper. A note fluttered to the floor when I removed these two items. It was from Anthea:

> *Hey chica,*
> *These arrived for you a few days ago. The big one was just left on the porch. I guess some people don't know you're out of town? Anyway, I hope your mom's doing better and that you're having a good time in the big city. Drop us a line sometime, we miss you.*
> *Anthea and…*

There was a kiss from Hermàn imprinted with gold glitter lip-gloss at the bottom of the note. Well, *besos* back to him, I thought. Ignoring my mother's watchful gaze, I opened the videotape first. When I saw the title and the director's name, I caught my breath: *Muses on the Margins: Women Artists Living on the Edges of Life, a film by Hyla Alexander*. It was Hyla's project. I wondered how long ago Hyla had finished it, and with unsteady hands, I opened the letter. It was the first time that I had seen Hyla's bold, angular handwriting. She wrote,

Herculine,

I feel badly about the way we parted. I knew you wouldn't understand my work, but maybe I didn't want to know. It's been a hard month, and I've missed you. I quit the café so I could finish my project and submit the tape to the Berkeley independent film festival, then I just had to get out of town for a while. I've been crashing with my brother in Mexico for a few weeks. I wanted you to see the tape, since you inspired me more than you knew. I hope to be back in time for spring semester; so if you want to see me then, you know where to find me.

Hyla

I read the letter over several times, tracing the lines of Hyla's pen strokes until the words lost their meaning. I took the tape over to my mother's VCR and for the first time, looked over at my mom, who was staring at me with an expression of concern.

"Um, I have a friend who's a film-maker," I said. "Do you mind if we watch her most recent project?"

She murmured, "Of course not, sweetheart. What's it about?"

"I'm not sure," I hedged, inserting the tape and moving back towards the couch, "Women artists living on the edge of society or something." I sat on the floor, leaning up against the couch where mom was reclining, and started the tape.

We watched in silence as the silhouetted figure of a female dancer filled the screen accompanied by haunting instrumental music – which I immediately recognized as another one of Linus' compositions. The light shifted and the dancer was revealed to be almost nude, on a small stage in an empty theater, body oiled, wearing only a black g-string. Even from the back, I knew it was

111

Hyla. As the title appeared over the image of her body, the dancer turned to face the camera, froze, and with the help of computer generated animation, she slowly turned to stone. I watched, rapt, as two tears trickled down the face of the statue of my lover.

Mom commented casually, "Beautiful girl…"

"That's my friend," I whispered, but the image on the screen had now shifted to a swirling mosaic of shattered mirrors, multicolored tiles, glass, and found objects, with lines of poetry embedded within the shifting patterns. The camera panned back to reveal a wall in an alley adjacent to a deserted lot on a city street upon which the mosaic had been installed. Several women artists sat on the sidewalk discussing their work. They said that they used only objects that they found in dumpsters, often smashing the pieces themselves, and they relied on acquaintances in the construction business to provide them with spare bags of the cement they used as mortar.

One woman said proudly, "We've been working on this wall for a year, and all kinds of folks come down to take pictures and ask us what it's all about."

Another woman added, "We tell them, 'This is our lives: broken dreams.'"

As the camera panned back to show a nearby burned out tenement building, the first woman continued speaking in a voice-over, "Yeah, we been living there for a few months now. It was hard when I was on my own on the streets but now with the three of us, it's better."

As the voices of the other women agreed with her, the scene changed again to a female chamber music trio playing on battered instruments in a dilapidated church basement while infants wailed in the background, and then again to a group of women in a park putting on a play and passing a hat for donations. Then there was an elderly woman singing the blues on a street corner for money, young female painters and sculptors working on their art in abandoned warehouses, a sidewalk saxophonista in fishnet stockings, bus station poets, graffiti artists, and of course, exotic dancers. Each woman said a few words about her art and her life on the streets, and then the camera moved on.

I looked at my mom – she was as absorbed as I was. The women's faces, voices, and the art they produced entirely on the margins of the city in which they lived, San Francisco – ironically, a bastion of arts endowment, wealth both old and new, and liberal

homeless policies – were mesmerizing. Each woman was barely scratching out an existence, yet willingly trading food stamps for art supplies or instruments, gladly forgoing meals for the sake of their art. Sex work, drug habits, physical abuse, and crime wove their way through many of the narratives, as did illness, mental health issues, and religion. There were pregnancies and abortions, pimps and boyfriends both good and bad, distant family relations, regrets, fears, and even some dreams that were still intact. Each woman's story seemed to hold up a mirror to me as I watched, driving home the uncomfortable truth of how fine the line was between their lives on the edge and those like my own which were cushioned in the comfortable viewing chairs of material privilege.

The film ended with a reprise of Linus' music and as I watched, the statue of Hyla began to re-animate and move again, superimposed over a montage of all the images of art showcased in the film, dancing until she turned back into a silhouette and froze against the swirling mosaic of mirrors and tiles. Embedded in the wall directly above her head was a handwritten dedication– written in what I now realized was Hyla's own hand: "For all the women whose voices are never heard. And for the one who helped me hear them." Tears ran down my face, and I wiped them away before I turned to face my mother, as the haunting strains of Linus's music faded out along with the image on the screen.

Mom asked gently, "Sweetheart, is everything okay with you and your friend?" I just shook my head and looked down. She said, "Well, should we show her work to some of my friends in the art film industry?"

I looked up, hopeful. "Oh Mom...would you?"

Clearly glad to be able to offer me some comfort, my mom beamed with benevolence. She said, "Of course I would, darling. We'll make a few copies and pass them around to all the right people. Something good is bound to come of it."

"Thank you so much," I murmured, and nuzzled my face into her shoulder before grabbing the other package from Anthea's box and heading off to my room. "I think I'll open this one on my own," I said, then added with a smile. "That one was enough drama to inflict on you for now."

My mom laughed; her whole life was filled with drama – by choice. I was the one who tried to avoid it, and she was evidently amused by the sight of me trying to cope with it now.

I climbed the stairs to my room. Unlike the rest of the apartment, the ceilings here were low and the room had both a skylight and a large arched window taking up one full wall. My futon was on the floor and a small heater filled the room with warmth and an amber light. I flung myself down on the bed and opened the letter attached to the hastily wrapped package:

> *Dear Herculine,*
> *I know you feel like your heart is broken, but I have the feeling it's not over yet. Don't give up.*
> *Love, Phoebe*

I tore open the slim rectangular package: it was an oil pastel portrait of Hyla. She was pictured dancing just like the night we saw her at the club, complete with mirrored reflections and the silvery green sheen on her skin. It was a skillful drawing, but why had she sent it? Why did she want to remind me of that awful night?

I lay back on my bed, exhausted from the sudden rush of unwanted memory and stared at the portrait of Hyla. If there had been a way to call her, I would have, but she was somewhere in Mexico, and I didn't know how to reach her. I felt my wounded pride and confusion give way to a flood of protectiveness and concern, and –I had to admit, traces of forgiveness that I knew would help me heal my heart. I propped the drawing up against the wall facing my bed and as I rested against the pillows and closed my eyes, I let my mind wander, imagining what Mexico must be like…warm breeze, hot sun, long white sandy beaches, beautiful blue ocean, thick green leafy rain forests, low sun-baked stucco houses with tiled roofs…but I had never been there. Where was Hyla now? The line from the "Persephone" poem, *the land of the sun*, seemed to fit all too perfectly – Mexico was a beautiful refuge and exile indeed.

I wrenched my thoughts away from Hyla and back to the "Persephone" poem. I had just realized why the scenario it narrated was even more tragic than the original story. At least the mythical Persephone could live in the land of the sun with her mother for half the year. The modern heroine in the poem, however, was trapped in a wintry underworld of an arranged marriage without possibility of release or escape. But why would her mother want her dead? What was the incriminating story her daughter could tell about her? And why would she ever betray her mother? In vengeance for selling her into a marriage that guaranteed her mother's escape from Vichy

France? Which side had her mother been on: was she collaborating with the Germans? If this was the information her daughter had, was it really worth killing her once she was safe outside the country?

In a flash, I had an inspiration. I ran down to the bookshelves holding my father's books and found an English to German dictionary. The fourth labor of Hercules, capturing the Erymanthian boar, might hold some clues in translation. I looked up "boar" in the dictionary and was greeted with two translation options: first, the linguistically obvious "wildschwein," and then the more cryptic "eber." There was something about this second term that felt familiar somehow, and it sent me back over to my pile of library books by the couch. Towards the bottom of the pile was a book called *Freedom at Any Cost: Currencies of Exchange in Vichy France*. I quickly turned to the page where I had noted a passage earlier in the week. Subjects were indexed in short paragraphs: Art collectors, Art dealers, Art galleries, Artists…and Auction houses. I turned to the page and read over the section I had marked in my notes:

Of the many auction houses that accepted art works confiscated from the homes of deported Jews, the house of Ebermann and Demetrius profited the most from the largest number of sales. The house was closed down after the war, due to the charges of collaboration with German SS officers during the Vichy regime who relied on local citizens for information for their raids. It is thought that the house of Ebermann and Demetrius assisted the SS by targeting the Jewish families who possessed the most valuable art collections in the city, which they would then auction to Austrian buyers.

This was the passage I had read, and had marked for its relevance to the Vichy era, but I hadn't realized its full significance at the time. Just to be sure, I turned back in my notes to my photocopy of my grandmother's obituary:

Sophia Danton, wife of Julien Danton, respected Vichy government official. Cause of death: suicide. Mme. Danton was suspected of politically subversive activities and anti-Vichy actions. Mme. Danton, née Demetrius, the daughter of Céline Demetrius, formerly of the reputable auction house of Ebermann and Demetrius, dissolved in 1942 due to the untimely death of M. Ebermann and the emigration of Mme. Demetrius in 1936.

Of course. I'd had had the answer all along. Sophia's mother was Céline Demetrius, the same Demetrius affiliated with the

unscrupulous auction house. This revelation was an unwelcome surprise, but it still paled in relation to the shock of reading Sophia's obituary again. I still couldn't believe it. What could have caused her to kill herself? Had my father known? I pushed the book away, frustrated once more by my father's secrecy. Why hadn't he told me or my mom any of this? Why hadn't he trusted us? Darkly I turned my concentration back to the rest of the obituary. What was that about Sophia's mother "emigrating"? Was there any way to find out where she went? And this Monsieur Ebermann, the auction house owner whose name translated to "boar man," could have easily been "Le Sanglier," someone feared by Jews and Gentiles alike – a man who preyed on his community and literally laid it to waste as he siphoned off its citizens and cultural treasures to the concentration camps and Austrian museums respectively. I had to find out more about him too.

I grabbed my coat and quickly scrawled a note to my mom: "I'll be back in a few hours!" Twenty minutes later, a cab dropped me off in front of the Columbia library and I headed straight down to the microfilm archives. If Céline Demetrius had left the country in 1936, perhaps there would be some mention of it in the art section of *Le Monde*? I requested the microfiche rolls from 1936 and began to scan patiently through the tiny print, looking for the capital letter D, hoping for an "arts section" where an announcement of change of management might have been placed. There was no arts section, and no mention of such a change anywhere in the advertising pages...After an hour, I began to give up. But then I found a weekend edition travel section with what would have been called a "celebrity gossip column" section, and there – in mid-February of 1936 – I saw that Céline Demetrius, accompanied by a host of other art world luminaries, had taken a cruise to the Gulf of Mexico.

Was Mexico in fact the "land of sun" where Persephone's mother in the poem, and Sophia Danton's mother in reality, had gone? Could she still be alive? She would be very old, but there was a chance. I left the microfiche booth and ran upstairs to the reference desk where I was directed to shelves of international phone books. Mexico was in several volumes, in Spanish, and far too vast for me to browse through. I found a small atlas and made a photocopy of the page where the Gulf of Mexico trailed off into the tip of Cancun. The cruise from Paris must have only taken a few weeks. But as far as I knew, Céline Demetrius had no plans to return.

I knew there were phone booths down the hallway and I let myself into one of them: a small, wood paneled, dimly lit cabinet, with a small wooden seat built into the wall. I dialed the operator, gave her my calling card number, and asked for directory assistance in Mexico. After what seemed like an endless series of clicks, buzzes, and recorded messages, I was prompted by a Spanish voice on the line that reluctantly switched to broken English when I inquired for the number of Céline Demetrius in Cancun.

The operator hesitated, then said, "You mean Demetrius-Odessa Enterprises in Cancun?"

"What?" I asked.

The operator repeated the name.

"Uh, yes," I stammered, "Please."

"Sorry, that number is unlisted."

There was a click and a dial tone. I sat in the phone booth, my mouth dry with disappointment. I had been so close. What now? I walked slowly back to the library's computer terminals and did a search on "Demetrius-Odessa Enterprises." The firm was listed in several business journals from the 1950s, and I tracked them down in an area of the library that held archives of periodicals. The business was predictably an Import/Export firm, vague enough to serve as a cover for any number of "enterprises." Whether it was still functioning was unclear. Somehow I would find out. And in the meantime, who was Odessa? What had happened to Ebermann? These questions would have to wait. I had a date with Ben and Lucy and didn't want to be late.

As I walked back out into the wintry night, I mused on the irony of my discovery: like Persephone, I not only felt caught between the two coasts of my life in both New York and Berkeley, but now Paris and Mexico seemed like diametrically opposed worlds of dark and light, and both were currently harboring women – Johanna, Hyla, and now possibly Céline Demetrius – who had something I needed.

The last week of my time in New York passed quickly. My mom was almost fully recuperated, and – after consulting with me – she had invited Ramon to move in with her. I was actually happy for my mother, and grateful to Ramon for staying by her side; I felt like I could leave her confidently in his care, and as the day of my departure approached, I realized I would even miss the easy camaraderie that the three of us had developed over the past month. After my breakthrough with the "Persephone" poem, I had put my

117

research aside and concentrated on getting Hyla's tape duplicated and distributed to several of my mother's friends, spending time with Lucy and Ben, and trying to extricate myself gracefully from Lyra, who had lately grown sulky, knowing that I would be leaving within days.

Due to this last entanglement, it was with more relief than I liked to admit that I boarded my plane back to California. A whole new semester was awaiting me, and I was anxious to see if Hyla was back in town as well. Anthea, Hermàn and Linus greeted me at the Oakland airport with a red balloon. I grinned as they hugged me and I relaxed into the refreshing waves of their light laughter as we drove home in the rain in Linus's car. Anthea probed me for details about my mom's health, Hermàn wanted all the dish about my "New York night life," but Linus just rested his hand on my thigh quietly as he drove us all home. His touch was distracting, welcoming, and held the promise of more.

Hermàn whined, "Hey chica, next time you go to New York, you better bring me too!"

I laughed, thinking of how much Hermàn would love my mother's friends, and said "Sure, you can all come! We'll party for a week!"

Anthea and Hermàn exchanged looks and raised eyebrows, but Linus just chuckled. Anthea said, "Honey, did they give you some happy drugs on the plane or something? What's up with all this new party girl stuff?"

I smiled to myself and gazed out the window as the lights of Berkeley came into view. "I'm just glad to be back," I said quietly.

Hermàn said, "So, is Hyla back on the menu?"

This time I did not answer. I looked at Linus and he smiled back at me encouragingly. He knew I was hoping that there was more than a menu waiting for me …I wanted a whole restaurant of Hyla, with maybe some Linus and Phoebe on the side.

But first, I needed sleep. After a celebratory glass of wine in our festive kitchen, which was decorated with colored lights and streamers to welcome me home, I led Linus upstairs to my room, layers of fatigue and jet lag weighing me down. All I wanted was to be back in the familiar smells and textures of my own bed. Before I could collapse into Linus's patiently waiting arms, however, I saw a blue airmail envelope marked "Express" waiting for me on my desk. My heart raced as I tore it open. Inside was a note from Johanna containing only two lines: *Hercule is alive and in Paris. Send another poem.*

118

The Fifth Poem: Echo
Berkeley, January 1990

Second semester started too soon for the first time in my life. Usually I was impatient for the beginning of classes, but this winter I would have liked a little more time to settle in and adjust to my life in Berkeley before I plunged back into my studies. Like Persephone, I felt as if I had left half of my soul back in New York and had to recover the other half I had stored in California while I was away. I knew that I had to reconcile and integrate my two worlds soon or the split within me would make it difficult to live in either one.

I had only been back in town for one jet-lagged day, and despite all my best efforts, I had been unable to track down any news of Hyla, whose housemates were still subletting her room and forwarding all her mail to a general delivery address in Mexico. At least they gave me the address. At the café where Hyla used to work, there was no word of her at all. Her "friends" at the video editing studio were too wrapped up in their own anxiety over their entries in the Berkeley film festival to care what had become of her, and when I finally worked up the courage to visit the Palladium Club, the bouncer wouldn't even talk to me.

Discouraged and rain-sodden, I trudged home from the BART station after my unsuccessful trip to San Francisco, but I was cheered to see the kitchen light on when I walked up the path to my house. Hermàn and Anthea were sitting at the kitchen table with Linus and several other friends, wine was flowing, and warm laughter filtered through the Cuban music playing on the stereo in the living room. I peeled off my wet jacket, and after a quick change upstairs into some dry jeans and a t-shirt, I joined the group at the table that welcomed me with a toast: "To the return of the scholar! Let the semester begin!"

I groaned, sat down next to Linus, and said, "Pour me a glass of whatever you've got that will stop time, will you?"

Anthea looked at me questioningly, "Girl? What's with you? I thought you couldn't wait to get into that feminist poetics course and the second half of that Greek whatever seminar that you were so crazy about last term!"

119

I slumped in my chair, all eyes upon me. "Yeah, yeah, I know," I said glumly, then felt myself blush as I chafed under my reputation as the "studious" member of the household. Linus put a comforting hand on my thigh, and I relaxed for the first time that day. Once the conversation had turned away from me and I finished my glass of wine, Linus and I slipped upstairs together to be alone.

He brought his guitar with him and we sat together on my bed, legs touching, as he played for me, and I lost myself in the dreamy rhythmical chord patterns of his music. The song was still weaving through my head after he stopped playing and pulled me close to him. Immediately aroused by Linus' graceful, wiry strength, I backed him gently up against the wall next to my bed, kneeling over him, holding his wrists above his head with one hand, as I pulled his t-shirt off with the other.

For a moment, I flashed back to another night, in a similar position, but the body beneath me had been Hyla's. As this image seared through my memory, I felt a sharp pang in my heart, and it was clear that Linus sensed this too as I released his wrists and sank my head down on his shoulder. He kissed my cheeks and neck, murmuring, "Hey…it's okay, it's okay…you'll find her."

I slowly relaxed as Linus undressed me, and I gave myself over to a singular concentration that I had not allowed myself with him before. All too soon we were resting quietly in each other's arms.

After a moment, I asked, "So, when is Phoebe coming back?"

"Probably not until the end of the semester," Linus murmured. "She's doing some research at UCLA, but sends her love…"

"So," I said, "it's just you and me, for a while, huh?"

Linus smiled, "Looks that way… Can you handle it?"

I nodded and said solemnly, "I can handle it. But there's something you should know."

Linus looked worried for a minute, but I smiled, and said, "No, nothing about you. There's this project I'm working on that takes up a lot of my time and sometimes I get really obsessed by it…" Then I told him about the poems.

When I was done, Linus let out a low whistle. "Damn. You've got your hands full, don't you?"

I sat up, pulled a blanket around me, and stared pensively out the window. "Yeah," I said, "And school is starting, and I don't know where Hyla is, and Johanna is messing with my head, and my mom is still recovering, and…"

120

Linus pulled me back down into bed and spooned me protectively, "Shhhhh," he said. "It'll all be okay. You can't do all twelve labors in one day, Herculine. Give yourself some time." He kissed the curls on the back of my neck and I smiled, snuggling back into his arms and feeling safer than I had since the morning back in November when I had almost told Hyla that I loved her. My sleep that night was deep, and dreamless.

The next day Linus and I walked to class together. We were both continuing the second half of Seidon's Archaic Poetry seminar. As the rest of the class rustled their notebooks and took out their texts, I was distracted by Linus' closeness to me and by the echoes of his music still in my head. I thought of Orpheus, who could make rocks move and animals weep with his music, who could even tame the winds and raise the dead when he sang and played the lyre. I felt like one of those stormy winds, or inert rocks that Linus was now taming with his art, and his touch. It was no wonder that Apollo, god of music, was also god of the healing arts. There was something restorative about Linus' music that had always calmed me. I resolved, as I shook myself out of my reverie and quickly opened my textbook, that I would resume my guitar lessons with him as soon as possible.

Our class seemed more rigorous this semester; Seidon expected our sight translations to be faster and more precise, becoming increasingly impatient when anybody hesitated or stumbled. He assigned twice as much work for us to complete before the next class, and my sense that the semester was beginning too soon was compounded by the weight of our homework. I heaved my book bag onto my shoulder when the class was over and groaned softly as Linus and I left the room.

As soon as we turned a corner, he pulled me close and whispered in my ear with a little bite on the lobe for emphasis, "You were brilliant in class today…will I see you later?"

Head spinning momentarily, my book bag dropped to the floor, and I pulled his hips up against mine. "Yes," I said, kissing him softly on his neck, "Yes, definitely. And hey – " He looked at me inquiringly, and I kissed him on the lips before I continued, "Bring your guitar tonight too."

He smiled and hugged me close before heading off to his next class. Turning in the other direction, I hoisted my bag onto my shoulder once more and walked briskly over to the library. As I strode through the thick glass doors, I hailed Joyce with a jaunty wink and a grin, and was soon immersed in the smoothly running system

of the library's vast machinery as seamlessly as if I had never left. Hours later, softly humming the haunting song that Linus had played for me the night before, I felt that I had come home on yet another level: the library was as much a haven and refuge for me as my own room.

I hummed to myself happily as I shelved books and entered new shipments of books into our computer system for several hours, and hardly noticed the time passing. When my work shift was over, I felt filled with energy and stayed in the library for another hour while I completed my translation assignment with ease. As a reward for my labors, in the remaining hour before Linus was due to come over, I took out my notebook containing my translations of my grandmother's poems, and the note from Johanna. So Hercule was alive and in Paris. The thought was dizzying in its significance. How old would he be now? Was he lucid, would he remember everything I wanted to hear from him about my father and my grandmother's life? For an instant I rashly imagined buying a ticket to Paris and missing the first week of classes just to find him and talk with him. My heart pounded with excitement for a few moments but then I remembered that the sentinel at the gate to Hercule was Johanna, and it was time to send her another poem. I sighed and leafed through the notebook to the fifth poem, called "Echo," and read it aloud.

I used to live
Where two rivers met.
The current was swift
And deadly:
Like two armies,
Poised for battle.
I lived in fear
Of flood.
Only the sight of him
Soothed me.
I waited every day.
I watched him gaze with ardor
Not at me, but at himself.
He couldn't see me.
But he could hear me,
So I whispered to him of my love.
I made him think his lover in the river
loved him too.

122

But it was only me.
Drowning in swift,
self-annihilating
Waves of desire,
I waited each day,
Almost wasted away.
Until I called to you,
And you forced the two rivers together.
The currents raged, foamed,
Overflowed the banks.
Lost in his own reflection,
He drowned in the flood
That washed the King's filth
From the stables
And the salt from my eyes.
You saw me then, as he never did,
And we ran together
To where the King's horses –
Freed from their squalor –
Waited for us on high, dry ground.
We rode to safety,
Far from the raging bloody tide
And days of whispering fear.
Now I speak out loud
And you see me
Clear and true,
Right by your side.

I shivered at the end of the poem. Echo had always seemed to be one of the most pathetic characters in Greek mythology. Once a lovely water nymph, but self-abnegating to a fault, Echo was reduced to a mere invisible shadow of a voice after wasting away for the vain young Narcissus, who could only love his own reflection in her river. But Sophia had changed all that. By intersecting Echo's sad tale with the fifth labor of Hercules – cleaning King Augeus' stables by redirecting two rivers to wash them out – she had created a new story for Echo that, granted, did not reach the same heights that some of her other poetic redemptions had, but many of the themes were the same. A trapped, potentially tragic female figure saved by a Herculean hero who, along with his strength and ingenuity, offers the heroine a level of validation and freedom that had not previously

been available to her. This Echo lives, while Narcissus drowns, and she rides to safety on a newly liberated horse, finally visible and speaking out loud – all symbols of power for women who could never take such liberties for granted. But what on earth did this have to do with the French Resistance?

I mused: the image in the poem of two rivers like two armies, forced together to clean out the stables of the King was enigmatic and compelling. The only two armies I could think of in Sophia's world were the Germans and the Allies. Could they have ever joined forces to fight an even greater source of oppression? If so, what shared enemy could that have been? It was unlikely, but I made a note to investigate this possibility. I knew there was more to this poem than I could see at the moment, so Johanna would just have to wait until I was ready to send it to her. After my work shift the next day, I would do some research on military strategy during the Vichy period and if that didn't yield anything, I'd even look up tidal patterns of the Seine. I was beginning to understand how my grandmother's mind worked. Sometimes the literal meaning was the most symbolic of all.

The first few days of the semester dragged on, leavened only by the occasional playful banter with Hermàn and Anthea and visits from Linus at night. In between my shifts at the library, classes, and homework, I somehow found time to practice the guitar and was working on a chord pattern based around E minor seven to which I would occasionally try singing the "Echo" poem. Maybe it was just Linus' influence, but this poem seemed more musical to me than the rest. And it was soothing for me to do something creative with it, since my research hadn't yielded any leads yet, and I didn't know what to say to Johanna in the meantime.

I read about the military maneuvers of the Vichy regime, and not once was there a mention of the German army joining ranks with any other force to fight together. Nor was there anything unusual about the Seine's tidal patterns during those years. Only dead ends everywhere I looked. After a weekend of writing a paper for my Feminist Poetics seminar, the "Echo" poem looked more like a coded narrative of resistance against the patriarchal commodification of the female body than anything else. I sighed. Why had my grandmother chosen Echo at all? She could have written about Medea or Antigone, or any number of other *real* tragic heroines. Why pathetic little Echo? Was it just because the fifth labor of Hercules had to do with rivers and Echo was a river nymph? Too easy, but

124

still…if she was a river nymph who "lived where two rivers met" maybe she was also in some way a member of both armies?

I went over to her bookshelf and looked at the books I had found on female double agents back in the fall semester. I pored over the titles again…*Torn Between Two Lovers: Collaboration and Espionage in World War Two; Both Sides Now: Female Strategies of Subversion in Vichy France*; and then one caught my eye and held it, *Meeting of Two Rivers: the Other French Underground*. I took all three books off the shelf but started with the last. This historian had evidence that there had actually been two Resistance movements in France during the occupation, one that was engaged in espionage and rescue missions, and another, more militantly radical faction called *Le Maquis* that took care of assassinations and sabotage missions involving explosives. There were often agents who worked with both of these branches of resistance activity, but rarely were they women. And even if individuals were involved in collaborative assignments, never had the combined forces of these two groups fought together en masse against the Germans. Or at least this historian had no evidence of such an event. But I was curious.

I went back to the first of the three books I had selected, and was intrigued to find out that the number of double agents was so high during the occupation that paranoia was severe and security measures were often known to reach absurd heights. Code names were hidden within encrypted missives, themselves encoded in Breton anagrams, using the linguistic irregularities of this obscure French dialect as one more veil of secrecy. There were many bloody purges of suspected double agents on both sides of the occupation: some even said that the Resistance purges were more ruthless than those of Vichy. I thought grimly of *Le Maquis*, the more radical resistance faction, and the level of brutality on which they operated as a rule. As my eyes skimmed through the chapters, I kept hoping I'd find an instance of outright battle between the underground and the Vichy forces, but it seemed that the first historian was right.

Then I read the chapter called "Red River: The Failed Espionage Armistice." In 1941 anxiety over double agents had reached such a fever pitch that the secret service wing of the Vichy government had called for a covert day of "Espionage Armistice": a day declared a "free zone" for spies to leave their posts in the opposition and escape back to the camp that held their true loyalty without repercussion or retribution. An idealistic notion and a desperate measure to be sure. Predictably enough, the day turned into

125

a massacre. As one eye-witness attested, parts of the Seine had turned red due to all of the dead bodies of spies suspected of betrayal who were shot then thrown over the bridges.

In a way, I could see that this was like a meeting of two rivers, battling against their own corruption, but then – to follow with the analogy in the poem – who was the King with the filthy stables and liberated horses? I turned to a reference book nearby that listed all of the officials in the Vichy regime and specifically looked for officers associated with the cavalry. My hunch paid off: I recognized a name from the list immediately – General Arnault. It had been this man who had called the "Armistice." He had been killed in its aftermath after agents exposed him as running a veritable "stable" of spies whom he had blackmailed to undertake their life-threatening missions. Ironically, he had been drowned in the very river that was running red from the blood of many of his own agents.

I paused. If "Echo," whoever she was, had been on the inside of this experience, someone who had known General Arnault but who had never been acknowledged by him, then what was her relationship to the Hercules figure who saved her? And if it had been Arnault who had called for the "Armistice," then was it Hercule himself who had yoked the two resistance rivers together? My mind reeled. Unless, of course, the massacre had been part of Arnault's plan from the beginning, and it was Hercule who harnessed the forces of both sides of the Resistance to undermine it. That way, he could make sure that as many of their own agents would survive the mêlée as possible.

I turned off my reading lamp, curled up in my dad's old leather chair, and leaned my head back against its broad, high leather padding. I stared with an unfocused gaze out at the wintry street and imagined myself in Paris, over forty years earlier, and could almost hear the sounds of old cars and trucks rattling over cobblestones. But it was just the rain against the roof and windows. I imagined myself walking along the poorly lit, war-torn streets in the cold rain, wearing only a thin wool coat and dress, scratchy wool stockings and thick-soled leather shoes. I could feel the wind whip between my legs and chill the exposed flesh of my upper thighs between my dress and the top of my stockings. I shivered and felt a phantom itchiness on my calves, thinking of the wool. Then again, maybe I would have been one of the braver female members of the underground who flouted feminine dress codes and risked arrest by cross-dressing in

126

men's clothing, if only for warmth and comfort, but possibly also in order to move undercover.

I saw myself again, this time in a man's cap, heavy wool jacket and pants, walking down the street, collar turned up against the wind, intent on making it back to the cell for food and the nightly strategy meeting. Or maybe I was on an assignment, on my way to rendezvous with another agent. All the doors and windows on the street were locked and barred, and all the cafés that used to spill out onto the sidewalk with warmth, light, and laughter were shut down early for the mandatory curfew. I shivered again and watched as I turned down a dark side street and knocked quietly on a small servants' entrance, looking side to side to make sure that I was not being observed. Just as the door opened to admit me, I turned with a start and woke up from my reverie as I heard the door to my own room open and was relieved to see that it was only Linus, not some Vichy Officer materialized from my vision. As I welcomed Linus into my room and my arms, part of my mind was still back in Paris: who had opened the door and where would it have led me?

For several more days, I hesitated before sending the fifth poem to Johanna. I hated to send it without feeling as if I had "solved" even a part of it and still didn't want to share any of the earlier poems either. My concern about "Echo" was that the story it encoded was not entirely clear: what part had Echo herself played in the purging of the spies? As if Johanna sensed my wavering on our bargain, at the end of the third week of classes another express airmail arrived from Paris. It said, simply, "*Julien Danton. Died 1946. Shot as a traitor. Look it up. Send another poem.*" Here was the lead I had needed about my grandfather. Time to go to the library, and fast. She'd get her poem, but only when I was ready to send it.

I immediately went downstairs to the microfiche archives and scrolled once again through old volumes of *Le Monde* from 1946, until I found the obituary for Julien Danton from April of that year. It read,

Julien Danton, Nazi collaborator and high ranking official in Vichy Regime, indicted for crimes against the state, most notably in league with war criminal General Auguste Arnault and other corrupt members of the Occupation. Shot as a traitor on April 23. M. Danton was a widower and is survived by no known family members. No services will be held.

"No known family members." Was there no record of his son's emigration? Just as Johanna had warned me, Julien had indeed been executed as a traitor due to collaborations with the Nazis, but the part that I couldn't believe was right there in print: "most notably with war criminal General Auguste Arnault."

Had my grandfather also been involved in planning the espionage armistice day massacre? If so, did that mean that it had been Julien Danton who was the Narcissus figure in the poem, and not Arnault, whom Echo had betrayed? I wondered again if something about my grandparents' marriage had not been quite right. If it had indeed been an arranged marriage, as suggested by the "Persephone" poem, it was entirely possible that there had been unequal or even unrequited love between them. It was remarkable, in fact, since their allegiances were to opposite sides of the war, that there had been any love at all. If there had been.

I thought about Sophia, and tried to imagine her life from the few clues I had pieced together from her poems. A young woman my own age, married off and abandoned by her mother in the middle of a war, utterly dependent upon the man she had been forced to marry for her safety. What if he had not wanted to marry her either? Had he been a cold, uncaring husband? What if he had been in love with himself, like Narcissus, or in love with his own power instead of her? As his wife, would Sophia have known about his plan with Arnault to undermine the Espionage Armistice? Perhaps. And perhaps, if she had known, would she have informed against Julien to her connections in the Resistance?

Was it possible that my grandmother, as a new, transformed "Echo," was alluding to the power that all women have to speak out in the face of oppression or corruption? In fact, could she have consented to the arranged marriage between herself and Julien Danton precisely because it would allow her to strategically infiltrate one of the central government strongholds? It was too much to hope for, but it turned the tables of the myth in exactly the way that I had come to expect from my grandmother. This time, Echo does not waste away or merely escape to freedom. She betrays Narcissus and her revenge is both total and liberating.

As soon as I got home that afternoon, I consulted my dad's translation of Ovid's *Metamorphoses*. I turned to the story of Echo and Narcissus and read it over quickly, realizing as I did so that for Ovid, Echo is a symbol of every woman who has ever sacrificed herself for love. Sophia must have felt that Echo was as much as part of herself

as all the other tragic heroines she wrote about, and for the first time I saw that Echo could also potentially be a part of myself too. Had I sacrificed any part of myself to Hyla, or to Linus? No, not yet. Echo was an important reminder and cautionary tale about the perils of doing so. I already felt that Linus was more of an equal to me than I had ever allowed a man to be before. While it was a new, and sometimes welcome balance, it also made me slightly uneasy. I resolved to see a little less of Linus for a while so that I could focus on the poems, as well as the rest of my academic work.

Like a young, female, intellectual version of my mythical namesake, I felt that I was in the middle of twelve laborious tests of my strength, and while I might not just have literally forced two raging rivers together to clean out a King's squalid stables, I felt as exhausted as if I had. In some ways, I had just as strenuously yoked together several different strains of research and analysis to understand the story behind the poem. I was finally ready to send it to Johanna.

I quickly wrote out a copy of "Echo" and an accompanying note:

Johanna, Here is another poem for you. Now I need to know more about Hercule. What was his connection to Sophia? Write soon. – Herculine

Sophia
Paris, 1937

Carefully placing the tip of her stocking over the toes of her right foot, Sophia slowly rolled the delicate silk up the length of her leg. Then she repeated her actions with her other stocking. She rose from the bed, careful not to disturb Esmée, who was still sleeping beside her, and fastened her garter belt around her waist, swiftly connecting each stocking to the dangling straps on her inner and outer thighs. She smoothed a slip over her lingerie and pulled on a tailored dress, grateful that she had chosen one that buttoned up the front rather than the back this morning. As she was about to put on her shoes, Esmée began to stir, so Sophia silently left the room in her stocking feet, her shoes in one hand, her coat and hat in the other. It was almost six o'clock, and Esmée's husband would soon be home.

Once she was safely standing in the hallway, a wave of dizziness passed over her and she swayed against the banister of the stairway. How long had it been since she'd last eaten? She couldn't remember. She hadn't had much appetite lately; the sight or smell of most food made her nauseated, no matter how hungry she felt. Maybe there would be something she could eat at the bakery on the corner... She quickly put on her shoes and coat, and walked as steadily as possible down the stairs, fixing her hat and veil in place as she descended.

She could smell the aroma of fresh baked bread coming from down the street as soon as she left the building, and it smelled so delicious it almost made her weep. Moments later, she was curled up in a chair in the far back corner of the patisserie, hungrily consuming bite after bite of warm bread dipped in sweet hot chocolate, and she felt better than she had in days.

She knew that Esmée didn't like it when she woke up and Sophia was gone, but Sophia feared that she would be late returning home, so she had let her new lover rest undisturbed. Esmée was the same age as Sophia – twenty-two – unlike most of Sophia's other female lovers, who were generally a few years older. Esmée's youth and innocence were valuable assets to Sophia right now. She was unmarried and childless – so there was little chance that she would

notice the subtle changes in Sophia's body, at least not for another month. Still, Sophia had not wanted to take any chances, and this was another reason she had left early.

At first she herself had not realized what was happening to her when her breasts became swollen and tender, her stomach became unsteady, and her head felt like it was filled with wet wool. She was so tired all the time; she could barely stay awake through dinner with Julien and ate next to nothing. He, of course, had not noticed. The sadistic pleasure he took from her body rarely involved full nudity. When it did, he did not linger over the details of her abdomen or breasts. The bruises he left on her shoulders and back were all that interested him.

But she had been surprised that Hercule had not figured it out yet. He had commented with pleasure one day during their lovemaking that her breasts seemed larger and more sensitive, but that was all. If he could see her throwing up in the morning, she thought bitterly, perhaps he would understand why. The real question was: why hadn't she told him? Or anyone else? It was still so early…she felt a strange mixture of protectiveness for the unknown life within her and a fervent hope that she would miscarry and be free from this overwhelming responsibility, this huge inconvenience. A child represented the end – quite possibly – of her double, and now, in some ways, triple life. She had her husband, her women, and for the past year, Hercule too. She had been surprised by the love she felt for him, first in gratitude for his caring protectiveness of her, then deepening into an intimate kinship and partnership that was even more unexpected. She had never thought she could love or trust a man again, but she trusted Hercule with her life.

Even so, there were times when she could barely remember who she was. And now this pregnancy. She had never wanted to be a mother. She and Hercule had taken precautions, and she avoided intercourse with Julien whenever possible. But now she was pregnant, with no idea whose child she carried. That was the other reason she hadn't told either her husband or Hercule.

Most of the time she simply wanted to leave the country and disappear. But even that was becoming increasingly difficult to do, especially if one's husband was a conservative government official. War was on the horizon. Germany and Italy were militarizing their nations and rumors flew about the drastic decrease of their citizens' civil liberties, particularly regarding the difficulty in crossing their

borders. Anxiety was in the air. People who could afford to were leaving the country in droves, like her mother had. But Sophia was trapped by Julien in more ways than one. Her former lover and dear friend Yvette had already left with her husband, and they were living in New York. Her letters were filled with relief at having escaped Europe, and she urged Sophia to flee and join them as soon as possible.

Sophia sighed and left the bakery. She knew it was impossible. Her greatest fear was not the possibility of war, or Julian's wrath if she were caught trying to escape. She feared only that if she did give birth to a child, that he might take pleasure in harming it too. *I will kill him*, she swore, clenching her gloved fists, *if he ever so much as raises a hand to my baby*. Despite her ambivalence toward the new life inside her, she placed one gloved hand protectively over her belly, and grimly set off for home.

The Sixth Poem: Galatea
Berkeley, February 1990

One of the oddities of winter in Berkeley, I soon discovered, is that the month of February is glorious. Not January, and definitely not March, when the rainy season tends to hit the Bay Area hardest, but in February, it is often the case that (as in mythical Camelot) it only rains at night and the sun invariably shines during the day. Flowers that I had only seen in florists' shops at this time of year in New York were blooming wild in almost every yard in Berkeley.

Plum and cherry trees were in blossom, their pale and dark pink flowers brightly set against wet slender branches like a living haiku; huge acacia trees exploding into fluorescent yellow pollen-laden boughs, some as big as a house; citrus-bearing trees heavy with fruit; and everywhere I looked, "merry wanderer" vines, with hundreds of bright purple blossoms twisting their way through every gate and fence in my neighborhood.

I shook my head in disbelief and plucked a small tea rose bud from the hedge next door as I walked to the bus stop one bright warm morning. I tucked it into the curls behind my ear, as Hyla had done so many months ago, so that its fragrance – and thoughts of her – could accompany me throughout the day.

I had been working hard this semester, trying to concentrate on my courses while making progress on the poems, balancing time between Linus and my other friends, keeping thoughts of Hyla alive in my heart while also keeping a distant watch on my mom, and carving out time for myself whenever possible.

During the afternoons, I had started going on long, rambling walks through the many neighborhoods of Berkeley, slowly acquainting myself with its architectural variations and themes, its socioeconomic shifts, and its eccentricities. But the day Linus drove me up to Tilden Park for the first time, a whole new appreciation for Berkeley opened up for me. My city girl's heart wondered at the hundreds of rolling acres of redwood and eucalyptus trees, the miles of winding trails, the hidden lakes and narrow beaches, and the small

133

handmade wooden bridges that led me into seemingly endless lands of different shades of green.

Unlike New York in February, with its bare trees, cold pavement, dead brown grass, and dirty snow, everything seemed greener and cleaner during the winter in Berkeley. The rain-washed light gave the city a blue-grey clarity on overcast days that intensified the hues of all the foliage thriving on long-awaited seasonal rainfall. On this day, the winter sun gave the wet streets a silver-green sheen as I rode the bus up to Tilden Park. I needed some time in the woods to clear my head, and a long walk on a new path was what I craved. I had awakened that morning to the realization that it was the eleventh anniversary of the day my father died, and my chest was heavy with grief that only the forest and its pure, fresh air could absorb.

I set off in a new direction once I passed through the trailhead. When I crossed from the wide, sandy jeep trail onto the single track hiking path, I felt myself begin to unwind as memories of my dad started to flood in. Here in the woods, I was transported back to being with him in Central Park. We had spent long hours there together when I was a child; he had played there with me – in the playgrounds and by the lake – and we had taken long walks too, roaming the pathways for hours at a time. It was one of these walks I focused on now, just over eleven years ago, in autumn.

The trees in the park had been in full glory, leaves flaming with colorful reds, golds, oranges, and yellows along every path. There was a crispness in the air and I remembered that I had been in high spirits that day, looking forward to seeing my dad, but he had been reserved when we met and our conversation had been slow to start. I realized that he must have something on his mind. So I waited, and walked with him in thoughtful silence until the moment when he reached out for my hand, cleared his throat, and began.

"Herculine, there's something I have to ask you."

"What is it, daddy?"

"Someday, when I die…"

"Daddy? Are you going to die?"

"Someday, sweetheart; but not for a very long time."

"Um, okay…"

"But when I do, Herculine, there's something I want you to do for me."

"Sure, daddy…what is it?"

"I want you to try and be friends with my wife, Johanna."

I was silent for a little while, nervous about the unpleasant prospect of attempting to befriend the Ice Queen, and unsure of why my dad was asking this of me.

I said, "Um, does she *want* to be my friend?"

Theo had laughed quietly, "She may not realize it now, darling, but when I die you two may find that you need each other. In fact, I am almost certain of it."

"But why, daddy? Doesn't she have any grownup friends?"

He smiled again, "Yes, honey – of course she does. What I mean is that there is a connection between you and Johanna that neither of you are able to appreciate at the moment, and I am simply hoping that after I am gone this connection will be a comfort and a help to you both."

I thought about this for a while, and then said with great seriousness, "Okay daddy; if she'll be nice to me, I'll be her friend. But I'll miss you so much I don't know how I could comfort her."

At this my dad knelt on the walking path, gathered me close in his arms, and held me tightly for several minutes. I could still feel his arms around me, and smell his wonderful warm scent of corduroy and wool.

I felt my heart constrict and my throat catch as I walked alone through the majestic eucalyptus grove. I rested against a tree that had shed its strips of pastel-colored bark and felt the smooth skin of the warm tree against my palms. The sun hit my face with pale heat and I breathed in the moist air deeply. My dad may have kept secrets from me, but on that day he had tried to open up his private world. He hadn't even known he was dying yet, or had the headaches already begun and he just hadn't told me?

I mused on the significance of my father's words as I turned around and made my way back to the entrance of the park. As I trudged up the hill to the bus stop, I realized that he had been right about so many things that day. Johanna and I did need each other right now, but maybe not in the way he had hoped. And yet, it was comforting in a strange way to know that she was out there, that she cared about the poems as much as I did, and that she held many of the keys to unlocking their secrets. Well, maybe "comforting" wasn't the right word. It was certainly motivating me to keep working steadily on the poems, but now my secret felt like a race. I tried to imagine who Sophia, or even my dad, would have wanted to win. I boarded the bus back down to campus, knowing full well that he would say that Johanna and I should be working together, not

competing at all. Perhaps that day would come. But for now, it was time to move on to the next poem.

I had read over my translation of the sixth poem, "Galatea," earlier that morning and I pulled my notebook out of my backpack and read through it again as the bus jolted gently down the winding hills.

He feeds on me.
I take shape
Under the cruel edge
Of his gaze:
Sharper than any chisel.
He sculpts me
With his eyes,
His hands,
His plans.
Every night,
All through the day,
He feasts on me.
But I am made of stone.
Others like him come to stare,
To try their wiles on me;
They cannot move me.
They preen their gaudy feathers
And glint their talons at me
But I do not fear them.
I smile and listen
And they wonder
Why their plans fail
Again and again.
He thinks he created me,
But he is wrong.
There is life within me.
You gave me the spark,
And I am creating it myself.
I am stronger than he is.
I will take his chisel,
And then his life.
There will be no more
Devouring of me,
Not by him or any other.

No more gnawing of bones.
Their curved beaks glistening
With my blood and yours.
We will clip their wings,
Tear out their talons,
Aim our chiseled arrows at their breasts.
And the land will be safe
For us to love
Again.

Translating this poem had given me some difficulty: "Spark" for instance, seemed like the best choice for *étincelle*, but it could also have meant "fire" or "excitement." Similarly, all of the bird symbolism and sculpture imagery had required several different French dictionaries to figure out. By this point I was used to Sophia's method of integrating the next sequential Herculean labor into the imagery of her heroine's transfigured narrative. But the combination of the story of Pygmalion's sculpture of the perfect woman who comes to life and Hercules' slaying of the carnivorous Stymphalian birds was disturbing to say the least. What I found most creepy about the poem, however, was that the individual Pygmalion had multiplied into a group of ravenous, objectifying men. Instead of just one apparently carnivorous and voyeuristic sculptor, Galatea was faced by the threat of a gang: a group of powerful men whose plans she – a rightfully resentful object of desire – had the power to thwart and subvert.

When I arrived back on campus, I headed over to the library to refresh my collection of potential research sources for this poem. While my stacks at home were growing higher, I had the feeling that "Galatea" was a different sort of puzzle than the rest. It seemed to be a more private poem somehow, more specifically about the struggle of an individual to fight for her own life. Was the "spark" within Galatea a glimmer of authenticity that she would risk her life to protect? I liked to think so.

As I roamed the seemingly endless shelves of World War II histories, I felt lost in the library for the first time. I honestly didn't know where to begin. Espionage and military maneuvers? No. Religious alliances against fascist forces? No. Cultural trends in fashion, design, and cuisine during the war? Definitely not. But wait...here was one: *Civic Art as Mythic Nation Building: Public Sculpture and Political Power in Vichy France.* Pygmalion was a sculptor after all,

137

and Galatea was herself a statue come-to-life. And in Sophia's poem, she was no obedient *objet d'art*, but a resistant self-creation that was set on destroying her master. This book could be a good start: it wouldn't hurt to know what was going on in the art world during Vichy, after all.

I hefted the heavy tome off the high shelf and brought it over to my favorite desk by a tall row of windows. The book was filled with hundreds of glossy black and white reproductions of public art that was commissioned during the occupation of France. It seemed that almost every town had been commandeered to produce a work of art – either a statue, mural, portrait, or monument – that was intended to usher in a new era of German-French aesthetic collaboration. The book was a potential gold mine. I checked it out at the circulation desk, hugging it to my chest as I walked home in the slanting late afternoon light, feeling its bulk protect me from the onset of the early evening chill with its weight and its promise.

That night I had plans with Anthea and Hermàn to go to a party at a gallery where a friend of Hermàn's was working. "Free food, fine wine, and tons of fab boys," he'd said. "What could be more fun?" Anthea and I had smiled and rolled our eyes, but agreed that we would join him. It would be refreshing to get out beyond our circle of grad student friends for a night and take in a slice of the upscale Berkeley art scene for a change. Linus showed up at our house after dinner to drive us all over to the party.

He hugged me as he walked in and said, "Hey, guess what I have for you?"

I smiled and shook my head, "No clue. What?"

He held a homemade tape out to me and said, "Listen to it later, I think you'll like it."

New music just for me? I wanted to run upstairs to my room and listen to it right that minute, but – my heart racing with pleasure at the gift – I tucked the slim plastic case into my jacket pocket and thanked him with a particularly long kiss. It had been a while since he'd had any new music to share with me and I had the feeling that whatever was waiting for me on the cassette might have something to do with my recent influence in his life. It would be interesting to see – or hear – what that turned out to be.

When we arrived at the gallery, the party was already in full swing. As promised by Hermàn, there were scores of handsome gay men in the room, laughing and openly embracing their boyfriends, and I breathed in the liberating air of the art world society that I had

138

come to know so well in New York thanks to my mom. I felt right at home. With a glass of red wine in my hand, I moved away from my friends to circulate, look at the art on the walls, and to admire the crowd of beautiful people with what I liked to think was my connoisseur's gaze. There were certainly more men here than women, and the reason was soon made clear. The majority of this artist's work was male nudes, in a variety of media. There were photographs, pastels, pen and ink, collage, even a sculpture or two.

I was particularly drawn to a series of small statuettes carved in wood off to the side of the gallery. They were sanded and polished to a silky, glowing smoothness, each one mounted on a different marble block – the stone chosen specifically, I noted, to complement the unusual grain of the wood used in each statue. The lines of the carved male forms flowed like silk, yet contained the strength and power of the exotically grained wood at the same time. I had to resist the impulse to reach out and caress these beautiful sculptures. Instead, I let my hand hover about an inch over the surface of one that was carved out of pale golden oak, depicting the elegant figure of a man reclining with the lower half of his body facing down, while his torso arched up and twisted gracefully around – the muscles of each arm flexed to support this motion – turning and looking back over his shoulder to see the artist.

The small sculpture radiated a heat, almost an energy field of essence, and as I let my floating hand glide over the curves of the form, I became aware of someone standing close by. I turned around to look behind me, unintentionally mirroring the exact motion of the statue I was admiring. I turned to see a tall handsome man with silver hair pulled back into a long ponytail, whose sharply defined, amber-hued features looked like those of Aztec royalty. He was wearing a floor length coat of sheared tawny fur, and he was smiling at me. I wondered at his striking appearance (wearing a coat like that in Berkeley, even in this crowd, was practically begging to have a can of paint thrown at him by a PETA activist), and smiled back. I assumed, rightly, that this was the artist.

I said, "I like your work."

He said, "I can see that. You're welcome to touch that one, if you like. It's from my private collection and isn't for sale."

I looked up at him in surprise, thanked him, and lowered my hand tentatively onto the surface of the statue I had been admiring. He was still watching me intently, which inhibited me, so I closed my eyes and let my hand glide freely over the form. As I did so, I

139

thought I could feel the organic medium beneath my fingertips take on the warmth of living, breathing flesh and move imperceptibly as I caressed its lines. I opened my eyes to see the artist staring at me, still smiling.

He said, "I can see that you feel the unique qualities of this piece. I call it 'Pygmalion's Dream.'"

Startled by the mythic reference, I looked at him with a questioning expression. He continued, "Think about it: what Ancient Greek sculptor in his right mind would have been sculpting the ideal *female* form? When all around him were beautiful young men, just waiting to be taken on as his muse? No, the real Pygmalion would have dreamt of someone more like this fellow."

Transfixed by this modern revision of the myth I was currently steeped in, I could barely speak. I said in a low voice, "Um, I'm actually a classics scholar; and it is exactly this kind of art – the kind that re-works myth into contemporary relevance – that I find most compelling."

"Really?" he countered. "Then I think there are a few pieces over here that you should see." He beckoned me over to a side room in the gallery and I followed, mesmerized by his magnetism, his penetrating gaze, and his confidence that what he had to show me would be exactly what I needed to see. The crowd parted as he led the way. As I glided through the room behind him, I saw Linus, Anthea, and Hermàn off to one side, laughing and talking, seemingly oblivious to my adventure. Before we entered the room, the artist turned to me and said, "The Nine Muses welcome you."

There were no other people in the side room, and I immediately saw why. These nudes were all female. And then I froze. They were studies, again in a variety of media, all unmistakably of the same woman. And that woman was Hyla.

Hyla's eyes, face, and body stared out at me from nine different poses, eight on the walls and one sculpture in the center of the room. And in each representation, I felt like I could see her breathing, could hear her saying to me, "I know you…I remember you…And you know me too."

I turned to face the artist and stammered, "H-h-how did you know? I mean, did you know that I know her?" I gestured around to the works on the wall and the statue mounted – as the ones of men had been – on a marble block, "You know…the model? Hyla?"

140

Now it was the artist's turn to look surprised. "You know her? Do you know where she is? I've been trying to find her for two months now, but she seems to have just disappeared."

I responded glumly, "Yeah, I know. I can't find her either. But she was...um, my..."

"Your lover?" he asked gently. In that moment, I realized that the artist was quite a bit older than I had initially thought. His smooth tanned skin had created an ageless effect on his appearance but there was a somber wisdom in his expression and a fatherly tone to his voice that caused me to look more closely into his face. There I saw the intricate network of lines around his eyes that had been caught up in his smile earlier, but now they were relaxed with the seriousness of his inquiring gaze.

"Yes," I said, meeting his eyes, feeling both sadness and defiance. "And I'm worried about her."

"I don't blame you," he said. "Let me know if there is any way that I can be of help in finding her." He reached into his coat pocket and drew out a turquoise colored card of heavy embossed stock that read, simply, "Chiron" with a phone number below.

"I'm Herculine," I said. "Thank you. I promise to call as soon as I know anything."

Chiron reached out a large, gentle hand and tousled my curls appreciatively. With a warm laugh, he said, "Herculine the androgyne. Perfect. And in the meantime, if you ever want to earn some extra money while you're studying the classics, I'd love to have you model for me. You're quite fetching, you know."

With that comment, he turned to leave the gallery and I looked back over my shoulder to watch him as he walked away. I stayed behind in the room filled with Hyla. When had she posed for these portraits of the nine muses? Why hadn't she mentioned it when we were together? Could she have been lovers with Chiron? There was something in the gaze of several drawings that suggested desire. But this could have been a result of the artist's own projections. Would I ever know? As I circled the room, appreciating the subtlety with which Chiron had rendered the images on the walls of Hyla as Clio, Terpsichore, Euterpe, Thalia, Melpomene, Erato, Urania, and Calliope. But my attention was finally drawn to the sculpture in the center of the room of Hyla as Polyhymnia, the muse of divine poetry. Larger than the male nudes in the rest of the gallery, this one was different also in medium. Whereas Chiron had

141

rendered his male objects of beauty in metals, woods, and clay, he had sculpted Hyla in flawless white Italian marble.

Even though the pose of the statue was ecstatically beautiful – Hyla, nude, reaching up to the skies with both arms upraised, her neck curved and her back slightly arched, leg muscles flexed as she surged her entire body up into the movement, perched on the tips of her toes – there was something that made me uneasy as I stared at the statue. Chiron had left Hyla's eyes blank, instead of inscribing them with pupils and irises as some sculptors do, and this made the figure seem spectral, her presence ghostly, and her beauty unearthly. Since no one was in the room, I glanced around warily, then placed both hands on the waist of the marble statue. Unlike the wooden sculpture of "Pygmalion's Dream," the statue of Hyla was cold. Still, I closed my eyes as I had before, and this time I could feel not only the familiar contours of my lover's body, but came away from the statue with the certain knowledge that the sculptor had known them intimately as well.

Dazed with the discovery of this new dimension of Hyla's private world, as well as the experience of such powerful art, I reluctantly left the room and went to find my friends. I had been gone longer than I realized and the party had dispersed. Chiron was nowhere in sight, and my friends were sprawled happily on a maroon velvet sofa against a wall, under a large painting of violently bright swirling colors depicting a group of naked male dancers. "Fabulous Fauves" was the title, and I smiled at Chiron's cheekiness. Nothing was sacred to him, apparently. How refreshing.

Linus looked up and saw me smiling. He rose to his feet and swooped me around in a low tango dip. Laughing, I kissed him and said to the group, "Hey, there's something you've got to see." I led them back to the Hyla room and they all stopped at the entrance, amazed. I leaned against a wall and watched them.

Anthea was the first to speak, "Did you know about these?" I shook my head. She looked mystified. "Well, damn; that girl sure got busy!"

Linus was standing in front of a gouache tint of Hyla reclining against pillows, posed as Erato, muse of love poetry, looking candidly at the artist, arms lazily posed over her head. He looked at me and I met his gaze; Linus could see it too. Hyla had been more than a model to Chiron. All this flashed wordlessly between us; protectively, Linus came over to my side and led me out of the gallery.

142

On our way to his car, Hermàn, who had seemed bored by the images of Hyla, asked me, "Who was that guy with the fur coat, honey?"

I shivered, remembering the look on Hyla's face in the "Erato" painting, and handed Chiron's card to him, saying, "He was the artist, Hermàn; you should call him – he's looking for fetching young models…"

Everyone laughed except me.

Back at the house, I lounged with Linus on my bed upstairs talking about the events of the evening and he said, "I want you to hear that song I made for you." Ah, I thought, it *was* just for me. I took the tape out of my jacket and slipped it into the small boom box I kept in my room. I pressed the "play" button, then curled back into Linus's arms. As the music began, I was instantly lulled into the trance-like sensuality that his music always aroused in me. I turned to face him and moved my hands to the waistband of his jeans, but then stopped. I recognized the song. It was my song, all right. But it wasn't just "for" me; it was based on the song I had written when I was working on the "Echo" poem. I had played the song for Linus once on the guitar, shy but proud, and he had been delighted by it, commending me for my interesting choice of chord progressions. Apparently he had been listening more closely than I had realized, and he had composed a complex variation upon my basic design.

I pulled away and said, "Hey: this is *my* song. Who said you could take it and change it into one of *your* songs?"

Linus put up his hands to shield himself in mock fear, "Whoah… no offense intended, I swear! It's a compliment. I loved your tune and I couldn't get it out of my head for days. I just had to build a riff around it. I didn't think you'd mind…I thought you'd like it."

I saw that he actually looked slightly hurt, so I relented, but not entirely, and met his jesting tone with my own, "Okay, okay: but if you ever put this on one of your tapes and sell it, I want royalties!"

Here I punched him playfully on the shoulder and he pretended to recoil in pain, yelping, "OW!" then he lunged at me and soon had me laughing and wrestling with him.

Even as our play fighting subsided into an embrace, a part of my mind remained removed and distant. That was *my* song. And he shouldn't have taken it. Royalties weren't the issue. It was the co-option of my creation, the disregard of my artistic ownership. A true collaboration would have been different, respectfully consensual. But

his gesture had not been. It had been an appropriation, even if unintentional.

An hour later, as Linus slept deeply by my side, I had more difficulty relaxing. I tucked the blankets in around him, pulled my jeans and a sweater back on and padded downstairs with *Civic Art as Mythic Nation Building* under my arm. I turned on a light in the living room and settled into a deep chair to read. But the meager text accompanying the photographs was overpowered by the force of the images themselves, and soon I found herself merely skimming over the words, and spending longer on each photo instead.

Propaganda can be endlessly fascinating to analyze, and I was glad I had taken the seminar at Columbia called "Ways of Seeing" about the power of the media in shaping cultural norms. The art that sprang from the Vichy occupation was not quite as overtly manipulative as the visual propaganda that erupted in Communist China or Soviet Russia, but it was close. I marveled at photographs of statues of women with babes in arms surrounded by a brood of children entitled "The New Motherhood," as well as a mural of a large Teutonic goddess presiding over an abundantly fertile agricultural scene in which archetypal French peasants worked in the fields under her benevolent Germanic gaze. In a time of war, hunger, death, and siege, these civic artists had been asked to summon up the most powerful counter-fantasies they could imagine to lull the French citizens into cooperation with the official vision of a prosperous Vichy nation that required their willing labor and fertility.

Interestingly, there was also a chapter in the book that documented the many forms of protest that were enacted against these works of "civic art," many of which were, in my opinion, exceedingly clever. For instance, in one town where a monument had been erected of a German general on horseback with a small band of French soldiers protecting him, some witty citizen had wrapped the general in a large strait-jacket, and then bound the soldiers to him in chains. Were the French thus imprisoned by madmen, or had they successfully captured the lunatic and were now leading him away to the prison in triumph? Either way, I thought wryly, this act of intelligent metaphorical sedition had probably raised the spirits of the French townspeople as well as infuriated the Vichy officials.

As I turned the pages of the book, I wasn't exactly sure what I was looking for, but I paid particular attention to the examples of civic art that portrayed images of women just in case there was a

144

direct connection to Galatea. I yawned as I leafed through a series of photographs in a chapter documenting the unveiling ceremonies devoted to each work of art that was donated to the many small towns in the country. All those faces of petty officials, now dead, so puffed up then in their pride, illusions, and arrogant sense of cultural mission. How many of these men had been shot after the war, like my grandfather had, as traitors?

As if my train of thought summoned up the words on the page, my eye was suddenly caught by a name I knew well. There it was, "Danton," twice in fact, under a formal photograph of four men and one woman from one of the unveiling ceremonies. The name made me stop and examine the photograph; but I was almost afraid to look too closely. Called "The Commission for Civic Art in Paris," the group was listed as including the following members: Léonin Schiffer, Jean Ebermann, Auguste Arnault, Julien Danton, and his wife, Sophia Danton.

I didn't move. I didn't want to breathe in case the book suddenly evaporated in my hands. I had never seen a photograph of Sophia before and now here she was, looking like a glamorous young female version of her handsome son, my father, Theo. Here was the same curly hair, the large lively dark eyes, and full expressive mouth that I had cherished as my father's features, which I had proudly inherited and now acknowledged as my own. I exhaled slowly, and combed my fingers gently through my hair as I gazed at the photograph, causing one of my own copper curls to fall upon the page. The thought of whether Sophia's hair might have been the same hue woke me up from my musings, and I realized with a start that every single one of the other names on the list was also familiar to me.

Leonin Schiffer was the general who had possibly been sabotaged by "Electra" in the first poem, Jean Ebermann was the unscrupulous co-owner of Sophia's mother's art auction house and the "boar man" from the "Persephone" poem, and Auguste Arnault was the official with whom Julien Danton had probably planned the failed Espionage Armistice in "Echo." And there was Julien: tall, handsome, and blonde, with a proprietary air in the way he held his wife's arm in his own. Blonde, I mused. That's odd. Dad's hair was so dark, and mine is the same color as mom's but with his curls. Who ever would have thought that Julien Danton was blonde? He looked Germanic in a way that puzzled me. Was Julien Danton of German heritage? Was this one of the reasons that Sophia's mother

145

had arranged a marriage between her daughter and this man? Had she thought that his background and his status in the government would be useful if the Germans took over France? Julien had probably been instrumental in Céline Demetrius's escape from the country, but I was merely guessing. If there was a way to know for certain, I would try to find it.

After staring at my grandmother's beautiful face for several more minutes, I carefully marked the page in the book and made a mental note to photocopy the image at my department the next day. This was a precious discovery: my first glimpses of my grandparents as well as a confirmation of my suspicions about my grandmother's role in the power brokering hub of Vichy France. Here were all the major players in the occupation, representing almost every facet of the dark political underside of the era. I scoffed: this was some "Commission on Civic Art." More like "Commission on Extortion and Massacre." Sophia was probably the only one of the whole group who really knew anything about art. Even Ebermann looked more like a thug than a curator. I hugged the book to my chest again and walked quietly back up the stairs to get a pen and a piece of paper. Sitting on the landing, I copied out the words to the "Galatea" poem, then composed a short note to Johanna.

> *Here is the next poem. I will come to Paris to meet Hercule as soon as possible. In the meantime, I need to see a photograph of Sophia Danton. Do you have one? Also, was Julien Danton German?*

Johanna responded in less than a week. During that week, however, I found that I was much less interested in seeing Linus than before the incident with my song. Except when we sat together in class, he left me alone at my request, with a sad, resigned look on his face. This I ignored as well as I could, focusing my energies almost exclusively on researching the activities of each member of the dubious "Commission on Civic Art." I was intrigued, but hardly surprised to find that every time there was an unveiling ceremony of a new public art installation, the festivities seemed to be accompanied, curiously enough, by coincidental police reports of often fatal skirmishes between Resistance and Vichy forces in the towns surrounding the lucky recipient city of the statue or mural. I could only imagine how hard Sophia was working during these months: keeping up appearances with her husband's cronies while feverishly attempting to alert the local resistance cells of the

146

impending threat. She must have had assistance. She couldn't have done it alone. She may have launched the arrows that killed the Stymphalian birds and brought them down, but it had to have been Hercule who helped her get the arrows – in other words, make the local connections, and plan the full range of resistance in each town. Hercule, who gave her the "spark of life within," which was the source of her strength.

There were days when all I could do was sit in my father's chair in my room staring out at the winter greenery and daydream about the day I would meet Hercule in Paris. Whenever I could afford to take the time away from my library job or my seminar papers and translation projects, I would make my way up to Tilden Park, to muse over the emerging patterns in the poems, and try to piece Sophia's story together more fully. Sometimes, I would just lie on my bed and think about Hyla, wondering where she could be and how I could reach her. Back in January, when Hyla's former housemates had grudgingly given me the forwarding address in Mexico, I had written to her immediately. But my letter had been "returned to sender."

Disgruntled, I pulled on my coat and went outside to take a walk through the neighborhood to clear my head. Just as I closed the door, I saw the mail carrier drive up and begin loading letters into the mailbox I shared with Anthea and Hermàn. A flash of light blue caught my eye. "Hey!" I called out for no reason to the stocky woman now driving away in the post office truck. In my excitement, I fairly sprinted to the mailbox and shuffled through the stack of magazines and junk mail until I saw Johanna's handwriting and the "Par Avion" stamp. Leaving the rest of the mail in the box, I ripped open the blue airmail envelope and walked back into the house.

Inside the envelope was a short note from Johanna that I skipped entirely in my excitement after reading the first line, *Here is a photograph*. I quickly put the note aside when I saw the photocopy that accompanied it. There was Sophia, dressed in the high fashion of Paris in the late 1930s, radiantly happy, and apparently arm in arm with someone who had been cut out of the picture. I couldn't tell if it was a man or a woman, but in my next note to Johanna I would demand to find out. The face was the same, though more animated, than the one in the *Civic Art* book (could this indicate that the other person who had been in the picture was not her husband?). I felt like I could gaze into my grandmother's face for hours. What year had

the photo been taken? How many years at this point did Sophia have left to live?

After sitting at the kitchen table staring at the photograph for half an hour, I returned to the note from Johanna. The tone of the rest of the note was very clear. It was a threat.

Here is a photograph. Research Julien Danton's national affiliations yourself. As for meeting Hercule, much will depend on you and whether or not I have all the poems by then. Send another, sooner rather than later.

I tensed, as if for a fight, and thought, Don't glint your talons at me, Ice Queen. I'm learning about creative forms of resistance from the master, and I'll send you another poem when I'm good and ready. I crumpled up Johanna's note and threw it in the trash, tucked the copy of the photo of Sophia into the breast pocket of my jacket, and headed back out into the glorious February sunshine for a long, refreshing walk.

Hercule
Paris, February 1990

The fine papery skin on the old man's hands and face soaked up the mid-afternoon sun in the courtyard. These were the only parts of his body that were exposed to the open air. He sat in his wheelchair, a wool cap protecting his head from the winter chill, with two thick wool blankets bundled over his flannel bathrobe, pajamas, and slippers. He still managed to look faintly debonair with the carefully folded tips of his clean white handkerchief arranged neatly in the breast pocket of his robe and a faded red silk scarf around his neck.

In his shaking hands the old man held a letter. He had received it eleven years ago. The fine tears along the creases of its folds as well as its pliant softness from being carried in the warmth of his breast pocket for so long were testimony to the numerous times he had re-read its contents.

Tears filled Hercule's eyes as he gently folded the letter back into its worn envelope and placed it back in his pajama pocket. Every time he read it, Theo's death filled him anew with grief. Johanna had mailed the letter the day before Theo died. She had called him to let him know that he had something to look forward to, and then she called him again the next day, disconsolate, barely coherent on the phone, telling him that Theo was dead. Hercule had been shaken by the news, plunged into a silent misery and remote state of grief that made his days go by in a sluggish blur of meaninglessness. Theo was dead. Those lively bright eyes, the warmth of his voice, extinguished. When the letter had finally arrived, it spoke to him from the grave, and Hercule realized that Theo had probably known that this would be the case. There had been so many times since then that Hercule had automatically picked up the phone to call him, only to be stricken again with the awful truth that Theo was no longer there to call. The world seemed empty. Even though Hercule had only seen Theo once or twice a year for a week at a time since he had moved back to Paris, they had called and written to each other regularly, and Theo had been a lifeline to Hercule in many ways – but mostly as a vital connection to his memory of who he had been in his youth, all that

he had fought for, all that he had loved, and—until Theo's death—had not entirely lost.

Hercule sighed and looked up at the sky. All forms of healing take longer the older one becomes, he thought. Even grieving. He had no friends from his own generation. They had all been dead for years. The others in the *résidence* were pleasant enough, but he never let anyone get too close. When one of them passed on, it was of no concern to him. But Theo had been so young. And there was something terribly wrong with the young dying before the old. Bitterly, he allowed self-pity to eclipse the purity of his grief for Theo, remembering how young he himself had been – only ten – when his own mother had died, leaving him to fend for himself on the streets of Paris.

Throughout Hercule's childhood, his mother never failed to remind him that if it hadn't been for his birth, she wouldn't have lost her figure and her beauty, and the attentions of his father, not to mention her other rich clients. Hercule, wounded by her accusations, still worshiped her and strove to be worthy of her inconstant affection. He couldn't help noticing that the steady stream of men coming to their apartment at all hours of the day and night didn't seem to think that his mother had lost her figure or her beauty. But he never said a word. He was under strict orders to make himself scarce and silent whenever his mother was "entertaining guests." Hidden behind a tall shelf filled with books left behind by the previous tenant of their apartment, Hercule had passed these lonely hours escaping into the occasionally incomprehensible but always fascinating worlds of Victor Hugo and Flaubert, De Maupassant and Rousseau, as well as translations of Dostoevsky, Tolstoy, and Dickens. Little Hercule often felt like he too was a character in a novel, one whose life was a mystery waiting to unfold and be revealed.

From little bits of information he was able to glean from his mother during her voluble drinking binges, he pieced together that in the year or so before his birth she had been the exclusive "mistress" of an important government official – married of course, with his own legitimate children, and very rich – and she meant "exclusive" in the sense that during those years she had only entertained him, although he may have had any number of other women in his life. But she had been faithful, she would cry, and then he had abandoned her when he discovered her pregnancy.

"Get rid of it," he had said.

"No," she had wept, "I love you…"

"Then it's over," he said, leaving several hundred franc notes on the table, immune to her sobbing imprecations, as the door closed with finality behind him.

One night, after reciting a particularly dramatic version of this story to her son, Hercule's mother had let his father's last name slip. It was "Vega," and Hercule privately adopted it as his own. After she died of pneumonia the winter he turned ten, Hercule began to follow news of his father in the papers that he found discarded in the trash bins of the orphanage where he was sent to live. It made him feel important somehow, and it helped him shield himself psychologically against the taunting of the other children he lived with there. "Son of a whore!" they would yell at him, "Bastard!" He was small for his age, but within a short period of time he had become a vicious and formidable fighter and the teasing soon stopped. By this time, however, the brand of shame that his mother had imprinted upon him had only intensified within him. "Bastard. Son of a whore." He knew it was true, and it ate away at him, causing him to isolate himself from others and to distrust everyone. At sixteen, he ran away from the orphanage just as they were about to take him out of school and hire him out to a factory, and he began his life on the streets of Paris.

After several weeks of starving and hiding, he joined up with a gang of young thieves he met at the market place as he was ineptly attempting to steal some bread. They helped him avoid getting caught and showed him more effective techniques that he picked up quickly. They liked him for his fast mind and ruthless fists and they took him into their life: picking pockets and shoplifting, even robbing the occasional home. They did all this for the men who worked on the docks: receiving shelter, protection, and occasional bottles of whiskey from them in return. Soon Hercule had gained renown among his new comrades for his nimble fingers, innocent looks, and daredevil courage. He would take on any job, no matter the risk, and always reaped the greatest rewards for his efforts. By the time he was eighteen, he was the leader of the group and decided to eliminate the dock workers from the equation altogether. He knew where they fenced the stolen goods, and within a few weeks, he and his mates had their own flat, were operating independently from the older men, and were keeping the profits of their exploits. During this time, Hercule had come to know the city of Paris more intimately than most of the regular citizens of the city could ever imagine. He knew

151

the vast network of hidden alleyways, sewers, rooftops, and cellars like a terrestrial network of constellations emblazoned on his mind. He knew everywhere there was to hide, and he knew everyone there was to know: every thief, fence, hooker, pimp, dealer, and crooked cop in the city. All of this would prove to be invaluable a decade later in his work for the resistance, but he had no way of knowing that at the time. All he knew was that he could survive better than most of the kids on the street, and that this was largely true because he trusted no one. Ever.

Until Henri. Dark and quiet, smaller than the other boys, but faster than they were too. When he joined the gang Hercule felt an immediate affinity for him and protected him against the other boys' hazing. Henri repaid Hercule with pure devotion. They made a perfect team: Henri would follow Hercule into any situation with complete faith and together they had never botched a job.

One night, they decided to burglarize some rich homes in the Sixteenth *Arrondissement* while the owners were on their summer vacation. While rummaging through the drawers of a large desk in the second home they hit, Henri said to Hercule,

"Hey, the guy that lives here's last name's Vega: just like yours!" He brandished a piece of stationery and Hercule snatched it out of his hands. There it was: Honoré Vega. His father's name. He folded the piece of paper carefully and put down the bag of silver that he had lifted from the dining room.

"Let's get out of here," he said brusquely, trying to hide the catch in his throat.

Henri just looked at him silently, picked up the bag of silver, and nodded. He didn't need to ask Hercule any more questions. As soon as he had seen his friend's face, he had understood in an instant that they had unwittingly been robbing the home that belonged to Hercule's actual father. Looking around, Henri gave a low whistle and said under his breath, but just loud enough for Hercule to hear,

"You've damn well got a right to this stuff..."

But Hercule did not agree. When it was time to fence the silver they had taken from the Vega home, he had Henri deal with it, and told him to dispense of the money how he best saw fit. Henri used it to pay up front for a small flat in the Latin Quarter that he and Hercule could share. Soon the two young men broke off from the rest of the group. Now that they were living on their own, they decided to steal only when necessary, and began spending their money on such novelties as respectable clothes, so that they could

152

eventually enroll in vocational courses at the local *lycée industriel*. Hercule had decided that it was time to learn a real trade, and the two young men began to imagine a life for themselves beyond the streets. Due to the infrequency of their thefts, the jobs they undertook had become increasingly risky: ironically, they had to steal more valuable objects to support their increasingly legitimate lifestyle.

One night, about a year after they had split off from the rest of their gang, as they were finishing a job in a mansion in the Fifth *Arrondissment*, Hercule could sense that something was not quite right. The street was just a little too quiet, even though it was the middle of the night. There was a watchfulness in the air, and he motioned Henri to stay back, but Henri didn't see his gesture and bolted swiftly across the courtyard. Suddenly lights flared, shots rang out, and he watched in horror as Henri crumpled to the ground.

Shaking uncontrollably, Hercule edged his way back into the house and groped his way through the dark and his tears, gasping for breath as he climbed out through an alley-facing window up onto the roof. He could hear the gendarmes below speculating that the guy they killed must have been a solo operator and he watched from the rooftop in silence and rage as they kicked his friend's body over to see his face. One of the cops said he'd seen the kid on the streets before. Another one shrugged and picked up Henri's limp body under his arms and dragged him to their car. As they drove away, Hercule allowed himself to weep for the first time since he had watched the men from the morgue carry away his mother's body eight years earlier.

There on the roof of a stranger's home he swore never to let another person into his heart. And for several years, desolate with guilt and blaming himself for Henri's death, he managed to stay true to this resolve. Working the streets alone, continuing his night school classes, women in his life had always come and gone: brief affairs, one night stands, sometimes he didn't even know their name. He liked women, but he didn't trust them. They always seemed to want something from him that he didn't have to give. So he took his pleasure from them, and if they took theirs along the way, so much the better for them. He had learned a little here and there about how to give pleasure too, that was easy enough, but that was all he had to give. They might want his heart and soul, but all they got was his body.

Then one night, on a delivery of a case of stolen silk stockings to an underground bistro where the *sapphistes* congregated,

he saw Sophie. Sitting at the bar alone, with a bottle of red wine and a glass in front of her, working her way slowly through the entire bottle by herself. He watched her drinking in silence for a while, then he ordered a glass too and sat down beside her.

He had seen women like her before: those glittering bourgeois beauties with the melancholy eyes, filled with a cold rage and courage that almost equaled his own. They chose to live double lives on the margins of society, risking their reputations – sometimes even their fortunes – for their passions. And their passions for each other flared much higher than anything he had ever known. They scared him, to be honest. All the drama and emotion. But this one seemed different somehow; there was a certain reserve about her, and most noticeably, when she pushed up the sleeves of her fashionably cut dress, he could see that there were bruises all over her arms. This was not something that he saw very often on rich women, but he had seen it all the time on the girls from the streets.

He watched her warily for many weeks. Every time he made a delivery to the bistro she frequented he always scanned the room to see if she was there. When she wasn't, he realized he was disappointed. Whenever she was, he would sit beside her at the bar and buy her a glass of wine. After over a month of observing her closely, he noticed that whoever was roughing her up was doing a thorough job. As he scanned her body he noticed not only the bruises and cuts on her arms, but similar discolorations on her calves as well, barely camouflaged by her dark silk stockings, and a trace of a bruise on one side of her neck. Hercule began to feel protective of her, and he felt a sense of kinship with her too: she might be dressed in silk, but her life was as rough as his in some ways.

They didn't speak much at first, but after he helped her out of a tight spot one day, when her husband was having her followed, he noticed that her eyes lit up faintly when she saw him in the following weeks, and this made him bold. He began to ask her about her life, and though her responses were initially terse and defensive, soon she began to confide in him like a friend. Ever watchful for the appearance of new bruises on what he could see of her body, Hercule summoned the courage one day to ask her who was harming her and if she'd like him to teach the guy a lesson. Sophie had laughed bitterly, and turned to face him with a mask of defiance on her face. But when she saw the kindness in his eyes, something in her softened, and after a few moments of gazing at him, she took a deep breath, and spoke with a cold, mechanical tone of detachment,

154

"It is my husband," she said. "I hate him. He is a *sadiste*. My marriage is a lie. His only pleasure comes from inflicting pain, and my pleasure only comes from women. If I could leave him, I would; but he is blackmailing my mother, so I cannot. He is a powerful man; I doubt you could teach him anything, but if you would kill him for me, I'd appreciate it."

The defiant gleam came back into her eyes with this last remark, and she took a long drink from her glass when she finished speaking, daring Hercule to respond. He merely held her gaze, transfixed by the loveliness of her face, imagining what it would look like without the hard lines of pain that shadowed her cheekbones and eyes. She was so young...too young to be able to handle such a monster of a husband. No one should be trapped in a brutal, loveless marriage. Hercule was irresistibly drawn to the pathos of her situation and admired the bravery he sensed in her. He officially took her under his wing that night.

He began bringing stockings and cigarettes just for her when he came to the bistro, then stopped using the excuse of his deliveries altogether, meeting her in parks, cafés, and even libraries, where she would recommend books to him that he would read when they were apart. The works of Colette were Sophie's favorites, and through her novels and stories he was transported into a world of sensuous complexity that he had never encountered before. He began to understand the love between women, and this helped him to understand Sophie too. Occasionally when Hercule dropped by the bistro to see her, he would catch sight of her in an embrace or dancing with another, equally beautiful woman but never the ones dressed in suits, always the other feminine ones. The fact that she was a *sapphiste* had confused him at first but it also made her seem safe to him; she didn't want anything from him that he couldn't give her. For the first time in his life, he had a female friend. At times he thought that perhaps she was becoming a substitute for Henri, but he would brush the thought away angrily. No one would ever get that close.

As their friendship grew and the more he understood about how dangerously she was living, the closer he felt to her. Years later, she told him that she had been drawn to the tragedy that she saw in his face because it seemed to mirror her own. He didn't understand what she was talking about at the time, because all he saw was her beauty, her fragility, and the white-hot iron cable of strength that ran through her and kept her going. If he had once noticed the tragedy in

her face, it had been replaced by the hopeful light that seemed to glow within her whenever she turned her face to his.

Their friendship grew into trust, and soon into love. Neither of them had ever let themselves be vulnerable to a member of the opposite sex before, so when they let down their guard, there was a flood of ardor as if their very souls were merging. And then after a year of clandestine meetings – hiding both from her husband and the *sapphistes* – Sophie became pregnant. She was both thrilled and terrified; Hercule was simply stunned. Whose child was it, his or Julien's? Sophie had no way of knowing, but at least the news had the unexpected effect of deterring Julien's sadistic tendencies from her for the next seven months – he told her he was repelled by her swollen body – and she was relieved when she realized that he had begun to turn to other women for inflicting his perverse pleasures.

After her son was born, Julien ignored his wife and child entirely, claiming that she was no longer beautiful and that the little brat need only be brought to his attention when they had to make a public appearance as an upstanding government official's family. In contrast, Hercule thought that Sophie was even more beautiful than before, and every stolen moment he could spend with her and little Theo was the joy of his life.

Two years later the war reached France and the Occupation began. Hercule and Sophie found a new purpose to their lives. Hercule couldn't bear to stand by impotently as his government capitulated to the Germans. He knew too many Jews who had been kind to him when he was struggling in his youth and wanted to help them somehow as the deportations began. His black market connections proved valuable when it came to forging visas and buying officials, and soon he found himself at the hub of a resistance network. Sophie's marriage gave her a more personal motive for her new political consciousness: she was protected by her husband's powerful position in the government, but many of her female friends who were being persecuted by the new regime were not. So she rejoined the *sapphistes* at the bistro, a few of whom had experience evading the law and the money to do so. They were fighting for truth and freedom in the name of love and felt as if they could never fail.

Around them, however, were forces that only wanted to destroy them. The Germans, the Vichy collaborators, Sophia's former female lovers, jealous and angry – some to the point of violence and treachery to the cause – and of course her husband,

who seemed to sense the new source of passion in his wife and began to harm her again, even more cruelly.

Hercule's rage against Julien mounted during these years: every bruise, every cut or burn that Hercule uncovered on Sophia's beautiful body seared into him too. Luckily Julien had never harmed Theo; if he had, nothing would have stopped Hercule from killing Julien immediately. He would kill the monster someday, he promised himself. But Sophia wouldn't let him yet. Julien was too useful, she said, and she dismissed her husband's torture as petty scratches and meaningless marks.

Hercule could not dismiss them. Whenever he touched Sophia's body and saw a fresh crop of bruises, he was filled with fury and vowed his revenge anew. In the meantime, Sophia was using her husband's government connections to help the resistance with crucial information that only someone with an insider's access could provide. As she did so, she was also learning more about how deeply he was involved in crime, corruption, and collaboration. Julien's activities increasingly became the target of their underground activities and Hercule began to let his personal vendetta cloud his judgment. He made a few tactical errors, too many innocent people died – people whom he had been helping to escape like those women crossing the border in the snow – and to this day he was haunted by their faces as the soldiers dragged them away.

Sophia had also turned away from him then. His errors had cost her terribly. Julien had realized that she was betraying him somehow, and she and little Theo were placed under government guard in their home. Hercule couldn't see them for a full year; she had ignored his stealthy attempts at communication through servants and market delivery boys, and he had gone almost insane with anguish. One night he had been able to climb up the fire escape and peer into Sophia's bedroom window just to reassure himself that they were alive and well, but the sight that met his eyes wrenched his heart: Sophia curled on the bed, clutching Theo to her chest, heaving with sobs.
Hercule knew he had to rescue them somehow.

He arranged everything. A small army of resistance comrades and grateful relatives of those whose lives he had already saved rallied together with transportation, money, and forged documents. One week later, Hercule sent a note through Sophia's laundress that he would be there at midnight, when she and Theo should be ready to escape.

157

When he had arrived, she had simply handed Theo to him, kissed him, given him the poems she had written, and turned away, promising that they would be reunited someday in America. Had she ever really planned to join them? Or had she known all along that she would have to sacrifice her own life to save her son's?

Hercule hated to leave her, had even briefly considered forcibly taking her with them. But he knew that she would have resisted, perhaps even fought him, and so he had bowed to her will, living for the day – against all odds – that they would be reunited. He had really only felt half alive since her death. He was haunted by his memories of her and had been grimly cheered when he read the news of Julien's execution. When Hercule had finally felt secure in the fact that Theo had found happiness with both Johanna and Clea, he knew he could leave New York and return to Paris to try and reclaim a little of what he had lost. To some extent he had. The topography of the city was relatively unchanged since his escape, though the culture had of course moved on and collective memory was short. But Sophie was everywhere he went, at least the ghost of her – still young, desperate and beautiful, enraged and trapped as she was when he last saw her over forty years ago. In many ways, his sense of himself as a ghost was only compounded. But at least he was here, where they had fought together and risked their lives for love.

Now there was more life. There was Theo's daughter Herculine. At the end of the letter, Theo had given him Clea and Herculine's address and urged him to write to her, but for years Hercule had not known what to say. "Hello, I am the man who raised your father and loved your grandmother and now I would like to meet you?" It was too awkward, too uncomfortable. What did he have to offer the girl other than his own need of her?

Maybe that was enough. "I need you," he thought. "Because I am broken with loss. I miss your grandmother, and your father, and you might be able to give some part of them back to me." If he wrote her, would she come to him? He had thought about asking Johanna to help him reach out to the girl, but she had never once mentioned either Clea or Herculine during her regular visits to him over the last ten years, probably assuming that he knew nothing and that she could simply deny their existence out of her own sense of pride. He relied on Johanna so greatly as his last connection to Theo that he couldn't risk alienating her. He would have to contact Herculine on his own. She would be about twenty years old now.

Maybe now she was ready to hear from him. Her name made him smile briefly. He would write to her, his namesake. Somehow he would find the right words to say.

And then he could only hope, and pray. Maybe if he did, somehow Herculine would come to him in time. Before he left this world too. His time was coming. He could feel it. He had lived so many lives already. Too much loss, too much pain. Not enough love. Perhaps she could change that.

As these broken fragments of thoughts went through his mind, a cold wind whipped across the small courtyard and the sun dipped behind the clouds. Hercule felt chilled to the bone. He motioned to the attendant to come wheel him back inside. There he would write to the girl and sit by the fire in the main room of the *résidence*. It was the only hope of warmth he had left.

159

"Hercules was strong, to be sure, but he was also ingenious. And like other notable classical heroes – like Aeneas, Perseus, and Odysseus – he had a great deal of support from almost the entire pantheon of gods and other gifted beings. His father, Zeus, gave Hercules a shield; Athena supplied him with impenetrable armor and helmet; Hermes provided him with a sword; Phoebus Apollo gave him a bow and arrows; Linus taught him to play the lyre, and Chiron – the centaur – taught young Hercules the arts. In fact, the twelve labors of Hercules can be read as the twelve stages of adolescent social development: a heroic journey that every individual goes through as a rite of passage, ultimately including a journey through the land of the dead, an initiation into comprehension of life and mortality and summons us not only into adulthood and responsibility, but also into thinking beyond our own narcissistic egos about the welfare of others."

Theodore Danton, *Redefining Heroism: Reclaiming Hercules;* Columbia University Press; 1968

The Seventh Poem: Ariadne
Berkeley, March 1990

My life had become complicated and confusing. I missed the simplicity of the years before I found the poems, before I left new York and moved to Berkeley, before I found and lost Hyla. There were even times when all that I had discovered about the grandmother I never knew I had, and the personal and political battles she had fought during the war seemed overwhelming. Struggling against the unexpected harshness of the winds and rain of March with my third broken folding umbrella of the month, my heart sank as I heard one of the vital metal arms snap, and I hurried home in the late afternoon gloom, holding what looked like the plumage of a storm-damaged cormorant over my head.

Anthea laughed out loud when she saw me come in the door and drop my wet bag and leather jacket in a sodden heap on the floor.

"Girl," she said kindly, "We have got to get you some rain gear, or you're going to turn into a walking puddle!"

I looked at her numbly. "Gear?" I asked, "Is that really necessary? I can just go to the bookstore and buy another umbrella…"

"No, no, no," said Anthea taking charge. "Put that poor excuse of a coat back on, and you can use *my* umbrella – which, I would like to point out, does not fold, which is why it does not break – and you're coming with me to the store."

Two hours later, I happily paid for my purchases at the register of the Coastal Sport and Survival Outlet store, looked at Anthea contritely, and thanked her. With the permission of the employee who rang up my new waterproof wardrobe, I put my old clothes and boots in the bag, and was wearing all my new gear out the door. I had even bought a "real" umbrella. Anthea just put her arm around me and smiled. I felt as if I had been outfitted in an exceptionally sleek new suit of urban armor, and was ready for any of the battles awaiting me– from the weather to Johanna.

But I was not ready, upon arriving home dry and fortified, to find – waiting for us on the front porch – Linus, Phoebe, and a slender young man who looked startlingly like Phoebe, except that instead of Phoebe's spiky hair and coquettish allure, he had a mane of dark curls and more classical beauty. The young stranger had to be Phoebe's brother Dion. I remembered Linus telling me that he was studying theater and film down at UCLA and that Phoebe had been staying with him for the last few months while she was doing her research. I paused before mounting the front steps. I noted that Linus had his arm around Phoebe and assumed with some relief that they were reunited. This would make my recent lack of interest in intimacy with Linus much easier on him, I realized, and with a new source of affection in my heart, I said, "Hi Phoebe, welcome back."

Phoebe's face lit up, as did Linus's when they saw us approach, and Phoebe ran down the steps to hug me. As I stood there in the fine drizzle of the early evening twilight, I looked over Phoebe's shoulder and met Linus's gaze. It was the first time he had been over to our house in several weeks, and there was hesitation in his eyes, but he also looked pleased to see such an affectionate reunion between me and Phoebe.

Anthea motioned to everyone, "Come on, let's go inside!"

When we settled into the kitchen, I noticed that Dion, who had only nodded silently to me when Phoebe finally remembered to introduce him, was carrying a large box with him. He set it on the table and said with a theatrical flourish as he sliced the top open with a knife, "An offering to the gracious lady Herculine…" and proceeded to empty the box of its contents: six bottles of Santa Barbara Pinot Noir. I blushed at this dramatic tribute, and – since all eyes were upon me – I said in the same theatrically formal tone, "Consider this a gift to the house: now, let us celebrate the return of Phoebe to Berkeley!"

At the word "celebrate," Hermàn padded sleepily into the kitchen. "Hmmmm?" he said, "Did I hear the telltale 'clink' of bottles?"

A half-dressed young man followed him into the room and Anthea's eyes widened. "Who's your friend?" she asked with a teasing tone.

Hermàn slipped his arm around the fellow's bare waist and said, "Oh, sorry honey, this is Percy. Percy, don't be shy; this is everybody. Want some wine?" He handed a corkscrew to me. "What are you waiting for, *chica*?"

162

I recovered my composure after my surprise at meeting Percy, took my cue from Hermàn's own nonchalance, and set about opening the wine while Anthea similarly busied herself getting glasses and setting out some bread and cheeses. We both knew that Percy was a precocious undergraduate in Hermàn's discussion section of "Latino Literature of Revolution" – the course for which he was a Teaching Assistant that semester. Hermàn hadn't stopped talking about him since January. However, Anthea and I both disapproved of Hermàn's flagrant disregard for the university sexual harassment policy. Having an affair with a student before the semester's grades were turned in exceeded even the tacit honor code among graduate students. However, I decided to keep quiet about it until our guests had gone. I was certain that Anthea was having the same thoughts on the other side of the room, since she was uncharacteristically silent.

As the delicious wine began to flow, and empty bottles began to line up on the windowsill behind us, the gathering took on a new level of festivity. Soon Linus and Hermàn were laughing, Phoebe and Anthea were bantering playfully with Percy, who had proved to be quite witty, and I found myself deep in conversation with Dion. He was in town for two weeks, researching the film archives at Berkeley, he said. His graduate work focused on performative representations of crowds and large ritual ceremonies on stage and on screen. He was attempting to theorize that these moments in film and theater played cathartic roles in their respective cultures, usually preceding the climactic redemption or resolution of a central social or political conflict. I asked Dion what kinds of resources Berkeley had that UCLA didn't.

He looked at me with some surprise and said, "Don't you know that Berkeley has the single largest collection of archival footage of anti-war movements in the nation?"
I admitted that I had not known this, but that it made perfect sense considering the city's own dissident history during the Vietnam era.

"Oh yeah," effused Dion, "But it goes way beyond that. Anything having to do with insurgency, resistance, counter-insurgency – fictional or historical – it's all there, ever since the Lumière brothers made it possible for us to film it."

Intrigued, I asked, "Seriously? Is there footage from Vichy France?"

Dion smiled. "They've got it all. And what they don't have you'd have to go to Paris to find. Is that what you're working on?"

Even though I had been gripping the arms of my chair a bit too tightly during this last part of the conversation, I didn't feel like telling Dion about the poems, so I took a deep breath and said dismissively, "Oh no, it's just a side interest of mine. I'm a classicist, like Phoebe and Linus."

At the sound of their names, Phoebe and Linus looked up questioningly at me. Hermàn took the opportunity of this break in the conversation to steer Percy back to his bedroom off the hallway, and Anthea also excused herself, yawning, "Time for me to call it a night too, y'all. *Bon soir…*" and she headed up the stairs to bed.

That left me alone at the table with Linus, Phoebe, and Dion. The room was quiet, but warm. I looked at Phoebe and said, "Thanks for sending me that drawing of Hyla. I have it up on my wall."

Phoebe said with a worried look, "Still no word?"

I shook my head silently, looking down.

"She'll turn up," Linus said quietly.

Dion, not understanding the context of their suddenly somber conversation, said brightly to me, "So hey, want to take me to the film archives tomorrow? Could be some cool stuff there for your project."

Linus and Phoebe looked at us in surprise, but I was glad for the unexpected distraction and accepted Dion's offer. He had an effusive, kid brother appeal; it would be a nice change from all the rainy gloom I'd been having lately.

Dion picked up his coat and moved toward the door, as did Phoebe, but Linus hung back and put his arms around me. He said, "So…Phoebe and I were thinking of inviting you over to spend the night with us…"

I smiled and gave him a quick hug, then pulled away, saying, "Thanks Linus, but I'll take a rain check." And at that moment a large gust of wind spattered rain against the window behind us. Linus bowed his head in acceptance as he, Phoebe, and Dion went out into the storm. I leaned against the door after I closed it behind them and sighed deeply. It was time to get to work.

Once I was upstairs in my room, I took out my notebook of Sophia's poems and turned to the seventh one: "Ariadne." Daughter of King Minos, whose wife Pasiphae had been seduced by a bull (possibly Zeus in disguise) and given birth to the monstrous Minotaur. Ariadne had assisted the hero Theseus in conquering the Minotaur by providing him with a ball of twine that enabled him to find his way back out of the labyrinth imprisoning the monster.

When Theseus killed the Minotaur, Athens was liberated from providing the annual sacrifice of nine young men and women to feed the beast. In thanks for her help, when Theseus escaped from Minos' kingdom after incurring his wrath, he took Ariadne and her younger sister Phaedra with him, only to abandon Ariadne on an island and marry Phaedra – who turned into another tragic heroine in her own right.

According to some sources, when Ariadne awoke alone on the island, she was soon discovered and beloved by the god Dionysus, who made her his consort. This part of her tale was rarely told, I thought wryly, since it is a happy ending. Why couldn't the Greeks ever let any of their legendary women have a good life? Is it just that contentment and fulfillment don't make good stories? I rather liked the way things worked out for Ariadne. And as I scanned through the lines of Sophia's poem, I had the feeling that my grandmother had liked it too. She wrote,

> *A tangled ball of thread*
> *On a sandy island shore:*
> *That's how you found me,*
> *After he left me there, for her.*
> *She was barely my "sister."*
> *He was never my "husband."*
> *Just a self-glorified man,*
> *Trying to be a hero,*
> *And a frightened young girl*
> *Irresistibly drawn to his flame.*
> *He thought he could save us;*
> *Stop the endless sacrifice*
> *Of youth to the killing beast.*
> *And she believed him.*
> *But I knew his idea of salvation*
> *Was really enslavement.*
> *Only, he needed my help to do it.*
> *"The monster is within us all," he said,*
> *But I didn't believe him.*
> *"The monster is just in you," I thought,*
> *As I handed him the ball of thread.*
> *Down he went, into the maze.*
> *He came back bloody, and exhausted.*
> *"It is done," he said.*

But I knew that it had only begun.
He didn't kill the right one.
Half-bull, half-man,
Offspring of deception,
Crazed with rage,
Wreaking vengeance on us all.
The truth went deeper, farther back.
You knew this as well as I.
The father had the answers,
Knew what it meant to be a gift of a god.
With a lasso made
From my strongest silk thread,
You captured him, and learned it all.
And now we stand alone on this island,
Drunk with the wine of love
Bathed in ecstatic oceans of life.
The maze is shattered,
And we are free.

At least this was one poem where the story of the heroine and the labor of Hercules were uncannily well-matched. The seventh labor of Hercules was to capture the Cretan Bull, which had been given as a gift to King Minos from Poseidon, but – in some versions of the story – it had also seduced Minos' wife and fathered the Minotaur, after which, the bull went mad, or Poseidon made it crazy, and it began terrorizing people in Crete and tearing up the fields. Hercules then captured the bull, but when they tried to sacrifice it to Juno, she refused the offering since it reflected too much glory on Hercules, and so they set it free, at which point the bull wandered peacefully throughout the land.

I put down my notebook and sat back, wondering what Sophia was up to this time. She began and ended the poem with Ariadne and Dionysus, who was curiously fused with the Hercule(s) figure that had played a similar role of savior and comrade in previous poems. Then there were those mentions of a sister and a husband, but were these just stand-ins for Sophia's husband Julien and another comrade-sister, as in "Electra"? As far as I knew, Sophia had no actual sisters or brothers. But what was all this business about killing the wrong man, whose father was the one with all the answers? In the symbolic realm of the poem, Julien/Theseus had apparently killed someone with Sophia's help, which had stopped

166

some of the bloodshed during the occupation, but Sophia seemed to be suggesting that it was this man's father, whom Hercule(s) had captured, who held the key to truly ending the war. Now the question was: who were these men, and what did the father know that the son did not?

I put the notebook down wearily and rubbed my temples. Writing the poems must have offered my grandmother an excellent source of cryptic catharsis; but for me, four and a half decades later, they were getting harder to figure out. Before going to bed, I looked over my Archaic Poetry translations for the next day and after polishing a few lines, I fell deeply into sleep, which was aided by the copious amounts of red wine I had enjoyed earlier in the evening. As the winter storm raged outside and sheets of rain washed against my bedroom windows, I dreamed of ocean waves and empty beaches, running after a rapidly unraveling yet seemingly endless ball of string.

In the morning, I was awakened by the sound of the phone ringing downstairs and the click of the answering machine as it finally picked up. The voice was male, and unfamiliar, but as he spoke, I realized that it was Dion, reminding me to meet him at the film archives.

As I reached for my jeans, I ran my schedule for the day through my head and was relieved when I realized that I could indeed meet him that afternoon. But first I had to put in my shift at the library, and make it through Archaic Poetry. I sighed, padded down the hall to the bathroom, and splashed some water on my face. By the time I got to the film archive, I would need a nap.

Sure enough, after class, Dion was waiting for me outside the film wing of the library, and his face broke into a large smile when he saw me approaching. "Hey," he said, "I was worried that you wouldn't make it! You know, I need you to get in there; I have guest privileges but need to be accompanied by a Berkeley student for full access."

"Sorry," I said, a little surprised and annoyed, "I didn't realize. I thought you'd been getting work done in there all day!"

"Nope," said Dion, as we passed through the magnetic sensors by the doorway leading to the film stacks. "Phoebe doesn't have an active ID since she's on leave, and Linus was too busy all day. You're my only hope. How long can you stay?"

Somewhat put off by Dion's sudden dependence on me, I told him that I only had about two hours.

Dion shrugged, seemed satisfied, and said, "Okay, cool. Let's get to work!"

He headed over to a computer terminal and started looking up films. I followed him, then tried a few entries of my own on the terminal next to his. I typed "Vichy," and the screen immediately filled with hundreds of entries. Overwhelmed, I redefined my search. Taking a chance, and thinking of the "Ariadne" poem, I typed first "Vichy," then "Bull." After the computer sifted through the thousands of possibilities it contained, I was surprised to see only one entry on the screen that read: "Papal Bull, Vichy France, Resistance Riot 1941." Had there been a Papal Bull issued during the war that had caused a riot? I had to find out. I quickly wrote down the location of the film in the archive and then tried another entry, "Danton." Again, the screen was filled with countless entries. My family name was evidently popular in France. Once again, I refined my search by adding one word: "Julien." Two entries came up this time, one that contained footage from an unveiling ceremony for public art commissioned by his bogus committee, and one that momentarily shook me: footage from his criminal trial in 1946.

I wrote down the entry locations with a shaking hand. I looked over at Dion who was printing out pages of listings and grinning. I turned to him and said, "I'm going to go find my films and maybe watch one of them before I go, but listen, it's fine with me if you stay after I leave."

"Wish I could," said Dion, "But they're watching us and will probably kick me out as soon as you go." I looked over at the media services desk and saw that the steely-eyed gentleman who had let us in was indeed watching us closely. Dion continued, "I've made a great start here; let's find some tapes and then meet up in the viewing rooms. We can always spend more time here tomorrow, right?"

As he went off by himself through the film stacks, I made a mental note to call Linus and arrange for him to take his fair share of babysitting Dion in the library the following day. In the meantime, it was time to watch some films. I eventually found the three tapes I was looking for, and when I reached the viewing rooms, I saw that Dion was already waiting for me there. When the media librarian assigned us to a viewing room with only one viewing station, I turned to Dion and asked him, "Aren't you going to watch some films too?"

"Nah, not today," he said, happily. "I'll just watch yours."

Incredulous that he didn't think to ask me if that was all right, yet also somehow disarmed by his easy self-assurance that of course I

would want his company, I simply shrugged after a moment and said, "Suit yourself."

We made ourselves as comfortable as possible in the hard plastic swiveling chairs in front of the viewing monitor, and I inserted the tape about the Resistance riot in 1941. Dion and I watched as blurry figures in black and white shakily moved through the city streets of Paris with an eerie silence that jarred against the frantic movements of their bodies. Rocks were thrown, windows were shattered, a flaming torch appeared – held aloft then thrown into a parked car, which almost immediately ignited, then exploded. The camera must have been heavy, I thought, since the frame shook even more than the figures themselves.

As if reading my thoughts, Dion said, "Isn't this amazing? The equipment they were using weighed over fifty pounds. Can you imagine what they would have been able to capture if they had the handheld cameras we have today?" He shivered with excitement.

I just raised an eyebrow at him and turned back to the screen. The scene had changed; the protesters were now in front of a church that looked as if it had already seen more than its fair share of violence and warfare. Its walls appeared soot-stained, its elaborately carved portcullis looked charred and hacked away in places too. The men gathered in front of the church were raising their fists in rhythmic unison and their silent mouths looked to be yelling, or chanting, the same unintelligible words. My French was good, but not good enough to figure out what they were saying by reading their lips, and I yearned to understand them.

When there wasn't much footage left on the tape, it looked as if a group of angry protesters pushed the film crew roughly to the side; they were so close that they were out of focus, and suddenly the frame went entirely askew. After being righted, the focus shifted again to a scene by a river where a body was being lifted out of the water and this time there were women present too, wringing their hands and holding each other up for comfort. Who was the drowned man?

Just as the film ended, I could see that the streets, now darkened, were ablaze, and many windows in the church by the river had been broken. Which church was it? How could I find out? That portcullis was distinctive…perhaps I could track it down in the religious architecture stacks upstairs. In the meantime, I rewound and froze the frame in order to make a quick sketch of the distinctive

169

features of the medieval entryway. Dion looked on approvingly, murmuring, "Nice work." And then, "Ever been to the Marais?"

"Huh?" I said.

"That church," he said, pointing to my notebook and to the screen. "It's in the Marais in Paris. Kind of a famous one. Saint Séverin."

"How did you recognize it?" I asked, amazed.

"Easy," said Dion nonchalantly. "The way it's placed on the street. There's nothing else like it."

"Thank you," I said, admiringly. "You just saved me a lot of work."

"*Mon plaisir, cherie*," said Dion with a charming smile. "Ready for the next one?"

Marveling at his peculiar combination of arrogance and charm, I slipped in the next tape, the one depicting the sculpture unveiling ceremony. Again, the footage was brief, in black and white, and silent, but it wasn't choppy at all. Of course, I thought, the camera could stay stationary this time, since it was a formal event. As the frame panned the audience of well-bundled burghers, then focused on the podium, I felt myself tense in preparation for a shock. I was going to see my grandfather again, but this time in motion, and it was entirely possible that Sophia would be by his side. My heart leapt: I wanted so badly to see my grandmother alive.

There were the officials…Ebermann, Arnault, and Schiffer, and the now familiar handsome face of my grandfather, but wait – I paused and rewound the tape– who was that woman clinging to Julien's arm? She was blonde, and she was laughing. I stared at her, motionless. Where was Sophia? And who was this woman? As the short film continued with the unveiling of a particularly uninspiring sculpture of a winged woman carrying a rifle in one hand and a scythe in the other, I reached for the cassette box and searched for a date for the footage. My heart sank when I saw that it had been filmed in September 1943. My grandmother had died several months earlier. And apparently Julien had already replaced her.

This thought sent a chill through my skin. Could this woman be the Phaedra to my grandmother's Ariadne? Had Sophia already known before she died who would replace her on Julien's arm after she was gone?

Just then, the image on the screen shifted; the crowd was gone and the square was deserted. The camera simply rested its gaze on the unveiled statue, now desecrated with large stains of what

170

looked like black paint (or could it be blood?) and the carcass of a dead, partially decayed animal at the statue's feet. I gasped involuntarily and leaned in closer to get a better view of what had been done to the statue. The animal looked like a cow, but I quickly realized that it had horns, and it did not have an udder. It was a bull.

I rose to my feet and ejected the tape, surprising Dion, and said, "Look, I have to go. I'm going to bring the last film home and watch it tonight. Sorry to leave so soon, but there's something I have to check out over in the book stacks."

Dion, looking at me with some wariness, said, "Aren't you going to tell me what this is all about? It's pretty freaky stuff…why are you interested in it anyway?"

"Not now," I said, grabbing my book bag and hoisting it over my shoulder, "I'll tell you later." And I was gone, furiously musing over what I had seen. The footage of the ceremony had apparently been preserved in the political resistance film archive because of what had been done to the statue afterwards. I hadn't seen a photo of this one in my book of *Civic Art As Mythic Nation Building*, but it was possible that I had overlooked it somehow. However, that wasn't what I needed to check. I had to find out about the symbolic significance of bulls in Vichy France.

Back up in the stacks, I went right to the section containing papal history. Who was the Pope during WWII anyway, and what stance had he taken on the war? The first book I found informed me that there had actually been two Popes during WWII; the first one, Pius XI, had died of old age in 1939, and then Pius XII had taken over. I looked up Pius XI first. And after reading just a few paragraphs, I had to sit down. His story held one of the missing pieces I had been looking for.

Pius XI had been born Achille Rati, and I smiled upon encountering another kindred soul both cursed and blessed with the legacy of a classical name. But this Achilles had not been much of a warrior before he became Pope; he had been a noted paleographer of ancient Christian texts, and had served for many years as the vice prefect of the Vatican library. I chuckled; we also shared a love of libraries as well as our classical names. In 1926, Pius XI had undertaken the first of many battles against the reactionary monarchist movement known as the *Action Française*, which had until this time operated with the support of a great many French Catholics.

Pius XI condemned the movement, declaring that the stability of France should not be tied to a monarchist restoration.

Although the condemnation caused great unrest among French Catholics, most obeyed his edict. That is, until the creation of the Vichy regime restored the hopes of former *Action Française* members, most of whom had become collaborationists in the hopes of reviving their nationalist and royalist dreams. In fact, many hoped that Pétain would simply restore the monarchy. I learned that the *Action Française* spearheaded the riot in 1941, which killed as many Resistance agents as collaborationists. After the war, all of the surviving members of the *Action Française* were condemned to death, and the organization was permanently dissolved. Sadly, I thought, Pius XI did not live to see the victory of his battle.

The part of his story that had caused me to sit down came next. Before Pius XI died, he had actively opposed the Nazi ideology of racism and totalitarianism by issuing a papal bull of sorts called an "encyclical" in 1937 that condemned the anti-Semitism of Hitler's regime. He also gave a public address that was soon published worldwide which contained the fateful words, "I say to you it is impossible for a Christian to take part in anti-Semitism. It is inadmissible. Through Christ and in Christ we are the spiritual progeny of Abraham. Spiritually, we are all Semites."

When I read this, I whistled softly. Those words were enough to start a riot. But this modern day Achilles had gone farther. During the year before he died, Pius XI had prepared another encyclical, condemning all racism and anti-Semitism; but this one was never published. The man who would soon take over the papacy, Cardinal Eugenio Pacelli, suppressed it, fearing an anti-Catholic backlash, or hostility from Nazi Germany. I couldn't help but notice that the Cardinal's first name, Eugenio, like "Eugenie" from the "Electra" poem, resonated with the murderous philosophy of "eugenics" that fueled Hitler's racism. Whose side had he been on, I wondered. As I scanned the page in the book, I was relieved to see that during the German occupation of Rome this new Pope had arranged that Italian Jews would be sheltered safely in convents and monasteries. Up to one thousand Jews were even concealed at his papal summer residence.

I knew I had struck a rich vein of informational ore, and with that certainty, I checked out several books and left the library with a lighter heart, which – though I didn't fully want to admit it – was partly due to Dion's obvious interest in me. I wondered idly how long he was going to be in town.

I had been in the library for longer than I realized and the sky was dark when I stepped outside into a cold, light rain. I felt a shiver run down my spine and I held my book bag close against my chest for comfort. Inside it I could feel the sharp edges of the third videotape that I had taken out of the library. I still planned to watch it that night. I hoped that neither Anthea nor Hermàn would be home when I returned. I wanted to watch this one in privacy. I had no idea what shocks my grandfather's criminal trial held in store for me. While having Dion by my side in the viewing room earlier that afternoon had been useful, I had the feeling that the tape in my bag might contain information that I would prefer not to share.

My surprise was therefore mixed with annoyance when I entered the house and saw not only Hermàn and Anthea sitting in the kitchen laughing and drinking wine, but Dion too. He had probably brought over a few more bottles to ingratiate himself with my roomates, I thought testily, as I picked up a pile of mail set aside for me on the counter. He apparently had an endless supply. But why was he here? Dion answered my unspoken question before I had even taken off my boots.

"Hey Herculine!" he called out happily. "I came by to see if you wanted to watch that video you brought home tonight!"

"Um, hi Dion," I hedged, avoiding his gaze as I sorted through my mail, "I don't know, I'm kind of tired. Maybe tomorrow…" most of the mail was headed straight for the recycling bin, but one letter puzzled me. The return address on the cream-colored business size envelope was "H. Vega" printed with a shaky hand above the embossed seal of a "Maison de Convalesance" in Paris. My own name had been typed out professionally above my mother's old New York address, which had been crossed out and forwarded twice to me: first by the Post Office to my mother's new address, then in handwriting I didn't recognize to my address in Berkeley. There was a faint European slant to the letters in the second address…could Ramon be handling the mail for my mother now? And who is "H. Vega?" I wondered as I headed to the stairway. Entirely preoccupied with opening the envelope as I began trudging up the stairs to my room, I didn't realize that Dion was right behind me until I reached the top. I turned around to face him when I reached the door to my bedroom and startled us both. He was holding a bottle of wine with two glasses and smiling irrepressibly.

Instead of the irritated words I wanted to say to him, I looked at his lovely face, shining with hope, and I gave in. There was

173

something about his unabashed attachment to me that melted my resistance.

"Okay," I said. "Just help me bring the TV and VCR up to my room, so we don't bug everybody in the house, all right?"

Beaming, Dion set the wine bottle and glasses on my desk and ran down to the living room to start unplugging the machines so that he could carry them upstairs. Meanwhile, I wearily straightened up my room so that Dion would not be forced to sit on any of my old socks or damp towels. I strategically placed my book bag and a stack of books on my dad's leather armchair so that he wouldn't be tempted to try and sit there. But that left only the bed as a viewing perch. I carefully placed two stacks of pillows at opposite ends of the mattress, encouraging a wide berth between us, and then I sat down to read the letter. It was written in French, in the same shaky hand and ink as the "H. Vega" on the envelope. I translated as best as I could...

Dear Miss Danton,

You do not know me, but I am an old friend of your family. I took care of your father when he was young, and I miss him more than I can express. I am embarrassed to admit that I have known of your existence for many years now; I apologize for not contacting you sooner. But now I am alone, and too infirm to travel to meet you. I wonder if you would care to come to Paris to meet an old friend of your father? It would mean a great deal to me if you would.

Yours sincerely, Hercule Vega

I sat on my bed in silence. All the sounds of the house seemed magnified as I contemplated the letter in my hand. Hercule was real. As real as Dion downstairs struggling with all the wires and cords of the TV and VCR. I hoped he would struggle a little longer. I needed time to think. In French, Hercule had written, *Il me manques plus que je peux dire*...which translated to, "I miss him more than I can say." Yes, I thought. I know what you mean, Hercule. His voice was so clear. It was as if I had been hearing it for months through my grandmother's poems. Or was that my father's voice I was hearing? Everything was starting to blur. Hercule had found me. I could meet him without Johanna's help. I felt a surge of triumph and hope. I would write to Hercule as soon as Dion left, and tell him I had the poems and had been wanting to meet him for months, and...

174

My bedroom door banged open as Dion lunged into my room carrying the TV and VCR, their cords strung loosely around his neck and shoulders like garlands of some exotic black-vined plant. He grinned at me and asked, "So, where do you want these anyway?"

I motioned vaguely to my desk, and as Dion figured out where the electrical outlets were, I continued composing my response to Hercule in my head and stashed his letter safely in my book bag. When Dion had finished setting up the machines, he came over to the edge of the mattress and sat down right next to me, handing me a full glass of wine with one hand and the remote control in the other. After pouring himself a glass, he pulled the stack of pillows from the far end of the bed where I had placed them and plumped them right next to me, settling himself in cozily, his thigh against mine. I rolled my eyes, wondering why I didn't just tell him to back off. I toyed with the idea for a moment and then shrewdly appraised his potential as a bed partner. His eyes were glowing, and his body was emanating an enticingly androgynous presence. I took a deep breath, smiled, and decided to just relax and enjoy the wine. Later I might even decide to enjoy Dion himself.

Apparently unaware of my ulterior motives in allowing him to stay by my side, Dion reached for the remote and said, "Hey, can you hit the lights? Let's start this, okay?" Bemused and baffled by his enthusiasm and more than a little affronted by his commanding tone, I obligingly switched off my lamp, and Dion pressed "play."

After some crackling and static, the frames settled onto a courtroom scene. A large bare room with a tribunal of dark suited men lining the rows of chairs along the perimeter, with a high table of older men in dark robes at the far end. In the middle of the room was one table with an empty chair and an antiquated microphone, awaiting a testimony. While the footage was in black and white, the major difference between this film and the other videos I had watched that day was that this time, there was sound.

A buzzing noise filled the courtroom, mingled with the impatient scraping of chairs and clearing of throats. Dion and I waited along with the assembled witnesses in the court for something to happen. It took a long time, but a door suddenly opened off to the side of the room, everyone stood up, and three men in pale shirtsleeves were led to the table. All three men walked with bowed heads.

I recognized Julien Danton immediately, due to his blonde hair – the other two men were dark – but other than this sole

175

distinguishing feature, I was shocked by how different he looked from the film I'd seen earlier in the day. Before his arrest, my grandfather had been a strapping, charismatic man with a wide, confident smile and large, easy movements. Here in the courtroom, stripped of his double-breasted suits and elegant ties, reduced to the status of a common criminal—granted, one that was on trial for treason—Julien looked beaten and crushed.

As if reading my thoughts, Dion murmured, "That's the same guy, isn't it? Damn. Talk about a shadow of his former self!"

I shushed him as the trial began. In a thick, fast, almost incomprehensible stream of French, the judges on the bench reeled off a list of the crimes of the first accused man. I picked up on counts of collaboration, plotting against the state, violence against officials, extortion. When asked how he pleaded to these charges, *"coupable ou innocent"* under pain of death by guillotine, the first man answered simply, *"Coupable."* And he was led away. The second accused man's arraignment proceeded with similar swiftness. But this one had been an arms smuggler as well as an extortionist, collaborator, and black market supplier. He admitted his guilt with the same *sang froid* as the first. He was led away to scattered applause, and then the room was silent with anticipation.

Julien Danton sat alone at the table. The camera re-focused its frame. It was clear that this was the trial that was being filmed for posterity. Dion nudged me in the ribs, saying, "Did you see that? Who *is* this guy?" I ignored him, and shushed him again, as the Judge said in a louder voice,

"Julien Danton, you are accused of the following crimes: collaboration, espionage, multiple counts of murder, extortion, and sexual slavery." *Esclavage sexuelle.* At this last accusation I gasped. There was no misunderstanding. Dion gripped my arm.
The Judge continued, "In light of your status as one of the highest ranking advisors to the Vichy government, the seriousness of your crimes, and the innumerable lives lost through your plots against the state, the court denies you the opportunity for mercy. The proof is irrefutable. We offer you only the chance to make a public apology to the citizens of France. Please stand."

Julien stood shakily, and drew a piece of heavily folded paper from his shirt pocket. He began to read:

"Gentlemen of the court, citizens of France, my beloved country, I only did what I thought would restore France to her former glory: the noblest monarchy in the history of western

civilization, the flower of culture in barbaric times. As a proud and loyal member of the *Action Française*," (here there was some hissing in the court), "I knew that all of my actions were justified if I could bring France to her destiny even one day sooner." Here he put down his paper and addressed the assembled crowd directly. "You mention lives lost; this was war, gentlemen. That is what happens in a war. As for the rest, it is trivial. These are desperate times, and call for desperate measures. I do not apologize so much as I exclaim my regret that I will not live to see the fruits of my labors: long live France! Long live the King! May God restore the divine lineage to its rightful throne!" The court erupted into mayhem as Julien sat down calmly.

The Judge banged his gavel for order, and silence was restored. He spoke in ringing tones, "Monsieur Danton, your confession is an outrage to the Republic. But there is one charge that we would like you to address specifically. How can you justify, in the name of your Catholic God" – here the judge's words were tight with contempt – "the murder of one Archbishop T____, an official of your own Church?"

The film had crackled at the sound of the Archbishop's name and I strained to hear more clearly. I rewound the tape and tried again, unsuccessfully. I impulsively gripped Dion's arm. I pressed "pause" and turned to face him.

"How good is your French?" I asked. "Are you getting all this?"

"It's pretty good," said Dion, "Why? What did you miss?"

"The Archbishop's name... Did you hear what it was?"

"Yeah, he said 'Toro,'" said Dion, "*Toro* in Spanish is like *taureau* in French, like in astrology, right? Taurus, you know...the bull."

I stared at him for a moment, my mouth slightly open in mute surprise. "Right. Thanks," I said, blushing with self-reproach that I – the classics scholar – had been too wrapped up in the drama of the scenario to translate this most elemental of romance language derivations. I turned back to the screen, my mind racing with images of the Minotaur, the Cretan bull, the desecrated public monument we had seen earlier in the day, and superimposed over them all – the sadness in my grandmother's beautiful face.

"Wait," said Dion, pulling me back out of my reverie. "What's this all about anyway? It's an incredible scene, but why do you care about it?"

177

I gave him a level stare and said, "I'll tell you later. Maybe. Now, just let me get through this, okay?"

Dion sat back dejectedly against the pillows. I ignored him, pressed "play," and the film continued.

Julien, still seated, was saying – with a slight trace of his previous arrogance – that he had done the republic the favor of killing Archibishop Taureau, who had been a true fanatic, an anti-royalist terrorist, but one who killed Resistance as well as Vichy agents; he was just out to get anyone who didn't put the church first. Julien admitted that he had thought that Taureau had been specifically intent on undermining the *Action Française*, but in fact, he had just been a pawn of the Pope – here Julien spat on the floor of the courtroom and the gathered citizens again erupted in shouts and tumult which only repeated poundings of the Judge's gavel could quell—and it had been the Pope, the one who signed the edict condemning the *Action Française*, who had been the real threat. Julien punched his right fist into his left hand at the end of this speech and his face was curled into an ugly sneer. It was easy to read his gesture and his expression: if he could have killed the Pope too, he would have.

The judge said, "Take him away. The guillotine is too good for him. He will be shot at dawn." Guards led Julien away and the crowd closed in behind him in a roar. The film ended with a crackle and blur. Unsteadily I leaned forward and turned off the machine. I fell back against the pillows and realized that I was exhausted. I looked over at Dion, who was staring at me intently.

He said, "I get it. This guy was related to you. Your last name is Danton too, isn't it? Who was he, anyway? Did you know any of this had happened?"

I shook my head, "Not really, no. He was my grandfather. I knew he was shot as a traitor, but the rest of this is new information."

Dion filled my glass with wine and said, "Here, drink this, it will help."

I held his gaze as I drank deeply. Then I set the glass down on the windowsill by the bed. Dion set his glass down beside mine, and kneeling on the bed, pulled me towards him. As I rose to my knees, I realized that Dion had the same full lips and delicately drawn cheekbones as Phoebe, though his eyes were slightly larger and more thickly lashed than his sister's, which gave him a curiously feminine beauty and yet a distinctly boyish allure. Slender as I was, and not

much taller, the strength of Dion's arms around my waist was unmistakenly masculine, as was the rough texture of his unshaven cheeks against my own.

Against my better judgment, my mind spinning with wine and the shock of my grandfather's trial, I welcomed the chance to escape into Dion's passion. Keeping one small part of my brain detached, at least for a few minutes before plunging entirely into the rhythm of our increasingly deep kisses, I thought of Hyla, and how she would laugh if she could see me now. Then, as Dion grabbed a handful of my curls with one hand and unfastened my jeans with the other, I surrendered that last shred of detachment, and let myself become fully absorbed in his androgynous charms, so similar, I thought, as I pulled his shirt off over his head, to my own.

The next morning, I awoke early to the sound of rain on the roof, and padded downstairs with my notebook, leaving Dion fast asleep in my bed. I curled up in the deep window seat in the living room, surrounded by Anthea's colorful pillows and quilt, and wrote my response to "H. Vega" in my best French:

Dear Hercule,

Thank you for contacting me. For months I have wondered how to find you and worried that I would never have the chance to meet you. The only reason I know of your existence is that I found the poems written by my father's mother, Sophia Danton. I think you knew her too. Did you ever see her poems? They are dedicated to you, and many of them are about you, I think. I am not sure. I would love to come to Paris to meet you this summer. I hope that you are in good health and that we can correspond in the meantime. There is so much that I would like to ask you.

Yours fondly, Herculine

Satisfied with my efforts, I tucked the letter into my notebook to send later that morning. Turning to the pages of my grandmother's poems, I looked over "Ariadne" once again and admired Sophia's cryptic perfection. She knew Julien had killed the wrong man, that his "father," the Pope, had been the real threat to the *Action Française* and to Vichy. But the Pope had been a friend to the Resistance, and somehow, Sophia and Hercule had benefited from his protection. Slowly, and with some relief, I copied out the poem in preparation for sending it to Johanna. As I wrote down the words, and came to

the reference to "slavery," I thought back to Julien's trial and the charge against him of trafficking in women, and I felt a chill. Was the woman by Julien's side at the art commission event a sample of his wares? Had he tried to sell his own wife's charms to others, just as she had been, essentially, sold to him in marriage? I shivered. As I finished copying the poem, I knew that there were some questions I would never find the answers to, and some answers I didn't want to know.

Theo
New York, 1978

Theo sat in the deep leather armchair in his study, staring out the window at the overcast sky. He had just returned from the hospital, where his internist had broken the news to him: the headaches he had been experiencing with increasing intensity were not migraines. He had a brain tumor. The cancer had already metastasized aggressively, and he had only a few months, possibly less, to live. His doctors had wanted him to stay in the hospital for observation and more tests, but Theo had staggered out the door before his internist could finish speaking.

The roaring of the void in his head that had begun in the medical examination room had receded now to a numb buzzing of fear. Tears ran unnoticed down his cheeks. He didn't want to die. He was too young, only forty-two... It wasn't fair, it wasn't right. All the hackneyed excuses made by every existential coward he had ever scorned now filled his head. He had thought he would never stoop so low. He, of all people, should know that no one is ever "too young" to die. But he was still filled with anguish and fear of oblivion. Now death was no longer an abstract concept, but his own ending, and he would have to face it. There was no way that he could ever accomplish everything he had still hoped to contribute to academia. But how could he leave when there was still so much to heal with Johanna, so much more joy to be shared with Clea, and so much to tell little Herculine?

A spasm of pain shot through his head and doubled him over, gasping for air.

He lurched towards his desk, his mind whirling, and unlocked the small center drawer, removing a slim sheaf of pale blue paper. He had intended to eventually give the poems to Herculine on her twenty-first birthday, but now that he knew he wasn't going to make it until then, he wanted to hide them somewhere Johanna would never find them. She would search through all his papers, he knew, but there had to be one place she wouldn't think to look.

Theo had already written into his will that he was leaving Herculine all of his books when she turned twenty-one, including the shelves of numerous first editions, which he knew was extravagant, but he wanted to give her something tangible and valuable from his

181

life. He had never told her about the poems, or about anything substantial from his past if he could help it, but he wanted her to have them. They were the only true heirloom he had to offer her. Everything else from that time had been lost. He knew that someday, when she was old enough to read them, Herculine would be drawn to the one book he had dedicated to her, so he pulled the slim volume from the shelf closest to his desk and slipped the poems deep into the center pages. Then, without disturbing any of the fine dust that had collected on the spine of the book or on the shelf in front of it, he replaced it next to the others.

Theo closed his eyes and sat back down heavily in his chair. He remembered when he had written the book, *Redefining Heroism: Reclaiming Hercules*. It was during the period when he and Johanna were not on speaking terms, due to his announcement of his intention to legally adopt Herculine as his daughter. As if acknowledgingthe sacrifice he had possibly made of his marriage when he made a place for his child in his heart, Theo had begun and completed his work on the book that would ultimately be dedicated to his daughter, but only he knew that he had also written it in honor of Hercule.

When the book was first published, and his colleagues read the inscription, a fairly extensive yet muted scandal reverberated throughout the international community of Classics scholars. At Columbia, where Theo was the well-loved Chair of the Classics department, the atmosphere was generally more solicitous. The Chancellor of the University even called Theo into his office not long afterwards, to assure him, with only the faintest trace of awkwardness, that his daughter would, of course, when the time came, be eligible for a scholarship to Columbia if merited by her eventual scholastic achievement. Theo had to smile at this rare expression of bonhomie from the Chancellor, and shook his hand warmly in thanks. It was the most overt form of congratulations he had received. The rest of his colleagues opted for a particular brand of professional yet congenial discretion that made itself felt through such barely perceptible signs as a touch on the shoulder, more inquiries than usual into his health, and even an entirely unprecedented bundt cake from his secretary that Christmas. He had delivered the cake to Clea and little Herculine, who was just three years old. They had both enjoyed it immensely.

Johanna, however, hadn't spoken to him for almost a full year. They had lived together in cold silence, except for the nights

182

that Theo had spent with Clea and Herculine, returning to the house on Riverside Drive before dawn, playing out the charade of his marriage. He and Johanna had always had separate bedrooms and independent lives, but during this period of their life together he watched with sorrow as the lines on Johanna's face grew deeper and her hair turned from pale gold to silver. He was causing her suffering, he knew, but he couldn't bear to leave her. Once she began speaking to him again and they had rebuilt their partnership, he understood that they had a bond that ran, in many ways, deeper than his passionate love for Clea. He and Johanna were both orphans of the war and now they were each other's family. Their marriage had been the only stable foundation in his life aside from Hercule.

Hercule... Through his haze of pain, Theo could clearly remember the night that Hercule had given him the poems. It was his twenty-first birthday and Hercule had taken him to a French bistro in Brooklyn that was owned by some of his French expatriate friends. They had ordered bottle after bottle of cheap burgundy and drank until they were weeping and laughing interchangeably. At the end of the evening, Hercule walked with Theo to the subway entrance and, as they were saying goodnight, he thrust a thin envelope into Theo's hands.

"Here, my boy," Hercule said in French, "There is not much that this old man has to give you, but this is one of the few treasures I own, and I want you to have it."

Theo was baffled, his head thick with wine, and he said, "But Hercule, you don't need to give me anything more; you've given me my life!"

Hercule shook his head sadly, and said, "No, Theo, your mother would want you to have this. She wrote these poems and gave them to me the night you and I left Paris. I can no longer derive any pleasure from reading them; I know them all by heart. It is time that they were yours. You have little enough to remember her by."

With that said, Hercule embraced Theo, kissed him on both cheeks, and turned away slowly into the night. Theo walked down the steps to the subway and read the poems on the train during the long ride back up town to Columbia. He translated them from the original French as he read, mystified by their significance, but intrigued by their radical departures from the original classical myths they were based on, which of course he knew well. It had been

183

painful for him to read them, and to see his mother's writing on every page. And she had dedicated and given the poems to "Hercule, who knows that love never dies." There had been many times over the years that Theo had wondered if his mother and his guardian been more than friends. Finally, here was the evidence.

Theo remembered the sick feeling in his stomach then, the obviousness of his discovery mixing unhappily with all the wine he had consumed, and realized that it wasn't so different from the nausea he was feeling now, facing the reality of his imminent death. How could he tell Hercule he was dying? How could he tell Herculine the truth about his past? She was so young...would she even understand? There were too many silences and secrets. There was so much that he wanted to tell her, so much that she had a right to know – but now that time was running out, he would have to rely on others to tell her his story. And who better than Hercule?

The time had come to ask Hercule for his help one last time. Theo reached for the pad of paper and pencil on his desk. He began to write.

Dear Hercule,

I am dying, and there is something I must ask of you before I do...

All too soon there was a knock on his door just as he was finishing the letter, and Theo realized that the sky was dark outside his windows. It was Johanna, bringing some soup for him from the kitchen. Had the doctors called her? She didn't seem too upset, but her face had a concerned expression.

"What are you doing, darling? You look exhausted," she said.

"I've been writing a letter to Hercule," he said.

"Hercule?" Johanna's eyes looked worried. "Why didn't you just call him?"

Theo cleared his throat and said, "Sit down, darling. I have unfortunate news. I've been to see the doctors..." At the alarmed look on his wife's face, he reached out his hand and said gently, "I had hoped that we would have a long life together, my dear. But it seems that I don't have much longer to live..."

He trailed off and Johanna whispered, "No...no, no – what is it? Why?" Her large grey eyes were wide with fear.

Theo told her all that he knew, and she begged him to call his doctors and consent to any procedure they recommended. He rested his head back against his chair, allowing the painkillers to provide him temporary respite for a few moments, then agreed. He could do this at least for her.

184

Johanna left the room to call the hospital, and her face was flushed as she turned away, which Theo knew meant that she was straining with the effort to hold back tears. When she returned, he could see that she was mustering all her self-control, and he admired her but also wanted to soothe her, so he said, "Thank you, darling. Please call Hercule also, tell him to expect a letter from me, and give him my love."

Johanna looked out the window and nodded her head.

Theo quickly sealed the letter in an envelope, addressed it, and handed it to her. "Would you do me the favor, my dear, of posting it for me tomorrow?"

Her eyes searched his face for a moment, then she took the letter from his outstretched hand and placed it in her bag. "Yes," she said. "Of course."

Theo winced with pain, suddenly fatigued, closed his eyes, and rested his head back against the chair once more. Johanna stood, stroked her hand across his brow, brushed back his mop of graying curls, and bent to kiss his forehead as his breathing grew deep and regular. One of her tears fell on his cheek, but he did not wipe it away.

When Theo woke in his armchair a few hours later, the first strains of dawn were streaking the gray sky with delicate fuchsia tendrils. He remembered that he was dying, and thought that really what he couldn't bear was to leave the beauty of the world behind. He remembered that before he had fallen asleep he had made a decision about Herculine, and that he had finally written to Hercule.

It would all work out in the end. He would go to the hospital in a few hours, they would take more tests, possibly even operate, and then he might have a few more months, even years to live. One had to stay positive, and although the pain was getting worse, he would do his best. As he reached for a glass of water by his chair and the bottle of painkillers, he thought of calling Clea to tell her, but he couldn't bear it. He would call her when the tests were over. She wouldn't be able to visit him in the hospital anyway, not while he was under Johanna's care. He longed to see Clea and Herculine one more time, just in case he died.

At this thought, a spasm of pain shot through his head, and Theo slumped back into his chair. "*Maman?*" he whispered, his native French returning in his delirium, "*Maman, tu es là? Aides-moi, aides-moi…*"

185

"Hercules' relationship with the Amazons was problematic at best. Threatened by their courage, strength, and independence from men, they represented a source of power that was almost unintelligible to him – and this fear of the unknown, the feminine, drove him to repeated acts of violence – and sexual violence – against them. By rights, the Amazons should have been his greatest allies: lovers of women, warriors of the highest order – they were in reality no threat to his homosocial world of rivalry and adventure. This is, no doubt, precisely why the Greeks pitted him so often against them: their own fear of the powerful women required retribution from their most extreme representative of masculinity. Only they didn't count on the fact that Hercules would admire Penthesilea and love Hippolyta, regretting his violence towards them to such an extent that there are two versions of his encounters with both figures: one violent, one romantic. Even history has not been able to preserve the misogyny that Greek culture attempted to project onto Hercules: his ambisexual indeterminacy has made him mythically elusive."

Theodore Danton, *Redefining Heroism: Reclaiming Hercules;* Columbia University Press; 1968

The Eighth Poem: Penthesilea
Berkeley, April 1990

As I kicked my way through puddles laced with petals from the purple magnolia trees along my street, I wondered, "Would the rains never end?" I marveled at all the flora in bloom, bravely holding up their slender stalks against the onslaught of the endless April storms. Daffodils, calla lilies, and fragrant freesias dappled the borders of every lawn, and even the redwoods and live oaks seemed to be pushing forward new pale green shoots. They were all drinking up the rain, and Anthea assured me that every year it was the same: dire warnings of drought during the halcyon days of February, only to be deluged in March and April, the end of which everyone was grumbling about how long the rainy season was lasting.

What a bizarre climate, I thought, and yet it was growing on me. The lush green hills in the distance above the university framing the abundant boughs of elegant wisteria adorning virtually every fence and trellis of Berkeley were a far cry from the bleak early spring mud and bare branches back east. As I approached our house, I cast a critical, appraising gaze over its fine, dark, craftsman style lines and large, diamond-paned windows. The broad eaves of the roof were as elegant as they had been back in the 1930s when it had been built, and with a little work the yard could look decent too. Wildflowers were blooming in the lawn, and tall oaks interspersed with ginkos and red maples flanked the sides and entryway. I made a mental note to get Hermàn and Anthea out in the yard with me as soon as the rains cleared up a little. Here I sighed: gardening would be nice, but I'd have to get some serious midterm studying done today. For the first time in my Archaic Poetry class, the professor had actually assigned the class a reverse translation for the final exam. It would be a lengthy selection from one of Pindar's Odes, but one that we hadn't worked through yet. The only way to prepare for the exam was to practice translating English versions of the Odes into Greek as often as possible. I was currently working on the eighth Olympian Ode, as translated by some Oxford don in the 19th century, and I was having some difficulty figuring out how to translate the word "Amazon" into Greek. The passage went like this:

Thus plainly spoke the god, and away to Xanthos and the Amazons of goodly steeds and to Ister urged his horses on. And the Trident-wielder for Isthmos over seas harnessed his swift chariot, and hither first he bare with him Aiakos behind the golden mares, and unto the mount of Corinth, to behold his feast of fame.

I knew that the god who was mentioned first was Apollo, and that the "Trident-wielder" was Poseidon, but only diligent research earlier that day had confirmed that Xanthos was the name used by the gods for the river Scamander, Ister was the ancient Greek name for the Danube, Isthmos referred to a waterway in Corinth, and Aiakos was one of the three judges of Hades. And since when did Poseidon have a bunch of golden mares trotting behind his chariot? I grinned at the image in my head, and thought for the millionth time that this was one of the reasons I loved Greek mythology: it never ended. There was always more to the story, more to discover, and more to learn. I worked on my translation until I was dozing off in my chair, pulled off my jeans and curled up in my bed, clad only in a pair of gray socks and my favorite green t-shirt, the comforter pulled close and snug.

Sleeping alone was not one of my favorite pastimes, I thought ruefully, as I settled in against my pillows, missing Dion's beauty and playful presence. I had actually ended up enjoying his company for the few remaining days he had been in town. It turned out that there was more to him than just the bright pretty face, dark curls, and velvet skin. He listened to me closely and thoughtfully, and showed a capacity for my own brand of passionate academic seriousness that I rarely found in men, even Linus. In this way as well as many others, he was almost the opposite of his sister Phoebe. Whereas Phoebe knew nothing of my work on my grandmother's poems, after my first night with Dion and our shared experience watching the video of Julien's trial, I had told him everything. He had listened to me solemnly, asking thoughtful questions, and was clearly caught up in the urgency of Sophia's story and my quest. For the rest of his visit, we had been practically inseparable, and when he left he had promised me that he'd keep an eye out for any potentially useful film footage that would shed light on my project. As I began to drift off, I thought of his full lips and his kisses, of his eyes closed, his thick dark lashes fanned out over his olive skin…and the distinctive hollow where his waist curved into his hip that had reminded me, all too

vividly, of the same curve of Hyla's. There was just enough time before I fell asleep to slip them both into my dreams.

The next morning, I wandered sleepily into the kitchen to sift through the previous day's mail scattered across the kitchen counter, hoping for a response from Hercule, and I caught my breath when I saw the corner of a blue airmail envelope sticking out of the pile. Suddenly wide awake, I extracted the short note, which – to my annoyance – bore Johanna's inimitable script, not Hercule's shaky hand. When I opened it I read:

> *You have deceived me. I have discovered the pattern in the poems and the first four are missing. Send them to me immediately, or I will make quite sure that you never meet Hercule.*

I had to think fast. I hadn't intentionally deceived Johanna; I just hadn't wanted to share the first few poems because they had become emotionally significant to me. This sentimental association was apparently no longer a luxury I could afford. Johanna was angry, and I knew that I couldn't risk her enmity. Not when I was this close to finishing. Quickly, I ran upstairs to start on the next poem, entitled "Penthesilea."

I had been preparing for this moment for several days, refreshing my memory about Penthesilea, one of the most illustrious Queens of the Amazons, heroine of the Trojan War – until she was cut down by Achilles. In the course of my research, I had made an unexpected discovery: during World War II, the beautiful German filmmaker Leni Riefenstahl, notorious for her Nazi sympathies and purportedly one of Hitler's mistresses, had managed to gain funding for a film version – casting herself in the lead role of course – of Heinrich von Kleist's early nineteenth century verse drama called *Penthesilea*. The film was never made, but I was intrigued, so I had looked up Kleist's book and found that – like Sophia Danton – Kleist had imagined an alternative scenario for his Amazon heroine, which was no doubt what had attracted Riefenstahl to the script. In Kleist's version, Penthesilea is not cut down in battle by Achilles as she is in the *Illiad*.

Instead she is thrown from her horse in battle by Achilles, who both spares her life and admits his love for her. Penthesilea, according to the Amazon code, can only love a man she has conquered in battle; so Achilles persuades her to accept his love by surrendering to her. They briefly enjoy their union until the battle between the Greeks

and Amazons starts up again. When Achilles approaches the Amazon camp with the intention of declaring his unconditional love for Penthesilea in spite of the war, she thinks he is coming to ambush her troops, so she shoots him in the neck with an arrow and then commands her dogs to tear him apart. After Achilles dies, Penthesilea learns the truth about why he crossed the battle lines, and she is driven insane by the revelation. At Achilles' funeral she flings herself across his dead body and dies in despair.

A bit melodramatic, I thought, but still interesting. Who would have thought that these two mythic figures would have been of interest to a tortured post-Romantic German poet such as Kleist, or for that matter, a woman of such conflicted ideologies as Riefenstahl? Especially, I thought with a smile, since both Achilles and Penthesilea had since been re-claimed by late twentieth century queer theorists as emblematic figures of ancient Greek homoerotics: Achilles with his beloved Patroclus, and Penthesilea with her lesbian community of women warriors. My grandmother's poem, of course, presented an entirely different spin on the legend:

I was Queen of the realm:
My stables were full.
My warrior mares
Were the finest in the land.
Fearless, fierce, and ruthless.
I rode them hard:
Till foam flecked their flanks.
I broke and trained them;
They fed only from my hand,
Their love for me
Was unwavering and pure.
We lived in a world apart from men.
But when you came,
Seeking shelter from the wars,
And claimed me as your own,
They turned against us.
You were their rival for my love.
These women of mine,
My wild mares. Once tamed,
Now completely mad.
They betrayed me, the realm,
And themselves.

They followed me back to the wars,
But they ravaged the land instead,
Eating the flesh of their kill,
Even when they killed their own.
You had to leave to calm them;
I had to stage my death to save us,
Fall to that fool Achilles;
He never could have
Bested me.
This is how we trapped them.
They thought they were free,
But they were wrong;
And they burned instead,
Their jaws still dripping with his blood,
On the pyre meant for me.
And we escaped.
Freedom was ours alone,
To dream of,
And to thrive.

I had to read the poem at least three times to reconcile
Sophia's juxtaposition of the eighth labor of Hercules – capturing the
wild, flesh-eating mares of Diomedes – with this radically revised
narrative of Penthesilea. I could see the basic connection: Penthesilea
was a skilled horse woman and warrior, training her own female army
– much as Sophia had probably trained other female agents in the
resistance – but "flesh eating" mares? Wasn't that a bit of a stretch?
Probably not, I thought grimly, when betrayal meant the death of
one's comrades. It was clear in this poem that Sophia and
Penthesilea were torn between two worlds: their Amazon community
(or the lesbian underground in Paris) and their partnership with
Hercules (or, in Sophia's case, the real Hercule). But I was still
disturbed by the violence of Penthesilea's sister-soldiers' reaction to
her alliance with a man, and the deranged extent of their mutiny.
Had my grandmother really experienced a rupture this severe and
destructive in her own community? Somehow I had to find out. If
there had been a large number of female agents killed around the
time of a specific battle, there had to be a record somewhere.

Over the next few days, I scoured for new sources at the
library. I read histories of women in warfare, I went back over my
books on the underground communities of women during Vichy, I

pored through endless databases of film footage in the resistance movement archives, and I even checked for fires or deaths in Parisian communities of women during the war years. Nothing. All dead ends. By the end of the fourth day, I was running out of options and turned with some trepidation to my last resort: my supervisor, Joyce. Without revealing too much about the nature of my project, I hoped I could pry from the library matriarch even the slightest hint of a possible lead. Cautiously, I approached Joyce during lunch break one day, humbly bearing a selection of her three favorite kinds of frosted pastries as an offering to the altar of her wisdom and beneficence.

Joyce received the gift graciously, and asked with some amusement, "What can I do for you, Herculine? Or should I say, what exactly do you need...hmmm? A day off next week perhaps?"

I stammered, "Oh no, Joyce, not me. It's not that at all, I ...uh, I just..."

Joyce was enjoying herself. "It can't be that bad, can it? Come on, sugar, what's the problem?"

This was exactly the moment, and the tone, that I had been hoping to achieve. Joyce had tucked in zestily to her first pastry and was licking her lips happily, apparently just waiting for me to ask a favor so that she could grant it.

"Um, what do you know about any connections between Amazons, horses, and um, World War II?"

Joyce laughed out loud, spewing pastry crumbs, which she dabbed delicately from the corners of her mouth, and brushed from the wide shelf of her breasts and lap with a napkin. She said, "I don't know anything about all three of those things *together*, honey, but I know who you should ask. Here's the number for Dorothea Equinette down in the archives. I bet she can help you out." Here Joyce scribbled a phone extension down on a notepad and handed it to me.

"Thank you, Joyce," I said, backing out of the room reverently, "This is great; you have no idea. Thank you so much..." and once I cleared the doorway, I turned and ran down the hall to the nearest university phone and dialed the number. A woman answered immediately, sounding surprised and faintly alarmed, as if no one had called that number in the last decade, but warmly invited me to come down to see her that afternoon. Heart racing, I shelved all the books in every cart at record speed and claimed a headache in order to leave my shift a few minutes early.

As I knocked on the small wooden door in the sub-basement of the library, I heard the faint whirr of a surveillance camera as it swiveled around to project my image beyond the door to the curator of the archives, who soon turned the lock and greeted me, smiling.

"Welcome," she said, opening the door, "Are you looking for something in particular?"

Struck by Dorothea Equinette's resemblance to a sweet-tempered, near-sighted Shetland pony, I immediately relaxed and said simply, "Hi. Yes, please. Amazons. Have you got anything here? Especially images of them in wartime, with horses?"

Dorothea's eyes grew wide. "Do you mean the Trojan war? Or other Amazon battles?"

Sensing that I might be stepping into more of a goldmine than I had dreamed, I said tentatively, "Um, really, any battle with Amazons would be great, but the Trojan war would be perfect."

Dorothea mused, tapping her fingers against her lips, slightly humming as her brain clicked and whirred through the vast holdings in the archive. I followed her through the maze of rooms, which was really no more than several large windowless storage spaces filled with long rows of shelves and cabinets, each labeled and numbered, but bearing – as far as I could see – books that looked no more valuable than some of those I had seen on my father's shelves. As for the cabinets, the doors were closed, and their contents were hidden from sight. Dorothea wandered slowly through each room, stopping every now and then to consider a neatly stacked set of objects under layers of insulating blankets. "Hmmmm, no, no, not these....maybe these...no, mmm, no, probably not."

Following behind her, and feeling like an eager border collie nipping at the heels of a stray mare, I mumbled, "Um, maybe we could at least try some of these? Just to see?" But Dorothea kept moving on. She led me through a door and down into the next level of the archive that was more of a warehouse, with racks of large flat panels leaning against all four walls.

Finally, with triumph in her eyes, she said. "Oh yes, yes, definitely these...right over here..."

She led me over to the far wall, switched on the lights directly overhead, and began pulling canvas storage covers off a large rectangular object. I was silent with anticipation, and then I felt an involuntary sharp intake of breath as Dorothea swept the cover from a gleaming mosaic. There, on the tiled panel, was unmistakably depicted an Amazon warrioress on horseback, her one remaining

breast bared, powerful bow drawn taut, framed against the backdrop of a kingdom by the sea and a group of women on horseback behind her. I had no way of knowing if the central female figure was Penthesilea, but her knotted gold headdress did look more elaborate than those of the others, who were only wearing simple laurel leaf garlands.

I asked Dorothea tentatively, "Do you think that's Troy in the background?"

"Oh, most certainly," said Dorothea, nodding her head vigorously. "The iconography of the ocean, the walled city, and the castle fortress certainly denotes Troy, and this panel was salvaged from a temple of Poseidon near the alleged site of the battle. The central figure is the Amazon Queen, clearly signified by the single left breast – as you know, they removed their right breasts when initiated to warrior status in order to be better archers: this way they could pull the bow string taut against their chests." Here Dorothea simulated the act of archery with a far-off look in her eyes, perhaps imagining herself on some ancient battlefield.

"It must be Penthesilea; I know a few things about Amazons," I said quietly.

Dorothea continued, nodding approvingly, "Yes, Penthesilea, who was known for her mastery of the horses gifted to the Amazons by Poseidon. But Penthesilea angered Poseidon by supporting Troy in the war, instead of his beloved Greeks, which is why he empowered Achilles to slay her."

Here Dorothea looked as sorrowful and pale with anger as if she had personally witnessed the killing of Penthesilea at Troy. I instinctively put my hand on the older woman's shoulder to comfort her. Dorothea looked at me warmly in response.

She asked, "So, is this the kind of artifact you were looking for?"

"More than I ever dreamed of finding," I said with genuine gratitude in my voice as I gazed transfixed at the vivid colors and gleaming individual tiles of the mosaic panel. I continued, "Just curious though, do you know anything about women and horses in France around the time of World War II?"

Dorothea's brow furrowed with concentration, and after a minute or two, she emerged from the archive catalogue in her brain, eyes slightly glazed with effort, to say, "No sacred artifact in particular comes to mind, I'm afraid; but I do know that there were several Sapphic cults of Diana in Western Europe in the early part of

194

the twentieth century which have endured into the present day." Here she blushed deeply, "They worshipped their goddess not only through rituals of hunt but also the, ah, distinctly feminine fascination for, mmm, shall we say, the equestrian sublimation of the libido. Perhaps there is evidence of such activity in France at that time, but I am not sure."

Wanting to avoid causing Dorothea any further embarrassment or discomfort, I thanked her profusely and promised to investigate this possibility further as I gathered my bag to leave, casting one longing look back at the mosaic as Dorothea gently arranged its cover back into place.

Dorothea, evidently pleased to have discovered a kindred spirit, generously offered to let me come view the mosaic whenever I liked. The look on the curator's shy, large-lashed face made me break into a smile and I had to restrain myself from enveloping the kind older woman in an energetic hug.

"Thank you," I said, instead. "I'm sure I'll be visiting you again soon."

After the door to the archives shut firmly behind me, I ran up to the stacks to look in one more place that hadn't occurred to me until now. It was time to take Sophia literally. Where were the horse breeding and training stables in Paris, and were any of them run by women during the Vichy regime? With most of the men off fighting, it was more than likely. I turned up a few books during my search, but the majority of them, like *A Girl's Best Friend: Women, Horses, and Coming of Age in Twentieth Century France*, were written for an audience of female equestrian aficionados, and none were overtly relevant to my project.

Then I saw a slim book about the history of cavalry battles called *Horses of War: The Real Heroes*. In this book there were two photographs of a well-known military stable that, after the horses had been vacated for safety during WWII, had burned down, possibly killing several of the women who worked there.

"Rumor has it," wrote the author, "that the empty stables were being used as meeting location for French Resistance fighters and that arson could have been involved." I made a quick note of the name of the stables, Elysian Fields, and raced downstairs to the microfiche archives. Certain that I was finally on the right track, I scanned through the Paris papers of that month and year for news of the fire.

Nothing, nothing, nothing. Why hadn't it been covered? Women had possibly been killed in the fire! Of course, I thought then, try the obituaries. But they were inscrutable; none of them, of course, came right out and said, "So and so, suspected resistance agent, killed in arson-related stable fire." I sighed with frustration and continued scrolling wearily through the seemingly endless pages of microfiche newsprint. Announcements for missing persons consistently ran along the sides of each obituary page, but I had disregarded these until one caught my eye, mostly because under the large title "MISSING" (in French, *PERDUE*) it featured a photograph of a fiercely beautiful young woman. Not someone who was likely to get lost on her own, I thought. And as I read the caption, I found what I had been looking for:

Helene Mendel, 24, noted equestrienne, missing for three weeks, last seen at the Elysian Fields stables. Distinguishing features: auburn hair, blue eyes, last seen wearing green riding jacket and skirt.

From the size of the reward and the address for the girl's parents, I deduced that Helene Mendel came from a wealthy family at the heart of Paris' cultural elite. What had become of her? And what had really happened that night at the Elysian Fields stables? I decided to comb back through the missing persons announcements for the rest of that month to see if there were any other young women listed who had been associated with the stable. There were three more. Four total. And here something jogged in my memory. How many mares of Diomedes had Hercules captured?

Somewhat fatigued by this point, I headed back up to the stacks to consult Apollodorus. I scanned the pages quickly and closed the book with a satisfying snap. Sure enough, there had been four mares. Four young women missing in the fire. And, apparently, four resistance agents who had betrayed the cause, and died for it. Which side had set the fire was still unknown, and despite the desperate stakes of their betrayal, I couldn't bear to think that Sophia and Hercule had intentionally rounded up their former comrades and killed them in a fire. But maybe they had. Not for the first time during this quest, I felt sickened by the reality of war and the brutality it brought out in ordinary people. Then again, how ordinary was my grandmother?

I gathered my coat and bag and left the library in the cool evening twilight. I gratefully filled my lungs with fresh air, still slightly

moist from the receding rain, and composed a note to Johanna in my head as I walked home along the now familiar streets behind the university.

> *Johanna,*
> *It was never my intent to deceive you. The first four poems simply have personal significance for me beyond the "pattern" that they fulfill. As a gesture of trust, I am enclosing the first poem now along with the eighth. If you will assure me that you will not breach our agreement, I will continue to send you an early poem along with each new one that I have yet to send you.*
> *In good faith, Herculine*

As soon as I got home and entered the brightly lit kitchen, filled with the sounds of Latin salsa music emanating from Hermàn's bedroom and the ring of Anthea and her friends' laughter coming from the living room, I sat down and copied out both the first and eighth poems to send to Johanna. Then I quickly scribbled out the note I had composed in my head and stuffed all three pages into an envelope. I would mail it the following day.

Standing by the kitchen sink, snacking on an organic carrot, I sifted through the newest stack of mail that had been left on the counter, sorting it into three separate piles—for Anthea, Hermàn, and myelf—still hoping to catch a glimpse of Hercule's cream-colored stationery. Under a sheaf of academic publication catalogues, bills, and credit card offers, I found instead yet another blue airmail envelope face down upon the counter. Annoyed, I thought, *Oh great. What is Johanna angry about now?* But when I turned the letter over, I was puzzled by the familiar handwriting that was definitely not Johanna's. And then I saw the postmark and distinctive stamps. It was from Mexico.

I ripped open the envelope and a quick glance at the bottom of the letter confirmed what I almost couldn't bear to hope: it was from Hyla. She wrote,

> *Herculine,*
> *I'm sorry. For everything. I've been gone too long. I meant to write. I think of you every day. I can't leave. But I want to come home. To you. Give me another chance. Help me get away from here. Come find*

*me. Come swim in the ocean with me. We can wash away the past. I
know we can.*
 Hyla

Another general delivery address followed the postscript, this time in
Tulum, Mexico. I read the letter over five or six times before I sat
down, shakily. Wash away the past? Come home to me? I closed my
eyes and rubbed my temples wearily. The reality of Hyla, alive and
well, and swimming in the ocean in Mexico seemed like such a distant
fantasy image, far away from the rainy winter months and dark
visions of Vichy France that had been the dominant palette of my
own life these past five months. In all honesty, I had to admit that
while I had been doing my best to hold on to my memories of Hyla
and the budding love that I had felt for her back in November, the
image of her had also become somewhat of a dream, the loyalty to
which had conveniently allowed me to keep myself aloof from any
other emotional entanglements since Hyla had left town.

    Now here she was, asking me to come to Mexico and rescue
her? Well, I thought, with some irritation, she would just have to
wait. The semester wasn't over until May, there would be no chance
to get away until June, and Paris was first on my list of travel
expenditures.

    Halfway up the stairs I stopped in my tracks. How far was
Tulum from Cancun? I fished through my bag and drew out my
notebook where the photocopy of the map of Mexico was still
slipped between the pages of the "Persephone" poem. Tulum was
less than a hundred miles from Cancun. I had dropped the lead on
Céline Demetrius's whereabouts back in January…maybe it was time
to pick it back up? After Paris, I reminded myself.
Maybe after Paris I would go looking for Sophia's mother, and for
Hyla too.

    As I carried my coat, bag, and the letter from Hyla upstairs to
my room, my thoughts shifting between shock, confusion, and
images of swimming naked in warm turquoise water, bathed in
sunlight and smiling blissfully into Hyla's eyes, I was oblivious to the
fact that my letter to Johanna was now buried, quite forgotten, under
a pile of junk mail on the kitchen counter headed for the recycling
bin the next day.

Hyla
Mexico, April 1990

She is dreaming that she is drowning. She has had this dream before.
She is kneeling on the bank of a river, the grass is muddy and she is slipping. All
around her are men, their arms reaching for her, pulling her down into the water.
They are grabbing for her and ripping her clothing, and she is pleading with them
to stop, screaming for help, screaming out one name only, "Herculine!" But
Herculine never comes. Instead, slipping from the muddy river bank into the
water as the men's hands grab her by the hair to force her head down, down, into
the waters where their blurred phalluses sway like submerged flowers, groping up
to the light, the reflection Hyla sees in the surface of the river before she goes down
is not her own face, but it is an anguished, panicked face. And it is Herculine's.

Hyla awoke with a start, covered in sweat. Though her room
in the hacienda was airy and cool, she was feverish with the aftermath
of guilt and anxiety from her recurring nightmare. Even after several
months in Mexico, the dream was always the same: relentless,
bringing her closer to drowning every time. She had taken to staying
up late into the night, avoiding sleep, trying ever increasing amounts
of cocaine and tequila to numb the dream away. But it was always
there, waiting for her. It always began the same way too. She and
Herculine are out in a forest, looking for something, and they decide
to split up for better results. Then Hyla hears the sound of rushing
water and thinks she hears someone calling her name. She follows
the sound and comes to the river, where at first she is alone, and she
bends over the water to splash her face with cool water. That is
when the first hand reaches up from the river.

She shuddered. At least the faces of the men in the water
were indistinct. Just vague composites of all and any men; but this
morning, she found that her forearms felt sore as if they had been
bruised, her knees ached, and she checked her skin for signs of
scratches. There were none. Of course.

She hadn't told Calypso about the dream. When she had
asked Hyla why she tossed and turned during the night so violently,
why she occasionally cried out in her sleep, Hyla had just smiled
evasively and said she had no idea; she never remembered her
dreams. One morning in bed, Calypso looked at her wide-eyed upon
awakening and said,

"Maybe the reason you don't remember your dreams is that they are so terrifying."

Hyla countered her concern with flippancy: "Huh, I don't know, Doctor Freud." Then, playfully switching roles from patient to doctor, she tapped an imaginary pipe and said in a mock Viennese accent, "Tell me about your mother and we can get to the bottom of this…" And she reached around Calypso's waist and grasped a handful of her well-toned and perfectly tanned bottom.

Taking the diversionary bait as Hyla knew she would, Calypso laughed and said, "Oh, I'll tell you about my mother anytime you want *quérida*; she was a piece of work all right. But I owe everything I have today to her – even you, if you think about it – so you won't catch me telling you any of her dark secrets."

Hyla's interest piqued. She knew that Calypso's wealth had been inherited from her mother and that the mansion they lived in was entirely paid for through the seemingly endless source of funds from her investments, but dark secrets? She began to fondle the long, hennaed curls cascading down Cal's back and shoulders and kissed her neck softly.

"Secrets like what?" she asked.

Calypso relaxed into Hyla's arms and said alluringly, "If you massage me out on the terrace, maybe I'll tell you about some of her less reputable moments…"

Hyla yawned performatively, "Sorry, too boring. It had better be juicier than that for a full massage. Now, if all you want is a foot rub…"

Caly pouted as she pulled Hyla out onto the patio where a sheeted massage table was already waiting for them, accompanied by a platter of fresh cut papaya and mangos on the table nearby.

"No baby," she said, "I want my morning massage. I'll tell you anything you want to know."

She said this with a wink as she placed a piece of papaya on her tongue and let her white silk robe drop to the ground. As always, Hyla was impressed by this fifty-year-old woman's magnificence. Calypso was in better shape than most of the twenty-year-old women Hyla had known, and was certainly more pampered and polished than anyone she had ever met. An open bowl of coconut oil was perched on a stool by the massage table. Hyla, clad only in a sheer white cotton shift, moved close to Calypso, dipped her fingers in the oil, and ran them along the older woman's clavicle and down to the lean muscles of her trembling abdomen.

"Then get on that table and start talking," she said, giving Caly an affectionate push.

As Hyla lay in bed three weeks later, still shivering under the silk sheets from the aftermath of her dream, she remembered their conversation as if it had been the day before. She hadn't had a chance to think it over carefully until now, but she couldn't avoid it any longer. Something had been nagging at the edges of her mind ever since that morning, and she had to figure out what it was.

Calypso had talked through the whole massage, which was unlike her. It was as if she had been bursting to tell the story for years, and had finally found the right confidante. Calypso's mother had been a formidable woman: a French expatriate living in Mexico, she had once been an elite art dealer and collector. Caly's mansion was filled with original Picassos, Cezannes, Riveras and Kahlos, as well as many others whose names Hyla did not recognize. Her mother had known most of the artists personally. But if they had known of her activities before the war, Hyla doubted that they would have let her buy their art, let alone deigned to socialize with her.

That day, out on the veranda, under Hyla's skilled hands, Calypso had told the story of her mother's money laundering art deals with the Nazis; how she had brokered ("You mean *fenced?*" asked Hyla) the sale and export of hundreds of paintings confiscated from rich Jewish family collections, for her own profit as well as that of the German war machine.

"How did you find out about all this? She didn't tell you, did she?" asked Hyla, confused.

"No, of course not," said Caly defensively, "Her friends told me after she died. She had to do what she did. She put self-preservation before everything else."

"Yeah," said Hyla with an extra deep thrust of her elbow into Cal's shoulder blade, "Before morality."

Calypso was quiet.

Hyla realized she had gone too far. She softened her touch and bent down to nuzzle her benefactor's ear. "I'm sorry," she said. "Did I touch a nerve?"

Calypso took a deep breath, raised her head from the table, and looked up at Hyla with large, sad, brown eyes. "More than you know," she said, and propped her chin up on her folded arms. "My mother escaped from Paris right before the war, it's true, but she also left her daughter there, my half-sister, and she died."

"Wait a minute," said Hyla, who paused mid-stroke along Calypso's back. "I didn't know you had a half-sister."

Calypso said in a low voice, "I don't talk about her. I never knew her. She was more than twenty years older than I was. Mama had married my father almost as soon as she settled here and taken his name – Odessa – and had started a whole new life for herself, but after her other daughter died, she was never the same..." Here she trailed off, and put her head down on the table again.

Hyla, too moved to respond, communicated her sympathy to Calypso the only way she knew how. She pulled off her shift and lowered herself gently onto the massage table beside her lover. Startled, Caly looked up, and once she saw the somber, caring look in Hyla's eyes, she relaxed and turned towards her, graciously accepting the younger woman's full body embrace.

Now as she went over the details of Calypso's story and the events of that morning again in her head, Hyla felt her own troubled breathing slow down and her temperature regulate. She knew the story was important, but didn't know why. If only Herculine was here, she would know. This was the stuff she was interested in after all. Paris and Nazis and family members dying.

Hyla paced the floor in her room. She had been on the verge of writing a letter to Herculine for weeks now. Ever since she'd heard the story, really. But something had stopped her every time. Sometimes it was just the pang of anger and shame at the memory of the condemning look on Herculine's face the last time she had seen her. She was just too sensitive, too intense. And yet Hyla longed for her at times, whenever Calypso gave her enough time to think of anything else but her needs. It seemed that whenever Hyla was about to sit down and begin a letter, or whenever she had carved out a little time to herself to gather her thoughts, Caly would appear with some extravagant plan or demand, and Hyla felt obligated to accommodate her. After all, she was only living in this luxurious hacienda, far away from her brother's ganja-dealing surf safari beach ghetto, thanks to Calypso's interest in her charms as a "domestic companion."

The night they'd met was almost mythical to her now. She had been hanging out at one of the local beach bars with her brother and his friends, some guys were playing guitar, and everyone was stoned and drinking tequila. Hyla had been feeling bored and restless all day, itching for some adventure, open to just about anything. Her life was starting to feel like a shipwreck on this endless beach of cloudless days and nothing to do. So when the beautiful red-haired

202

woman in a flowing white dress appeared at the door, she was immediately curious, and aware that the woman was gazing directly at her. Never one to give anything away without a chase, Hyla turned away nonchalantly and walked over to the chairs where the guitar players were sitting.

"Play something I can dance to," she commanded in Spanish, and they complied.

One guitarist strummed a sequence of haunting minor chords as the other played a solo of such sensuous beauty that Hyla was moved to dance in a way that she hadn't since leaving California. She walked slowly to the center of the room, lifted her arms, and began to move. All eyes were upon her, and this was how she liked it. The mysterious woman in white was the only other female in the bar. And Hyla was dancing just for her. At first she barely moved, shifting her body ever so slightly, swaying dreamily to the rhythm of the chord pattern, but then she turned to face the woman, and saw that she was mesmerized. Hyla beckoned to the woman to join her, and expected her to demur. But lifting her chin defiantly, with the hint of a confident smile, the woman walked to the center of the room and accepted Hyla's hand. All the men in the room looked like they were in a trance.

The two women danced as if their bodies had known each other for years. Perfectly matched in height, agility, and grace, Hyla was soon breathless with admiration for her new dance partner. After ten minutes of sinuous improvisation together, the woman in white said, "I'm Calypso. Come with me." And Hyla went.

In the chauffered car that drove the two women up the hill to the hacienda, Calypso made her move, pulling Hyla up against her, clutching a fistful of her now shaggy sun bleached mane, and kissing her passionately for several minutes. When they paused for breath, she said, "I've been looking for someone like you. I need a companion, a playmate, a lover. It gets lonely up here on the hill, but I think you could make it quite enjoyable indeed. Tell me, can you give a decent massage?" Hyla just smiled and began kneading Calypso's shoulder with her long, dexterous fingers. Calypso closed her eyes and purred like a cat. "Excellent," she said. "I'll send the driver down for your things in the morning. But tonight you'll stay with me." And so she had. Hyla had't ventured down the hill since.

In the intoxicating weeks that followed, there had been more massages, much passion, and even some dancing, though it was usually Calypso requesting a private performance from Hyla, which

she only joined on rare occasions. But it had now been almost four months since Hyla had been living up on the hill, completely isolated from the rest of the region, all her needs met by the small army of servants, as if she and Caly were on their own island paradise resort retreat, complete with a vast infinity pool.

It was time for her to get away. She wanted to swim in the ocean, have some time to herself; even a few hours with her brother and his stoner friends would be a refreshing reality check to all the opulence here. But Caly would not be pleased if she asked her permission to go away for the day. On previous occasions, when faced with such a request, Calypso had wheedled and cajoled, and Hyla had ended up staying. But this time, she would just leave a note and go. She'd borrow a bicycle from one of the kitchen boys and be back before sunset. Cal would just have to survive for a day without her.

Twenty minutes later, coasting down the hill from the house to the town, and then to the beach, Hyla felt exhilarated with a level of freedom she had almost forgotten was possible. Her head seemed to clear with each level of elevation that she descended, and the lazy, languorous spell that Calypso had cast over her evaporated the closer she came to the ocean, flying her bicycle through the glowing fields along the winding country roads.

She rode straight to the local post office and bought a piece of paper, a few stamps, and an airmail envelope. She wrote for several minutes, carefully choosing her words, licked the stamps, addressed the envelope to Herculine, and tossed the letter into the "out" box. As she did so, she felt a weight lift from her heart and mind. Calypso might be up on the hill fuming and storming, but as Hyla ran down to the beach and threw herself into the ocean, all she knew was that she felt alive and free for the first time in far too long.

The Ninth Poem: Psyche
Berkeley, May 1990

A pale layer of marine fog rolled off the San Francisco Bay and blanketed the Berkeley campus with a grey quietude that permeated my soul. I felt calm; perhaps the calm before a building storm, but calm nonetheless. I stopped along my morning run to enjoy the scent of a variegated pink and yellow rose bush in bloom at the corner of Calpurnia Street and Euclid Avenue. Its heady perfume complemented the cool moisture of the fog, and even though I knew that the grey veil would burn off by late morning, it still softened the impending heat of the rest of the day and soothed my mind for the moment.

There was simply too much happening at once. The semester was quickly drawing to a close, which meant final mid-May deadlines for seminar papers and translation projects. The letter from Hyla had been sitting on my desk for two weeks, waiting for an unambivalent response that I hadn't yet been able to muster. My work on Sophia's poems had also been stalled as I struggled to keep up with my academic workload. I still hadn't heard back from Hercule and had even sent him another note, expressing my hopes that he was in good health as well as my concern over not hearing from him. Part of me wanted to ask Johanna if he was all right, but I dreaded letting the Ice Queen know that Hercule and I were in communication and had circumvented her entirely. If another week went by, I promised myself that I would contact his *Maison de Convalesence* directly.

On the afternoon that I finally handed in my Archaic Poetry take-home exam – a twenty-page reverse translation exercise – I trudged home exhausted and dragged myself up the stairs. I curled up on my bed, holding a pillow close, remembering the silky texture of Hyla's skin and the fullness of Dion's lips. Within seconds I was sound asleep and dreaming deeply.

I was a little girl again, swimming in the warm ocean water at Coney Island with my dad, clasped to his back, riding in to shore on small waves, over and over. I was laughing with excitement and the deep sense of safety I felt as he swept me up in his arms and whirled me around in the water, creating a glittering shower of spray that

cascaded down upon us both. The droplets fell upon my mom too, there beside us, laughing – her hair long, wild, and wet – looking like a mermaid emerging from the waves. I dreamed with vivid sensory detail as dad and I encircled mom with our arms and felt the wet heat of her body against our skin, the salty kisses shared between us, the heavy tendrils of mom's cool, damp hair wrapping around my little arms as I was suspended between my parents' torsos, arms, and lips. And then I was in the water alone, sinking fast, eyes open in the clear green liquid ensconcing me, wondering at the beauty of this new, strange, watery world where tiny silver transparent fish darted close to the surface. I mused, "Where am I? Can I breathe down here? Where are my parents? Do they know I'm here?" And just as the sunlit green clarity began to darken at the edges of my mind, I felt the pull of strong arms under my own, and the sensation of surging up into the air: Ah! Breath! And the faces of my parents, ashen with panic, quickly melting into relief as they saw my face and heard my laughter.

"Mommy," I said in my dream, "It was so beautiful there. Where were you? I wanted you to see too!"

And the rest of the dream was spent in the shallows by the shore: my mom and dad taking turns underwater with me, teaching me to hold my breath as I opened my eyes and marveled at the world beneath the surface of the sea.

Two hours later, I awoke. Groggily, still half asleep in my dream world with my parents on the beach of my childhood memories, I reached up to touch what felt like dampness on my face, and I realized that it was wet with tears that were still softly streaming from my eyes. That dream...was it a real memory? Had that afternoon really happened? It seemed like something I had dreamt before, but I wasn't sure. It had felt so real. I had been dreaming of waves that kept getting bigger, crashing into the shore around me as I ran away up the beach, over and over, but soon I realized that it was actually the pounding rhythm of a bass guitar under my bed that I heard: a party downstairs had started without me.

It was dark outside, and from the level of noise coming up the stairs, it sounded like there were at least fifty people in the living room. I padded down the hall to the bathroom, and quickly showered, relishing the warmth of the water on my skin even more than usual. After drying off, I put on some party clothes, which meant a black tank top instead of a grey one and a pair of jeans that had been laundered sometime in the past month. As I headed

206

downstairs, I quickly realized that there were significantly more than fifty people in the house. The party guests were spilling out onto the porch and the lawn and there were people that I had never seen before in the kitchen and living room.

"Meet the neighbors!" yelled Hermàn, as he flounced by in a yellow mariachi blouse over red lycra cycling shorts, and I smiled politely at the jovial drunken strangers packing the hallways of my home as I edged my way through to the dancers in the living room. I spotted Linus and Phoebe by a window in the dining room and waved to them to join me in the kitchen. They immediately began wading through the bodies towards me, and by the time they reached me, I had poured three glasses of sangria.

"Hey Herculine," said Phoebe, as I handed her a glass. "Great party...thanks for inviting us."

Since I hadn't even known there was going to be a party, let alone handled the invitations, I just smiled weakly, and said, "Oh sure...glad you two could make it."

Phoebe murmured, with seriousness in her eyes, "I'm sure Dion would have loved it if he were here. All these people, the dancing, the wine. This is exactly his kind of scene."

"Right," I said awkwardly, "We, um, would have invited him to come up from L.A. too, but it all kind of came together at the last minute."

Phoebe continued with a hint of protectiveness in her voice, "You know, he's pretty smitten with you...I hope you won't break his heart." Here she smiled, as if even she knew that the likelihood of this was slim.

I bantered back, "Oh yeah, right: that's me, the heartbreaker." But a quick glance at the look on Linus' face told me that this particular quip might not be perceived as funny by everyone in the room. "I mean," I continued, "I was thinking of giving him a call to see if he'd like to come up and visit sometime..."

Phoebe looked somewhat reassured, and heartened by this, I finished my glass of sangria and continued, trying to muster a casual tone, "Speaking of upcoming visits, guess who wrote me a letter? Apparently Hyla is alive and well in Mexico after all..."

Both my voice and social armor broke as I admitted this for the first time to anyone since I had received the letter, and the looks of caring and compassion that I saw on my friends' faces were too much to bear. The next thing I knew, Linus and Phoebe had enveloped me in an embrace and were literally holding me up in their

207

arms as my knees wobbled and I sobbed softly on Phoebe's shoulder, stammering out words past the enormous lump in my throat.

"She's been gone for months, and now she expects me to actually go *down* there to Mexico and *rescue* her or something…" As the brandy in the sangria began to spin my head, I felt Linus' long fingers combing through my curls soothingly, and I heard his voice saying,

"Come on, Herculine… It's not so bad. At least she's okay; that's what matters, right? And she still wants you, which is even better. Let's go dance and get some of these blues out of your system."

I nodded my mute assent, snuffled a bit, and allowed myself to be led to the living room where the music was blaring so loudly that it could almost drown out my self-pity and confusion. All I wanted was to lose myself in the crowd of dancers and feel Linus and Phoebe's bodies close against me. But the room was too crowded and filled with strangers, so – turning towards Linus and Phoebe, and regaining some of my composure – I said, "Actually, I've got a better idea. Let's go upstairs."

Phoebe and Linus exchanged questioning glances. I held my breath, hoping that they would join me. To my relief, Phoebe smiled, and at this signal Linus pulled both of us towards him and gave us each a long, lingering kiss in turn. Phoebe then did the same. Our common attraction re-established, we ascended the stairway holding hands. While the party throbbed on downstairs without us, Linus, Pheobe, and I healed old wounds and deepened our bonds with as much grace and far more passion than that displayed by any of the dancers at the party below.

The next day, true to my word, I called Dion and invited him up to visit. Knowing his interest in wine, I suggested that we celebrate the end of the school year by taking a few days together in Napa – there was a special archive at Sonoma State that I was interested in checking out, and while I was doing research, he could be wine tasting. He agreed so quickly that I wasn't sure if he had heard me completely, but he promised to drive up by the end of the week when we were both done with exams.

The day Dion arrived, I was waiting for him, packed and ready, out on the lawn in front of my house. Filled with excitement about going up to the special archive, and intrigued to see what the chemistry would be like between us, I had been too restless to stay indoors. As he got out of his car, an old black convertible Porsche, I

208

was impressed once again by his androgynous beauty, and I pulled him close in a warm embrace.

"Hey there, Herculine," said Dion after a long kiss. "Um, I see your bag and everything, but I just drove seven hours from L.A., and I need to rest for a little while before we head up to Napa..."

I grinned, took his hand, led him inside the house and up to my room. I didn't even remember that I had left my bag out on the lawn until we came back down an hour later. There hadn't been any napping involved, but we were rested and refreshed. In fact, I was positively glowing: it was going to be a great little getaway after all.

As we drove up to Napa, Dion told me about his final documentary film project on anti-war riots during the 70s, and I caught him up on the latest developments in my own research too. He was rapt and silent for a good forty minutes while I talked. It was as if I couldn't stop. The story just became deeper, and as he listened, it was clear that the danger around my grandmother's life heightened with every poem. No wonder I had put them aside for the last few weeks. I had started to feel a growing anxiety as I approached the last few poems, knowing that Sophia's death was foreshadowed more urgently with every line. Dion's eyes grew wide as I ended with the story of "Penthesilea."

He let out a low whistle and said, "Okay, so this just keeps getting bigger, huh? How much of this does the lady in Paris know?"

I smiled wryly and said, "Too much, I'm afraid. But I'm still a few steps ahead of her." I continued, telling Dion about my last exchange of letters with Johanna. "I'm just trying to keep stringing her along until I can get to Paris and meet Hercule. Frankly, after that, she can do whatever she wants with the poems."

He looked at me skeptically, but I said quietly, "It's really okay. The world needs to read them. They belong to all of us. Especially those who have ever fought for something they believe in, in love or war. Johanna's a famous scholar; if she publishes them, the world will read them."

I turned away then, feeling hot tears well up in my eyes and spill over onto my lashes and cheeks as I watched the rolling hills of Sonoma county begin to surround us on the drive. The idea of giving up the poems to Johanna made me miss my father suddenly with an ache in my chest that was so painful that my ribs actually hurt. I hated to give away anything that had been his. But I meant what I had said to Dion. Johanna was the best person to take the poems public. I just wanted to complete my work on them and learn

209

whatever private message they had to tell me about my family, and possibly even myself.

I wished that my dad could be with me, so that he could see how the golden grasses dappled with clumps of dark green oaks looked like a pastoral Greek countryside, but without the rustic ruins. Instead, ranches and farms gave way to grand mansions and vineyards, and Dion curved his car around the glowing landscape with smooth confidence, comforting me silently as he drove with one hand on my thigh and the other on the steering wheel.

To calm myself during the remainder of the drive and to do something productive with the longing in my heart for connection with my dad, I took out my notebook and began reading over the next poem in the series, entitled "Psyche."

I doubted you.
I almost lost you.
They filled my head with lies.
You came to me
In darkness always.
How could I know
That you were filled
With only light?
I loved you freely.
When you asked
For the ropes of gold
I wore around my loins,
I did not complain.
I did not explain
That I could not die
As long as I wore them,
Protected by her power.
I unclasped the belt,
Handed it to you, trusting.
Not knowing why.
Who betrayed whom?
You sold my gold
To buy their freedom.
The price was only mine:
Shame and danger.
You'll never know
The trials I had to pass

210

To regain their trust.
You exposed me,
But I saw you for what you are:
No hero. No god.
Just a child-man,
Beautiful and rash.
I didn't mean to burn you:
I didn't know
The heat of my tears
Was more than you could bear.

Great, I thought. This one was even more cryptic than the rest. The ninth labor of Hercules — stealing the magical golden girdle from the Amazon Queen Hippolyta — combined with the myth of Psyche and Eros. The analogy between the modern day relationship of Sophia and Hercule and that of Hippolyta and Hercules was troubling to me; it was hardly a positive comparison. I knew that one version of the legend of this labor is that Hercules conquered and raped Hippolyta in order to steal her magic girdle, while another version presents them as lovers and equals, but still has him force the girdle away from her. Either way, this poem was one of the first indications that there was an element of tension, even coercion between Sophia and Hercule, and that upset me. The properties of the magic girdle varied according to legend, but the line in the poem explaining that she "could not die" as long as she wore it suggested that Sophia was alluding to the version of the story in which the girdle protected the wearer against death. If so, when Sophia relinquished her equivalent or symbolic girdle, she opened herself up further to mortal danger. I shivered involuntarily.

All of that made sense, but how did Psyche fit in? Psyche, the beautiful but foolish young mortal woman whom Eros, the god of erotic love, takes as his wife. Afraid to frighten or overwhelm her with his godly raiment, Eros insisted on only visiting his young wife at night to make love to her. Hearing that she had never seen her husband in daylight, Psyche's jealous sisters filled her with doubt about her mysterious spouse, speculating that since she'd never seen him, he might really be a monster and not a god at all. One night, to prove her sisters wrong, Psyche took a candle and looked at her beautiful young husband for the first time while he was sleeping, but a drop of the burning candle wax fell on his skin, awakening him, and he fled in despair over her betrayal. In order to regain him, Psyche

had to perform several impossible tasks set for her by Aphrodite, Eros's mother, who was dangerously envious of the young mortal woman's beauty. With helpers such as an ant, a river-god, and an eagle, Psyche went so far as to brave the underworld, ultimately prevailing and regaining her husband's trust.

Why had my grandmother chosen this myth for her poem? Psyche was such a foolish girl, hardly a heroine at all. But Hippolyta: she was someone who I would have loved to read a poem about. How did it all fit together?

This poem seemed to be written directly for Hercule. I wondered if Sophia had written from the perspectives of both Psyche and Hippolyta because she felt as if she, usually a great warrior queen herself, had acted like a foolish girl in some way due to her love for Hercule. Perhaps she had even paid for her rashness with shame, increased danger, and, it seemed, a slight loss of respect for her heroic lover. Then there was always the possibity that she had been coerced. Perhaps she simply had not felt as if she could refuse Hercule anything after all they had been through together. Love during wartime couldn't have been easy even if they hadn't been members of the underground resistance, risking their lives almost every day. But these two…I shuddered just thinking about the risks and stresses they had faced. Now that I had started the poem, I regretted being so far from the Berkeley library. My mind was beginning to race down my memories of the familiar stacks of books in search of possible clues to the poem's meanings. Hopefully the special collection at Sonoma State would be worth the trip; and if not, we could head back to Berkeley sooner than planned. But in the meantime, I had a new library to discover and a poem to solve.

When Dion drove me over to Sonoma State the next morning, I daydreamed about Psyche's story as the glowing hills rolled by. I thought about what it meant to believe that one's lover was a god; and how it would be more than difficult to trust someone so implicitly when all voices spoke to the contrary. Would I have done the same in the foolish girl's place? What would my grandmother have done? She had taken a leap of faith of her own, believing in Hercule over and over, through years of wartime, risk, and danger.

When Dion pulled away from the curb, dropping me off in front of the campus, I kissed him in thanks for his indulgence of our day apart while I was doing research. He was the perfect companion for this excursion: undemanding, yet ready to fulfill my every need, as

212

well as most of his own. I felt lightheaded both from the kiss and with excitement for the day in the library awaiting me. I checked the campus map I found at an information kiosk, and realized that the library was straight ahead. I walked quickly up to the large concrete edifice, somewhat put off by its stark industrial design, but was pleasantly surprised upon entering the main hallway to discover a wide central stairway lit by a spacious light-filled atrium. In order for me to love a library, it had to give me a sense of possibility, which was often achieved architecturally by high ceilings or large windows. Symbolically, these structural features gave my brain room to roam, even to soar. This library had clearly been built for my level of flight, and I was relieved to feel that this was a place where I could think clearly.

After presenting my Berkeley I.D. to a kindly older gentleman staffing the circulation desk and receiving permission to use the library resources for the day, I walked slowly around the first and then the second floor – a map of the library stacks in hand – trying to decide where to begin. My mind kept drifting back to Hippolyta's girdle and the "ropes of gold" in the poem that Sophia's Psyche had worn around her waist but then had given freely to her lover, who had sold them. Was it possible that in real life Sophia had allowed Hercule to sell some of her family jewelry to help the cause of the resistance?

I went to a computer terminal to try a search on jewelry auctions from early twentieth century France and found the call numbers for several shelves on the first floor that held numerous catalogues and glossy-paged books filled with photographs and drawings of the estate jewelry of the period, much of which turned out to be lavish art nouveau brooches and pendants. Bored by such extravagant opulence, I idly flipped through the pages of several thick tomes until I came across an index at the back of the third volume, *Immortal Raiment,* that in addition to a much more diverse catalogue of designs, listed the sales of certain pieces at auctions from 1900 up through the 1950s. Running my finger down the listings for the late 1930s, I caught my breath when I saw that several Parisian auction houses, including Demetrius-Ebermann, had profited during the war from the sale of gold jewelry as well as private collection art and furniture. However, none of the entries for any of the auction houses listed the item I was hoping to find there. Something like: "solid gold rope design woman's belt or ornamental girdle." That would be too much to wish for, but I wondered where I might be

213

able to find a more comprehensive list of all the gold jewelry sold at auction in France during the war.

I walked up to the second floor where I had seen the microfiche collection on the library map, and spoke to the reference librarian in charge there about my search. The small middle-aged woman listened quietly behind her half-moon glasses, nodded once or twice, and then – with swift methodical efficiency – walked over to a long wall of card catalogue drawers and began to comb through their contents. I hadn't received personal assistance like this from a librarian in my entire life, and found myself feeling somewhat akin to Psyche in this moment, remembering the many helpers that had assisted the distraught girl in her efforts to placate Eros's mother.

Much like the ant that helped Psyche winnow through and separate an entire room filled with different grains, this kindly reference librarian was culling through the information hidden in the drawers at a rapid pace, and she had already assembled an impressive stack of possible leads. The librarian explained as she worked that the Sonoma State library had only recently begun its transition from card catalogue to computer database and that she still (with a sigh) preferred the older system. With this, she snapped the last drawer shut, turned to face me, and presented me with a small stack of cards.

"This should get you started," she said, with a modest ring of triumph in her voice, and I smiled with amusement as I thanked my helper, imagining the understated pride of Psyche's ant as it completed the first of her laborious tasks.

While sifting through the cards and following their call numbers, I saw immediately that they were leading me into a completely different area of the library. I was in war history now, and the books on the darkened shelf were dusty. The section in which most of the books the reference librarian had found for me were economic studies of investments and industry during World War II, many of which contained at least a chapter on the black market economies and war profiteering. I was intrigued and sat down near a window to begin the day's serious reading. I learned about all the ways that major U.S. corporations still flourishing fifty years later had shamelessly invested in Nazi Germany and even provided them with equipment and services at a reduced rate, but in such volume that their profit was massive. Until the discovery of the concentration camp horrors – in some cases, literally not until after the war was over – the economic boom experienced by industry tycoons while

214

the rest of the U.S. and Europe's citizens were living on rations was staggering in its unethical inequity.

I rubbed my eyes. This was interesting, but where was the lead I needed? I began to skim the indexes of all the books I had taken off the shelf for entries related to "Jewelry," "Gold," "Belt," even "Girdle," which led to an unexpectedly fascinating discourse on the value of black market silk stockings during the war. Nothing else was holding my interest though, and I was almost ready to give up and start scanning through microfiche newspaper entries for possible estate jewelry auction announcements.

As I wearily ran my finger down the index of the seventh book in my stack, entitled *Alternative Economies: Life on the Black Market in Vichy France*, past the "B's" (no "belts" listed) and on my way down to "G" for girdle, I was passing by the "D's" when something caught my eye: "Demetrius, page 124." I stared for a moment in disbelief, then turned to the page. There was the name "Céline Demetrius," and beneath it a lengthy description in italics opposite a black and white drawing depicting a delicately twisted braid of three thick, presumably gold chains, joined at the center by a classic art nouveau knot, the clasp resembling a gracefully woven cluster of wheat. The description explained that this was the only surviving illustration of a solid 24 karat gold belt that had been designed for "infamous art world diva" Céline Demetrius because it had been missing since the war. The editor commented that,

Many jewelry and black market historians assume the masterpiece had been melted down for its gold value in desperate times, which had been approximately four thousand francs per ounce. The belt, estimated to weigh almost thirty-five solid ounces of gold, had never been officially auctioned, but as with so many precious possessions during the Occupation, the likelihood of theft was great.

I exhaled slowly, unaware that I had been holding my breath as I was reading the words on the page. Could this be the family heirloom that Sophia had sacrificed to Hercule? If so, it had been worth almost one hundred and fifty thousand francs. A fortune. I thought back to the lines in the "Psyche" poem, "You sold my gold/To buy their freedom." How would Hercule have bought freedom, and for whom? I rested my head back against the wall behind my chair and thought about Vichy France. The kinds of people who might have needed freedom during that time included most of the citizens of the

nation. But in particular, I thought of the resistance agents and Jews in hiding who would be living in the most peril.

What was the price of freedom during the war? Sophia's poem somewhat self-indulgently suggested that the real price she had paid for others' liberty was her own shame and increased danger. But the cost of fake passports and citizenship papers must have been exorbitant. In order to discover who and how many people had gained their freedom thanks to Hercule's resourcefulness and Céline Demetrius' gold belt, I would need to find out the price for forged identity papers during World War II, and then I could factor that number into the worth of the belt, possibly revealing how many lives Hercule and my grandmother had saved.

I went back through the books on black market economies during the war to look for information about fake passports. There were many references to the dangers of producing and selling them, as well as data on the numerous arrests and resulting executions related to this trade, but no numbers or sales information. Trying not to be too discouraged, I tucked *Alternative Economies* under my arm so that I could photocopy the pages I needed, and neatly placed the other books back on the shelf. After making the copies, I went back to the reference desk in hopes of finding the librarian who had helped me earlier, but she was no longer there. Standing in her place was a tall man with a wild mane of salt and pepper hair and large, watery blue-green eyes that were magnified by the thick lenses of his wire-rimmed glasses.

He smiled at me vaguely, "May I help you?"

Glad to meet yet another member of my bookish tribe, I smiled back and explained my quest. The librarian raised his eyebrows and said, "Not many people know about our archive. Did you make the trip here to see the special collection?"

Heart beating fast, I admitted that I had indeed.

The librarian, who introduced himself as Louis, came around from behind his desk and said simply, "This is your lucky day. I'm the curator, and the only one with a key to the room. Follow me..."

As we walked downstairs, through rows of shadowy, unlit stacks of books to the far corner of the library's east wing, Louis explained that over forty years ago, a formerly wealthy Jewish wine merchant had fled France just as the Nazi threat was becoming apparent and settled in the Napa Valley, where he had rebuilt his fortune in wine importing. As the years went by, his family expanded the business into a winery of their own, and when Sonoma State

216

opened in the early 1960s, the merchant had set up a trust for the maintenance of a collection of his own documents and journals, as well as those of other European Jews whose escape he had helped to fund throughout the war.

My eyes widened. The kind, soft-spoken man standing in front of me literally held the key to a treasure trove. Like Psyche's second helper, the river god who made the reeds sing with instructions for gathering the golden fleece, this librarian was the resident deity presiding over a veritable stream of valuable information, and only he seemed to know how to make the reeds in his library sing.

He stopped in front of a door at the end of the long hallway, selected a small silver key from the large ring hanging from his belt loop, and opened what I could see was an unusual lock: the key slid into a stainless steel panel on the door with Swiss precision, and I thought I could hear a complex tumble of mechanisms falling into place as Louis turned the key first to the left, then twice around to the right, and back again to the left. The door quietly swung open, and I entered the room as he flicked on an array of soft track lighting overhead. I was faintly aware of the thick pile of plush, plum-colored carpet under the leather soles of my boots as I walked expectantly to a table at the center of the room and took a seat.

Louis moved quietly over to a row of mahogany file cabinets arrayed against the wall at the far end of the room. He unlocked one of the drawers and, after donning a pair of thin white cotton gloves, carried a stack of slim leather journals as well as a thick leather portfolio to the table and placed them before me. As he did so, he also handed me a pair of gloves, which were required, he explained, if I wanted to handle the collection.

He said softly. "It's two o'clock now, and the library closes at five. I'm afraid I can only allow you to stay in the archive for an hour today, since I have other responsibilities to attend to. I will return for you at three. Good luck." With that, he left the room.

Completely mystified by both my good fortune and Louis' treatment of this collection as a high-security government archive, I put on my gloves and began leafing through one of the journals. The handwriting was masculine, angular, and difficult to read. I skimmed through the pages, looking for numbers. I found some, but they were mostly property records, and lists of items sold on the black market, but nothing that would require such elaborate protection in this archive. As I continued sifting through the documents, enjoying the

smell of the old, supple leather as I handled them, I became aware that there were very few journals here written by women. I wasn't sure why this troubled me, but I had the feeling that I might find something – more of a personal story perhaps – in a woman's journal. Since my time here was limited, I began to go through the sheaves of papers in the large leather portfolio, looking for women's names, even for handwriting that seemed more overtly feminine. Some were loose pages, others were fragments of paper torn from books covered with writing and numbers, still others were letters, and all of them bore meticulously affixed catalogue numbers.

I began separating the letters out from the rest, following my intuition and curiosity, with a slight voyeuristic thrill as I noticed that the majority of the letters bore women's names. One letter in particular drew my attention: written in dark lavender ink on a tissue thin blue envelope postmarked 1941, addressed to one "Cassandra Lanvin" with no return address, it had an air of intrigue and romance that called to me immediately. There was also something vaguely familiar about the European slope of the handwriting that made me think of my grandmother. I opened the envelope, and as I unfolded the letter inside, a smaller, tightly-folded piece of paper fell out onto the table. I quickly scanned the letter for a clue to its enclosure, but it was scrawled in hasty French: *"written last week, lost then found– may it find you in safety."* The enclosed note had been folded and re-folded into such a small square that the edges of the folds had begun to tear. As I gingerly opened this second letter, I couldn't help but notice that it did not bear a catalogue number as the outer envelope had. Then as I read the words written in French, my heart began beating faster with each line:

> *My darling Cassandra,*
> *Word has reached me that you are safe. I will wait with trembling arms every day until I see you again in New York and we are both safe and free. You are in my soul and my heart. Of course H. did not believe you when you warned us of the danger, but I know better. I will make sure that he follows your instructions and we will all be reunited that much sooner. I send you my undying love.*
> *Sophia*

Now I knew why I recognized the handwriting of the poem. It was my grandmother's. I hadn't looked at the original manuscript of Sophia's poems in several months – once I had completed my

working translations of the poems in the fall, I had stored the originals safely in my father's book, deeply hidden in my closet at home. But I was certain that my grandmother had written this letter. The capital "H" and "S" were distinctly similar to those on the title page of the manuscript of her poems: larger and more flowing than the rest of her evenly balanced orthography.

For a moment, I flashed back to the day in late August in my father's study when I had seen the poems for the first time. Page after page filled with my grandmother's writing. And after "Psyche," the next poem in the series was entitled "Cassandra." There had to be a connection. I cast a quick glance around the room and made sure that the surveillance camera mounted in the far corner of the room was aimed at my back as I did something I would never have considered before in my life. I re-folded the letter into its tiny square and, heart pounding with the unethical enormity of my actions, tucked it quietly into the front pocket of my jeans. The letter was unnumbered. It was written by my grandmother. No one else knew of its existence, and no one would ever miss it. After jotting down the address for Cassandra Lanvin and casting a cursory glance at the remaining contents of the portfolio, I went back to the journals, but found that I could barely concentrate on anything I saw. Soon I heard Louis knock on the door, and I quickly composed myself to seem discouraged and ready to leave. When Louis saw my crestfallen face, he seemed genuinely upset.

"No luck?" he asked, furrowing his brow. "Hmmmm. Well, let's see what we can do about that…" And he opened a different drawer in the file cabinet, from which he removed a long metal box. As he turned to the side for a moment, I noticed with some pleasure that his profile resembled that of a hawk – or an eagle, just like Psyche's last helper, the eagle who flew to the River Styx and filled a crystal vial of water for her to give to Aphrodite.

"I was hoping that we wouldn't have to handle these directly," Louis said, turning back to face me, "but I would hate for you to leave here empty-handed." At these words, I felt a sharp pang of guilt and thought of the precious square of paper in my pocket, but Louis' air of mystery as he plumbed the hidden depths of the collection quickly muted any regret I might have had about the purloined letter in my jeans. Maybe there were more clues for me to discover? I watched, mesmerized, as Louis put on his white cotton gloves and drew out from the box several piles of what were clearly identification papers, passports, and other forms of travel visas – all

old, faded, and worn. Many were bound with other papers as well. He turned several over in his hands.

"This one cost five thousand francs; and this one three thousand. This one was twice that, for some reason, but this one was much less."

I could barely speak, and asked in a whisper, "How many are there?"

"About fifty," said Louis proudly. "These are the jewels of the collection. Our patron contacted all of the people who accompanied him during his escape and asked them to donate their forged identity papers to the collection."

"Are there any belonging to women?" I asked, slightly more boldly.

"Let's see..." he mused aloud, as he turned each delicate artifact over in his hands. "Yes, yes, here's a Lourdes, and an Yvette, a Sylvie, and a Françoise. And here's a Cassandra – that's an unusual name!"

"Cassandra?" I said, feeling faint. "Um, I'd like to see that one, if that's okay..."

"Certainly," said Louis, placing the passport into my gloved hands.

I turned first to the photograph. Cassandra Lanvin was a beauty with large, haunted eyes. A few stray tendrils of dark curly hair fell onto her high forehead, and a shadow of anxiety seemed to hover over her serious gaze into the camera. Then I looked at the official information. Cassandra Lanvin, born 1915, had emigrated to New York in 1941. Two years later Sophia would die, probably never having seen her again.

I turned to Louis and asked, "By chance, do you know if this entire group emigrated at the same time?"

"Yes," he responded with certainty. "It was one of the largest coups of the French underground. Our patron worked with his connections in the Resistance, the wine community, and the Parisian art world to raise the money. At least fifty of his Jewish friends and relations escaped safely."

I heard the words "Parisian art world" and knew that I had been luckier than Louis would ever realize.

I asked Louis if there was time for me to copy down all the prices of these passports, and after checking his watch, he looked anxious for a moment, then offered to help me. We sat down side by side at the table and made a long list of names, then Louis handled

220

the delicate documents, and I wrote down the numbers. We worked quickly and efficiently: our two systematic researcher's minds perfectly harmonized in taxonomic collaboration.

When we were finished, Louis turned to me with a satisfied smile, saying, "You know, this is actually one of the rare opportunities I've had to use this collection for academic research. Whenever you publish, please be sure to mention the collection in your acknowledgements. I'm sure that our patron would be very pleased."

I blushed, not wanting to disabuse Louis of his assumption that my research was related to my scholarly work, but I told him that he had been more helpful than I could express and promised him that if indeed my work was ever published I would be sure to acknowledge not only the library but his own and his other colleagues' most generous assistance. It was Louis' turn to blush.

As we left the room and shook hands, I turned and walked away with a bounce in my step out into the sunlight to wait for Dion to pick me up. As I was waiting, I added up the numbers on the list, and found that the price of fifty forged identity papers came roughly to one hundred and fifty thousand francs, just slightly more than the probable price of Céline's belt's weight in gold. It all began to fit together. Sophia had surely known some of people, besides Cassandra, who had escaped thanks to the library's mysterious patron. And Hercule had helped her to make their escape possible. But what was the "danger" about which Cassandra had warned them?

I lay down in the grass and took Sophia's letter to Cassandra out of my pocket. I read it over again and lightly stroked the paper with my fingertips. If I could have kept the whole envelope and enclosing note, I would have. Ethics be damned. These words were some of the only existing traces I might ever find of my grandmother. I wrote out a quick translation of the letter in my notebook and then put the small re-folded lavender square back in my jeans. I would tackle the questions it raised later, when I was ready to work on the "Cassandra" poem. In the meantime, I still had "Psyche" to solve.

I stared up at the cloudless sky as long shadows began to edge over the golden hills surrounding the college and thought about the story behind my grandmother's ninth poem. Possibly against her will, but at the very least, without realizing the considerable danger in which it would place her, Sophia must have given Hercule her

mother's belt to be melted down and sold for its cash value. Hercule must have then used the cash to finance forged passports for a large group of French Jews. Somehow this act must have increasingly threatened Sophia's safety at home, and she had to work hard to redeem herself with Julien and his cronies. Recalling the lines from "Psyche," a chill ran along my skin...

You'll never know
The trials I had to pass
To regain their trust.

How had she done it? I wondered...More fake "spying" for the Vichy regime? I could barely imagine the risks that my grandmother had taken every day, and even then I knew that my imagination certainly fell short of the real danger Sophia had known. Hopefully she had some helpers other than Hercule, so – like Psyche – she had not been entirely alone when faced with her husband's wrath and suspicion.

Dion arrived then, right on schedule. Cheeks flushed with sun and wine, he was bursting to tell me about his day: the delicious food he had eaten, the wine he had tasted, and all the gorgeous vistas he had seen. Since he had been tasting wine all day, I decided that it was my turn to drive, and I basked in his glow as he gushed about his adventures. Only after twenty minutes did he remember to ask me if my own quest had been a success. In response, with a satisfied grin on my face, I said cryptically, "More than I can even tell you."

As I drove his convertible slowly over the ridge, and Dion napped in the passenger seat, I mulled over the "Psyche" poem in my head, as well as Cassandra's letter, wishing again that I could turn back time and watch all of these events unfold. But if I could, I wouldn't be able to just sit passively as my grandmother moved ever closer to her death; I would have had to save Sophia somehow. I gazed into the hills, my mind on the road, yet also thousands of miles and almost five decades away from the sun drenched valley unfolding around us.

After we returned to the inn, we went upstairs to our room, undressed, slid into the cool sheets, and had a private wine tasting party of our own. Later that night, as I slipped off into sleep, a stream of images from our afternoon and evening together coursed through my mind. Dion across from me at dinner, our legs touching underneath the table as he fed me peaches soaked in Cabernet

Sauvignon for dessert; walking and laughing together while stargazing after dark; and finally, Dion by my side, his curls framed by candlelight, his face relaxed in contentment that mirrored my own.

Soon I was dreaming that I saw him lying on a long white couch, draped only in a simple tunic, as I leaned over him, holding a candle up to the delicate lines of his face. Just as I was about to lean down and kiss him, a drop of wax fell on his shoulder and startled him awake. He sat up with an anguished look on his face and ran from the room. I followed him out into the street, where it was cold, dark, and slick with ice. Soon I lost sight of him, but I was still running, naked, through the wintry city streets calling his name. As I ran around a corner, I stopped dead in my tracks at the sight that awaited me: a floodlit street and a circle of soldiers converging menacingly, rifles aimed upon a solitary figure shivering in a thin white tunic just like the one Dion had been wearing. But it wasn't Dion. It was Hyla. She was turning towards me, her arms held out to me, imploring me to save her.

I awoke in a cold sweat. Hyla. She was trapped. Maybe not on the unforgiving streets of occupied France, but her plea for me to come and rescue her a month ago had been real. And I had done nothing. As my breathing slowed to normal and I settled back against the pillows, I resolved that it was time to act. I reached for my notebook and finally wrote the beginning of a response to Hyla's letter.

Forgive me. For everything. I will be there as soon as I can.

Wide awake now, and staring at the ceiling, my dream still vividly clear in my head, I silently thanked Dion for leading me back to Hyla, and felt a wave of relief wash over me now that I knew what I must do. As soon as Dion went back to L.A., I would be on my way to Mexico. I would find Hyla, and maybe even track down Céline Demetrius. Paris and Hercule would have to wait.

Heart still beating audibly in my chest, I reached for a book to soothe my mind. My worn old copy of my dad's early edition *Bulfinch's Mythology* was the first at hand, and I turned to the pages I had marked which related to Psyche. Bulfinch's account of Psyche's marriage to Eros, her unintentional betrayal of his trust, and her labors of atonement for his mother, surprisingly seemed much more meaningful than it had before. Suffused with the resonances of my grandmother's life, Psyche's trials seemed almost heroic to me now: a

clear trajectory from romantic innocence to the wisdom of soul partnership.

Despite the seeming maturity induced by her dangerous life choices, Sophia had been so young – in her early twenties like me – when she began working for the resistance and falling in love with Hercule. As she approached the end of the poems, it was no wonder that she had chosen Psyche's tale to illustrate her own journey to wisdom and her fall from innocence.

Musing over the many stages of Psyche's story, I wondered why Sophia hadn't mentioned the finall labor Psyche had performed for Aphrodite, which was closest of all her trials to that of Hercules' last labor. Both Psyche and Hercules, like every epic hero before and after them, had to travel to the underworld and back and brave the temptations of its realm in order to reach their goal. Psyche had to bring some of Persephone's immortal beauty to Aphrodite in a box and almost died in the process, only to be rescued by Eros just in time. Hercules, in his twelfth labor, had to go to Hades and capture the three-headed dog Cerberus. Maybe Sophia had simply wanted to wait until the twelfth poem to explore this connection? I quickly took out my notebook to check: sure enough, the last poem in the collection was entitled "Eurydice," implying the story of Orpheus and his own underworld journey to rescue the woman he loved. Hmmm, I thought. Something to look forward to. For the time being, I had no doubt that Sophia, like Psyche, would have risked death for the man she loved. But what if Hercule, unlike Eros, could not save her? I shivered. What if something had happened to Hercule? I could only hope that there would be a letter waiting for me upon my return to Berkeley.

As I settled back against the pillows again and re-read the section in Bulfinch that recounted Psyche's reunion with Eros, Dion stirred in his sleep and I kissed his lips goodnight once more. I thought again of Sophia and Hercule, and how they were not only fighting a war for freedom, but a war for their love as well. Psyche is, of course, I reminded myself, the Greek word for the soul. And when the soul is joined with erotic passion, the result is divine. When Eros and Psyche had a child, Bulfinch tells us, they named her accordingly: "Bliss." As I finished reading the myth of their union, I closed my sleepy eyes with a smile, snuggled up close to Dion's warm body, remembering Hyla's velvety skin and golden green eyes. As I fell asleep, I dreamed that warm turquoise ocean waves washed over us, reunited once again.

224

Sophia
Paris 1941

Sitting in a dark, smoke-filled room, slumped over her glass of wine at the bar, Sophia held her face in her hands and cried. Eugénie was dead. She felt broken by the news. Several friends at the bar tried to comfort her, but she refused their gestures. She was waiting for Madeleine. Only she would understand. She had loved Eugénie too.

Eugénie had been working undercover in a Vichy household, gathering information for her comrades in the underground. She had been discovered, publicly denounced, and had killed herself rather than informing on any of her comrades. A pall had fallen over the Paris underground at the news. Eugénie had been young, beautiful, and from a good family, which Hercule and his friends had managed to smuggle out of the country as soon as she was caught. But the papers that had reported her death hadn't known the real double life that Eugénie had lived and risked everything for. She too was a *sapphiste*, and had been Sophia's lover ever since Esmée had left the country.

There were no words, no comfort to be had. Madeleine would just hold her, and let her cry as long as she needed to. It was already late in the afternoon, and Sophia had hated to leave little Theo with the servants, but she noticed that he became anxious whenever he saw her weeping, and she couldn't bear to worry him. She had fled, rushing down the street to the grocer whose assistant took a note to Madeleine for her, in the hopes that she could meet here, the newest and most hastily assembled of the *sapphiste* haunts – and the only one that had evaded the rash of raids and closings begun with the onset of the Vichy regime. Sophia shuddered.

This war could very possibly be the end of her. It was straining the already taut tension wires in her life to the breaking point. Many of her friends here tonight were meeting in back rooms every day, working with the men in the Resistance underground to undermine the government and protect those – like themselves – who were being persecuted. She joined her sister-comrades when she could, supported them with Julien's money, and – as often as possible – passed them information from his papers or the meetings he held in their home late at night. But unbeknownst to most of her

friends, the most important contribution she made to the Resistance effort was through Hercule.

Sophia wiped her tears and took a deep breath. At least Hercule was safe. He had become more than a lover, more than a friend, and far more than a comrade. His tireless courage and life-risking fearlessness had inspired her to take previously impossible risks herself. Smuggling forged passports and stolen jewelry to upscale Resistance contacts who didn't want to be seen associating with the likes of Hercule or his friends, she had become one of his cell's most trusted agents. But balancing these activities with the rest of her complicated life – the brutal pretense of her marriage, her genuine love and concern for her son, her relationships with the women whose lives were also being torn apart by the war, and her changing feelings for Hercule – was becoming increasingly difficult. There were days when she could barely get out of bed to face the demands and fears awaiting her.

She feared dying. She feared abandoning little Theo to Julien's cruelty. Her husband had not harmed the child yet, but Sophia knew that if Julien discovered her betrayals and she were to die, Theo would suffer for her crimes. She had made Hercule swear before every mission she undertook, no matter how small, that if mischance were to befall her, he would rescue her son and keep him safe. Even take him out of the country if he had to. Hercule loved Theo; when the boy was younger he had often met the two of them in parks and had played with him like a father. But then the war began, and those happy, light-filled days had ended. Sophia grieved for them now, and this sorrow brought back her pain over Eugénie.

Sophia felt tears gather in her eyes again as a wave of despair washed over her. At least some of her lovers had escaped: Yvette, Esmée, and most recently Cassandra. At the thought of Cassandra, Sophia's heart lifted slightly, and she wrenched her thoughts away from Eugénie. Cassandra's escape had gone smoothly; she was thriving in New York and waiting with open arms for Sophia to come join her with little Theo, as soon as she could get out of France. *Someday*, thought Sophia wistfully. *Someday I will go.* But for now she knew there was still work she must do. Others she must help before she risked her life and her child's life to leave. She laughed bitterly then, as a sour taste rose in her throat: it would take a miracle to get away from Julien. He practically kept her locked in the house. Thanks only to the pity, good will, and Resistance sympathies of her carefully hired servants, Sophia was able to have rare moments

of freedom, but she could be betrayed by any one of them in a moment, and that vulnerability only added to the tension of her life. Where was Madeleine? Would she ever come?

As if in answer to her thoughts, Sophia suddenly felt gentle hands caress her shoulders, and she could smell Madeleine's musky perfume as she leaned down to whisper into the curls tangled around Sophia's ear, "I am here, Chérie. Let me hold you. Come to the floor and dance with me."

The last thing Sophia felt like doing was dancing, but the music was slow, and she knew it was a way to be close to Madeleine and to whisper to each other more privately than if they were to sit anywhere else in the crowded room. The *sapphiste* world was breaking down under the tension of the war too – distrust and rivalry were escalating, and there had even been rumors of Vichy infiltrators in the bistros that had already been shut down. Understanding the risk Madeleine was taking by meeting her openly here, Sophia turned, rose, and looked gratefully into her friend's beautiful face.

Madeleine was tall and dark, with a touch of severity to her features that only made her more striking. She was a major Resistance operative and had benefited greatly from the information Sophia gleaned from Julien and passed along to her. As they danced and murmured in each other's ears, Madeleine told Sophia that she was afraid that she had been discovered.

"This may be the last time we meet, darling. Like our poor Eugénie, I know too much, but I won't endanger you or the others. They won't get anything out of me, no matter what they do," she grimaced.

Sophia clung to her tightly, saying, "No, you mustn't let them catch you. Let the brothers help you. Go into hiding…"

Madeleine sneered, "Brothers. Bah. You trust the men too much, *ma petite*. They only want one thing from us, don't kid yourself."

Sophia shivered in her friend's arms. She couldn't bear to believe such cynicism; she knew many men of integrity and courage, especially Hercule.

Madeleine continued, her voice rough with contempt, "I work with the boys when I have to, but this is their war and sometimes I think they are actually enjoying it. All the danger and secrecy. It's like a game to them…"

Sophia nodded; this she understood. But she had seen the same reckless gleam of pleasure in Madeleine's eyes upon receiving a

particularly difficult assignment that she had seen in the eyes of some of their male comrades.

She said quietly, "Don't you enjoy it too?"

Madeleine chuckled and held her closer, "Yes, I enjoy killing Nazi bastards and sympathizer dogs, but never hiding or running all the time." She steered Sophia over to a table and took a long drink from her glass of wine. "I will cross the border tonight and then will help comrades smuggle guns in and people out." She looked at Sophia somberly, "We will find each other again when this madness is over, I promise."

Sophia held her friend's gaze as long as she could before tears welled up in her eyes, then she rested her head on Madeleine's shoulder, repeating quietly, "Don't go, hide here, we can still be together, don't leave me..."

Madeleine stayed until dark, then she was gone.

Sophia, frantic with distress over Eugénie's death *and* Madeleine's departure, had finished two more glasses of wine and did not trust herself to walk home quickly and steadily enough to get there safely before Julien's return. She hailed a cab and allowed herself the expense just this once; Julien tightly controlled her weekly stipend and punished her if she asked for more. But the long ride in the privacy of the taxi would give her time to compose herself before seeing Theo, so it was worth the risk.

As the car wound through the darkened streets of Paris, Sophia closed her eyes and thought about Hercule. She remembered how she used to tease him about his name, yet gradually she had come to see him as more of a hero than the legendary Greek warrior. Out of curiosity, a few years earlier, she had bought an old copy of Apollodrus' *Encyclopedia of Mythology* to learn more about Hercule's namesake. She had been immediately absorbed in the legend of his twelve labors, had wept over his unwitting betrayal by the beautiful Deianeira, and had found small comfort in the knowledge that the gods had immortalized him in the stars. This reading, during the long, sickly winter of her pregnancy with Theo, had led to other books – Ovid, Homer, Virgil, Aeschylus, Sophocles, Euripedes, and Sappho – and Sophia had plunged hungrily into the rich lore of Greek myth and legend.

She had always loved books – as a child, reading had been her only escape from her domineering mother – so when she was racked with morning sickness and sleepless discomfort, the world of the passionate gods and the mortals who loved them called to her like a

true siren song. The stories had seemed alive to her, so relevant to her own world, as if the primitive cruelty of these ancient people had never truly been tamed or refined by so-called modern civilization, but had only – as Doctor Freud liked to point out – gone underground.

She smiled wryly at her pun. Lately her own immersion in the underground world of the Resistance had seemed like an endless mythic cycle of corruption and redemption, a series of labors in which neither Hercule nor Hercules was the only hero. There were countless women in her world who were heroic too, and they each had a story, not unlike the women in the myths; but they were the minor heroes, the everyday saviors – too often sacrificing themselves for the ones they loved. Like Eugénie.

With a sigh of frustration, Sophia noticed that her cab had stopped and was wedged stuck in traffic. She sank back against the cushions of her seat and thought of Eugénie, now dead, and wished that she too, like the mythical Hercules, could be preserved in the heavens as a constellation for eternity. *If I were a god*, thought Sophia, *I would do it.*

A sudden clarity struck her. There was something she *could* do to immortalize Eugénie – maybe not for the world to see, but at least for herself in her own brief lifetime…Sophia fished through her slender handbag for a pencil and scrap of paper, anything would do, and she found a receipt from her seamstress – a large sheet of paper that had been folded several times over. *Perfect*, she thought, as the cab lurched its way through the crowded streets, *for I am like a seamstress now too, stitching together the past and the present, the mythic and the real…*

And she started to write. The words came haltingly at first, only because the images were flowing too quickly through her head. Eugénie, sacrificed like Iphigenia, so that the men's war could go on; she herself like Electra – left behind to go mad after her sister died. *My sister: the virgin sacrifice for good sailing wind. Iphigenia, nobody knew what we shared.* How to tie it to the hero's story though? Sophia combed back through her memory…The first of Hercules' labors was the Nemean Lion. Yes. That would work. She remembered with a shiver her last night of passion with Eugénie. *We were like lions, hunter and prey, prey and hunter.* And the rest of the poem flowed from her pencil as if past and present, myth and truth had always been one, just waiting for her to reunite them.

229

"Calypso is the most intriguing of all the classical seductresses: not vengeful, but deeply sorrowful; powerful, but not magical; offering Odysseus immortality if he would consent to be her eternal husband: a very mortal sort of proposal. After being lovingly imprisoned for seven years on her island, in the back of his mind Odysseus was always trying to get home to Penelope, but was never quite capable of leaving. Finally Zeus sent Hermes down to tell Calypso to release him, and this time she couldn't refuse. Ultimately, the story of Calypso is less about Odysseus than it is about her opposition to Penelope: Calypso is immortally youthful, whereas Penelope is aging every year; Calypso has infinite independent resources, whereas Penelope is struggling to survive in the absence of her husband and son; Calypso represents the infinite vacation from worldly care, whereas Penelope embodies the burden of the mortal coil in all its complexity and strife. Certainly Penelope is faithful, but so is Calypso, and even better – she would have been faithful for all eternity, which is not something that most mortal women can promise. The question is: why does Odysseus want to leave the island? On some level, do all mortals need their fantasies to come to an end?"

Theodore Danton, *Sirens, Nymphs, and Mortals: A Study in Seduction;* Yale University Press; 1966.

The Tenth Poem: Cassandra
Mexico, June 1990

I waited until the plane leveled off in the sky to tilt my seat back as far as it would go. I turned my head to the side and stared blankly out through the small oval window, feeling like I was in a magical time machine, at the mercy of mysterious and whimsical designs beyond my control. This flight felt like the beginning of an unmarked, uncharted voyage: hurtling off into the sky towards an unknown destination on an uncertain mission. I surrendered to the moment and watched as the Bay Area receded farther and farther away, until all the cars, houses, and highways blended into a smooth carpet of golden brown hills dotted with clusters of dark green trees. Within moments these too were lost below a fine layer of cumulus clouds, completing the illusion that I was flying through another temporal dimension: on my way up, perhaps, to Mount Olympus, rather than heading south down to Mexico.

I had sent a telegram with the date and time of my arrival to the general delivery address on the back of the envelope of Hyla's letter. A two-hour drive in a cab from the airport in Cancun would take me right to the town of Tulum, and hopefully Hyla would be waiting by the post office to meet me when I arrived. In the meantime, I had over five hours of flight time to breathe deeply, and prepare myself for the unknown.

I decided to take out my notebook of my grandmother's poems and start working on the tenth one, entitled "Cassandra." Ever since I had found the letter Sophia had written to Cassandra Lanvin, I had been looking forward to seeing what this next poem would reveal. Layered with references to Hercule's tenth labor – capturing the rare herd of red cattle owned by the three-torsoed red giant Geryon – the poem also contained references to the mythical Trojan princess Cassandra, and the story of how – thanks to Apollo, whose advances she had spurned – she became a famous prophetess, yet cursed by Apollo never to be believed.

In preparation for my trip, I had brought along a few of the books that had been most helpful to me in my work so far: my own dog-eared translation of Ovid's *Metamorphoses*, as well as my father's

231

old copies of *Bulfinch's Mythology* and Apollodorus. Turning to the page in Apollodorus where I had marked Cassandra's story, I re-read his condensed version of the tale: "Apollo desired Cassandra and offered to initiate her into the arts of prophecy; but after she had learned all that he could teach her, she refused to submit to his desires. In revenge, Apollo cursed her with the power of prophecy that would never be believed." Rough justice, I thought. Cassandra should have known better than to break a bargain with a god. Shaking my head at Cassandra's hubris, I turned to Sophia's version of the story, and read:

> *I tended his shrine:*
> *Humble and obedient,*
> *In appearance only.*
> *My heart was still free.*
> *He owned my body,*
> *But I denied him his pleasure,*
> *As well as my own.*
> *In revenge, he cursed me:*
> *Through his eyes,*
> *I could see the truth and*
> *I knew danger was near.*
> *I could tell the world*
> *The truth I'd seen,*
> *But they would never listen.*
> *Why did I think you would be different?*
> *Setting off across the desert*
> *Heedless of the danger I saw ahead.*
> *On your hero's quest*
> *To fight not just one monster,*
> *But three in one; his skin red like blood.*
> *You found him,*
> *And you gored him*
> *Through his three greedy red hearts.*
> *Leading his precious herd*
> *To freedom,*
> *You wouldn't believe me*
> *When I warned you:*
> *These would not go free*
> *As had the others.*
> *No, you had to watch*
> *As they were sacrificed*

Upon the altar, one by one.
Their blood indistinguishable
From their beautiful red hides.
And he looked on and laughed.

I gazed out the window into the soft mountains of clouds. People
had died, that much was clear. I was getting better at reading the
poems' coded layers by now. The familiar triad – Sophia as the
mythical heroine, in this case Cassandra; Hercule as Hercules; and a
third threatening male who could be anyone, but I was betting on
Julien – caught in another scheme to help people get out of the
country. But this time, for some reason, they had not succeeded. My
questions were: who were the people? Who or what was the signified
by the triple bodied giant? Why had the plot failed? Why hadn't
Hercule believed Sophia when she had warned him? Had the "real"
Cassandra—Sophia's friend and possible lover Cassandra Lanvin—
warned them about this plan, or was the mythological Cassandra just
a symbol here for Sophia? Something inside me bristled at Sophia's
analogy drawn between people and cattle, but from my research I
knew all too well that millions of Jews, Gypsies, homosexuals, and
prostitutes had been transported by cattle cars on trains across
eastern Europe to concentration camps. So perhaps the poetic
comparison was more apt than I liked to think.

    It would be days, if not longer, before I would have access to
a library again, so this poem would have to simmer in my brain for a
while before I was able to figure it out through research. For the rest
of the flight I sketched out possible scenarios in my notebook and re-
read the stories it involved: first the story of Cassandra and then the
tale of Hercules' tenth labor, musing while I did so about the parallels
with my own mythic quest down to Mexico. Hyla probably wouldn't
appreciate being compared to a herd of cattle, but I did feel as if I
was crossing a metaphorical desert to rescue her, and hoped that if I
succeeded, I wouldn't have to lose her once again. These thoughts
continued to worry me as I fell into a fitful light sleep, interrupted
only a few hours later by the bump of the plane touching down on
the Cancun airstrip.

    A blanket of hot air enveloped me as I walked out of the
airport entrance to the long line of cars waiting at the taxi stand. I
regretted not changing into my shorts and sandals when I got off the
plane and felt my black jeans and t-shirt stick to my skin with sweat
almost immediately. There was no air conditioning in the cab I

chose, but looking around at the other cars, I realized that the rest of
them had their windows down too. The heat was simply a fact of life
here. It was no use trying to mask or escape it. As my driver wound
his way through the maze of highways around the airport and headed
out to the coastline, I felt my anxiety rise. What was I doing here?
What if Hyla wasn't there to meet me? How would I ever find her?

But as soon as we made it past the congestion of high rise
resorts and tourist attractions, we started driving on the coast road to
Tulum, and the sight of the ocean – vast, transparent, pale green-blue
with waves breaking softly on the beach – calmed my fears. At one
point, after an hour of driving and gazing longingly out at the water, I
surreptitiously placed my sweater over my lap and – keeping one eye
on the rear-view mirror to make sure that the driver couldn't see
what I was doing – I pulled off my jeans to change into my shorts.
Then I asked him in rusty high school Spanish to please pull over to
the side of the road and wait for me for just a few moments. The
driver rolled his eyes and muttered something I didn't catch, but he
pulled the taxi alongside the sand, I leapt out of the car barefoot and
sprinted to the ocean, reveling in the feeling of using my muscles so
freely after hours of being cramped inside a variety of moving
vehicles.

I splashed the warm water on my face, neck, and shoulders,
arched my back, and stretched my arms up to the sky, laughing out
loud at the wonder of being alive in such a beautiful place. Shaking
my curls out in the sun, droplets of water sprayed out around me,
and I returned to the cab, slowly this time, refreshed and renewed,
but also grounded. I was really here in Mexico. I had anointed myself
with its waters and was now open to the adventure that awaited me.
In fact, it had already begun.

The town of Tulum was small, sleepy, and drenched with
heat. As requested, the cab driver dropped me off in front of the
small building that served the town as a post office, but Hyla was not
waiting there. Grimly hoisting my bag onto my shoulder, I realized
that I was not surprised. Somehow I had known that this wasn't
going to be easy.

Just as I was about to enter the building to inquire into the
whereabouts of a young American woman named Hyla, I heard a low
whistle and turned around to see if it had been directed at me. The
only person I saw on the street was a teenage kid who looked like a
street urchin: skin and bones over dark brown skin, a hungry look on
his face and a shock of silky black hair falling into his eyes. He was

standing next to an ancient, rusted old blue moped, the kind that had been popular in the 70s in the U.S., but which no one had ever really taken seriously as a mode of transportation. This one looked like it had been used as a workhorse for the past twenty years. The boy climbed on and said to me, in broken English, "Come. I take you."

"Where?" I asked. "Where will you take me?"

The boy said, "Hyla. She is waiting."

I summoned all of the courage I had learned from my grandmother's poems and walked over to the boy. Trusting in fate, I climbed onto the moped behind him and encircled his slim waist with my arms. Like my grandmother and her pantheon of mythic heroines, I too could risk my life for love.

"Take me to her," I said, and the boy started the bike.

We wound through the village streets and gradually up into the inland hills, climbing slowly as the valiant moped chugged steadily along. Occasionally trucks and buses passed us on the road coughing black smoke, the passengers and drivers waving and calling out to us gaily. My mysterious young chauffeur only raised one hand silently in greeting. I was relieved to see that he kept his other hand steadily on the handlebar as the road grew narrower and more winding the higher we climbed. Finally, the boy rounded a bend and a lush grove of flowering trees came into view, with the rooftops of a vast estate looming over them.

It was my turn to let out a low whistle. What kind of scene had Hyla become involved in? Was this a home? A resort? A rehab center for the rich and strung-out? A lunatic asylum? How was I ever going to get her away from this place? My concerns were only compounded when the boy steered us away from the heavy iron gates of the main entrance around back to the servants' gate, which was also locked, but swung silently open when we approached and heavily clanged shut behind us . My anxiety returned full force.

The boy parked the moped against a shed on the edge of the property and he motioned for me to follow him. We passed through several different gardens, up a series of terraced patios, and, once we were inside the mansion, through a series of hallways until we reached what seemed like the servants' quarters. The boy led me to a small sunny room with its own tiny bathroom and pulled a thick white cotton towel from a drawer, placing it on the bed as he left.

I stood in the center of the room in mild disbelief. Where *was* I? And for that matter, where was Hyla? I gazed out the window at the sky, which looked like it was gathering clouds for a late afternoon

235

storm. I felt stiff and grimy from my travels as well as from the moped ride up the mountain, and the thought of a cool bath beckoned to me seductively. I undressed as I ran water in the tub and was soon floating on my back, languidly running a new bar of coconut scented soap over my skin.

Half an hour later, my body relaxed and refreshed, but my mind filled with mounting trepidation, I lay on my bed in fresh clothes, staring out the window as the sky grew darker and more foreboding. There was a quiet knock on the door. I immediately stood, and whispered in a low voice, barely daring to breathe, "Come in…" The door opened, and there was Hyla.

All I could see at first was the blaze of green from her eyes. As she stood there, framed in the doorway, I marveled at how long her hair had grown since I'd last seen her. It was still a tawny mane, bleached blonder by the sun, but now it reached her shoulders, and hung in soft uneven waves around her face. She was wearing only a thin white cotton sarong and a pale blue bikini top that offset the deep golden tan of her skin. She was barefoot. Neither of us smiled.

Hyla closed the door behind her and stood expectantly in the room, her face serious, her eyes wide and questioning. I had no answers for her. We opened our mouths to speak at the same time, stammering out apologies, awkward greetings, regrets. And then we were in each other's arms. Bodies pressed forcibly together, our hearts pounding against each other's ribs, our faces pressed gently into each other's necks, tears mingling on our skin.

Hyla kissed my wet cheek and turned to face me without loosening her grip around my torso. We softly touched noses and lips and gazed searchingly into each other's eyes.

"Do you forgive me?" asked Hyla.

I said quietly. "I'm here."

She said, "I was worried you wouldn't come."

I pulled away slightly, staring at her intently, and burst out with a string of questions. "Hyla, where are we? Why are you here and why couldn't you leave? Are they going to let you go just because I'm here or do I have to figure out a way to abduct you?"

Hyla relaxed her hold on my body and looked down at the ground for a minute before she looked up to meet my gaze again and answered.

"It's complicated," she said, "but the reason I needed you to come here is that there is someone I think you should meet." Still holding on loosely to my waist, Hyla took a deep breath and told me

236

about Calypso. She started with the story of the night they met, and as she described dancing at the cantina, I flashed back to the night I had seen Hyla performing at the Palladium Club as Medusa, and I could easily imagine the allure of her sinuous, graceful body in a little beach-front bar.

Hyla's next words snapped me out of my reverie, when I heard her say something that sounded like, "Caly's just a lonely heiress with an unbelievable art collection and more money than she knows what to do with, but not many real friends or people she trusts."

I looked at Hyla in disbelief for a moment and pulled away. "Are you telling me that I came all the way down here to 'rescue' you from a rich old lady? Is that why you can't get away on your own? She doesn't trust you? How much does trust cost, anyway?"

"Hey…calm down," said Hyla. "It's not like that at all, I swear. I haven't taken any money from her. I'm just her guest, and I earn my keep giving her massages and being her companion."

"Her *companion*?" I sneered, crossing my arms defensively across my chest and taking up a fighting stance. "So do you two play cards and go to the movies a lot? What's the matter: are you getting bored of your life of leisure?" I felt like I was daring her to respond.

She sighed and leaned against the wall. "No, no…give me a chance to explain. I was miserable for months, missing you, trying to just lose myself in oblivion down here, drinking way too much tequila, getting high, trying to forget the pain of that night…" She trailed off and looked away, wrapping her arms around herself protectively.

I felt cold and angry and didn't say anything to comfort her. We had to get through this, and this part definitely wasn't going to be as easy as I had hoped.

Hyla cleared her throat and continued. As she did this, I realized that she was fighting back tears and that there was probably a lump in Hyla's throat at least as large as the one I had in mine.

Hyla said, "But it wasn't working, and I kept having these dreams—these nightmares, really—and you were always in them, and I was just trying to get back to you but could never find you, and then, and then, I would always just…drown." She shuddered and began crying quietly, hugging herself even closer as she leaned her head back against the wall, eyes closed, tears trickling down her cheeks.

I watched silently, feeling Hyla's suffering, and then I took a step towards her, saying, "I've had nightmares too. All different kinds. But I was always trying to rescue or protect you, and there were always so many obstacles, I…" I choked, and held out my arms to Hyla, who stepped forward into my embrace. "I could never save you, and the dream would just end, and I would wake up miserable too…"

We stood in the middle of the room holding each other again, tears in our eyes, foreheads pressed together, murmuring our forgiveness.

I asked quietly, "Why do you want to leave?"

Hyla said, "I love you. I don't belong here. I want to be with you, and I can't let hurt pride keep me away from you anymore."

She loved me. That was all I could hear for several moments. Then I told her I loved her too. Finally, the truth was out.

But I had to ask, "If you love me, why didn't you just leave and come back to Berkeley?"

"Two reasons," she replied calmly. "First, I had to see if you felt the same way as I did, and if you really wanted me back."

I smiled and stepped gently on Hyla's bare toes with a teasing nudge, "You know I do."

Some light came back into her eyes at this return to our playful banter, and she said, "Well, I hoped you did, but there's another reason. I think Caly might be able to help you with that project of yours, you know – your grandmother's poems. Her mom was an art dealer in Paris who escaped before the war, and…" she trailed off.

Warily, I arched an eyebrow in response.

She continued, "And, I don't know, I guess I just thought she would be interesting for you to meet. Come with me," and she took me by the hand, leading me out of the room.

"Wait," I said, "where are we going? Do you have some kind of plan?"

"Not really," she said hopefully. "Just intuition."

I went back into the room, pulled my shoulder bag off the bed, and took Hyla's hand, saying, "I don't know what we're doing, but I'm trusting you…"

"Good," said Hyla. "That's all I'm asking." And she flashed a hopeful smile that almost threw me off balance with its beauty.

I pulled her close, burying my face in her hair, inhaling her scent, "And I'm getting you out of this pleasure dome, whether Circe,

238

or Calypso, or whatever her name is, will let you go peacefully or not. And if I have to meet her before we escape, so be it; but I wish I didn't."

Hyla laughed quietly, took my chin in her hand, and kissed me full on the lips. I closed my eyes, stopped breathing, and let the electric waves of sensation course through me. She pulled away, eyes glowing, and I took a deep breath.

She held out her hand and I took it. Her eyes were simultaneously challenging me to trust her and reassuring me with the promise of a renewed commitment between us. I met her gaze steadily and accepted the challenge, following her lead down the hallway. Soon we turned down a corridor that I had not yet seen, and climbed a flight of spiral stairs inset with swirling patterns of turquoise blue tiles. The stairway deposited us in a large room with a vaulted ceiling, open on three sides to the gardens around the house, with long white sheer curtains blowing idly in the pre-storm breeze.

Over in one corner of the room, surrounded by large potted palms and antique wicker chaises, I could see a woman reclining on a divan with what looked like an ice pack on her head and a drink in her hand, a half empty bottle of tequila sitting on the low glass table beside her. Her long white dress draped in loose folds over the curves and lines of her body, and her whole frame quivered as Hyla and I approached her.

Without turning to face us, the woman said flatly, in a clipped monotone of contained anger, "Where have you been. I've been asking everywhere for you. And you're with someone. Who is it. Send them away. I don't want to see anyone. And I want to know where you've been."

Hyla said gently, "No drama, Cal, please. I've just been downstairs. And a friend has come to see me. Someone I want you to meet. Her name is Herculine."

Calypso lifted the ice pack from her head and slowly sat upright on the divan, turning her body around to look at us. Her long, hennaed curls were in disarray around her shoulders and her large, dark eyes looked vaguely wild and unfocused. For a strange and fleeting moment, I thought I was looking at a deranged version of my own mother, but noted quickly that Calypso's features were vaguely European and her skin was bronze.

Calypso was silent as she appraised my appearance then turned to look at Hyla accusingly, saying,

"I don't want to meet her. Send her away."

"No," said Hyla. "It's not that simple. When she goes, I go too."

Calypso picked up her glass of tequila from the table and took a long drink. When she finished, she held the glass in her hand for a moment, as if testing its weight, and then – just as a flash of lightning crashed through the sky and the building storm finally broke – in one swift movement with perfect aim, Calypso hurled her glass at Hyla's feet, causing it to shatter all around us.

I yelled "Hey!" as I saw the glass coming and reached to shield Hyla's face. Unlike Hyla, who was barefoot, I was wearing sandals, so I quickly lifted her and carried her to the edge of the room. Then I strode back to Calypso, who was standing still, aparently in disbelief at her own actions – and struck her on the face with full force. She reeled from the slap and collapsed on the divan, sobbing in what I now realized was a drunken despair.

I snarled, "I don't know who you think you are, and I don't care. Don't ever think you can treat *anybody* like that again."

Calypso just cried, and said, "Get out of here. Take her with you and just get out of here. Just go…"

"Come on," I turned and said to Hyla. "Let's get out of this place. Is *this* who you wanted me to meet? You've got a weird sense of humor…"

Hyla didn't move. "No," she said. "This isn't how it was supposed to happen." She walked towards Calypso, carefully avoiding the shards of glass, and said, "Caly…listen. This is important." She turned back to me and said, "Please, Herculine, tell her who you are. Tell her about your grandmother."

"*What?*" I asked incredulously, "Why?"

"Trust me," said Hyla, imploring me. "Please."

I scowled impatiently, and said, "Why should I tell this harpy *anything?* And why would *she* care about my grandmother?"

"Please," whispered Hyla.

I looked at her, then back at Calypso, who was just staring at Hyla. And more to protect Hyla from the fury of the disheveled woman's gaze than because I wanted to appease her, I growled at Calypso, "Okay, okay…my grandmother's name was Sophia Danton." I turned to Hyla, "Now can we get out of here?"

But Hyla was looking at Calypso, who had raised her head and was staring at me.

"What?" I asked, "Does this mean anything to you? Who are *you*, anyway?"

Calypso looked back at Hyla, "What have you told her?" she demanded.

"Nothing," said Hyla, "I swear."

Calypso turned back to stare at me suspiciously. "Prove it," she said.

"Prove what?" I asked. "That Sophia Danton was my grandmother? Are you joking? Why should I prove anything to you?"

"You see," said Calypso to Hyla. "She is lying."

Hyla looked anxious and asked me, "Do you have any proof in your bag?"

My mind was racing with anger and confusion. For some reason, this crazy red-haired lady was really interested in my grandmother. Why? And why couldn't Hyla just tell me what was going on? But I realized that I did have something that might at least convince Calypso that I was no liar.

"Hold on," I said, and fished through my bag for my wallet. I drew it out of the bag and found the photocopy of Sophia that Johanna had sent me back in the winter, which I had cropped and slipped behind my driver's license so that I could have it with me at all times, like a talisman of my father's love. I removed the small piece of paper and slowly handed it to Calypso.

"This is her," I said, "My grandmother, Sophia Danton."

Calypso's eyes looked panicked as she held the photocopy in front of her. She looked wildly back and forth between me and Hyla, then back at the photo.

"Where did you get this?" she demanded hoarsely.

"It belonged to my dad, Theodore Danton. I never knew her. But I wish I had." I said this wistfully, but then I lost my patience and asked Calypso directly, "Why? Will someone please tell me why you care about this?"

Calypso sat down wearily, holding the photo in her hand, then met my gaze, saying, "Here is the final test. What was your great-grandmother's name? This is something that *she* could not have told you," here she nodded condescendingly towards Hyla.

"*She* happens to be the woman I love," I snapped. "And I am not impressed at all by how I've seen you treat her. You don't deserve any more answers from me, but since *she* wants me to tell you: my great-grandmother's name was Céline Demetrius, and that is all you are getting from me until you explain what is going on. Give

241

me back that photograph." I took a combative stance and held out my hand.

Calypso sagged back onto the divan.

"What? What did I say?" I asked Hyla.

Hyla said quietly, "You are her great-niece, Herculine. And she is in shock. She never met her half-sister. Her mom left Sophia in France and came down here to Mexico. She married again and then had Calypso with her new husband, so her last name is his — Odessa — not Demetrius."

Now it was my turn to feel shock. I sank to the floor, faintly aware of tiny glass shards biting into the bare flesh of my legs, and knelt there, staring at Calypso. Demetrius-Odessa Enterprises. This was Sophia's younger half sister? How was that possible? Had Sophia even known of her existence? But even stranger, could this violent, sodden, but admittedly beautiful woman actually be my own great-aunt?

I turned to Hyla, "How long have you known all this?"

Hyla responded, "I wasn't completely sure. But I've had a feeling I might be right ever since I sent you that note."

Here Calypso looked up jealously, "What note? When did you send her a note?" But then she saw my angry face and dropped her head back onto the pillows behind her. "It doesn't matter... You were right. I needed to meet her. She even looks like Sophie..." her voice broke with emotion and she turned towards me, holding out the photograph of Sophia. I took it with relief.

"Forgive me.," she continued. "My parents died when I was young; I have been raised by servants, and generally I...I trust no one." Here she gazed balefully at Hyla, and said, "I trusted *you* though. I loved *you*."

Hyla walked around the perimeter of the room, still wary of the glass on the floor, and approached the divan from the other side, kneeling down beside Calypso and taking the older woman's hands in her own, "And I love you too, Caly. I always will. But I loved Herculine before I met you, and it is time for me to go back to my life with her."

"What about *me*?" whispered Calypso. "What will I do without you?"

I regarded my relative somberly. So, Céline Demetrius was dead. And her one surviving daughter had been left alone in the world for far too long; that was clear. I wasn't even sure if she was entirely sane.

242

"Come on, Hyla, let's get out of here," I said, and began walking towards the door, slipping the photograph back into my wallet.

Calypso looked dazed. She wrapped her arms around herself and rocked slowly as she sat on the couch, closing her eyes and retreating into a private world of pain, saying, "No...no, don't go... I need to think. This is too much all at once..."

Hyla sat down next to Calypso and held her until she leaned her head slowly onto Hyla's shoulder. I met Hyla's eyes, and silently we nodded in unison. We would at least make sure she was all right before we left.

A light rain was falling, and a cool breeze flowed through the room. As Calypso's eyes gradually regained clarity and focus, she also regained some of her poise.

She shuddered, then said, "I have behaved appallingly. I hope you will be able to forgive me. I must leave you now, but we will talk tomorrow. You are welcome to stay the night." She rose unsteadily from the table, turned to look at Hyla one last time, and moved slowly off into her private wing of the house.

Hyla said, "I'm glad you trusted me."

She stood up and I took her in my arms. "Me too," I murmured. "But this is all much stranger than I had ever imagined."

The sky was dark and the rain had stopped, filling the air with a freshly washed fragrance of sea air and wild lilies. Hyla said, "Let's get some sleep. It's been a long day." And she led me downstairs to her small room.

As we shed our clothes and washed the small cuts on each other's legs and feet from the broken glass before we went to bed, I had never felt so raw yet healed, so vulnerable yet safe.

"I just want to hold you tonight," I said to Hyla. "Any more would be too much."

Hyla nodded, and curled up next to me, holding me close as we slept deeply through the night, exhausted from the ordeal we had both endured and from which we had emerged not only intact, but closer.

The next day Calypso did not emerge from her side of the house until late in the afternoon. In her absence, we spent the day by the pool, taking leisurely walks around the expansive grounds of the estate, sharing stories of our lives during the months we had been apart as well as our visions for the rest of the summer we hoped to spend together. Hyla told me more about what Calypso had confided in her about Céline Demetrius's wartime activities, and I

243

listened grimly as my understanding of the extent of my great-grandmother's war-profiteering deepened. The wealth that surrounded us seemed tainted by blood money, and I began to feel restless and uncomfortable in the midst of such luxury bought with death. When I explained this to Hyla, she reminded me that Calypso was the beneficiary of two fortunes: her father, Señor Odessa, had been a successful luxury resort developer in Cancun, and as I already knew, her parents had run a lucrative import/export firm together for many years. Most of Calypso's inheritance came from her father's legacy. The art collection that adorned the walls was more like her "trust fund," that she only dipped into when necessary.

"You know, she has all this money, but she hasn't had a happy life," Hyla said.

"Poor little rich girl," I said bitterly. "There's no excuse. She could have been doing something to help people with all her money then; that would have made her feel a little more useful, at least." Having been raised by my mom to be practically Marxist in my political and social values, I shuddered and realized that reconciling myself to the complex reality of my newly discovered relative would be challenging in ways I had not yet considered.

However, Calypso's existence made Sophia seem more real to me, and that was both comforting and strangely disturbing at the same time. I realized that during all the months that I had longed to have known Sophia, the dream-like quality of my grandmother's life had become darker and more terrifying the closer I approached. But now that darkness seemed muted by Calypso's vitality, as if her half-sister lived on inside her and was somehow more knowable than before.

I could feel the "Cassandra" poem calling me. I couldn't wait to get back to the university library in Berkeley, and then to Paris, where I was determined to meet Hercule. I had called the *Maison de Convalesence* before I left for Mexico, but had only been able to leave a message on an answering machine. If Hercule had responded, I wouldn't find out until I returned to Berkeley. It had been over a month since I'd heard anything from Johanna though, which had to be a good sign. I shivered and shrugged away the thought of the Ice Queen and focused my attention back to Hyla, the sun-drenched gardens, and the contentment that was enveloping me so entirely.

We heard a splash come from the pool area. Hyla and I exchanged a glance: it was time to confront Calypso. We hurried over to the pool and there she was, taking her afternoon swim, as if

everything was fine. We sat together pensively on a chaise lounge until she finished her laps, and as she emerged from the water, Calypso wrapped a towel around herself and approached us.

"I have arranged for a plane to take you home," she said. "The driver will take you to the airport in an hour. Then she addressed Hyla, "Thank you for all of your services…you may go."

She began to turn away, but I called to her, "Wait! How dare you talk to her that way! I thought you *loved* her. And what about me? Doesn't it matter to you that we are related?"

She gazed at me thoughtfully. "What more do you want from me, Herculine? Aren't you already taking enough?" She glanced at Hyla. "Do you want money? Fine. Name your amount, and my lawyers will contact you." Her face was hard and expressionless. "Now leave."

"No," I said, "I don't want any of your money, and I'm not taking anything that's yours. Hyla is free to go as she pleases – or should have been." Calypso winced, and I continued. "All I want from you is some information about my family. Can you handle that?"

Calypso raised her chin defiantly, but remained silent.

I went on, "After my father died, I found a collection of poems written by his mother, Sophia…"

Calypso drew in her breath sharply.

I hurried on, "I've been working on them for months, trying to figure out what they're about, and I think I've almost finished ten of the twelve, but I need to know if you have any information about Sophia, her husband Julien, what they were doing during the war…anything."

Calypso shook her head, and there was a haunted look on her face. "No, no," she said. "I know nothing except what my mother told me…"

"What was that?"

She spoke so quietly I could barely hear her, and her eyes looked far away, as if she was hearing something in the distance, "After we heard that Sophie had died, *maman* used to drink tequila and cry for hours, blaming herself for marrying Sophie to that bastard husband of hers, double-crossing us, never letting Sophie leave France. *Maman* said that it would have been easy for him to get Sophie in and out of the country but he wouldn't, just to spite us…She used to say that he knew that once we had Sophie, we'd

245

never let her go back. He wouldn't even let her write... We never even knew how she died. Or that she had a son."

I thought I saw a flicker of pain cross Calypso's brow as she spoke the last few words. But they were valuable words, confirming what I had conjectured regarding the conditions of my grandmother's marriage, as well as her conflicted relationship with her mother.

"Thank you," I said. "I know this is painful for you, but I need to know as much as possible."

"I understand," said Calypso wearily. "Is there anything else?"

"Yes," I said, hoping that her goodwill would hold out for a few more minutes, "There was a man named Hercule who was a close friend of Sophia's, and I wonder if you ever heard anything about him?"

Calypso stood motionless and closed her eyes. Then she opened them slowly and looked at me. "No," she said. "I never heard *maman* mention a man with that name. Who was he?"

"He took care of my dad here in the states," I said, "and I think he and Sophia may have been active in the underground resistance together. I'm not sure; I'm still trying to piece it all together."

"I'm sorry," said Calypso. "I cannot help you."

And then in a rush of words and emotion I hadn't planned to express, I stammered, "Look, Calypso, I'm sorry for what happened last night. I didn't know what I was walking into. If I could have met you some other way, I would have preferred that, I assure you."

Calypso, evidently wishing that she too could erase most of the memory of the previous night, merely said with stiff formality, "I accept your apology. I also regret the circumstances under which we met." She shot Hyla a sharp glance. "Perhaps we will meet again." She stopped and thought for a moment. "Please give the butler your address before you leave. Now, farewell." Then she turned and walked back into the house.

I watched silently as my great-aunt walked away from me, wondering if I would indeed ever see her again. She didn't seem to care. But it was hard for me not to. Despite her violent temper and fierce attachment to Hyla, I was drawn to Calypso somehow, and wished that there were a way to draw her out of her protective fortress. I sighed and looked at Hyla. It was time to leave, and while I hadn't gained much new information, I felt closer to Sophia and had Hyla by my side once again, and that would have to be all that mattered.

On our way to the airport, Hyla asked the driver to pull over by the ocean one last time. She assured me that Calypso's chartered plane would wait for us, and we ran out onto the sand, shedding our clothes, and dove into the ocean together, as I had dreamed of doing all winter long. We floated in the soft waves for as long as we dared, holding each other and soaking in the beauty surrounding us. Hyla's golden skin glistened in the water and her eyes glowed with emotion.

"This is what I imagined," she said softly. "This is what I wanted to happen."

"And this is what I dreamed," I said. "I can barely believe its real."

"Thank you for coming to get me," she whispered.

"Thank you for coming back to me," I said.

Our kisses were salty and sweet, then we ducked under an incoming wave, rising to the surface and shaking out our hair in a spray of sparkling droplets, laughing and splashing each other in relief, joy, and gratitude.

"Come on," said Hyla, "Let's get back to the car and catch our plane…"

"I'll race you," I dared her.

But she just laughed, "I'm the one that's been swimming laps each day, babe; you might want to rethink that dare!" And she dove off in the direction of Calypso's car waiting for us on the shore. I kept up, just barely. When we were reunited, fully clothed, and ensconced in the back seat of Calypso's car, we were driven swiftly to the local airstrip where a small plane flew us back up to the States, to California, and to the life awaiting us there. We were the only passengers on the plane, and we spent the flight resting in each other's arms.

Upon our arrival in Berkeley, we took a cab to the house, which was uncharacteristically empty. I took Hyla's hand and led her inside. We carried our bags upstairs and when we entered my room, Hyla held me in her arms.

"It's good to be here," she said, looking deep into my eyes. "Nothing has changed."

"Well," I said, "It's about time there *was* some change around here…"

Just as I was about to pull Hyla down onto the bed with me, I noticed that in the small pile of mail waiting for me by the door to my room there was a small blue envelope sticking out – and it wasn't airmail from Mexico this time, it was Johanna's stationery.

247

"Sorry," I said to Hyla, pulling away gently. "There's something here I have to deal with."

I knelt down to open the letter and was horrified when I read the following words:

Herculine,

You never responded to my last note. If I don't hear from you by the end of the month I will take legal action. Those poems were part of my husband's estate, and therefore my property, which you have stolen. Contact my lawyers at the number below and arrange to meet me in New York to hand over the originals. This farce has gone on long enough.

Johanna

I sat down fully on the floor and read the letter over again. *What on earth was going on?* Was this some kind of stunt that Johanna was pulling? It seemed much too serious for that. "Stolen?" The poems I had found in one of my dad's books? I turned to look at Hyla, who was gazing at me with concern.

"What's wrong?" she asked.

I explained that the complicated arrangement I had with Johanna had somehow had gone awry.

"I have to contact her so that she doesn't take legal action," I said, "but it looks like I'm going to have to go to New York next week."

Hyla said, "You mean *we're* going to New York."

I smiled. "Thank you," I said. "I guess things really have changed."

Hyla, still looking serious, said nothing.

It was too late on the east coast to contact Johanna's lawyers to ask them for her phone number in Paris, so I tried to relax and took Hyla in my arms. When Hermàn and Anthea came home an hour later, we were showered, dressed and waiting for them downstairs. They were so surprised and excited to see Hyla that they immediately began calling friends to come over for a welcome home party. Linus and Phoebe showed up, as did Percy and a new flame of Anthea's named Antony. Hermàn whipped up a big batch of strong sangria and when Antony's reggae band mates showed up, we danced out on the lawn and the party went on for hours.

Early the next morning, I left Hyla sleeping and tiptoed quietly into the kitchen to call Johanna's lawyer in New York. Heart racing as I spoke, I asked the legal assistant to give me Johanna's

phone number so that I could attempt to settle the matter with her peaceably.

"Dr. Danton is currently residing in Manhattan for the month," he informed me, "so that she can bring this matter to a timely resolution."

Surprised, I asked for Johanna's contact information there, but the assistant said merely that I was welcome to write to Dr. Danton in care of the legal offices and that the message would reliably be delivered to her.

With a sigh, I hung up the phone and drafted a quick letter:

Dear Johanna,
There must be some misunderstanding. As you know, I found my grandmother's poems by chance, after you had moved out of the house in one of my father's books in his personal library, all of which he bequeathed to me. And I did respond to your last letter and sent you the first and eighth poems as a gesture of goodwill. I've been meaning to send you the ninth poem but have been caught up in some unexpected traveling which has prevented me from doing so. I will enclose it now and hope that when I come to New York next week to resolve this matter with you we can do so civilly.
Herculine

I included a copy of the "Psyche" poem, and my mother's address and phone number so that Johanna could reach me. Then I called my mom to tell her that not only had my trip to Mexico been successful, but that Hyla and I would be arriving in New York the following week. Mom was thrilled that she would be meeting Hyla and seeing me so soon: just in time for the opening of her dance company's summer season.

I smiled. Same old mom: she always has to be center stage. Hyla would probably love her just like the rest of my friends always did. The question was, what would mom think of Hyla? My mother had never met any of my lovers before. Which role would she perform in honor of the occasion? Cool parent, nonchalant in her matter-of-fact acceptance of her daughter's female lover? Maternal yet protective earth mama, enfolding Hyla into a deceptively nurturing embrace while shrewdly analyzing her appropriateness for me? Or would she go into her "youth culture" routine, trying to impress Hyla and pretend she was her new best friend? Was my mom even still capable of this particular performance after her heart

attack? I shuddered, remembering the times I had seen my mom assume each of these various roles with her young dancer friends. While the household was still sleeping, I slipped out to mail my letter and get to the library as soon as it opened. It had been too long since I'd done any work on the poems and I was grateful that Hyla had said she wouldn't mind if I was gone most of the day. I jogged lightly down the hill to the university, filled with anticipation for the discoveries awaiting me there.

As soon as I walked into the library, I took a deep breath of the familiar scent of the marble walls and leather bound spines and felt even more at home than I had at the house. I sat down in my favorite chair in the atrium and reviewed Sophia's tenth poem once more. The nagging question of who or what the "three greedy red hearts" of the giant Geryon symbolized raised an uncomfortable possibility. If somehow this threatening figure represented Julien Danton, I had to be prepared for more unwelcome information about his corruption. Discovering my grandfather's criminal record had been the most difficult part of my research so far: I was ashamed of him, and feared what more I had yet to unearth about him. It was with trepidation that I walked downstairs to the film archives to watch the footage of Julien Danton's trial once again, this time without the distraction of Dion's attentions, to see if there were any more clues to be found there.

As I sat in the darkened cubicle, watching the film of my grandfather arrogantly defying the court, all I could think about was the women whose lives he had destroyed in his prostitution trade. Collaborating with the Germans, killing the archbishop, and all of his spying were awful, but somehow the inhumanity of trafficking in women's bodies and lives seemed to me – and possibly had to my grandmother as well – to be his greatest crime. If his profit from these women's exploitation was one of Julien's three symbolic "greedy hearts," it was easy to see that there were many options for the other two: extortion, collaboration, espionage, and murder, among others.

I thought about the image of the cattle in Sophia's poem – precious and trusting, herded away by Hercules, only to be sacrificed in the end. Then I combined this image with my fears about Julien's prostitution ring – was it possible that the people the resistance were trying to save this time weren't simply Jews, but the women entrapped by Julien? My head was suddenly filled with a vision of battered exhausted women, possibly Jewish women, transported in

cattle cars to the German military brothels, or concentration camps, and something in the way my palms were sweating made me know that I was on the right track.

I wrote down my ideas and headed back up to the stacks to find out as much as I could about prostitution during the Vichy regime. I found several books that mentioned the subject, noting that officially it was illegal, but that there were regular reports of disappearances of women from the city, which were usually explained away as white slavery abductions. The women never resurfaced. Only one text, *Crimes of War: The Traffic in Bullets, Bodies, and Bombs*, hinted at a larger systematic network that had ties to Vichy administration officials. The author mentioned Julien Danton in a footnote along with the names of other high ranking individuals implicated in prostitution rings, but that was all.

As I leafed through the book, I found a few rare testimonials of Jewish women who had survived the concentration camps and who told of being taken off the trains headed to the camps and diverted to military brothels instead. One survivor had written:

Only young women and older girls were taken by the soldiers. I was fourteen. Many girls were killed before they ever reached the camps. I once heard a story, I don't know if it is true, about a group of women being sent to the camps who were aided by the resistance fighters; they killed their guards and tried to escape by crossing the border, but they were caught, imprisoned, and executed. We used to tell each new girl the story to give her hope, but maybe it really just kept us scared and docile.

I shivered as I read these words, imagining being only fourteen and repeatedly subjected to the violence of rape, possibly for years. I marked the page and closed the book, bowing my head for a moment in silence.

With weary steps, I carried *Crimes of War* over to the library's photocopy machine and made copies of this testimonial along with several others. It was more than I wanted to know, and it was all I needed to confirm that my hunch about the meaning of the "Cassandra" poem was right. Once Sophia and Hercule had discovered Julien's involvement in sexual slavery, they must have tried to sabotage it and, despite Cassandra Lanvin's warnings, had almost succeeded. If the story in the survivor's testimony was true, perhaps Hercule had managed to help a group of young Jewish women who had been forced into prostitution overcome their guards

251

and get to the border, but then they were caught and executed while he had somehow escaped. It was a stretch, but it fit the poem's cryptic lines:

> *Leading his precious herd*
> *To freedom,*
> *You wouldn't believe me*
> *When I warned you:*
> *These would not go free*
> *As had the others.*
> *No, you had to watch*
> *As they were sacrificed*
> *Upon the altar, one by one.*
> *Their blood indistinguishable*
> *From their beautiful red hides.*
> *And he looked on and laughed.*

Just as the mythical Hercules had to stand by and watch as Geryon's red cattle were slaughtered, had the "real" Hercule witnessed the execution of the women he had attempted to rescue? Hopefully not. But Sophia must have felt all too similar to the mythical Cassandra. Knowing the full extent of Julien's influence, and possibly tipped off to other risks by Cassandra Lanvin to which she alluded in her letter, Sophia had probably tried to warn Hercule that this plan wouldn't work – too many high officials risked being exposed if the women got away and told their stories – but he wouldn't listen to her, and the women lost their lives.

After this disaster, Sophia's relationship with Hercule must have been strained. Estranged from her husband at home, and now from her lover underground as well: who did Sophia turn to for support after this crisis? Cassandra Lanvin, whom she had addressed as "My darling" in her letter? Could this have been when their friendship blossomed into something more intimate? I quickly turned to the copy I had made of the letter in my notebook, having secured the original with the manuscript of Sophia's poems deep in the recesses of my closet at home in a box containing keepsakes and photographs from my dad. I marvelled at the letter each time I read it:

> *My darling Cassandra,*
> *Word has reached me that you are safe. I will wait with trembling arms*
> *every day until I see you again in New York and we are both safe and*
> *free. You are in my soul and my heart. Of course H. did not believe*

252

you when you warned us, but I know better. I will make sure that he follows your instructions and we will all be reunited that much sooner. I send you my undying love… Sophia

I noted grimly that Cassandra had apparently warned Hercule of the peril of his mission but that he had, of course, disregarded her advice and Sophia had to take up her torch as the unheeded prophet of danger. Was there yet another plot for Sophia herself to escape that was never undertaken? If only…I thought. But if Sophia had escaped, would she have gone to New York? Would my dad ever have met my mom, and would I even exist? *Probably not.* I thought again of the mythical Cassandra, taken as spoils of war from Troy by Agamemnon, only to be murdered by his wife Clytemnestra upon their arrival in Thebes. If Sophia had attempted to escape, she might have died a few years earlier – and who knows if my dad would ever have escaped.

Turning away from these confusing existential conundrums back to the political level of the poem, which seemed relatively clear to me now, I regretted that there were still levels to the poem's personal meaning that I could never understand. For instance, what did Sophia mean when she wrote that she "denied him his pleasure as well as my own"? Was "him" Julien? Was she denying him sex? And had he actually "laughed" upon finding out about the failed escape of his prostitutes? I was feeling sick with loathing for my grandfather's inhumanity, and for Hercule's hubris too. How had he dared to take these women's lives under his protection and not listen to Cassandra or Sophia's warnings, only to lose them all?

I trudged home without the usual elation I felt upon discovering the key to one of the poems. This one was just too disturbing; its implications were more than I could bear. It had been harder than usual to re-enter the brutal world of my grandmother's life during wartime, now that Hyla was back and joy was in my heart again. This was as much research as I could take for my first day back. I headed home, my mind dark with imagined horrors of the holocaust, but by the time I reached the house, my glowing anticipation of the sight of Hyla had eclipsed them all.

She was upstairs waiting for me and welcomed me into her arms, sensing from the look on my face that my day at the library had been difficult. But I didn't want to talk. I nuzzled into her neck, weaving my hands through her sun-bleached mane, and kissed her. After resting quietly in each other's arms for a while, Hyla asked me

253

what had happened during my day at the library. I told her about my grandfather and the prostitution ring, shame in my heart, and Hyla held my gaze steadily.

"You are not responsible for his crimes," she said.

"I know," I said. "But I hate him. And that's just really hard."

Hyla nodded. "It's okay to hate him. Sometimes members of our own family are the most messed up. That's why we go out into the world and create a new family for ourselves..." She pulled me close and held me until the windows grew dark, and hunger drove us out for some savory Thai take-out from town.

"Did you figure out the poem?" Hyla asked as we walked down the stairs.

"I think so," I said. "I'll tell you about it later. Right now, I'm just really glad you're here."

Hyla stopped and turned to me with a smile, "We're home, Herculine. Everything's going to be all right. And hey – isn't that how a mythic journey is supposed to end?"

"Yeah," I said. "But this one isn't quite over yet."

Looking up into the clear night sky, as we walked to town, I could see the brightest stars in the constellation named after Hercules that my dad had taught me as a child – and I thought of the mythical hero, returning home empty-handed after the beautiful cattle he had captured had been sacrificed to appease Juno's wrath. Then I thought of Hercule, returning to Paris to face Sophia's despair and disappointment after the women he had tried to save were murdered. Unlike my namesakes, my hands were not exactly empty upon my return home from my quest for knowledge today, but nor were they full. I had almost solved all of the poems, but in solving this last one, I felt like something – certainly any obligatory sense of love for my grandfather – had been lost.

Also strangely, even though I had felt Sophia coming closer and into clearer focus after meeting Calypso, now I felt as if she was slipping further away. Why was this happening? Was it that I was coming close to the end of her manuscript? Or was it the knowledge that her death was approaching with increasing speed as each poem came to an end? If I never finished the poems, could I keep my grandmother alive somehow?

No. Just as I couldn't bring my father back to life by solving the poems or learning about his mother, or even by patching things up with Johanna and ultimately meeting Hercule. But wasn't that

why I was doing all of this? Studying classics, researching the poems…anything to keep my dad alive in my life, in my heart, in my mind? Silent tears trickled down my cheeks in the darkness. I turned my face away from Hyla, but I knew she was watching me carefully. I held her hand as we walked to town and thought of the hurdles ahead. I didn't know how many more of them I could take.

Calypso
Mexico, July 1990

Calypso was folding her clothes methodically and placing them carefully in her suitcase. There was no one else in the room to see her, so her expression was an impassive mask of emotionless concentration. The light in the room was unsparing, and every line in her face stood out in stark relief. In public, she performed glamour; but when she was alone, her face and her posture betrayed not just her age, but the weight of despair and guilt that she carried within her.

Calypso had more guilt than anyone suspected. More, in fact, than anyone would ever know. It had been a strain keeping up appearances during her conversation with Herculine. When she saw Hyla and Herculine together, her heart had contracted painfully and she found it difficult to talk, much less act civilly and look unconcerned. But she had done her best, and had given up Hyla freely, grieving the loss of her privately, and deeply. But even more than Hyla, it was Herculine who had caused Calypso the most distress. Simply the fact of her existence was a shock to her sensibilities, and set off loud psychological alarm systems in her head so often that she had actually been suffering from the migraines that she had managed to elude for years. She hadn't had one since her mother died.

She had never felt loved by her mother. Céline Demetrius had been cold, imperious, and remote. She had only been interested in her lonely child from her second marriage when Calypso was silent, obedient, and subdued into a pretty caricature of a little girl – and even then only for very brief periods of time. Calypso's childhood had been racked with illnesses and maladies, perhaps in the hopes of obtaining rare affection and maternal concern from her otherwise indifferent mother. All of the ailments had felt entirely real, and many had been quite serious: but the migraines were the worst. Confined to a dark room in isolation for days at a time, they seemed to undermine the very effect they had been intended to produce. Her mother avoided her during her migraines, which had only made Calypso languish longer in their thrall.

256

It had been a particularly serious bout of pneumonia that had finally ended their torturous relationship. Céline's lungs, weakened by decades of smoking strong cigarillos, had contracted her daughter's lung infection and died after a long suffering month in which she dramatically and deliriously railed against her teenage daughter for killing her, as if that had been her intention. Calypso often wondered: had it?

For a few years Calypso was able to live alone in relatively affectionate peace with her father in the shadow of his own waning health, and his emotional pining for his once charming, seductive, and much younger wife to whom he had been devoted. She had probably kept him on a starvation diet of love and affection too, thought Calypso bitterly. She remembered her elderly father with compassion, but their relationship had been distant in its own way too. When he had died a few years after her mother, she had felt only slightly more alone in the world than she had felt before.

She had made the house on the hill her emotional fortress, penetrated only by occasional affairs—at first, older male friends of her father who had hovered over her protectively after his death, but she had little interest in them after she learned all they had to teach her about handling her estate, and her body. She began to travel the world then, aimlessly searching for something, but she didn't know what. The family lawyers made sure that she was provided for, and she eschewed formal education, reading idly at times, voraciously at others, traveling alone, until chance romantic encounters provided her with temporary lovers, traveling partners, and occasional house guests in the years that followed. She attended lectures at major universities in several countries; she spoke French, Spanish, a smattering of Italian, and English. She even dabbled in art herself. After her mother's death, she was free to express herself without the fear of Céline's mockery or censure. After several years abroad, Calypso returned to the villa in Mexico, unequipped for any kind of lasting relationship, true bond, or intimacy, but certain that love would somehow find her someday. And when it did, she would never let it go.

It was then, upon her return from her wandering, that she received the letter from the man named Hercule, who had been a friend of Sophie's. Somehow he had tracked her down to tell her that Sophie had a son, who was only a year older than Calypso. Hercule had written that he hoped Calypso would be reunited with her nephew so that Theo wouldn't be alone in the world. The humor in

the situation was dry: Calypso was more alone in the world than anyone she had ever met. What kind of familial comfort would she be able to offer this unknown nephew who was old enough to be her brother? It was terrifying. Part of her wanted to fly to New York immediately, to find Theo and claim him as her own, both of them abandoned in different ways by these two cold French women. But she couldn't bear it. She was afraid to meet him, to know him and be known by him. She wasn't sure which she was more afraid of: to possibly be rejected by him, or to be loved by him. It was too confusing.

For years she lived with the knowledge that Theo was alive and living in New York, that he was married, a professor, and oblivious to her own existence. If she revealed herself to him, would he claim part of her wealth as his own? She had enough to share, but it was something else that she didn't want him to have... a part of her. Her pain. Her loss. She didn't want to meet someone who had known her half sister, someone Sophie had loved. Calypso had hated Sophie her whole life. Céline had made no secret that the daughter she had left in France was her favorite child.

Calypso never responded to Hercule's letter. Instead she dreamt of Theo, she paid detectives to spy on him, she even traveled to New York once and secretly attended one of his lectures. She came close to revealing herself then, after watching him for an hour, admiring both the kindness of his face filled with passion for his subject as well as the humility behind his intelligence. But once the lecture was over, the terror over took her again and she had fled from the room. She returned to her villa, her tequila, her lovers, her art, her emptiness, and her pain. Because it was hers. It was all she had.

Until this girl, this Herculine. Calypso had not known that Theo had a daughter. Somehow the detectives had missed this crucial fact. It took her completely off guard and had almost shattered her. At first she had feared Herculine too. But now she saw that behind her angry front, this girl Herculine was different. She wasn't like the others. This girl was a part of her. Calypso felt it. Herculine felt and looked like the daughter she never had, the one she might have wanted: proud, beautiful, and fiercely loyal.

Calypso had done what she needed to do. She had lied to Herculine, yes, but that was unavoidable. There was no real reason that the girl needed to know that Hercule had contacted her. Or if there was, it wasn't her responsibility to tell her. The last thing she wanted was for Herculine to know that she had known about Theo's

existence for decades and hadn't done anything about it. She couldn't bear it. She had no explanation, no excuse.

All Calypso knew was that she needed to ensure that her sister's grandchild was safe: that she was provided for. This was the only way she could make amends with her conscience. She felt weighted down by her guilt over her bitter resentment of her mother's obsession with the ghost of Sophie, and her shame over having denied her connection to her dead nephew Theo. But it was not too late. She had called her lawyers and set up a trust for Herculine. She had made the girl her sole heir and beneficiary. She would atone. She would atone. In her bedroom, on her knees, head in her hands, shoulders bowed over her suitcase as she wept, longing for the loving touch of anyone…the forgiveness of everyone. She would give anything she had.

A few minutes later Calypso composed herself, closed her suitcase, called for her butler, and requested that her driver be ready to take her to the airport momentarily. A few weeks in the Greek islands should clear her mind, and a new lover would clear her heart. She strode outside and straightened her shoulders, holding her head high and wiping the tears from her face before her servants could see her. Her car was waiting.

The Eleventh Poem: Atalanta
New York, July 1990

New York welcomed me home with a fanfare of summer glory. As Hyla and I stepped out of our cab from the airport onto the curb in front of my mom's loft in Greenwich Village, it was like there was an impromptu parade going on all around us. There were banners and streamers flying from lamp posts, balloons floating outside shops and stores, a small band of steel drum musicians on the street corner, and women wearing colorful summer dresses looking like wildflowers of every shape and hue. The late afternoon sun was gilding the city and I felt its glow suffuse me.

I had been raised to think of New York as the mythic city of every artist's dreams: a post-modern fortress town built on layers of fortunes made and ruined, loves found and lost, the cradle of contemporary western civilization and apex of modern culture. I felt all of this complexity vibrating in the air and around me, emanating from the warm stone and concrete of the buildings, rumbling beneath the layers of rock, earth, cobbles, and pavement. But mostly, I just felt like I was home again, and whole, in a way that I realized I did not yet feel in Berkeley. Whole, that is, except for the glaring absence of my dad. At least in California I didn't feel his absence so acutely. He was simply inside me there somehow, while here...I looked around thoughtfully as if I imagined I might glimpse a trace of him. Here, I would always be seeing the city partly through his eyes. My foundation was still here – in this rough and beautiful place – no matter where I chose to live the rest of my life, precisely because my childhood with my dad had been here. This was clear to me.

The last time I had been in New York, tending to my mom after her heart attack and nursing my own broken heart after Hyla's disappearance, I had been too emotionally overwhelmed to feel my deep connection to the city in its harder, colder winter guise. But now in summer, it came rushing back like wine in my veins: every hot summer night of my childhood and youth, long afternoons in the leaf-laden parks, climbing trees and riding my bike, sailing my toy boats with my dad on the lake, and later – as a teenager –the secret trysts on park benches, beneath trees, in secluded Gothic courtyards

and Greenwich Village nightclubs. It was all here: every corner a landmark of my life. It was more than I could even begin to express to Hyla. So I just smiled and took her by the hand as we walked inside mom's building and up the stairs to her loft.

As expected, there was a note – but no mom or Ramon – waiting for us inside. They were out enjoying the afternoon, the note said, and we should all meet up at their favorite Mediterranean place on the corner of Spring street at nine o'clock. I shrugged and put down my bag. Hyla did the same and looked around the loft wonderingly. Its high windows were gleaming with light, and the place reflected mom's signature style of abundant bohemian chaos: her big cozy sofas strewn with pillows and afghans, there was dramatic abstract art on the walls, her tall wooden bookcases overflowing with my dad's books, and the large meandering plants and vines were curling around any available surface or corner. And the long wooden dining table, centerpiece of all her late night dinner parties, was laden with flowers, last night's wine glasses, theater programs, and notes for her company's most recent performance. Hyla looked enchanted.

"This is how you grew up?" she asked.

"Well, not quite so luxuriously," I admitted. "Mom struggled for a while when her company was just starting out, and our apartments were usually a lot smaller, but the troupe really took off, and then…" her voice caught on her words, "and then Dad died and he left her some money, and she bought this place and the studio next door, so she's really set now."

Hyla nodded quietly. I knew that she was probably thinking of the series of depressing foster homes she had lived in. She didn't mention them often, but when she had, she told me they had been grim, dismal places, without any traces of art or cultural beauty.

"This is where you should have grown up too," I said to Hyla.

She nodded. "I know. I feel it. I've always wanted to live in New York. It's every film maker's dream."

"Well," I mused, "Maybe we can live here someday, if you really want to. I'm not sure how I'll be able to earn a living – every academic in the world wants a job at a university in New York – but hey, I could always teach at a private school or something."

"Whoah, slow down," smiled Hyla. "We're getting ahead of ourselves. Let's just enjoy the fact that we're here now and take a long walk. I'm dying to see this city of yours."

261

I grinned. I had been waiting for this moment since the early stage of our romance: the day I would take Hyla around New York for the first time. Within moments, we were out on the streets in the glorious sun, amidst the mid-summer revelers, young and in love in New York City. I knew it didn't get much better than this.

We wandered arm in arm around Greenwich Village for hours. I showed Hyla landmarks both historical and personal, we drank iced mochas at an outdoor café, listened to street corner guitarists, and watched dancers in Washington Square Park. Hyla bought us matching studded leather bracelets from a street vendor, and we witnessed several different forms of street theater within a five-block radius. We were unaware of the passing time and sunset came late; it was almost nine o'clock before we realized it was time to meet my mom. When we entered the Mediterranean restaurant and found mom and Ramon there, already carousing with a group of friends at a table filled with plates of food, we happily tucked right in to the feast.

My mom embraced us with a dramatic flourish, Ramon greeted us warmly, and the rest of the dancers immediately drew us into the conversation and laughter. I was relieved to see that my mom seemed to be handling the moment well, and that Lyra was not among the group that night. She was still a member of mom's dance company, so we would definitely see her at the performance in a few days, if not before. I had already told Hyla everything that had happened while we were apart, so she was prepared; it was Lyra that I was worried about. I was also feeling confused about whether or not to contact Ben and Lucy to tell them that I was in town. While it would have been great to see them, I was feeling so deeply committed to Hyla – truly monogamous for the first time in my life – that the thought of seeing my former lovers was just to complicated to consider. I would see them when I came back from Paris, I decided, and hopefully they would be open to meeting Hyla too.

After the dinner ended around eleven, we all decided to go out dancing at a small club nearby. A crowd was already filling the floor and moving to the sultry trance beat of electronic house music, and although the interior was dark, I could see the familiar features of the lounge, bar, and dance floor. I had spent countless evenings here, and knew every hidden corner and discreetly placed banquette intimately. It was the first time that Hyla and I had been out dancing together since our reunion, and the moment was charged with significance. We separated ourselves from mom's entourage and

found a secluded area of the dance floor. Hyla pulled me up close against her and whispered,

"I like your world."

I kissed her while smiling, and said, "My world is better with you in it."

Still pressed close together, we began to move our bodies to the music. Soon we were dancing as if we were magnetically fused: at least one part of our bodies was touching at all times, preferably as many as possible. If there was desperation to our savoring of this long-awaited moment, there was also joy, release, and a welcoming of all that was now possible between us.

The trance-inducing songs ran into each other seamlessly with only slight variations in the driving beat. We lost track of time, and only when our clothes were soaked with sweat did we break contact, gasping and laughing. Hyla went to the restroom to splash herself with cool water and I went over to the bar to get us some cold drinks. Out of the corner of my eye on the way to the bar, I spotted Lyra across the room, dancing with a handsome African American man. Their bodies were moving together like a honey slide: slow and sensuous, matching each other's graceful moves with muscular strength. Lyra's partner was evidently a dancer too. I was glad and relieved to see her so evidently absorbed in a new interest, and I nodded to Lyra with a smile when she turned her head and looked questioningly in my direction. Lyra returned the smile as her dance partner dipped her deeply towards the floor, arching her back with tender precision.

My mom came over to my side at that moment and caught me gazing at Lyra as she danced.

"Any regrets there, sweetheart?" she asked.

"No," I said, "just relief that there are no hard feelings on her side."

"At least not now," mom commented, "but she was down for a few weeks after you left in the winter. Then Jason joined the troupe, and they've been inseparable since. Their duets are really quite beautiful. You'll see one at the show."

"Will you be dancing, mom?" I asked.

"Just wait and see," she said with a mysterious smile. "I have a surprise for you."

"Oh great," I said. "I should have known…"

263

"You'll love it," she said. "I promise. By the way, your friend seems very nice. This is the first moment she's taken her hands off you, so I guess that's a good sign?"

Feeling like a teenager who's been caught necking in the car, I whined, "Mommmmm...come on...Cut it out, please?"

"Okay, okay," she conceded, "But am I ever going to get some quality time with you while you two are in town?"

"Sure..." I said, looking at her curiously. "Hyla's kind of independent like me; I'm sure she'd be glad to prowl around the city on her own one of these days."

"*One* day?" Mom said with a sarcastic edge to her voice. "Is that all I get?"

My jaw dropped. Was she jealous? This was the first time I had ever brought anybody home to meet her, the first time I had ever been serious enough about anyone to bring them home with me at all. Couldn't she relinquish center stage just this once? I could tell that I had to handle this situation very carefully.

"Mom?" I asked tentatively. "Hyla means a lot to me. You know that. But you come first. You always will. So, don't worry, okay?" I put my arm around her narrow waist. "I mean it. Just let me know when you want some time together, and I'm all yours."

She looked at me, her edges softened by my reassurance, and I saw Hyla emerge from the restroom and begin walking towards us. With a start, I remembered the drinks that I was supposed to be getting, and quickly ordered two glasses of wine at the bar. When I turned around, I saw Hyla talking with my mom a few feet away. Mom was nodding and Hyla was reaching out her hands to her. Mom took them and then smiled at her with what looked like gratitude. I was baffled: what was going on? I walked over to them with the glasses of wine, handed one to Hyla, and said,

"Hey, what am I missing?"

Hyla put her arm around my shoulders and kissed me on the cheek, "Nothing, babe. Nothing that concerns you anyway. Your mom and I are just making sure that she and I get some quality time alone during this trip. We really want to get to know each other." Hyla winked at my mom and they exchanged grins. I just raised an eyebrow at them.

Mom said, "See you in the morning, darling," then she kissed me and embraced Hyla, "Welcome, dear. We'll all have a wonderful time..." And she was gone.

264

We watched her walk away, her long, slender frame encased in a shimmering green sleeveless dress with a multi-layered chiffon skirt, her auburn hair coiled up in an intricate knot with wispy tendrils carefully framing the delicate nape of her neck.

"Your mom's quite an original," said Hyla admiringly.

"Um, thanks. I think," I said, sipping my wine. "Does meeting her explain everything you've ever wondered about me?"

Hyla smiled, put her glass down on the bar and took me in her arms. "No way. You're still a complete mystery." The twinkle in her eyes became serious for a moment as she paused and said, "But I would have liked to have met your dad. I think that would have explained a few things."

I closed my eyes and pulled her close. I felt deeply understood in that moment, far more than Hyla knew. My heart ached at the thought of my dad, and I realized that more than anything, I just wanted to leave the club and walk around in the balmy night air. We finished our wine, danced to one more song, then emerged from the club, the fresh air engulfing us with a refreshing warmth and fragrant urban edge: restaurants, late night flower markets, cigarettes and perfume. I was in heaven.

The next day, still on California time, we woke late to the sun high in the sky, and when we padded out to the kitchen in search of tea and breakfast, mom and Ramon were already long gone. We had the day to ourselves. I wanted to take Hyla uptown, and to museums, and to the Park, and to the library, and…Oh. The library. I had to get there soon. My meeting with Johanna was in three days, and I wanted to get as much work done as possible on the poems before then. But I also wanted to run around the city with Hyla …was there any way I could do both? I looked over to the window seat where she was idly paging through an art journal and drinking a glass of juice. I had an idea.

I walked over to my shoulder bag, rummaged through it, then carried a book over to Hyla and handed it to her.

"This is *Bulfinch's Mythology*," I said. "My dad's copy. It's kind of an encyclopedia of Greek myths, but it's still really interesting. I was thinking that maybe if you read the parts about Atalanta you might want to help me with my research…"

Hyla's eyes widened, then she laughed and asked mischievously, "Oh really? Hmmmm. Let me see, what's the going rate for research assistants these days?"

I felt myself blush, but continued, "And when you're finished with that story – it's pretty short – then maybe you'd like to read Apollodorus's account of the eleventh labor of Hercules: stealing apples from the garden of the Hesperides. The same kind of apples, in fact, that ended up being Atalanta's downfall. Both stories are woven into the eleventh poem that my grandmother wrote, and, I thought maybe you'd like to know what I'm working on. I'll give you my translation of the poem to read as soon as you're done with those, okay?"

Hyla looked bemused as she took the book from my hands, and then, as I waited for her begin reading, she laughed and said, "Oh: you mean you want me to read it right *now*? Ahhhh, I see. Okay, okay...I'm reading! See?"

She theatrically opened Bulfinch to the page that I had marked and bent her head over it in mock studiousness. I turned away, exasperated, but when I looked back a moment later, she seemed genuinely absorbed in the book. At my sigh of relief, Hyla looked up and winked at me. I left the room with a lighter heart, and as I showered and dressed, I went over the familiar mythic details in my head while Hyla, I knew, was encountering them on the page for the very first time.

Atalanta, proud daughter of a ruthless king. She ran more swiftly than any man in the kingdom and refused to marry anyone unless he could outrun her in a race. All the unlucky suitors who tried and failed were executed by her father. Atalanta, free and unfettered by a man, did not care. But finally one young man loved her so desperately that he prayed to Aphrodite to aid him in his race to win her. Aphrodite heard his prayers and gave him three golden apples from the garden of the Hesperides, Hera's sacred grove, where there grew immortality-granting golden apple trees. Atalanta loved this fearless young suitor too, but she begged him not to race her, knowing that he would lose and be killed. He persisted, and with the aid of Aphrodite's apples, he knew that he would prevail. During the race, the suitor distracted Atalanta three times by throwing an apple in her path – causing her to stumble, slow down, pick them up, and ultimately lose the race – winning her hand in marriage. Atalanta was too proud to have let her beloved suitor win intentionally, but neither could she refuse the lure of the golden apples. It was said that many years later the lovers were turned into lions by Aphrodite for not honoring her sufficiently, and I loved the image of the two golden immortal cats, running like the wind by each others' side into eternity.

The eleventh labor of Hercules may have involved the same golden apples, but it was a different kind of story entirely. Well, there was still a connection: both stories involved deception, but with Atalanta it was in the name of love. With Hercules, it was out of desperation. The garden of the Hesperides was also the location where Atlas held the heavens up on his shoulders. The Hesperides nymphs who guarded the grove were none other than Atlas's daughters, so when Hercules went to steal the apples, he knew that Atlas would be an invaluable ally. When he finally found the remote, sacred garden, Hercules tricked Atlas into picking some of his daughters' apples for him by offering to hold up the heavens for him while he did so. Atlas did him the favor, but then decided that he would take the apples for himself and leave Hercules to the arduous task of holding up the heavens: he had done it long enough. Hercules, frantically trapped and longing to rid himself of his crushing burden, tricked Atlas yet again by agreeing to take his place permanently if only Atlas would relieve him for a moment so that he could adjust his cloak because he was cold. Atlas, a strong but not terribly intelligent fellow, fell for the ruse, and ended up (of course) holding up the heavens for the rest of time while Hercules pocketed the apples and fled. Not my namesake's finest hour.

Sophia's poem took this fact into account unsparingly. I had re-read the eleventh poem, "Atalanta," on the plane to New York several times while Hyla had slept. On the surface, it seemed to be the least political of the poems that I had translated so far. And I couldn't help but marvel at Sophia's skill in weaving together the two apple-centered tales to tell her own desperate story. I glanced out into the living room where Hyla was still intently reading. I took my notebook out of my bag and read the poem once again.

Running like the wind,
I hold the heavens on my shoulders,
A woman in a garden
Soon to be alone.
In every life, they have undone me:
Those golden spheres
With their gleaming perfection.
Life after life, time after time
Endlessly tripped up, tricked,
Seduced by them.
What did I think they'd give me?

What did I think you would give me?
Freedom, love, knowledge.
They gave me nothing,
The nothingness that is death.
You gave me life,
And that is why I am running.
My burden is heavy,
They are close on my heels,
They say I know nothing,
But they are wrong.
I know enough not to let go
Until the time is right.
I know that each time you
Toss a glowing orb at my feet,
I must catch it,
As if my life depends on it.
Because it does.
You almost caught me.
If you had,
I would have shared my knowledge,
My life, and each apple with you,
Willingly.
I did not think that they
Could kill you too.
Forgive me:
The heavens are falling.
You must leave the garden,
And I must go on running.
No one can catch me now.

The poems were definitely getting darker, I thought grimly. This one was on the verge of total breakdown. *"They are close on my heels... The heavens are falling...No one can catch me now."* That couldn't be good. Sophia was either in crisis or saw a dire situation approaching, and she was pushing away Hercule's help for the first time. Interestingly, she had fused Atalanta and Atlas, the two figures who had been tricked by men and apples, into a figure of a hunted, burdened exile. And these two figures were meant to represent Sophia herself. I shuddered each time I read this poem, filled with the foreboding that my grandmother had attempted to sublimate through her poetry. The personal element seemed dominant this time; the

political level was almost completely obscured. Where to begin my research at the library? Apple orchards in Vichy France? I snorted derisively as I walked into the living room, towel-drying my wet curls.

Hyla looked up and beamed at me, "This is amazing... what a great story. I love Atalanta, and how her suitor risked his life for her... do you think she let him win on purpose?"

Such a romantic, I thought. *Just like me.* "Yeah, I think maybe she did," I said aloud. "I always loved her too. I tried to run super fast when I was a kid, pretending I was Atalanta. But nobody ever tossed any golden apples my way..."

Hyla laughed, put down the book and kissed me lightly before she went off to the shower. "If you're lucky," she said over her shoulder, "I might just toss you an apple or two someday when you're not expecting it..."

I had never felt luckier.

Twenty minutes later we left the apartment, ready for the city. Instead of taking the subway uptown, I caught a cab so that Hyla could see the sights as we rode all the way uptown to Columbia. I pointed out the Empire State, the Chrysler building, and asked the driver to go through the park so I could show her some of my favorite haunts.

When we finally pulled up in front of the main university gates, I saw the familiar neo-classical buildings, statues, and endless flights of long marble steps throbbing with people and activity and I was filled with heightened excitement. I stuffed a handful of bills in the cab driver's hand and rushed out of the taxi. Hyla had to run to keep up with me as I jogged off in the direction of the library.

A few minutes later, we entered the main reading room, and Hyla's eyes shone. The high arched ceilings, vast windows, glowing wood-paneled walls and marble floors were magnificent as always.

"This place is gorgeous..." she whispered.

"Let's get started," I said with a grin.

I led her over to a bank of computer terminals and said, "Use your imagination. Think of anything from the poem, the Atalanta story, or the eleventh Hercules labor that you might want to search under, and try it, okay? See what comes up, and if any of it looks interesting, write it down" – I tore a piece of paper out of my notebook and handed it to Hyla with a pencil – "and we'll check it out later. I'll be looking for Vichy France connections..."

Hyla, evidently amused by my fervor and efficiency, saluted solemnly and went to work, while I began searching at the terminal

269

beside her. Coming back to the Columbia library had galvanized me and cleared my head. I placed my translation of the "Atalanta" poem between us on the counter and glanced over it quickly, looking for the reference that had been tugging at the back of my mind the whole afternoon: "The heavens are falling." What would happen if Atlas or Hercules had let go of the sky? It would have fallen. I knew it was a stretch, but had there been any unusual astronomical events during the Vichy regime? Maybe Sophia had simply been talking about falling bombs? But no, of course, no bombs had fallen on Paris. Though the price France had paid for that privilege had been far too high.

I gritted my teeth and looked for almanacs from the years 1940-43. I scribbled down their call numbers and continued searching for anything else that seemed like a possible lead: races, Olympics, French athletes, golden trophies, famous gardens, apple orchard regions in France, and even admission rates for women in French universities at the time. All the references to contested "knowledge" in the poem made me wonder if access to education had been an issue for my grandmother. Occasionally a title came up that looked interesting, but mostly I only found dead ends. After an hour, shoulders hunched and fingers cramped, I had scrawled down about thirty titles. I turned my unfocused eyes away from the computer terminal and looked over at Hyla, who was leaning back in her chair perfectly relaxed, gazing at me with bemused patience.

"You know, Herculine, " she said, "This is *really* exciting, but this is my first time in New York, and I'd like to see more of the city today, okay? I'm going to take off, and I'll meet you back at your mom's place tonight."

"Really?" I asked, hoping that my tone didn't betray too much of my delight at the thought of an afternoon to myself in the library. "Will you be all right on your own?"
"I'll be great," she said with a confident smile, kissed me, and strolled out the door.

Watching her go, I wondered if she had even bothered to do any searches while I had been working. I looked over at the piece of paper I had given her and it was blank. Trying not to be too disappointed, I went in search of the library's collection of French Almanacs, and sifted through a stack of them, looking for signs of the "heavens falling" during the Vichy regime. It turns out that there *had* been an unusually high occurrence of meteor showers in the summer of 1942, but whether or not this had influenced Sophia was

impossible to know. I shifted my focus to the Olympics, but another dead end immediately presented itself: the 1940 Olympics had been cancelled due to World War II and had not resumed again until 1948. I wondered about all the athletes who had been unable to compete for those eight years…had any of them been women? More important, had any of them been runners? A search for female athletes in the 1940s yielded a book of biographies of women Olympians called *Lighting the Torch: Women in the Olympics, 1900 through 1980*. I ran up to the stacks to find it.

I was astounded to learn from this book that thousands of women had taken part in the Olympic games since the turn of the century, and I skipped ahead to the notorious 1936 Berlin games, Hitler's propaganda vehicle, boycotted by many athletes and nations alike, to see if there had been any distinctive female runners from France.

There certainly had. Most notably, there had been Evelyn Landys, record-breaking swimmer, runner, cyclist, and gymnast. Parisian party girl, arrested several times for driving at unsafe speeds in sports cars, motorcycles, and speedboats; married twice yet often accompanied by female "companions too, ultimately barred from the Olympic team for her Nazi affiliations and unconventional lifestyle. After providing the Gestapo with valuable information about the French army that was used in the 1940 invasion, she had lived through the German occupation of France with the impunity of a valuable *collaborateur.* Considered a traitor to the state and an enemy of the people, Landys and several of her comrades were killed by the Resistance in 1944.

I closed the book and put it back on the shelf. I wasn't sure what the connection was, but I had the feeling that somehow Sophia had known of Evelyn Landys. Before the war, could they have encountered each other in the lesbian underground? And afterwards, when divided loyalties had riven even the most radical communities, had they found themselves on opposing sides? The photograph of Evelyn Landys in the book – long-limbed, muscular, beautiful and laughing, her face turned up into the sun and her thick blonde hair blowing around her face as she prepared for a race – was everything I had always imagined Atalanta to be, even including the slightly cruel curve of her lips.

Had she and Sophia been lovers? Had there been contact between them during the occupation? My mind raced with possibilities. Would there be any way to find out? During the period

when Sophia had been infiltrating the Vichy government and elite society as a spy for the Resistance, it was possible that she could have used her connection to Evelyn profitably. Perhaps something regarding Julien's specious "arts commission" would yield a clue...I wished for a moment that I was back in the library at Berkeley, where I would have known exactly where to find the book I was looking for. Columbia must have it too, but where? I searched under "arts and Vichy," and several books in the same area of the stacks came up, but in another part of the library. I raced over to the other stacks and quickly found all three, then sat down on the floor between the tall shelves with the books in my lap as I scanned their indexes for the names Landys or Danton.

The first book yielded the same photo I had seen of Julien and the unnamed woman in the video that I had found several months ago. The second book contained a photo of Julien and his cronies, but no Sophia. The third book had no photos, but in the index I found the name "Landys, Evelyn," and immediately turned to the page where the author recounted an eyewitness account of an event that took place at a private art opening in 1941:

All the Parisian luminaries were there: government officials and their wives or mistresses, financiers and industrialists, actresses and actors of the stage and screen, writers, musicians, artists – including those whose art was on display – and even a famous athlete or two, including Evelyn Landys, the scandalous Olympic champion, with her husband on one arm, and her female escort on the other. Arts commissioner Julien Danton and his lovely wife Sophia hosted the evening, which was an elegant affair, creating the illusion, as their parties usually did, that the war could not possibly be converging upon us, but was a distant nuisance at the most.

So they had been thrown together at least once. I was elated by this discovery and dismayed by its elusiveness. There was no way to find out if they had exchanged any information that evening...or was there? I checked the date of the party and headed downstairs to the microfiche room, where I scrolled through the Paris newspapers for that week in June 1941. Nothing, nothing, nothing, and then...possibly something interesting. A building at the edge of the city blown up by resistance forces said to have been a warehouse filled with German munitions. The explosion had been enormous, shaking the foundations of several other buildings nearby and destroying many others. One photograph of the area was displayed

272

on the microfilm: the charred ruins of the warehouse and the remains of two buildings on the next block – both missing their rooftops as well as parts of walls and floors. The sky had certainly fallen here. I wondered how many innocent people had been killed, but the article said there had been no casualties. Perhaps Sophia's comrades had been able to warn them to evacuate – to run – in time.

If there had been contact between Sophia and Evelyn that night, there might also have been a favor exchanged for old times' sake. A fleeting image of my beautiful young grandmother in a passionate pre-war embrace with the "scandalous Olympic champion" streaked across my mind, and I knew that if Sophia had been desperate enough Evelyn would have helped her. Perhaps there were bonds between women that transcended men's wars after all.

Far from having "solved" the poem, but finished with my work for the day, I left the library pensively, lost in thought as I rode the subway back to the Village. Hyla was waiting for me impatiently at mom's loft, eager to tell me about her day and to venture out together into the evening. It was hard for me to muster the enthusiasm to listen thoughtfully to her effusive account of all the sight seeing she had done, but I nodded and smiled at the right moments and could see that Hyla was wrapped up enough in her own excitement not to notice, or at least not to mind. As we dressed for dinner, I told her about my discovery of Evelyn Landys.

"So is she Atalanta?" she asked, as we walked downstairs and out onto the street.

"I don't think it's as literal as that," I mused, "and the heroines in the poems usually stand in for my grandmother in some way. But I think that Sophia may have been inspired to write about Atalanta partially due to her connection with Evelyn."

"I wish there was some way to know what really happened," Hyla said, and I could tell that even though she may not have been as caught up in the research process as I was, she was still intrigued by the mystery of the poems that had been driving me for the last ten months.

"Me too," I said, taking her hand. "But it just keeps getting harder."

We met with mom and Ramon for a relatively early dinner that night, but the meal turned out to be fraught with tension, because my mom was insisting that she had to attend my meeting with Johanna. By the end of the evening, we were both furious.

"Absolutely *not*," I seethed.

273

"You don't have a choice," she stated firmly. "I'm coming."

"No, you're not!" I slammed my fist against the table. "It just doesn't concern you."

"It most certainly does," she insisted. "I refuse to let that woman take anything away from you. You've worked too hard on those poems for her to simply force them out of your hands!"

"Mom, look," I said. "I'm going to do my best not to let that happen. Don't you realize that she probably hates you even more than you hate her and that being there will only make her want to hurt me?"

Mom was momentarily chastened by this, but she recovered quickly, and said, "I won't let her hurt you. And if she and I have a score to settle, this seems like the perfect time to get everything out in the open. I just want her to treat you with respect for once, sweetheart. If it hadn't been for her, your relationship with your father could have been so much closer."

Knowing I was treading on thin ice, I said quietly, "It was his choice too, mom. We can't blame *her* for the way he chose to live his life."

I watched mom closely as I spoke, but my words did not have the expected effect. In the past, whenever I attempted to puncture the idealized bubble my mom kept around her vision of my dad, she usually responded with white-hot fury. This time, her face just looked sad and weary, and she passed a hand over her brow. Ramon looked at her in concern as she murmured, "I know, you're right…" and closed her eyes, leaning her head on Ramon's shoulder, ending the conversation.

I was barely breathing. I was *right?* Right about something concerning my dad? I looked at Ramon and Hyla in disbelief. Either my mother was more stressed out about this upcoming confrontation with Johanna than she admitted, or her heart attack in the winter had altered her perspective on life in ways that I hadn't realized. My mom always seemed to want to turn my dad into some kind of a god, but I knew that he was a fallible mortal like everyone else. His death had proven that definitively. I felt hot tears well up in my eyes and I brushed them away roughly. Hyla's arm protectively encircled my shoulders.

"Okay mom," I said gently. "You can come with me, but please let me handle it. I'm just worried that you might add a dimension of revenge to Johanna's agenda that could ruin my chances of getting out of there without a court case."

Mom raised her head and nodded solemnly.

Three days later, we were almost late to meet Johanna because mom changed her outfit six times before we left. She finally emerged from her room wearing a magenta silk wrap-around dress with a flared skirt. It clashed stunningly with her auburn hair, and made her look like she was on the verge of bursting into flames. This was probably exactly the effect that she wanted to achieve, I thought sourly.

Hyla headed off to a dance class with Ramon, promising to meet up with us later in the afternoon. I watched them walk off down the street together laughing, wishing that I were going with them instead. I would have much preferred to observe Hyla's body going through the motions of a dance class than watch all my work of the past ten months evaporate in Johanna's hands. Just in case, I had brought with me not only the originals of Sophia's poems, but also copies of the originals, as well as copies of all my translations. I would try to bargain with Johanna somehow. I hadn't figured out the best angle yet, but I did have a plan, providing mom didn't derail my efforts.

Our cab ride uptown to Columbia, where we were meeting Johanna in the French department conference room, seemed interminable. I stared out the window and sulked, feeling like a thirteen year-old on my way to the dentist, while mom idly hummed and played with her hair. By the time we arrived, the button-down shirt I had reluctantly donned for the occasion was sticking to my back with anxious sweat, and mom and I had barely exchanged a word. Irene, the trusty French department secretary, glowered then ushered us into a plushly carpeted, oak-paneled meeting room, and we sat down silently at the long, highly polished table. A few minutes later, through a different door, Johanna entered the room. Tall and elegant, resplendent in a grey silk dress, jacket, and pearls, her silver hair softly framed her handsome, angular face upon which there was an enigmatic mixture of rage, condescension, and curiosity.

I stood up and looked over at mom, who had a faint smile playing on her lips, and who motioned to me to relax and sit down. But I continued to stand. I walked over to Johanna and held out my hand.

"I'm sorry that it's come to this, Johanna," I said.

Johanna said nothing, ignored my hand, and sat down at the far end of the table.

I remained standing tensely, my hands clenched by my sides.

"Look," I said to Johanna, "I don't know how these things usually go, but I would just like to talk to you directly and resolve this peaceably. Are you willing to meet me halfway?"

Johanna replied coolly, "You are correct. You do not know how such matters are handled. So sit down and learn."

I looked at my mother, who was watching the whole exchange with fascination in her eyes, and looked back at Johanna, who seemed to be mocking me with her now impassive expression, and slowly took my seat.

Mom said lazily, "Hello Dr. Danton. I don't believe we've met. I'm Herculine's mother, Clea Coleman."

As mom spoke, Johanna turned towards her with a stare of irritation, and I realized that, of course, she had never met my mom before. I saw Johanna's mouth twitch slightly as she scanned mom's dramatic appearance and then give way to a wry smirk.

"How convenient that you are here," said Johanna. Then she turned to me, "Your mother's intrusion on our meeting couldn't have come at a more convenient time. If I have to take legal action, now I know that your mother was complicit in your deception of me and I will press charges against both of you."

Mom leaned forward, eyes blazing, and said, "*You're* the intruder, Johanna; you're intruding on my daughter's life, and neither of us have deceived you in any way. State your business and then have the dignity to drop this matter before *we* press charges against *you!*"

"You can't press charges against me," said Johanna, regally settling herself into her deep leather chair. "The poems belong to my husband's estate, and I am the executor."

Through tightly clenched teeth, I said, "The poems belong to *me*."

Johanna retorted, "You are not only ignorant of property law, you also underestimate your own ignorance. I knew of the poems' existence before you did; I simply did not know where they were. You claim to have found them in one of your father's books, but how do I know you are telling the truth? Somehow you managed to extract them – probably with your mother's assistance, which would make her an accomplice to your crime – from my husband's personal papers, which were expressly left in my care, and I demand that you return them to me."

Mom's voice rang out in the room, "Your *husband*? He was her *father*! Don't you *dare* imply that my I or my daughter would ever steal anything from you!"

She was sitting on the edge of her seat, pale and shaking with rage. I moved over to her side and held her in her arms, whispering,

"Mom, mom, your heart…hey, take it easy, please…this doesn't matter at all, okay? Please?"

Johanna watched them, her face an impassive mask. She said sharply, "I think you'll find that this matters quite a bit, Herculine. Now, return my property to me. I'm tired of this drama and it is time for your little game to end."

"It's not a game, Johanna," I said quietly. "If the poems belong to anyone, it's Hercule. I found them tucked into the copy of Dad's book that was dedicated to me that he had in his library. You know, the one on Hercules. I found them after you had already moved out of the house. If there were any 'personal papers' there, I have no idea where they could have been. The place was empty except for the book shelves, and you know that he left all his books to me."

Johanna looked thoughtful, appraising my somber face as she spoke, only wincing slightly when she heard me call Theo "Dad." But she apparently knew the truth when she heard it, and said shrewdly, "How could they possibly belong to Hercule?"

"You've never seen them then? There's a dedication page…" I said, fishing through my bag for the copy of the originals. "My grandmother's poems are dedicated to Hercule." I handed the photocopy to Johanna across the table. "He must have given them to Dad or something. I don't know. I also don't know why Dad didn't just give them to me…I guess he knew I'd eventually look at his copy of the Hercules book, but he was taking a real chance."

"He probably did mean to give them to you, sweetheart," mom said, extricating herself from my protective embrace and settling herself again proudly in her seat. "He had to go to the hospital so suddenly at the end, I'm sure there were hundreds of things that he wasn't able to accomplish before he died."

Johanna looked pale while mom was speaking. Between gritted teeth, she said, "Stop it. Stop talking about him like he was yours. He was *mine*. I was the one they called when he died. Not you. I was the one who handled all the arrangements, who had to watch them take his body away…who…" and here she broke,

277

turning her face to the side and resting it in one of her hands, as she clutched the arm of her chair with her other hand for support.

I gazed at my enemy with surprise and concern. I had never thought about the agony Johanna must have gone through after my dad's death. For the first time the image of his body being wheeled out of an anonymous hospital room and down to a holding chamber, soon to be driven to a crematorium where his wasted beauty was consigned to flames became clear to me. The reality of Johanna's grief had never presented itself to my imagination this vividly or viscerally. Did she still have the urn with his ashes? I felt a pang as I realized that I didn't even know where my father had wanted his ashes to be scattered. Had Johanna already done it?

"Johanna," I said softly.

The older woman looked up wearily, her large grey eyes tinged with red from crying.

I continued, "There's something I have to tell you. When I was little, before my dad died, he asked me a favor. He asked me to try and become friends with you someday. He said that we were going to need each other. I didn't understand him then, but I think I do now. Maybe we can help each other."

Johanna looked at me in surprise and murmured, "He asked the same favor of me. And I had no intention of honoring his request." She raised herself from the deep chair and began to smooth the folds of her suit in preparation for leaving. "I don't even know why I care so much about those poems. They have nothing to do with me. They were..." her voice faltered with emotion, "...somehow just a part of him that I couldn't bear not to have. But perhaps they really are yours. I have to go now, I don't feel well. Forgive me..." She stood up and moved hurriedly away from the table.

As Johanna headed towards the door, I ran after her and caught her before she could leave. I clasped both of her arms and said, "Don't go! Stay. Let's figure this out. Please. I *do* need you. And the poems need you too."

Johanna resisted as I tried to lead her back to the table.

"Listen," I said urgently, "I've thought about this, and I've made a decision. I want you to be the one to publish the poems. I think the world needs to see them and to know Sophia's story. But I've done so much work on them already and I only have two more to figure out. Please let me finish my work and then I will give you

everything. It's turned into kind of a personal quest for me. Can you understand that?"

Mom looked shocked and started to speak, but I held up my hand and motioned her to be silent.

Johanna pulled away from me, but she murmured, "Perhaps."

"Good," I said softly. "Then you will consider my offer?"

"I will consider it," she said, taking a deep breath, and walking back to her chair. "There is still much to discuss. I decided to take action through my lawyers because I hadn't heard from you after my last communication in April. Why did you renege on our agreement, and where are the poems you owe me?"

I defended myself, " Johanna, I assure you that I sent you the first and eighth poem and fully honored our agreement. My letter must have been lost in the mail. When I hadn't heard from you for so long I just assumed you were traveling. Please believe me. This is far too important to me to treat it lightly."

Johanna looked at me evenly and said, "I would like to believe you. Letters have been lost in the mail before. But I had no way of knowing. As a gesture of trust, please give me the rest of the poems now. The originals."

I sifted through the papers in my bag and selected the photocopies I had made of the originals for this very purpose. "I'm sorry Johanna," I said, handing them to her. "But the originals stay with me. I hope these will suffice."

For a moment I wasn't sure if she would accept them or not, but as soon as she saw the first page, she was utterly absorbed. I let her read for a few minutes, then she looked up and said, "Yes, this will do."

Mom and I exchanged a glance. The tone of the meeting had just shifted.

Turning to Johanna, I said, "Now there is something that I need to discuss with you. I must meet Hercule before he dies."

Johanna looked away and nodded thoughtfully, "How soon can you come to Paris?"

"Is it urgent?" I asked. "Is he in bad health? Should I go immediately?" I paused, took a deep breath, and continued, "I have to tell you, Johanna, I received a letter from Hercule several months ago and sent him two letters in response, but I never heard back from him. I even left a message at his residence, but he didn't return my call."

279

Mom looked startled by this information and looked back and forth from me to Johanna expectantly.

Johanna frowned, "I owe you an apology, Herculine. I know that you wrote Hercule, but I didn't know until now that he had initiated contact between you. I pick up his mail every day from the concierge, and she gave me your phone message as well. He never saw the letters you wrote him and doesn't know that you called." She looked down at her hands, which were gripped together so tightly that her knuckles were white. "I just couldn't bear to lose him too."

I sat still and silent, trembling with the effort to control my rage. I closed my eyes and tried to breathe deeply. After a few moments, I opened my eyes and said to Johanna with controlled fury, "You mean you couldn't bear to lose your control over me…"

Raising her face to meet my glare, Johanna quickly pulled herself together and squared her shoulders, saying, "I refuse to respond to that accusation."

Mom was fuming, "How dare you interfere with my daughter's life! She has every right to know Hercule – even more than you do!"

I intervened again between my mother and Johanna before Johanna could respond. I kept her anger in check as I said, "Johanna, what you did was wrong. And you probably knew it. But I will forgive you if you promise to take me to Hercule. I'll come to Paris as soon as I can."

Johanna nodded, looked warily at me, and said, "Yes, please do. We are fortunate that Hercule is well. He is frail, but healthy, and I am sure that a visit from you would be, ah, rather invigorating for him. Herculine, if you don't mind – " here she looked questioningly at my mom, "I'd like to talk with you about what you've discovered about the poems so far."

Taking her cue, mom kissed me on the cheek, saying, "Good work, darling. I'm going to go back to the apartment to rest. Come back and meet up with us soon…"

"Thanks mom," I said, but she had already turned to Johanna and was speaking to her now.

"Make sure that you do right by my daughter, Johanna. Otherwise you'll have *both* of us to deal with," and she walked out of the room in a flourish of fuschia.

After the door closed behind her, Johanna said, "Herculine, your father asked that I make an effort with you, and I am willing to fulfill that request. But I made no such promise regarding your

280

mother." She grimaced, but recovered and said, "Now, tell me what you have discovered about the poems."

I was nervous, but excited, and Johanna listened intently as I related the developments of my research and the web of stories that encompassed each poem. By the time I had ended my tale, I saw a look of appreciative admiration on Johanna's face and felt my heart surge with pride.

She said, "This is more important than I realized. And your work has been exemplary. In my own investigations I see now that I have missed several levels of significance. You have earned your publication credit, Herculine. But I am glad to report that I have my own missing pieces to contribute to the effort."

Now it was my turn to listen as Johanna explained more in detail about the wealth and political connections that wove through the subterranean Sapphic world of Paris in the 1930s, and the complex ties this community had with the resistance as well as the art world at the time.

"So you see," Johanna concluded, "Sophia was poised at a powerful quadrivium, a four-way vortex, if you will, with connections among the politicians, the resistance fighters, the artists, and the social elite of Paris. And each sector wanted to use her for its own interests. I am not surprised that her poems increasingly show the tensions she must have experienced as the occupation became more conflicted."

I gathered my courage and asked her, "So, when you – or we – publish the poems, would you consider writing the contextual essays accompanying each poem and then I can provide interpretive explanations?"

Johanna smiled for the first time, her expression reserved but still genuine. "I would consider that…yes."

We both knew our work was done for the day, so we shook hands solemnly and were about to say goodbye when I remembered, "One more question," I said. "If you wouldn't mind telling me…Where did you scatter my dad's ashes?"

Johanna looked away and said, "I haven't yet. They are in Paris with me still. He wanted them scattered in the Seine, but somehow I haven't been able to do it."

I said softly, "Maybe we can do it together when I am there too…"

Johanna looked sad and said nothing. I touched her shoulder, then watched as she turned away and left the room. I felt something

melting inside me: an old wound that I had carried around my whole life. I felt closer to my dad in this moment than I had in a long time. One of the barriers that had always stood between us was finally coming down. Making peace with Johanna was filling me unexpectedly with the full force of his love and pride. The Ice Queen had been deposed, and summer was returning to the land of the sun, which I now knew was in my own heart.

Later that night at our celebratory dinner, mom and I laughed and kissed each other on both cheeks; we were a formidable team, and after today, we knew that we could survive just about anything together. Hyla and Ramon listened raptly as we took turns describing the afternoon's events, but I tactfully left out most of my private conversation with Johanna. Mom was glowing with triumph, and I couldn't bear to temper her radiance by revealing my newfound alliance with my former rival.

I didn't see much of my mom for the next few days while she took over the final rehearsals for her dance company's upcoming performance. When the opening night finally came, I was fidgeting and nervous. I knew mom was planning some special "surprise" for me, which was nerve-wracking enough, but my work on the "Atalanta" poem had not yielded any fruitful results, so I was feeling irritable as I sat with Hyla in the darkened performance space, waiting for the show to start. Hyla, however, was excited and unfazed by my moodiness.

"You'll solve the poem soon; I just know you will," she said with a mysterious smile.

But I just slumped in my seat and glowered.

I sat that way through the first three dances – a duet featuring Lyra and her lover Jason, and then two full ensemble pieces – including a *pas de quatre* performed by four men dressed in bold primary colors, who lifted and dipped each other joyously to the accompaniment of a be-bop medley, bending the conventional rules of gender and power on stage with evident glee. The final piece of the evening was, of course, my mom's "surprise."

I watched with bated breath as long panels of double-sided mirrors suspended from heavy silver chains were lowered down slowly all around the stage, hanging and swaying gently, like a bizarre forest in a breeze. Then mom entered alone, and there was a loud smattering of applause from her devoted fans in the audience, and she stood still, looking off into the wings, until it subsided. As she

stood and waited, the music began, and as the first few haunting measures wove their way through the air, she began to move.

She was wearing a long silver mesh dress that clung to her torso and fell in evocative folds around her elegant legs, and she was dancing with and between the mirrored panels in a way that refracted her reflection hundreds of times around the stage. In fact, I realized that mom was actually dancing with her own reflection, flirting with it, beckoning to it, teasing it, even flouncing away from it in mock resistance to its infinite allure. She was mesmerizing. Hyla sat with her mouth slightly open in awe. I was barely breathing, and the audience was completely caught in mom's spell.

Then the first phase of the piece – the courtship – ended and shifted into a new phase – what I could only describe as marriage – when mom slipped smoothly behind one slender piece of mirror, unhooked it from its suspending chain and used another to ingeniously attach it behind her, so the chain was wound around her torso, shoulders, and waist, and the mirror seemed fused to her spine. Her movements were intentionally labored now, less graceful and smooth, but still she danced – swirling through the forest of mirrors, searching for something with increased anxiety behind every dangling reflection. And then I realized what mom was seeking: she wanted to see the reflection of the empty mirror attached to her…she wanted to see the face of her partner – who, because it was fused to her too closely – she would never be able to see, and – the narcissist's nightmare – it would never be able to reflect herself back to her, as she so evidently craved.

This dance was the most daring self-revelation I had ever seen her enact on stage, and I had been watching my mother evolve through performance my whole life. She was simultaneously Narcissus and Clea, everywoman and herself, a cautionary tale and a mythic truth embodied. The final phase of the dance came when mom hurtled through the mirrored forest, her mane of auburn curls now flying wildly around her face as she came to a stop at center stage, her chest heaving with exertion, her eyes beseeching the audience with desperation, the perspiration on her skin shining as brightly as her silver gown. Then she slowly unwound the chain and carefully lowered the mirror onto the floor. As she did so, the other mirrors hanging from chains slowly lowered also, and slid down onto the floor until they too were lying flat. Mom was surrounded by a river of light. She seemed bewildered at first, running to each corner of the stage looking for the mirrors in which to see herself, but

finding none, she began a tentative, delicate dance between the mirrors on the floor that soon grew into a full-bodied expression of freedom, liberation from illusion, and self-love, as she celebrated the absence of the tyranny of the mirror in her life as a woman, as a dancer, and as an individual. I felt a tightness in my chest, then hot tears sliding down my cheeks, and soon I was up on my feet beside Hyla, cheering along with the rest of the audience as the performance ended and mom stood alone center stage receiving bouquets, graciously accepting the tributes of her fans.

The rest of the company soon joined her for their curtain calls, and after several rounds of bows, the lights in the house came back up and everyone moved out to the lobby for the reception. I found that I was incapable of speaking as familiar faces hugged me and congratulated me on my mom's spectacular return to the stage. I merely nodded and smiled and tried to inconspicuously wipe the traces of tears from my cheeks. Somehow in the melée I became separated from Hyla, but soon spotted her across the room with a tall European-looking man with artsy glasses who was gesticulating emphatically. Hyla seemed absorbed and was nodding earnestly at him, so I took the opportunity to break away from the crowd to find my mom.

She was in her dressing room, taking off her stage make-up while Ramon rubbed her shoulders with soothing ointment. She was purring softly, and I wasn't sure if she should interrupt. But she turned and greeted me with a wide smile and held out her arms to me. Ramon gave mom then me a kiss on the cheek and left the room. I knelt by her chair and buried my face in her shoulder, still unable to speak.

Mom stroked my curls lovingly and said, "I thought you'd like it, darling. It was inspired by you and your father, you know. All those myths you two were always talking about. I guess something sunk in along the way. But, like your grandmother, I like the idea of reinventing them to tell a story that means something to me now. I was glad to see that it evidently means something to other women too."

I raised my head and met her gaze, "It meant something to everybody there," I said. "But it meant the most to me. Thank you, mom. It was beautiful. You were beautiful."

We left the dressing room and I steered her through the admiring crowd for about half an hour, when I realized that Hyla was

284

still over at the edge of the room talking to Euro-guy. I asked my mom, "Who's that man talking to Hyla? Do you know him?"
She looked in their direction and said, "Oh good, I'm glad they found each other. That's my friend Yuri who runs the film festival every summer. Remember? You asked me to give him Hyla's tape back in January. He told me that he was really impressed by it, and it was a runner-up in the competition. I told him that she'd be here tonight. He must have recognized her..."

I remembered with a shiver Hyla's haunting dance at the opening and ending of her film. If he had seen that, he had seen too much.

I told mom, "I'm going to see what this guy and Hyla are carrying on about, okay? Can Ramon prop you up for a while?"

She shooed me away and was immediately engulfed by an entourage of adoring dancers. As I approached Hyla and the man from the festival, I could see that now Hyla was nodding enthusiastically at whatever he was still so emphatically suggesting to her.

She turned a shining face towards me, "Herculine! You won't believe this! This is Yuri, and your mom gave my tape to him and he loved it! He wants me to assist him on a project that he just got a grant for here in the city for a few months...isn't that amazing?"

I looked in astonishment at Hyla, then at the man beside her – who seemed like a decent guy, if perhaps a little too aware of his own good looks – and then back at Hyla. I was having difficulty speaking again. Hyla seemed to sense this, and took my arm.

"I know," she said. "It's a big change. It took me by surprise too, but we've been talking for a while, and I'm beginning to think that this is something I'd really like to do. There's even a place for me to live with some of the other interns. Maybe you could stop out for a semester and we could live here in the city and you could do research at Columbia or something while I work on the project?"

My brain was swirling. This really was moving much too fast. I mustered my composure and said quietly,

"Let's talk about it later, okay? It does sound amazing," I nodded at Yuri, "but I'm kind of overwhelmed right now... I think I need some air. Do you want to go for a walk?"

Hyla nodded and said she'd meet me outside in a few minutes. As I walked away, I saw Hyla shake hands with Yuri, and then take his card. When I stepped outside, I wasn't sure that there

285

was actually sidewalk beneath my feet. Everything suddenly felt extremely unstable.

But when Hyla joined me, she was trying to be somber and attuned to my distress despite her evident elation.

She said, "I'm sorry, babe. That really came out of the blue. I need to think more, before we even talk about it. A walk is a great idea. And hey – I'm really hungry too!"

We headed over to a brightly lit Korean market on the corner a few blocks away and Hyla heaped her take-out box with savory vegetable stir fry, but I did not feel hungry. I could barely feel anything at all. Hyla staying in New York? It was too much to even comprehend after all we had just been through. I had committed myself to her, and I thought she had committed herself to me. But it looked like even that had been an illusion. Was I the one in a hall of mirrors now, projecting my own desires onto Hyla?

I waited outside the market while Hyla paid for her meal, and as we walked away, I looked on, horrified, as she casually reached into a display of golden delicious apples, gleaming under the lights, and pocketed one of them.

I hissed at her, "Hey, put that back! Or go pay for it! This is my neighborhood, remember?"

But Hyla just looked at me mischievously as we rounded the corner and bit into the apple, crunching it salaciously and licking her lips. Then she offered the apple to me, reciting quietly as she did so, "*In every life, they have undone me: those golden spheres, with their gleaming perfection...*"

I stood still as the significance of Hyla's words dawned on me. Then I recited the rest of the line from my grandmother's poem: "*Life after life, time after time, endlessly tripped up, tricked, seduced by them. What did I think they'd give me?*" There was another ancient story involving a woman and an apple, and it had never entered my mind. After a moment, I asked Hyla,

"How long have you known?"

"That the third figure in the poem was Eve? Since that day in the library, I think. But I dismissed it, since you never seemed to consider the possibility of a Christian dimension."

"Well," I said, "I think it was more of an Old Testament, *Judeo*-Christian element, but still – you're right, I never even considered it. And it helps to explain so much..." I reeled off a few more lines from the poem, "*A woman in a garden soon to be alone... You*

286

must leave the garden, and I must go on running... Running? So Evelyn Landys was really Eve...*and* Atalanta..."

It was all too much. I sat down on the steps of a nearby brownstone and put my head in my hands, raking my fingers through my hair. Hyla sat down beside me and put a comforting arm around me, saying,

"See babe? I knew you'd solve it..."

I shook my head, "No, you're the one who solved it; it was right in front of me and I didn't even see it. Evelyn must have been much more important to Sophia than I realized, and her sense of betrayal when Evelyn sided with the Nazis must have been devastating. A true fall from innocence, leaving her – Sophia – alone in the garden, and running for her own life."

We sat quietly for a while on the steps. I let the warm summer evening air soothe my over excited mind, but I could tell that Hyla and I were off in different places – she was probably thinking about the film project and the life in New York that she now longed for, while I was transported back to pre-war France and a summer night there long ago...seeing young Sophia and Evelyn walking arm-in-arm along the Seine, as European women tend to do, only the current between them was electric, and their hearts were pounding beneath their thin silk dresses, barely able to contain their anticipation for the evening that awaited them...

My reverie was broken by Hyla pulling away her arm, and turning towards me with a pensive expression on her face, saying, "I hope you won't mind if I don't go to Paris with you, Herculine. If it's okay, I think I'd like to stay here and sort things out while you're gone. I'll see if this project is really something I want to do and then we can talk about it all when you get back. You won't be gone long, right? How do you feel about this?"

Looking at my lover in dull dismay, I said nothing, but thought to myself: *I feel like a woman in a garden, soon to be alone.*

Theo
New York, 1978

Theo awoke, feverish and sweating in the hospital bed, from a dream about his mother. They had been playing together in shallow waves at the edge of the ocean, laughing and splashing, and he could still feel the warm wet sand running between his fingers and toes. He thought he could taste the salty ocean water on his face, but realized that what he was tasting were his own tears.

He closed his eyes and tried to go back into the dream. Perhaps he could trick the morphine into letting him slide in right where he had left off, but the dream was gone. He twisted in his bed with frustration, straining against the oxygen tube in his nose. He would have liked to rip the tubes out of his arms and rush out into the street, filling his lungs with fresh morning air, so that he could go to the ocean and feel its life force surrounding and infusing him once more.

He had been so happy in the dream. All he wanted was to see his mother again, to hear her voice, her laughter, to feel the warm sun on his body, to see her loving eyes. All of his anger towards her seemed to have dissolved in the salt water around them, in the tears now trickling down his cheeks. He had been angry for too long. Underneath all the adult rationality and knowledge of historical contingency, a small child had been raging inside him all his life. Raging at her for abandoning him – first by sending him off to America without her, and then for killing herself instead of coming to find him. How could she have done it? Hadn't she loved him enough to persevere? He reached back into the dream world of his earliest childhood sense memories and he could faintly remember feeling loved by his mother: her warm embrace enfolding him in soft blankets at night, and just now, in his dream, the memory of her sun-kissed laughter and the love in her eyes.

Of course she had loved him. Everything she had done must have been for love. Even sending him away. He knew that, wanted to believe it somehow, and the effort to accept it as truth calmed him.

His mother's face was etched into his mind, but he would have loved to see the photograph he had of her in his desk, to hold that old leather frame once again and feel the weight of it, of her, in

288

his hands. He would have to remember to ask Johanna to find it and bring it to him. Would she be able to do him this favor? Or, once she saw the photograph, would she be too shocked by the resemblance between Sophia and Herculine to bring it? It was true: every time he saw Herculine, it was as if he was looking at a cropped-haired version of Sophia as a child. He wished his mother could have known her – so fiery and proud, so bright and confident. She was exactly what Sophia would have wanted in a granddaughter.

He started in panic: he must tell Herculine about the poems…or had he done so already? He couldn't remember. Ever since he'd been admitted to the hospital the previous day, the combination of morphine, antibiotics, and blood thinners had addled his usually lucid mind. He had played the scene out in his head so many times, telling Herculine about Sophia and the poems…and Hercule. Hercule…had he ever sent the letter? Yes, thought Theo, as he dozed off in the dark room, he had. And he smiled. His last conscious thoughts were the memories of the warmth of the sun on his skin, of Herculine as a baby, and the first time he held her against his bare chest as she slept in his arms.

"As with every other epic hero in Greek mythology, as well as in virtually every other heroic tradition around the globe, Hercules must conclude his twelve labors, his ultimate quest for validation from the gods, by successfully journeying through the land of the dead. But unlike other heroes, such as Aeneas, who must make peace with his dead father Anchises – or Jesus – who must "harrow" hell so that Christian souls can pass through on their journey through purgatory and up to heaven – Hercules must simply capture a dangerous dog. Where is the archetypal symbolism, or heroic virtue here? Part of the answer lies in the journey itself: Hercules must first be initiated into the Eleusinian mysteries of the cult of Demeter and Persephone in order to enter and leave the underworld while still alive. This initiation involved absolving him of his "blood guilt" from his many murders, a ritual of purification that both healed him and opened up to him for the first time the vision of ultimate spiritual rebirth: the intellectual capacity for immortality. Our Hercules, hero of the body, conqueror of the physical plane, was ready to embark on the final, metaphysical, stage of his epic journey towards ontological wholeness and, paradoxically, philosophical transcendence."

Theodore Danton, *Redefining Heroism: Reclaiming Hercules;* Columbia University Press; 1968

The Twelfth Poem: Eurydice
Paris, August 1990

Paris in August was deserted. Hot, dusty, and silent, with only an occasional pair of overheated tourists on the streets, while most of the Parisians were on their *vacances* – cooling off in the turquoise waters of Corsica, Cannes, or Biarritz. The city itself felt dormant; the shopkeepers grumbled and opened late; even the waiters were slightly more supercilious than usual. Barely a breeze stirred the leaves in the *Bois du Bologne*, and many of the famous ornamental fountains adorning the city were shut off to conserve water. The mood of the city matched mine perfectly. Like Paris, I was *vide*, emptied out, on a very strange sort of summer vacation – knowing that I had to be here, but wishing I was anywhere else, and not alone.

To be fair, I wasn't really alone; I just wasn't with Hyla, and her absence after several weeks of uninterrupted intimacy left me feeling even emptier than the city of Paris. I had been relieved when Johanna had graciously sent a driver to pick me up at the airport and had offered for me to stay in her guest room. Even so, our acquaintance was still new, and I sensed that adjusting to such a dramatic change would take time. After spending the night in Johanna's elegant, immaculate apartment, and most of the morning out wandering the streets of Paris alone, I could feel that Johanna and I would slowly but carefully continue building on the fragile new trust between us. However, in the intervening week since our breakthrough in New York, it seemed that Johanna had receded from me a little. Once or twice I had caught her staring at me thoughtfully, and her eyes had even lit up in the morning when I walked into the kitchen, but she had looked away hurriedly. I couldn't help but wonder if it wasn't a bit like having a glimpse of my dad in her home again. Perhaps she would come to enjoy it.

In the meantime, I was here in Paris to bring my work of the last eleven months to a conclusion. I was impatient to meet Hercule later that afternoon, and hoped that Johanna would let me help her scatter my dad's ashes, but most of all, I felt ready to come to terms with Sophia's ghost – on every street corner, it seemed, as I grappled

291

with the multiple meanings contained in the final poem in the collection, "Eurydice." I had spent the whole morning walking around the Marais, following a list that Johanna had given me of locations which had served as underground resistance cells, and I had the unnerving feeling of being covertly followed down the silent streets, or that at any moment the specters of long dead Vichy agents would lurch out at me from behind a doorway.

On the plane from New York I had mostly nursed my wounded heart, numbed from repeated rationalizations and justifications for Hyla's decision to stay behind. I had helped her get settled in her new room in the film assistants' apartment, and was miserable when we said goodbye. After just having found her, it felt like losing her all over again, despite Hyla's repeated reassurances that this was not the case. I felt like Orpheus in the "Eurydice" myth, deserted and bereft, and spent most of the flight re-reading the last poem in my notebook and trying to figure out what my grandmother was trying to communicate, or to conceal. Combining the stories of Hercules' twelfth labor – the abduction of Cerberus, the three-headed dog who guarded the gates of Hades, land of the dead – with the tale of Orpheus' journey to the underworld to rescue his dead bride Eurydice, Sophia had woven a somber web of allusions into the "Eurydice" poem that seemed to be entirely personal. Aside from the stale truism that "war is hell," and Paris during the occupation must have seemed like a kind of hell to her when she was also entrenched in the "underworld" of the resistance, I couldn't find a single trace of a political dimension to the poem.

Even here in Paris, on an empty park bench in a small shady courtyard, the poem seemed more mysterious than ever:

> *You came to find me*
> *To bring me back to the light,*
> *Back to the life we had together.*
> *But I didn't want to go.*
> *You didn't expect that, did you?*
> *I followed you with dragging steps*
> *Hoping you would look back*
> *As I lingered,*
> *So that you would fail the test,*
> *And lose me forever.*
> *I cannot leave; I know that I must not.*
> *This is my destiny,*

292

But I have something that you want.
And I will let you have it.
But you can't have me too.
In order to take him,
You must prove yourself worthy.
Purify yourself for past sins,
Initiate yourself into the mysteries
Of my soul.
Only then will I teach you
How to enter and leave this place,
My prison, my hell,
Unscathed, newly burdened
With the three-fold emblem of my love.
One is for loving me too much:
You must learn to love another.
Two is for trying to bring me back to life:
You must learn to live on memories.
Three is for looking back:
You must learn to let go.
He will help you.
Take him.
He will not struggle, as I have,
Or lag behind you, as I do now.
In his love for you,
Mine will never die.

What surprised me most was that beside Eurydice, there was another heroine also enveloped in this poem: Persephone, now Queen of the Underworld and owner of Cerberus, who had helped Hercules with the completion of his final labor and who had negotiated with Orpheus for Eurydice's release. Persephone's voice distinctly emerged in the second half of the poem, offering to deliver up Cerberus to Hercules, and blended smoothly with the voice of Eurydice, who for some reason was resisting rescue from her supposedly beloved Orpheus. My question was, why did Eurydice want to stay in hell? What kind of destiny did she feel compelled to fulfill there? I assumed that the "you" in this poem was, as usual, directed to Hercule and his heroic namesake Hercules, but he was also blended with Orpheus here – the idealistic lover and musician who thought his devotion could transcend the boundaries of life and death, and which almost did. If he hadn't looked behind him to

293

make sure that Eurydice was following him as he retraced his steps out of hell, thus breaking the bargain he had made with Persephone for freeing Eurydice, he would not have lost her. As the poem suggested, neither Orpheus nor Hercules knew know how to *"laisser,"* to let go. I thought wryly: I could relate.

But more than the presence of Persephone and the question of why Eurydice didn't want to be rescued, the part of the poem that baffled me the most was the transformation of the terrifying three-headed dog Cerberus into a powerful three-fold emblem of Eurydice/Persephone/Sophia's love. In this poem, each head of the beast, instead of a threatening nightmare of slavering bloody jaws, was a profound symbol of life-renewing devotion. This final labor and journey to the underworld was now conceived as a rebirth for Hercule(s), or at least that was how my grandmother wanted it to be.

I walked back slowly to Johanna's apartment in the *Place des Vosges* in the mid-afternoon heat, lost in thought, and the streets and buildings of Paris soothed me with their deeply saturated beauty and history. Even in the sun-drenched afternoon of a peacetime summer over fifty years after my grandmother's death, everything seemed vaguely familiar to me; after all, for the last twelve months my head had been filled with visions of Sophia's life during wartime on these streets. When I was little, I knew that my dad had often gone to Paris, "to visit friends," he had said, and it pleased me now to imagine him here, walking these very streets, perhaps thinking of me back home in New York. Once I had asked him to take me with him to see the Eiffel Tower, but he had kindly but firmly refused. "Someday when you're older," he said. And I had pouted impatiently.

Now I realized that he had probably made those trips to visit Hercule; but why couldn't he have told me this? Why all the secrecy? Why hadn't he wanted me to meet the man who had raised him? Johanna was close with Hercule; even my mom had met him once. Why was I the only one who had been left out?

Perhaps at dinner that night I would ask Johanna. We were planning to see Hercule later this afternoon, and I felt strangely disassociated from this impending reality. It was almost too much, too impossible that this man of myth whose life I had been following in my grandmother's poems for a year would be sitting in front of me, flesh and blood and probably much smaller than I imagined him, in only a matter of hours.

As I entered Johanna's apartment, I sensed that something was not quite right. The windows were all left open to the heat, as if someone had forgotten to close them that morning, and there were signs of a hurried departure: the contents of a handbag emptied out on the table in the foyer, some water spilled from the vase of fresh flowers as if they had almost been knocked over in haste, and a pair of Johanna's white silk house slippers kicked haphazardly under the table. She had evidently been in a hurry to leave.

Sure enough, there was a note scrawled on a sheet of paper left on the table:

Call this number and take a cab to this address. Hercule is not well.

Below these words were a phone number and street address. I sat down on one of the graceful upholstered chairs next to the delicate table in the hallway and held the note in my trembling hands. Damn, I waited too long. And now he's going to die, and I'll never meet him, and... No. I pulled myself together and ran back down the stairs to hail a cab. I would get there as fast as I could and hopefully make it in time.

I explained in my best French to the cab driver that I was in a terrible hurry and that it was a matter of life and death, but he just looked at me in the rear view mirror and rolled his eyes wearily. He'd heard it all before. Sure, a matter of life and death, *mademoiselle*. Right. So he took his time and possibly even the longest route to Hercule's *résidence*, or at least it seemed that way to me, sitting in the back seat wringing my hands in frustration.

Once we arrived, I bounded up the stairs of the stately looking building and after identifying myself to the *concierge*, I sprinted through the courtyard into the rear building and up two flights to Hercule's room. When I reached the door, it was closed, and I stopped still in front of it, my heart racing. What would I find on the other side: my destiny? No, only a part of it: an essential piece that had been missing for so long that I hadn't even known it had existed. I closed my eyes, took a deep breath, straightened my shoulders, ran my fingers quickly through my tangled curls, and knocked softly on the door.

"It's Herculine," I said.

Johanna opened the door.

She looked pale and tired, but she nodded and motioned for me to enter the room. It was small but very clean, cool yet filled with light, and there – resting peacefully in a narrow single bed near the

295

window – was a frail old man with wisps of curly white hair. He was breathing deeply. I let out my own breath. Hercule was alive.

"How is he?" I asked quietly.

"He will be fine," murmured Johanna. "But he had a bad fall. The doctors didn't want to bring him to the hospital because he is so frail, but they think it's a minor concussion from which he should recover in a few hours..." she trailed off, looking worried, and gazing at the sleeping old man with tears in her eyes.

"You love him," I said, understanding this for the first time.

"Yes," said Johanna. "He's been like a father to me since I was your age. And he has been all the family I've had since..." she looked at me with a pained expression, "...since Theodore died."

I sat down heavily in a chair with my head in my hands and then I turned back to Johanna.

"Is there anything we can do?" I asked.

"Just sit here and wait," Johanna said sadly, "And be here when he wakes up."

"We can take shifts," I offered.

Johanna responded softly, "I will not leave. You may come and go as you please."

I felt chastised by her words, but continued to sit silently by her side. We sat for several hours, alternately reading, resting, and eating gratefully when a kind nurse brought us a small meal.

"How did he fall?" I asked as we finished our bread and soup. I gestured towards his empty wheelchair in the corner. "I didn't think he was still walking..."

Johanna looked towards the sleeping form in the bed as she answered, "Apparently during his nap this morning he was dreaming that he could walk, because when he awoke, he took several steps from the bed and then collapsed." She shook her head sadly. "They found him on the floor over there." She pointed to the small hand-woven area rug about five feet from the bed.

I gave a low whistle. "That must have been quite a dream."

"Yes," said Johanna wistfully. "I like the idea that in his dreams he is still a young, able-bodied man" – her face became somber – "but I hope this doesn't happen again. They may decide to continue keeping him restrained, which I know he will detest..." Here she motioned to the thick fabric straps that I had not previously noticed, which secured Hercule firmly to the bed. I shuddered.

But as I did so, I noticed a faint movement in the bed, as did Johanna, and we both sat up, immediately alert. Hercule stirred,

296

moaned softly, and tried to turn over, but when he found that he could not, due to the restraints, his eyelids fluttered and he looked around in panic, crying softly, *"Qu'est-ce-que-c'est? Qu'est qui c'est passé? Aidez-moi, quel qu'un…"*

Johanna hurried over to his side and rang a bell for the nurse. In flawless French she soothed Hercule and wiped his brow with a cool wet cloth, saying, "Shhhh, my dear. You had a bad fall today, and you hit your head, but you are fine, and you will be perfect soon. They have restrained you for your safety, but only for a little while… and look, I have brought a visitor for you…"

Johanna turned and gestured towards me. Hercule's eyes tried to focus as he scanned the room in the direction that Johanna was pointing, and when his gaze found me his whole body started forward, as if shocked.

"Sophie?" he cried. *"Sophie? C'est toi?"*

I was speechless, and entirely unprepared for this reaction. I looked worriedly over at Johanna, who also seemed surprised and concerned. She took Hercule's face in her hands and looked at him carefully. We were both hoping that he hadn't injured his head more seriously than the doctors realized.

Johanna said, "Hercule. No, this is not Sophia. She died many, many years ago. This is Theo's…Theo's daughter. Herculine. I told you she was coming, remember?"

Disoriented and bewildered, Hercule turned back to gaze at me.

"Theo? Is Theo here too? Where is Theo?"

My heart sank. Hercule was lost in the past. He had no idea who I was. I took a deep breath and walked over to where Johanna was sitting, then knelt beside the bed, and took one of Hercule's frail hands in my own. When I saw that the thin strap prevented me from lifting his hand from the bed, I gently unfastened it, and he looked up at me with gratitude.

Then I said the words I had endlessly rehearsed in my best French over the last few days, joined with a few more phrases that this unexpected situation now demanded.

"Hercule, I am Herculine, Theo's daughter. I am here to meet you because I know that you are someone he loved very much, and someone who my grandmother Sophia loved too. You wrote to me several months ago and I wrote back to you but…" and here I cast a sidelong glance at Johanna, "but my letters were returned to me unopened. I have wanted to meet you for a long time, and I

know my father would be glad that we are finally together… How are you feeling?"

Hercule's eyes seemed to clear as he gazed at me and listened to my words, and his breathing became calmer too. As I held his gaze, feeling the life force pass between our clasped hands, I also felt his confusion, fear, and despair subside and I tried to infuse him with my own love, hope, and strength.

Finally, after a few minutes, he spoke, at first in French, and then in halting English, "*Bonjour*, Herculine. I have wanted to meet you for a long time." He paused, then looked questioningly at Johanna, "Tell me what happened. I remember nothing…"

Johanna gently recounted the story the doctor had told her, and as she finished, two nurses came into the room and bustled around Hercule, attending to his needs and making sure that he was comfortable. They untied his other restraint, but affectionately admonished him that he was not to try to go dancing again anytime soon. Hercule chuckled faintly, and I could see that he was a bit of an old charmer with the nurses. When they finally left, I resumed my position by his bed.

Much restored, but still fatigued, he grasped my hand with more strength this time and said, "Tell me. Tell me all you know…"

I was momentarily taken off guard by this request. I looked quickly at Johanna, who raised her eyebrows and shook her head, so I asked him, "All that I know about what, Hercule?"

"About me, *cherie*; about me, and your father, and…" He paused and looked at me piercingly for a moment before he continued, "Sophie."

I gave a nervous laugh and said, "That's why I'm here, Hercule – to ask you the very same questions."

He scowled, so I tried again, "Well, um, it wouldn't take very long for me to tell you what I know about my father; I was very young when he died. And I barely know anything about you and Sophie…except," she looked over at Johanna, "I have the poems."

"Ahhhh," said Hercule, closing his eyes and resting his head back on the pillows. "So you know everything."

I protested, "No, hardly anything, really – I mean, I have the feeling that you and my grandmother loved each other and worked together in the resistance, but almost everything I've tried to figure out is speculation at best at this point. I was actually hoping to discuss the poems with you and see if you could help me understand them."

298

Hercule looked at me shrewdly. "You are smarter than that, *ma fille*; if you are Theo's child you can do better. You ought to be able to understand the poems without my help."

I blushed with shame and felt suddenly angry. How dare he challenge my intelligence? I tried to withdraw my hand from his, but he gripped me more tightly.

"Do not be upset," he said. "Of course I will help you. But I want to see how much you know first."

Johanna and I exchanged glances, and Johanna said, "Herculine and I would like to publish the poems, Hercule. But you are the only one who knows their true meanings, and they are dedicated to you, so we need your permission. We think they are important academically and historically. The world needs to see them."

Hercule nodded silently, and looked out the window as he spoke,

"Everyone is dead now, except me, so it does not matter if you publish them. Go ahead... Those poems are not mine." He gave a short harsh laugh, "They are Sophie's. That is why I gave them to Theo." Broodingly, he looked at me before he continued, "But I am glad that he gave them to you. Sophie would have liked that."

Confused by Hercule's shifting moods, I just nodded, and said, "Thank you."

Johanna seemed to pick up on my discomfort and touched me on the shoulder as she said to Hercule, "Now that you are awake, Hercule, Herculine and I should go home and get some rest. We've been here for hours. We'll come back in the morning and visit with you longer then."

Hercule looked disappointed, but he waved us away dismissively, "*Oui*, yes, come tomorrow." He turned to Johanna, "But I need to see the girl alone first. Meet us later in the day."

Clearly flustered by this exclusion, Johanna nodded silently, turned towards the door, and closed it softly behind her.

Surprised by Hercule's callousness, I lingered behind and said to him, as respectfully as possible, "Hercule, excuse me, I know we just met, but couldn't you have been a little nicer to Johanna just then? She's been here for nine hours. You didn't even thank her. You're the only family she's got. I mean, I'm glad you want some time alone with me. That's why I came here. But you should be kinder to her...she really loves you."

Hercule looked at me and said, "*Il se faut laisser, ma petite.* How you say? *Laisser?*"

I translated softly, "*Laisser* means 'to let go.'"

"*Oui,* yes, she must learn to 'let go' of me. And of Theo too," he said flatly. "You know this. You have read the last poem, yes?"

I nodded, my mind whirling with the significance of the fact that Hercule had remembered the exact words of the "Eurydice" poem: *You must learn to let go...*

"Did you memorize every one of them?" I asked quietly.

"Yes," he said, smiling. "That is why I could give them away. I have them here," he patted his heart.

I felt my own heart constrict with pain and admiration for this enigmatic man who had committed twelve poems to memory for decades, in pure devotion to the woman who had written them.

"I'll see you tomorrow," I said, barely able to speak.

"*Bon,*" he said, "Be here at noon," and looked at me with a challenge in his eyes.

I hoisted my bag over my shoulder and walked out of the room, utterly baffled by my encounter with this strange, volatile old man. The corridor was empty when I closed the door, so I leaned against a wall and took a few deep breaths to steady my nerves. This was the man I had been reading about and imagining all year. He didn't seem like much of a Hercules anymore, but he still had a powerful will, and an almost irresistible magnetism. I could imagine him when he was young and vital, his curls dark and glossy, his bright eyes flashing. No wonder Sophia had fallen for him. I pushed myself away from the wall and walked outside to find Johanna.

She was waiting for me by the concierge, nervously tapping the heel of one of her fine Italian leather shoes. She looked grim when she saw me and said, "He's never been that way before. I think he may have really hurt himself in his fall. If he's not back to himself tomorrow, I will take him to the hospital. He's usually so kind..." she shook her head.

"I'm sorry he was rude to you," I said. "He's not what I expected at all."

Johanna said, "I could see that. But don't let him fool you. He's a sentimental old man. Now come, let's have some dinner." As she turned and set off down the street, I fell into stride beside her and together we walked in silence for several blocks to a nearby Moroccan restaurant.

Once we were seated, Johanna ordered a glass of red wine and I said, "He knows every word of the poems by heart."

She raised her eyebrows, clearly impressed.

I continued, "I'm going to bring them tomorrow and see if he'll help me fill in the gaps."

"Excellent," murmured Johanna, back to her professional aloofness. "That will be invaluable for our project."

I felt warmed by Johanna's use of "our" when referring to the publication of Sophia's poems, and we spent the rest of our meal of richly spiced *cous cous* and luscious lamb *tagine* discussing our proposed timeline and ideas for the book.

Later that evening, as I was falling asleep in the crisp white sheets of Johanna's guest room bed, I realized that she was turning out, ironically, to be the academic colleague of my dreams: unsentimental, yet passionate; a purist for concept and design; a rigorous yet inspired collaborator; and adamant about equality in every aspect of the project. I was becoming fond of Johanna, and protective of her too, in ways that I had never expected.

The next morning, when I showed up alone at Hercule's *résidence*, I found him waiting for me, dressed and ready to go out in his wheelchair, at the entrance to the courtyard.

"Good morning," he said tersely. "There is somewhere we must go. Please notify the concierge that we are ready for her to call us a taxi."

Taken off guard once again by Hercule's curt, commanding tone, I did as he asked, and we waited together in silence until the car came to pick us up. The driver lifted Hercule into the back seat, fastened the seat belt around his small frame, and loaded his folding wheelchair easily into the trunk of the taxi. I sat next to Hercule and wondered where he was taking me. Feeling slightly annoyed by his dominating behavior, I sulked and looked out the window as the driver headed away from the city and out into the suburbs. After about twenty minutes, Hercule asked me gently,

"Don't you want to know where we are going?"

I responded coolly, "I'll find out soon enough."

"You are angry at me," said Hercule.

"I don't know you," I said.

"What do you want to know?" he asked.

"Actually," I said, "I'm wondering why my dad didn't tell you about me, and why we never met until now."

"Ah," said Hercule thoughtfully. "I will answer that question soon."

"Okay," I replied, feeling annoyed. "Then I wonder why I'm here at all, and why so many people love you, when you seem kind of like a mean old guy."

Hercule laughed heartily at this, and covered my hand with his own.

"I like you," he said. "I liked your mother too. You are like her, you know that? Very candid. Very bold. In some ways, you are like Sophie too. So sensitive, so quick to take offense…"

I absorbed these comparisons thoughtfully. Here was a man who had intimately known my dad and my grandmother for years and had even met my mom. He potentially held the answers to so many questions that I had about my past that I was puzzled as to how to proceed with him. I felt like just handing him a questionnaire: What was my dad like when he was a little boy? A teenager? My age? Was he always a reader, like me? What did you two *do* together during all the years that he was growing up? What kinds of things did you do when he came to visit you in Paris? Why did you leave New York? Why were you the person who raised him? Did you know my grandfather? What happened to those women you were smuggling out of the country? What really happened to Sophia? What was the nature of your relationship with her? How else am I like her? Did she have female lovers too? Did you know any of them? Why didn't my dad tell me about her? Why didn't he leave Johanna so that he could be with me and my mom?

There it was. The question that had caused me continuous pain throughout my childhood. No answer had ever made sense. If my dad had really loved me, wouldn't he do anything for me? For years I had wondered if the reason he hadn't left his wife had actually been my mom's fault. But when I was older I saw that this was not the case. I began to see that my dad was a man living a lie, many lies really, and I doubted as to whether even Hercule would be able to shed light on the reason why. But maybe he could. And yet, had I come all this way just to confront that unanswerable childish question yet again? Why didn't he leave her to be with me? Lost in my thoughts and in my childhood pain, I did not even notice until the taxi stopped that we had been driving through a cemetery.

As I got out of the car and stretched my legs after the long drive, the driver unloaded Hercule's wheelchair and then lifted

Hercule back into it. The two men spoke rapidly in French for a few minutes, and then Hercule handed the driver some money.

"*À bientot,*" the driver called as he drove away.

"He'll be back to get us in an hour," explained Hercule. "Would you mind pushing the chair for a while? I'll let you know when to stop."

"Okay, I give up: where are we?" I asked, as we wound our way down a long path through various clusters of tightly packed gravestones, some of which looked hundreds of years old.

"We are in the Saint Denis cemetery," said Hercule. "In the section where Parisian Jews were buried after the war."

I stopped pushing and walked around the chair to face Hercule.

"Who is buried here?" I asked.

"You will see," said Hercule. "Now push."

Frustrated by his cryptic answers, I returned to my post and continued pushing the wheelchair in stony silence. Finally, after about ten minutes of winding through narrow, well-manicured pathways between endless rows of gravesites, Hercule said, "Stop." I locked the brakes on his chair and once again walked around to face him.

"What should I be seeing here?" I asked, looking around.

"Over there," pointed Hercule. I followed his gesture and walked over to a gravestone made of elegant black marble. It read simply, "Julien Danton, 1905-1946," with a small Star of David carved beneath. It was evident that the stone had been tampered with and then repaired where cracks had been sealed and scratches mended.

I looked at Hercule and asked, "But wasn't he Catholic, and shot as a traitor to the nation? Why is he buried here?"

Hercule's eyes twinkled, "Ahhh, so you do know a few things. I thought so. He may have converted to Catholicism in his youth, but his surviving original family members were Jews, and they were proud, with influence. They were some of the first ones who got out of the country before the Germans came. When they returned after the war, his family had both of them exhumed from the common cemetery outside the city and buried here with the rest of the family. Aren't you going to look at the other grave?"

I froze. Both of them? The other grave?

I turned to look where he was pointing. A few feet away from Julien's plot, on a lighter stone of simple granite was engraved, "Sophia Danton, 1915-1943," with a matching Star of David.

My legs felt weak and I knelt down unsteadily in front of the gravestone.

I took a deep breath and tried to comprehend the enormity of what I was seeing and where I was. I was kneeling on my grandmother's grave. And my grandmother was Jewish. Of course. Why hadn't I guessed?

I turned to Hercule and managed to stammer, " So...she was...? I...I thought, I mean, I just assumed that she had been Catholic too...I don't know why."

He smiled at me kindly, "I didn't think you knew. Yes, Sophie was a Jew, but passing as a gentile. Just like her mother. Johanna does not know, but your father did. We came here together often. It is a nice place."

I looked around. My father? He knew his mother was Jewish? But that meant that he was Jewish too... and that meant that I was... what? Half Jewish? Did that even count? I knew all too well that it would have counted to the Nazis.

What was I supposed to do with this information? I felt the world spin beneath me as I knelt onto the earth covering my grandmother's grave. It took me a few minutes to pull myself together as more questions hurtled through my mind, but once I opened my eyes, I noticed that what Hercule said was true: I was having an identity crisis in a "very nice place." The cemetery was peaceful and lovely, with trees and simple gardens interspersed throughout the plots of graves. I could see why my dad might have wanted to come here. There was a timelessness to the place that made the impermanence and surreality of existence seem benign somehow. I felt like I was in a bit of a time vortex myself.

Beneath me lay the remains of the woman whose life and passions I had been tracing for almost twelve months – all those adventures, all the risks taken, lives saved, lives lost, lovers and enemies, now re-framed by the fact that she was in far greater danger, as a Jew passing for Catholic, than I had ever imagined – and it all came down to this. A plot of ground and a stone. Sophia had been more alive to me over the past year than most of the people I encountered in my daily life: mythic even, larger than life, on a par with the classical heroines with whom she had identified in her poems. And now she was just earth. *As we all will be.* I realized that

304

my hands were shaking as I raised myself to my feet and faced Hercule.

"Thank you, "I whispered. "Thank you for bringing me here and for telling me the truth about my family. But I'm overwhelmed. I feel like I need to re-think almost every conclusion I have drawn about the poems now that I know Sophia was Jewish, and I can't help but wonder why my father hid this from me too." I looked at Hercule imploringly, "Do you understand why?"

"*Ma fille*," murmured Hercule, "How can you know what it was like for him? To a child in the war, being a Jew meant only two things: shame and fear. For Theo, it also meant losing everything. He grew up in that house of lies, but I – who am not a Jew – told him the truth and tried to raise him to respect all people. After the war, there was still anti-Semitism in the U.S., and your father was filled with fear. So he tried to put it behind him. After all, he had not grown up knowing he was Jewish, so I suppose it was easier to renounce it once he knew. Even so, the shame of his choice must have been what kept him from telling you. *C'est compliqé*; it is complicated, *ma fille*, but that is my guess."

I pondered his words for a long time, wishing that I could have talked about this with my father and reassured him that I wouldn't judge him for his choice. He had been acting on a survival instinct, and I could see now that this was why he couldn't bear to lose either of his worlds – the one he shared with Johanna or the one he created with me and my mom. He had already lost the most important world of all – the one he had known all too briefly with his mother—and that was enough for one lifetime.

I turned to face Hercule and asked him, "You just said that my father grew up in a 'house of lies.' What did you mean? I know that my grandfather was a liar and a criminal; while researching the poems I have come to despise him and feel ashamed to be related to him. He was a terrible man, and caused so many deaths…but was Sophia dishonest too, just because she was passing as Catholic?"

Hercule looked stricken and said, "*Non, non, pas de tout*… that is not at all what I meant. Come here, *cherie*. I do not want you to be ashamed of your grandmother *or* your grandfather…"

As I walked towards Hercule, I watched as he reached into the breast pocket of his shirt and pulled out a square of neatly folded paper. He unfolded it gingerly and handed it to me with a different sort of challenge in his eyes.

I took the piece of paper and began to read. I immediately recognized my father's handwriting, quickly glanced to the top of the page and gasped as I noted the date— the day before he died—and looked quizzically at Hercule again before I looked back at the letter. He gazed at me calmly and nodded at me to continue reading.

Dear Hercule,

I am dying, and there is something I must ask of you before I do…I have many regrets, but one of the most acute is that I will not have the chance to see you again before I die. You are my oldest friend, and what I learned from you about love I have tried to pass on to my own daughter (yes, Clea and I have a daughter), who I named after you, in honor of you. Her name is Herculine Danton. You would love her. She even looks like maman in a certain light. I need you to find her, Hercule; make sure that she comes to you when she is grown…there is so much that I haven't told her. So much that I need you to explain to her. Forgive me for not being able to do so myself. Out of my own selfishness I have created an impossibly divided life, and I have caused all of those I love more pain than I ever intended.

And this is why I need to write to you, to explain why I have not told you about Herculine before, why I haven't told her about you, and why I am asking you to find her now. You are the keeper of my past, but Herculine is my hope for the future. She knows nothing of my early life, and she sees me only for what I am in her eyes: her loving, if often elusive father. So you must tell her the truth. However, before that can happen, there is something that you and I never spoke of, and now it is time. I wish that I could be looking into your eyes and seeing your face, which I hope would soften with love as you hear my words and not harden into denial. I can only tell you that I have known for some time that you are more than a family friend. Your love for my mother was too evident, too profound for friendship. I believe that the two of you were lovers. And I believe that I am your true son.

There is no shame in this, Hercule. There is no shame in matters of love. There is only shame in the conventions and institutions that stand in the way of love's full expression. Just as you and my mother were not married, nor am I married to Herculine's mother, Clea, who I brought to meet you just over ten years ago. Your warm welcome and immediate acceptance of her in my life meant more to me than I can express; I am sorry that I did not allow the two of you to know each other better. I did this for Johanna's sake, for you are like a father to her, and I could not risk dividing her from you for my own selfishness.

My love for Herculine is more perfect than anything I have ever known. I wonder if this is how you felt about me, watching me grow – yours, and yet not yours – for that is how I see her, and why I have come to you now to tell you that

306

I understand. I understand and forgive you for never telling me that you are my father. You couldn't risk my rejection, I know. It was safe to be a loving family friend to whom I would always be grateful for saving my life. But I am grateful to you for far more than this. I am grateful to you for teaching me how to love, and how to live my short life to its fullest. I have tried to convey at least some of this to Herculine...I hope I have succeeded. And if I have not, I pray to some benevolent pagan god that you will find her and that she will learn it from the same deep source as I was fortunate to have as my teacher.

My life may be ending, dear Hercule, dear father, but as we know, my love for you will never die. Live well.

Your son, Theo

My father's words blazed through me. *My love for Herculine is more perfect than anything I have ever known... I understand and forgive you...* Hot tears gathered in my eyes, and I wiped them away fiercely, trying to concentrate on what has happening; it felt like the earth was shifting beneath my feet once again. My dad was Hercule's son. He had known for years. This was the reason that he hadn't told me about Hercule...but why? Because...because, this meant...that the old man sitting in the wheelchair in front of me was...

"My grandfather?" I whispered to Hercule. "*You? You* are my grandfather? Not Julien Danton?" Relief flooded my whole body and overwhelmed most of the confusion coursing through my mind. I looked wonderingly at Hercule as he sat silently nodding in response to my question, tears in his eyes. I kneeled down beside him and took his hands in mine.

I asked him, "Is that what you meant by 'house of lies'? How could you bear not telling my dad? Didn't you want him to know?"

"Of course, *cherie*; of course I wanted him to know," Hercule said gently, "but I didn't want him to feel ashamed of his parents. Sophie and I were not married..."

"Well, neither were my parents," I said defensively, "and I was never ashamed..."

"It was a different world back then; you can't understand," Hercule answered wearily and passed his hand over his eyes. "Adultery was a punishable crime during Vichy, and there is a word for children like you, like Theo, and like me: we are all *bâtards*. I had to live with that word my whole life; if I could spare my son from its cruelty, it was a small sacrifice. Now, if you please, my letter," he said brusquely, and gestured for me to return it to him.

I was reluctant to surrender this artifact of my father's last day of life, this intimate document that I could imagine him writing...I could see his hand holding the pencil, the concentration in his eyes as he wrote... But then I looked into Hercule's eyes and saw the panic rising there. This letter was *his* lifeline to my dad, not mine. I handed back the letter respectfully and watched as Hercule immediately relaxed as soon as he held it in his hands, re-folding it lovingly and placing it back in his breast pocket over his heart. He patted his chest where it was securely tucked away and sighed, smiling up at me, and said, "We are finished here. Shall we go?"

"Finished?" I said, smiling at my grandfather. "We've haven't even begun."

Every day for the next two weeks, I met with Hercule. Sometimes we just sat in his room talking about the poems, sometimes I pushed him in his wheelchair as we went for walks in the neighborhood, sharing memories of my dad. Sometimes in the evening I would wheel him to his favorite *bistro*, where we would share a bottle of wine and he would tell me stories of his own life, the war, and his love for Sophia. Occasionally Johanna would join us, but most of the time we were alone. Sometimes when we talked about events that had happened during the war and I could not comprehend the decisions that he had made, there were sparks of temper on Hercule's part, or stormy silences on mine, but we emerged from each of these episodes with deeper respect for each other's complexity and sensitivity.

He confirmed most of my theories about the first eleven poems, making occasional small corrections and filling in key gaps that I was always grateful to understand. For instance, in the "Galatea" poem, the "spark of life" that the speaker mentions (*There is life within me. You gave me the spark, And I am creating it myself...*) was not just vitality, or the love that brought the statue to life, as I had assumed, it was literally Sophia's realization that she was pregnant with Theo! Similarly, in the "Penthesilea" poem, when Sophia wrote *This is how we trapped them...and they burned...on the pyre meant for me,* Hercule clarified that of course he and Sophia had not rounded up their comrades and killed them in a fire. Instead, when they found out that four female comrades had betrayed the resistance and endangered the cause as well as the lives of their others in the underground, they let the information leak to the Vichy officials. Once the Germans knew that their double agents were no longer useful or trusted, *they* burned down the stable while the women were

inside. Hercule looked miserable as he told me this story and told me that Sophia had never forgiven herself for their deaths.

I admittedly felt relieved upon hearing this, and was duly saddened when I learned of the rift that developed between Hercule and Sophia after the border crossing disaster narrated in the "Cassandra" poem. I asked Hercule if he had ever found Cassandra Lanvin once he emigrated to New York.

He shook his head sadly, "No, she had died of pneumonia before we arrived. I found others in her group, and they told me. But I grieved her loss. She was a true friend, and a great beauty." He added wistfully, "As were all the women she loved…"
We sat in silence for a moment, and then I realized that I hadn't yet mentioned Calypso. Tentatively, I asked him if he knew that Sophia had a half-sister.

Hercule's eyes lit up and he said, "You found her? How? I wrote to her once, years ago, but there was no reply…"

I knew enough about Calypso not to be surprised that she had lied to me about never having heard of Hercule, but I kept this to myself. "Yes, I met her," I said, "And she is a complicated person; the war took its toll on her too."

"Perhaps," said Hercule dismissively. "She does not concern me now. She is alive, but Sophie is not. She should have made contact with Theo, but he never mentioned it so I can only assume she didn't."

"Then again," I said, "There are many things that my dad didn't mention. So you never know…"

Hercule smiled and shook his head. "This family of ours has too many secrets, *ma fille*, you are right…"

Too many secrets, indeed. But many of them were finally coming to light. Hercule and I had covered each of the poems in depth, and it wasn't until the end of my final week in Paris, two days before I was scheduled to leave, that we finished discussing all but the last. On that night, I unraveled my theory about the eleventh poem, "Atalanta," and Hercule was beaming at me with pride. More than a few times he seemed transported into the past as I described to him the scenarios I had deduced.

"You *do* understand," he said, as we sat in the *bistro*. "You have seen what it was like then, for us."

"No," I said, "I have only tried, wondered, and hoped; but I can never really know."

309

"That is for the best," said Hercule gravely. "I would not want you to have known it as we did."

I saw the shadows in his eyes that haunted him sometimes, and I thought of all the death that he had seen, all the suffering and fear, and I knew that he was right. I was glad I had not known it, but I said, "I still wish I could have known *her*."

Hercule nodded. "She would have loved you, *cherie*. She was more remarkable than I can ever tell you."

I smiled and said, "I believe you. I feel like I have come to know her through her poems and she has filled me with a different kind of awe in every one."

Hercule reached for my hand and said, "And now, it is time for the last poem."

I returned the reassuring pressure of his grasp then withdrew my hand, took out my notebook, and turned to "Eurydice."

"This one seems entirely personal," I said. "Am I missing something? Are there any references to the war?"

"No," said Hercule, shaking his head, "You are correct. This one is just for me. Or just for her. Depending on how you read it."

I told him how I read it: Sophia casting herself as both Eurydice – the reluctant bride of Orpheus, half-dead half-living, longing to stay in the underworld, beseeching him to let her stay – and simultaneously as Persephone, the Queen of the underworld herself, who offers Hercules her own pet as a consolation for Eurydice's desertion.

"So that makes you both Orpheus and Hercules," I said. "Was that how you felt at the time?"

Hercule shrugged and said, "I never felt like much of a Hercules; that was just her perception of me. And I didn't know the story of Orpheus until years later in New York, when I went to the library and read books to understand all the references. But looking back, I can see how she would have seen me that way: wanting to rescue her, when she didn't want to leave."

"Why?" I asked quietly. "Why didn't she want to leave?"

"I don't know for certain," Hercule explained haltingly, "but what I was able to piece together is that she was planning something too secret to share with me…a plot to expose her husband's crimes so that the authorities could easily prove his guilt, but I do not know how she managed it. I think she succeeded. And I think he found out."

310

I shivered, then took a deep breath and asked, "Is that why she killed herself?"

He stared fixedly at his glass of wine and held onto it tightly as he said, "She did not kill herself, *ma cherie*. That is only what the report says. He slit her wrists in the bath...That is how they found her." And then a bitter shadow fell over his face, and he looked up at me with haggard eyes, saying, "I had friends in the police who told me that there were rope burns around her wrists as well as the lacerations. He made it look like suicide, but he murdered her."

"He?" I choked. "You mean, Julien?"

"Yes. I mean the beast she married; he was killing her for years, slowly. He finally finished the job that night. Some days I am glad that he did it this way, rather than handing her over to the Germans, as he was always threatening to do...But you see, I always thought she would join us; I believed her when she said she would. We waited a year...she wrote every week, and then..."

As Hercule trailed off, I noticed that tears were trickling slowly down the furrows in his deeply lined cheeks. I reached out and held his hand, which was still clutching his wine glass. Our eyes met, and a look of loss and understanding passed between us. I was horrified by what Hercule had just told me. I had to revise so much of what I had imagined about my grandmother's life now. If my dad had known this too, would he still have been angry at the thought of his mother or ashamed of her actions?

I managed to ask, "So, my dad never knew that Julien killed her?"

Hercule took a deep breath and said, "No, I thought it was better that he didn't know. When he was old enough to ask how his *maman* had died, I told him that she had killed herself like Roman heroes did, nobly, before their captors could kill them first. He knew that she had been a hero of the resistance, so he seemed satisfied and never asked again."

I pondered this information. My dad should have been proud to tell me about his mother. His illegitimate birth, hiding her Judiasm, and her alleged suicide were nothing compared to all the good that she had achieved during the resistance. And she hadn't even killed herself after all. She probably had meant to rejoin him and Hercule in New York eventually, but had been prevented by Julien's vengeance.

"Was it possible that my dad didn't know the extent of his mother's heroism?" I asked Hercule, who admitted sadly that Theo

had only listened skeptically to him when he had tried to praise his mother's wartime efforts. His anger at her abandonment had been too deep to understand the sacrifices she had made. I had no choice but to revise my understanding of my father also, and the man emerging from the shadows of the past was more troubled and complex than the man I thought I had known.

As I was filled with these thoughts, Hercule turned his attention back to our discussion of the final poem.

"When I read this one the first time," he said, "I didn't understand the last part. But I do now. She knew she would never join us; she was trying to help me let her go. She gave me Theo so that I could love him instead, and keep her love alive in me."

"So my dad – Theo – is …is Cerberus?" I asked in disbelief. "Her own little son, the vicious killer three-headed dog of hell?" I laughed aloud incredulously. Hercule saw the humor in my words and joined me, chuckling first at the absurdity of the substitution, then laughing as loud as I was, slapping his hand on the table for emphasis, and after a few minutes we both had tears in our eyes of hilarity mixed with grief.

"I guess it was him," said Hercule, after recovering from his laughter, "but I think she meant it to…how you say?"

"To transform the image?" I offered.

"Yes, yes exactly," nodded Hercule. "The love for a child can be terrifying, and painful. But there is more to it than that…"

I mused, "She gave you her son, a symbol of her three-fold love, and sacrificed herself so that her son could live, and so her love could live through him." Then I paused. "Kind of a nice inversion, if you think about it, of the patriarchal Christian myth structure in which a father sacrifices his son so that he can live on in three-fold eternity, and not always in a loving way either."

"Don't forget the most important part," said Hercule. "He wasn't just *her* son. He was *our* son. *My* son too."

I shook my curls in embarrassment; I had been so used to thinking about Hercule simply as a family friend or Sophia's lover for so long that sometimes I still forgot that he was Theo's father, and my own grandfather…

"I'm sorry, *grandpére*," I said, looking contrite.

Hercule waved his hand graciously, and said, "You are correct about her changing the Christian story. This was something she would talk about with me. How a mother would never do it…sacrifice her child for anything, anyone. How she would sacrifice

312

herself first, always. And she knew I was the same: a father who would die to save his child. I almost did, that night…"

I sat silently at the table watching Hercule's face as he relived the events of the night that he attempted to rescue the two people he loved most in the world, but had to leave one of them behind, just like Orpheus. And then I thought I understood on yet another level why my dad had not been able to leave his wife to be with me and my mom.

I asked Hercule, "Do you understand why my dad didn't tell us about each other?"

Looking deep into my eyes, pulled back from his reverie by the urgency in my voice, Hercule said, "Yes, I believe that I do. Theo lived in two worlds. He had to keep them apart, because if he didn't, he would have had to choose one over the other, and he could never do that. Just like his mother. She… Sophie…could never choose. She loved me, and she loved her women, and she loved her son – she lived in three worlds – and she never wanted to hurt anyone. Neither did Theo. He loved you, but he loved me too, and you and I were in separate spheres."

"And now we are here, together," I said sadly. "Without him." And I wondered if Hercule was thinking what I was: that I would give up this night, these last few weeks, all the poems, grandmothers, and lovers in the world, just to have my dad back again. But Hercule was smiling at me, so perhaps I was the only one having such thoughts.

He said, "Your father would be so glad to see us together like this, *cherie*; he would be so glad…"

As I reached for and held my grandfather's hand gently on the red and white checkered cotton table cloth, I saw my life in palimpsest form: layered translucently over a visual map first of my dad's and then of my grandmother's lives and loves. I saw for the first time that I was like them in the way that Hercule had described. I lived in several worlds too – New York, Berkeley, and now Paris – and I never wanted to have to choose between them.

"I think I'm part of the family tradition," I confessed to Hercule wryly, thinking of Hyla and how – like Orpheus and Eurydice – I couldn't seem to let her go. And yet Hyla, like me, was not someone who could be kept very long. I would give her what I had required of all my lovers before her: I would love her *and* let her go. I turned back to Hercule and asked him earnestly, "Have you ever

been able to choose between your worlds or to let go of someone you loved?"

"No," he shook his head. "Of course not. And you will be the same. We cannot let go of that which defines us, that which is at the core of us, or we would turn to... to dust, and blow away, just like that," he snapped his fingers and made another dismissive waving gesture with his hand.

A shiver went down my spine. I knew what he meant. But I also knew that I was different. I would find a way to let go and still love. I gazed at my grandfather, so proud and fierce in many ways, though age and pain had visibly diminished his strength and health. It might be too late for him to know this, but there was still time for me. We parted ways that night with great warmth mixed with sadness, knowing that the following day was the last of my visit.

The next morning, Johanna went with me to pick up Hercule. She walked by my side as I pushed Hercule's wheelchair, heading towards the banks of the Seine. When we reached the edge of the water, Johanna opened a small silver urn containing my father's ashes and handed it to Hercule, who solemnly reached in and scattered a trembling handful into the river. Hercule handed the urn back to Johanna, who did the same, her face an impassive mask behind her large black sunglasses. Then she handed the silver box to me and I repeated the ritual. Then carefully, slowly, I shook the rest of the remains of my father's body out into the air, the sky, and the water.

That evening, Hercule and I said goodbye. I promised to come back to see him in the spring and to bring my mom someday too, and we pledged to write and talk on the phone as often as possible. But it didn't feel like enough. I felt like I was leaving a piece of my heart with Hercule when I left him in his room, and I sobbed all the way back to Johanna's apartment in the cab.

For the first time, Johanna put a comforting arm around me and drew me close, saying, "You must come back soon. You're always welcome here. You must see Hercule as often as you can, and we must work on our book."

I nodded gratefully, marveling that this moment was even happening. I thought for a fleeting moment that I could feel my dad there in the cab with us, beaming with pride and love.

During that last night in Paris, I woke up a few hours before dawn, feeling as if warm, strong hands were lifting me out of my bed. I realized that I had been dreaming of my dad and had thought for a moment that I was a little girl again, and he had just been lifting me

314

out of the window seat where I had fallen asleep reading so that he could carry me over to my own bed and tuck me in for the night. He would then rest quietly by my side, and I would entwine my small hand into his in the hopes that he wouldn't be able to let go and leave. But he was never there in the morning. And he wasn't here now when I awoke from my dream. But he was in my heart. And I had emerged from my journey through the underworld more confident of his love for me than ever before.

I felt my breath rise and fall under the blankets and I thought about Hercule, sleeping deeply – I hoped – on the other side of the city. I thought of the night that he had come to rescue his son and his lover and take them to safety in America. He had rescued one, but had to leave the other, and he had remained torn in half for the rest of his life. Unlike my grandfather, I felt more whole, and more at peace, than I had ever imagined was possible. Lying awake in the dark of a deep Parisian summer night, I stared out the wide window in my room, and saw the sky as clearly as if I was lying in a field in the countryside on a warm summer night.

The stars were large and bright, I could feel the earth warm beneath my body, and I knew I was a part of it all: the myth, the truth, the history, and the fiction that were woven together to make up the vast and varied tapestry of mortal life. I was my grandmother, feeling the muse course through me; I was Hercule, risking his own life to save the ones he loved; I was my father, loving us all and incapable of hurting any of us; and I too was a member of Sophia's alternative pantheon of mythic heroines. Confident in our knowledge that although we pass on and off the stage of life so quickly, our lights flickering out almost as soon as they are lit, there is one part of us that makes our brief stay worth everything. It may not last as long as we want it to, and we may not be able to keep the ones we share it with by our sides, but if the feeling is true, then so is this: only love will never die.

315

Sophia
Paris, 1942

Sophia sat at her writing table in her room, late at night, staring out the tall, open window at the stars filling the sky. The city was dark and silent and the stars were bright. She had just finished writing the twelfth and last poem of her *Nouvelle Panthéon,* and in less than an hour Hercule would be here to take them away. He thought he was coming for both her and Theo, but he would only leave with the boy. Somehow she had to make him understand why. A tear spilled over onto her cheek and ran down toward her chin before she brushed it away angrily. There is no time for tears, she thought. They are a luxury. She must make sure that everything was ready before he arrived.

She went into Theo's room and checked one last time through all the items in the bag she packed for him: clothes, boots, a blanket, food, money, his identification papers – false and true – and a small packet of photographs that she hoped would not be lost along the way. One was of her holding him when he was three years old and both of them were smiling; another was of her with Hercule before Theo was born; and the last was of the three of them on one of the only days they had been out in public together.

She rubbed a dark purple bruise on her arm absent-mindedly. She could hear Julien's snores from down the hall. She had drugged his wine at dinner so that he would sleep through the noise of Hercule's entrance...and of his departure. With Theo. Her darling boy. Sophia knelt by her son's bedside and watched him sleep. He looked like a delicate fairy child while sleeping, with his coppery curls, high forehead, delicately drawn eyelids, thick lashes, and fair skin. She caressed his brow, which furrowed slightly under her touch, ran her fingers lightly over his curls, then laid her head down beside his, breathing in the freshly washed, warm sleeping child smell that is ambrosia to every mother. Her heart contracted with pain: how could she let him go? Once more her mind raced with all the reasons that she couldn't leave with them, the danger that her presence would add to their escape; the unnecessary risk that her son would face – ironically – if his mother was by his side. If she left, Julien would have her hunted down within a few hours. He wouldn't even notice

316

that Theo was gone for days; he barely paid any attention to the child at all – and his disregard would be long enough for Hercule to get him out of the country safely, leaving her to pay the price. She knew what awaited her. And now she rubbed the bruise on her arm consciously. But she had work to do.

With great reluctance, Sophia pulled herself away from her son and went back to her room where she sat at her writing desk once more. She quickly wrote out a dedication page and sealed the twelve poems in an envelope to give to Hercule. Then she took a bound sheaf of official papers and placed them in another envelope, for Hercule to deliver to a resistance comrade once he crossed the border. These were the documents that would lay the groundwork to bring down Julien and the rest of them. Beasts. Tears came to her eyes again as she thought of the women she saw on the train that day, months ago now, their eyes haunted and pleading, their bodies gaunt with malnourishment and fatigue, calling to her to help them, to save them. But she could do nothing for them, standing like a puppet, like a statue in a mask by Julien's side. Until now.

Her grief over the immediate loss of little Theo was now subsumed in a greater grief: the loss of the innumerable lives she wasn't able to save, as well as the imminent loss of her own life, compounded by her fear of oblivion. It will be a release, she thought, an end to the fear, and the suffering. At least she had managed to salvage fragments of her life and turn them into something useful. She who had been used like a pawn by her own mother and then abandoned, sold to a man who didn't love her but used her as a screen to keep up appearances, masking the twisted cruelty of their union. Healed and strengthened by all the women who had loved her over the years, finding a purpose from her work with her comrades in the resistance, and finally, given the gift of life and a deeper level of love than she had ever imagined possible from Hercule and Theo. She had taken the broken pieces of her life and made them into art.

What does it mean to be a hero, she wondered, staring out into the night sky… Is it to be brave and strong and glorious, like all the male heroism in the myths she loved to read to Theo at night? Or had she been a heroine herself, in her own quiet persistent way… What would Theo think of her life when he was older? Would he say, "My mama was a hero in the war, and thanks to her, hundreds of lives were saved"? That depended on how the war ended, she thought bitterly.

She looked at the stars and prayed to them that her son would grow up in a time of peace, that his children would live in safety and freedom, and that when they thought of her they would know that what she had done, she had done for them, for their futures, as well as for those she had saved. She had fought for her own freedom and for theirs, and she loved them even though she would never know them. Perhaps one day Theo would read her poems and understand, and he could tell his children the story of his mother, who had been a heroine too, in her own way.

At the sound of Hercule's muffled step on the fire escape outside, Sophia flinched. The time had come.

Herculine
Berkeley, 2000

Walking back to my office after teaching my seminar on Ancient Greek Poetics, I crossed the Mills College campus, and the balmy air around me was filled with the petals of budding plum and cherry blossom trees blowing in the warm spring breeze like delicate pastel snow flurries. Undergraduates were lounging on the grass, reading and talking; some of them even waved to me as I passed. I returned their greetings absentmindedly, however; my thoughts were intent on reaching my office as quickly as possible. There was a letter that needed my immediate attention.

I had stopped at the Classics department before class and picked up a large stack of mail that had been waiting for me for several days. The recent publication of my second book, *Mythic Truth*, had caused some sensation in the academic world. Once the reviews in several academic journals had hit the shelves in university bookstores, invitations to speak at conferences around the country had begun to pour in.

The best part about the offers, I thought as I walked briskly across the courtyard, was all the fully funded travel they implied. One conference was in New York, which would be a great opportunity to visit with my mom and Ramon for a while; another conference was in Los Angeles, where I could see Dion, who was running an independent film studio; then there was one in New Orleans, where I could see Anthea, who was teaching at Tulane and raising her daughter. One was even in Austin, Texas, where Hermàn had already been tenured at the state university.

As I reached my office and searched through my shoulder bag for my keys, I thought wistfully of all my far-flung friends. Phoebe was in London working at an investment firm, to everyone's surprise, and Linus had been composing and struggling to make it in the recording industry in Berlin for several years now. I hadn't received invitations to conferences in either of those cities yet, but I was still hopeful. Out of all of my friends, only I had stayed in the Bay Area, fortunate enough to be hired as the new classicist at Mills, and deeply tied to my home on Calpurnia Street.

Most of the traveling I had done over the past few years had been the summers I spent in Paris with Johanna and Hercule, becoming almost as close to him as I had wished I could have been with my dad. My relationship with Johanna had transformed during our preparation and publication of *La Nouvelle Panthéon*, which had been hailed as a critical success by historians and literary scholars alike. We had decided to dedicate the book to the memory of Sophia Danton, and to Hercule, who had lived to see the poems published, and who wept when he held a copy of the book in his hands. On the front cover was a grainy enlargement of the photo of Sophia and Hercule in a passionate embrace that had been hidden behind the photo of them laughing arm-in-arm in my dad's small leather frame. The book was a tribute to their love as well as an academic breakthrough, and my only regret was that my dad hadn't lived to see it come to pass.

When Hercule died during the winter of 1995 of a swift and deadly pneumonia, I was devastated, and had to take a leave of absence from my new teaching job at Mills. It was as if all of the remaining grief from my dad's death came back to me with double force, paralyzing me with despair for weeks at a time. I stayed in Paris for a month with Johanna—who was also in deep mourning—and we arranged his memorial, which ended with the two of us scattering Hercule's ashes over Sophia's grave, according to his wishes. Then I took refuge for a few more months in New York with my mom, who rose to the occasion of nurturing me with grace and understanding. During this time, I began to work on my second book, *Mythic Truth*, as a way of coming to peace with both my dad's death and Hercule's, as well as my own mythic legacy. This was the book I would dedicate to my father. It brought me scholarly fame, tenure, and most importantly, peace to my grieving heart.

Surprisingly, Hercule had appointed me his sole heir, and the money he left me had enabled me to buy the house on Calpurnia Street that I had rented for so many years with a varying constellation of roommates. These days, I shared my home with the laughter and companionship of visiting colleagues and friends whenever possible. Original work by local artists adorned the walls, the wood floors gleamed, there were plenty of comfortable chairs, sofas, and deep window seats for reading, and the whole place was filled with a spacious light-filled grace. I had converted one of the bedrooms into my study, and another into my own master bedroom, but the rest had been appointed as guest rooms ready for any number of visitors on a

moment's notice. And then, when Deni had moved in, everything finally felt complete.

We met during my third year at Mills. Deni was a new hire in the Philosophy department and we had struck up a friendship during a humanities faculty meeting. There was something magnetic in the sultry curve of Deni's mouth, defiant stance, leather coat, and wry, intelligent voice tinged with a faint French accent that had drawn me in immediately. It was only a matter of time before we were involved and living together, and before we knew it we had fallen effortlessly into a passionate yet deeply peaceful and mutually supportive domestic routine. Our academic lifestyles provided the structure that fueled our tranquility: teaching during the school year, and traveling, researching, and publishing during the summers. During our first summer together, we had traveled through the Greek islands for a month. The following year it was Tuscany. This year we were planning a trip to the south of France.

As I let myself into my office, I was off in a daydream, thinking of the way Deni's skin tanned to golden caramel in the summer sun. But when I closed the door behind me, I took a deep breath and returned to the present moment. I dropped my bag to the floor, placing the large stack of mail I had been carrying across campus onto my desk chair, then ran my fingers through my curls to clear my head.

There was one letter in the stack of mail that was not from an academic conference. I had noticed the exotic stamps and foreign postmark on the blue airmail paper immediately, and this is what had caused me to return to my office in such haste. As I reached for the envelope, the sight of Hyla's handwriting caused my fingers to tremble. It had been months since her last letter, and the sight of her angular script still had a profound effect on me, even after all the years that had passed since I'd last seen her.

Our parting in New York ten years earlier had been painful: we had tried to maintain a long distance "open" relationship while she pursued her film career and I finished graduate school, but the strain of the distance, brief visits, and unexpected scheduling changes had worn us down quickly. When Hyla finally took a job with a documentary film crew in Indonesia, I tried to let her go for good.

Or so I thought. Anytime she had a layover in San Francisco, Hyla would show up on my doorstep, and our reunions were still so charged for me that I couldn't turn her away. One night I had even had to ask another lover to leave when Hyla showed up

321

unannounced, even though she had suggested that he stay and join us. But when I met Deni, everything changed. It was with relief that I had bid farewell to my seemingly endless stream of part-time lovers, but breaking the news to Hyla that I was now in an exclusive relationship was more difficult. Since then, five years ago, Hyla had kept in touch sporadically by letter only, since the locations where she was filming were becoming increasingly remote. There was no way for me to contact her – no stable address, post office box, or internet connection – and somehow, I found that I preferred it this way.

From the postmarks on her envelopes, I could trace the trajectory of Hyla's career, and even occasionally saw her films in documentary festivals in New York or San Francisco. But as I watched my former lover's life soar further and further away from me, I savored my own life even more fully as my roots deepened and my love with Deni flourished.

The letter in my hand was a perfect example of what I had come to expect from Hyla… just one line sprawled across the delicate paper: *Mythic one, you are in my dreams as always…keep me in your heart forever.* Heart pounding, I read the line over several times, then tucked the letter back in the envelope. I kneeled down, unlocked the lower drawer of my desk, and placed the letter deep in the back with all the rest. I closed the drawer firmly and locked it again before I rose to my feet.

Leaving the rest of my pile of mail untouched, I picked up my bag and walked out of my office, locking the door behind me. Taking a deep breath of the late spring afternoon air, I felt my heart expand as I walked through the blossoming trees. It was time to go home.

30038363R00183

Made in the USA
San Bernardino, CA
04 February 2016

Imprimé sur du papier 100 % recyclé

Pour obtenir des informations concernant les prochaines activités de Brigitte Langevin, veuillez communiquer avec elle à l'une des adresses suivantes :

Courrier postal :

**Brigitte Langevin
6, 25ᵉ Avenue
Bois-des-Filion (Qc)
J6Z 1X9
Canada**

Courriel :

contact@brigittelangevin.com

Site Internet :

www.brigittelangevin.com

- *S.O.S. Cauchemars* permet de comprendre la cause des différents cauchemars, de les interpréter et de leur donner un sens. L'ouvrage propose également une méthode efficace pour s'en prémunir.

- *Recueil de 500 postulats*, pour trouver des solutions tout en dormant.

- *Mon premier journal de rêves*, outil simple et original conçu pour toutes les personnes désireuses de noter et de comprendre leurs rêves.

- *Le rêve et ses bénéfices* expose des témoignages inspirants qui vous donneront le goût de vous occuper de vos rêves. Ce livre expose avec simplicité une méthode que chacun peut mettre en pratique pour comprendre les messages de ses rêves et en bénéficier pleinement.

- *Comment aider mon enfant à mieux dormir* offre aux parents et aux éducateurs tous les outils pour surmonter les différents problèmes liés au sommeil des enfants. Ce guide dénonce les pièges qui guettent les parents et leur offre des stratégies éprouvées pour surmonter les difficultés.

- *Mieux dormir… j'en rêve !* propose de répondre aux questions les plus fréquemment posées sur le sujet. Ce livre traite du sommeil de chacun : celui de l'étudiant, de la personne âgée, de l'homme d'affaires stressé, de la femme enceinte, etc. Il fournit des informations essentielles sur les conditions d'un bon sommeil et guident aussi le lecteur vers des moyens concrets pour mieux dormir et offre des solutions thérapeutiques pour venir à bout des troubles du sommeil.

À PROPOS DE L'AUTEURE

Brigitte Langevin agit à titre de conférencière et de formatrice au Canada, en Europe et partout à travers la francophonie. Elle partage ses connaissances dans le but de favoriser un meilleur sommeil et de permettre une compréhension plus profonde des bienfaits d'un travail sur les rêves. Également, à travers son parcours et ses recherches, elle a développé une expertise dans les questions touchant la discipline et les enfants.

Elle est recherchée pour son dynamisme, son humour et sa facilité à vulgariser des concepts théoriques et scientifiques. Elle amène ainsi les individus à prendre en charge leur sommeil, leurs rêves et aussi à assumer positivement leur rôle de parents ou d'éducateurs.

Auteure prolifique, elle a publié à ce jour huit ouvrages :

– *Rêves & Créativité* s'adresse à tous ceux qui ont à cœur de développer leur potentiel de créativité par les rêves, tant dans le domaine personnel, artistique et professionnel que scientifique.

UNELL, Barbara et Jerry WYCKOFF. *Se faire obéir des enfants*, Montréal, Éditions Le jour, 1993, 192 p.

Autres

Psychologies magazine, n° 228, mars 2004.

BOURCIER, Sylvie et Germain DUCLOS. « La fessée au banc des accusés », *Magazine Enfants Québec*, novembre 2004.

BIBLIOGRAPHIE

BACUS, Anne. *L'autorité : Pourquoi ? Comment ?*, Paris, Marabout, 2005, 286 p.

BENOIT, Joe-Ann. *Le défi de la discipline familiale*, Montréal, Québécor, 2005, 221 p.

DODSON, Fitzhugh. *Aimer sans tout permettre*, Paris, Marabout, 2005, 352 p.

DOLTO, Françoise. *La cause des enfants*, Paris, Librairie Générale Française, 1986, 634 p.

DUCLOS, Germain et Martin DUCLOS. *Responsabiliser son enfant*, Montréal, Éditions du CHU Sainte-Justine, 2005, 185 p.

FERLAND, Francine. *Grands-parents aujourd'hui, plaisirs et pièges*, Montréal, Éditions du CHU Sainte-Justine, 2003, 144 p.

GAGNIER, Nadia. *Ah ! non, pas une crise*, Montréal, Éditions La Presse, 2006, 75 p.

HOGG, Tracy. *Les secrets d'une charmeuse de bébé*, Paris, J'ai lu, coll. « Bien-être », 2004, 317 p.

LANGIS, Robert. *Savoir dire non aux enfants*, Montréal, Québécor, 1996, 159 p.

LANGEVIN, Brigitte. *Comment aider mon enfant à mieux dormir*, Boucherville, Éditions de Mortagne, 2009, 208 p.

ANNEXE : AIDE-MÉMOIRE

- ➤ Votre poupon de moins de dix-huit mois vient de faire une bêtise ? Pour bien se faire comprendre de lui, il faut l'interpeller par son prénom, aller le chercher par la main, se mettre à sa hauteur, capter son regard, lui faire de gros yeux, prendre sa grosse voix et lui expliquer ensuite la règle avec des mots simples.

- ➤ Complimenter et encourager son enfant par des paroles ou lui faire un sourire complice, un clin d'œil, un pouce levé ou un « high-five » signifiant « bravo ».

- ➤ Donner du temps de qualité à son enfant est aussi une expression de l'amour qu'on lui porte.

- ➤ Si les règles sont clairement expliquées et si les parents montrent qu'ils ne permettront pas qu'on les transgresse, une situation problématique ne durera pas très longtemps.

- ➤ Un enfant, un jeune ou un ado qui négocie, parce qu'il croit qu'une règle n'a pas ou n'a plus sa place, mérite d'être entendu.

- ➤ Une stratégie qui a bien fonctionné avec un aîné peut ne pas obtenir de succès dans une situation semblable avec un cadet. Il ne faut donc pas hésiter à varier les stratégies ou à les adapter.

- ➤ Lorsqu'une crise familiale perdure ou s'aggrave et que la vie devient infernale, le recours à un professionnel devient alors nécessaire.

- ➤ Enfin, voici les principes essentiels pour bien exercer vos fonctions de parents : beaucoup de tendresse, un brin de fermeté, des moments spécifiques de disponibilité, le moins d'angoisses possible, un sacré bon sens et pas mal d'humour.

Une discipline sans douleur

facilement cet état. Quand nous leur interdisons une chose, ils répliquent par un « Je te déteste! », puis, une heure plus tard, ils nous soufflent un « Je t'aime »...

> L'utilisation du marchandage, des cris ou de la fessée est souvent une réponse inappropriée à un sentiment d'impuissance. Ces façons de faire enseignent la violence à l'enfant et ne sont que des exutoires à la colère des parents.

> Les mains des parents sont faites pour soigner, pour caresser, pour tenir l'enfant lors de ses premiers pas, pour le guider, pour l'inciter à découvrir les merveilles de la vie. Bref, elles sont faites pour exprimer tout leur amour.

> Soyons conscients de nos limites, de nos besoins et de nos propres désirs, afin d'éviter de faire des gestes répréhensibles ou de prononcer des paroles très regrettables. Les propos blessants (menaces, humiliations, critiques, etc.) sont aussi préjudiciables qu'une fessée.

> Bébé qui pleure ne veut pas dire mère indigne.

> Quand un parent interdit quelque chose à son enfant, il peut se demander : suis-je en train de lui imposer une fantaisie purement arbitraire ou est-ce une règle qu'adopte la majorité des parents ?

> Quand un parent se questionne sur la légitimité d'une intervention auprès de son enfant, il peut se demander : va-t-il blesser quelqu'un d'autre, se blesser lui-même ou briser quelque chose ? Et aussi : si je n'interviens pas, cela aura-t-il un impact sur sa vie dans dix ou vingt ans ? Si la réponse est NON à ces deux questions, il y a lieu de ne pas intervenir. Par contre, s'il répond OUI à l'une des deux questions (ou aux deux), il doit intervenir chaque fois que son enfant adopte ce comportement.

Annexe
AIDE-MÉMOIRE

- Un parent parfait, cela n'existe pas. Il est néanmoins possible de devenir un excellent parent. Viser l'excellence, c'est se donner le droit à l'erreur, tout en se responsabilisant et en faisant tout en notre pouvoir pour améliorer nos aptitudes parentales.

- Les enfants veulent être l'objet exclusif de l'amour de leurs parents. Le travail des parents est de les ramener à la réalité. Les limites servent à cela et elles sont donc une dimension essentielle de leur éducation.

- En posant des limites, le parent joue son rôle ; en protestant, l'enfant joue le sien.

- Le rôle du parent est de prendre soin de son enfant, non pas comme ce dernier le désire, mais comme il en a besoin. Son rôle consiste donc à faire respecter les règles établies et non à uniquement rechercher l'affection de l'enfant ou à lui faire plaisir.

- Il est normal que les enfants puissent ne pas nous aimer et, parfois même, qu'ils nous détestent. C'est « l'ambivalence des sentiments ». Les enfants expriment très